BEYOND HERE BE MONSTERS

I0636714

OTHER BOOKS BY GREGORY FROST

Rhymer
Rhymer: Hoode
Shadowbridge
Lord Tophet
The Girlfriends of Dorian Gray
Fitcher's Brides
Lyrec
Táin and Remscela
The Pure Cold Light

Praise for
Beyond Here Be Monsters

"Greg Frost sets his fantastical stories in the equally strange re-
alities of history. Other times, other cultures. But I always know
that however it goes, I'm in for a good ride."
—Maureen McHugh, author of *China Mountain Zhang*

"*Beyond Here Be Monsters* is an abode of dark, dark parables. In
these stories Gregory Frost demonstrates craft, intelligence, a
sense of humor, and a willingness to cross genre borders without
a visa. Trust me, you've never read anything like 'Ill-Met in Il-
lium,' a secret history of the Trojan War—with vampires—told in
Homeric verse. Nor 'The Seals of New R'lyeh,' in which two petty
criminals attempt to pull a heist in a New York City transformed
by its new ruler, Cthulhu. In 'The Dingus,' hard-boiled 40s-Bog-
art-movie boxer-turned-cab driver Meyers tries to find out how
his protégé Kid Willette managed to get himself torn to pieces at
Red's Roadhouse. Frost is a master of the small details that make
a character come to life, that take a story from merely entertaining to haunting. Plus, when he isn't scaring you to death—and
sometimes in the midst of it—he is very funny."
—John Kessel, award-winning author of *The Dark Ride*

"*Beyond Here Be Monsters* . . . Well, yes. But in addition to
downright delicious suspense, terror, tragedy, and horror, here
also be pathos, retribution, the occasional satisfying survival of
dire circumstances, at times great heart, and even some good
comedic fun. Frost is a consummate storyteller who excels in
embedding you in exquisitely detailed unusual settings, intro-
duces you to riveting characters, and then spins out the immer-
sive and often terrifying, situations he visits upon them. This is a
treasure of a collection!"
—Michaela Roessner, author of *The Stars Compel*

BEYOND HERE BE MONSTERS

A COLLECTION OF CREATURES AND CURIOSITIES

GREGORY FROST

FAIRWOOD PRESS
Bonney Lake, WA

For B

CONTENTS

THE DINGUS

All Meyers wanted to know was how Kid Willette, that he'd personally educated in the ring his last two years as a trainer, had ended up dead—and not just dead, but beaten, mangled and dismembered dead. It didn't make sense. It shouldn't have been. Nobody could put a glove on Willette unless he wanted them to. Unless he'd been bought. That was the only time he'd ever gone down. Meyers knew that better than anybody.

So when he walked into the 6th District Station to find Detective Bulbitch, he just wanted a simple explanation: Kid had been doped; Kid had been drunk; Kid had been wounded. He thought he would hear an answer that would let him go home from his nightshift in the taxi, hoist a farewell shot of bourbon in commemoration, and then go to sleep untroubled by impossibilities.

He found Bulbitch at his desk, sharpening a pencil with a pocket knife. The shavings were sprinkling down onto his belly. His pink skull, graced with all of seven remaining hairs, glistened as if the pencil was giving him a very hard time.

Meyers drew the folded *Inquirer* from his armpit, opened and tossed it in front of the detective. Bulbitch looked up. For an instant Meyers saw fear—the same fear he glimpsed in people all the time when they first got a look at him. Then Bulbitch's face widened into amusement. "Well, if it ain't my most favorite pugilist. How you been keepin'?" Meyers made a nod at the paper, where the front page headline proclaimed "Roadhouse Horror." It was so big that even the national story following up on Truman's kicking McArthur out of command had been squeezed into a sidebar.

Bulbitch didn't bother to look. "You still driving the cab?" he asked; and when Meyers persisted in saying nothing, he folded the knife and sat upright. He brushed the shavings like crumbs off his shirt and tie. "Yeah, all right," he said, "okay. I figured you'd hear about it. Expect the word's out everywhere from Jack O'Brien's to the Christian Street 'Y' by now."

And so the story unfolded.

Red's Roadhouse out in Paoli was one of those two-story places slapped together with boards that had probably started life as a barn. The main hall had sawdust on the floor and a bar that was big enough for a catered wedding party to circle. On the second floor and in the back were the rented rooms, one of which they even had the chutzpa to call a "suite." It was to this suite that Cody Aldred and his three enforcers had retreated for some R&R after a few weeks of breaking legs. The owner of the place, amazingly enough named Red, swore up and down that he didn't know that Cody had brought in any working girls. How was he to know the women weren't the men's wives? It was a question that nobody answered as they were too busy laughing, seeing as how Red employed a half dozen chippies of his own in the second floor rooms.

So, a little past midnight the night before, in the main room at least two dozen people were lounging in various states of blur. Those who still remained in the aftermath—including ever-reliable Red—agreed that no one else had come in. Nobody at all had entered Cody's suite.

And yet, in something like five minutes, according to everyone in the place, Cody and all three of his boys had been butchered. Torn to pieces. The three chippies were unharmed, and not one of them could explain what had happened.

There'd been noise, something that howled like a gale and rattled the brass knob and shook the door on its hinges. The screams, someone said, were the screams of men being slid quick into hell. Only when it was over—and silent—did Red work up the gumption to go look. He didn't even reach the door before the three chippies in there started their own caterwauling. Red

paused with his hand on the knob, and that was when he noticed that the sawdust under his feet was turning wine dark, the
stain spreading outward. The shrieking went on and on, but Red
backed all the way to the bar, where he grabbed some change and
hurried to the pay phone on the outside wall. Nobody else went
for the door in his absence, although maybe one or two sidled on
out of the roadhouse.

"Tough guy, old Red," said Bulbitch. "Uses himself a little
baseball bat with a rebar center when somebody acts up in his
establishment. But even he wasn't gonna open that door. And,
Meyers, you ought to leave it closed, too."

Meyers kept his hands shoved deep in his pockets. He rocked
like a punching bag, his mind sifting the details. Bulbitch grabbed
a pack of Camels off his desk, jerked one cigarette out, and put his
lips around it to draw it from the pack.

"So," Meyers finally, casually said, "Kid was with Cynthia,
huh."

"Yeah." Bulbitch's fingers had just scissored on the cigarette,
but stopped. He scowled with the realization that he'd been
played, and he stared up at Meyers without lifting his head. "And
you have now got all the information you're getting, Mr. Meyers." He rose up, his head even with Meyers' neck. "You listen to
me now. Leave it. This isn't Montgomery versus Mouzon at Shibe
Park. Ain't any rules here. This is somebody did something so awful we're gonna have to invent a new word to call it. And anyway,
Kid Willette *ruined* you in the fight biz, so what in hell is it you
think you owe his ghost?"

Meyers pulled the newspaper to himself. The picture on the
front page was of a pile of trash beside what might have been
a body under a sheet. "Nothing," he said. "Not a God damned
thing. I was just curious, was all." He took the paper and left.

The following night, whenever he had a fare that dropped
anywhere close to Third and Race Streets, Meyers trolled over to
the DR bridge and drove the Crawl. He had no idea where Cynthia lived, but he knew where she worked when she hadn't been
hired for a night and hauled out to Paoli.

The third time through the Crawl that night, one of the working girls hailed him and told him to take her to Spruce and 22nd. On the way he asked if she'd happened to see Cynthia.

She told him, "Not tonight, I ain't, on account of her pimp dragged her over to South and Second till things settle down. And you didn't hear that from me."

After dropping her off, Meyers cut over to South and then drove straight down toward the Delaware; about the time he crossed Broad he remembered to turn off his light.

He parked the cab and got out, then strolled north along Second. This was the turf of old money, and a hooker had to blend a bit. He knew he might not find her—she might have scored a john already. But he got lucky.

Cynthia had a little dog on a string, a Pekinese, and she was walking it up and down the sidewalk between South and Lombard. Her platinum hair all but glowed under the streetlights. Meyers wondered what she did with the dog.

As he came nearer, she paused and made a show of taking out a cigarette. He shook his head in the darkness as he drew up. "You know, I still don't smoke," he told her.

Her pose relaxed, and she stared hard at him. "Oh, *you*. I mighta known." She pulled out a lighter and torched her own smoke. Her hand might have been shaking. "You looking for a tumble tonight, Pants-on-Fire?"

"Not really." He held out his hand as if inviting her to dance. Between two fingers was a folded ten dollar bill. "I need to talk to you, Cyn."

"You think so?" Her jaw clicked, and she shifted it from side to side. Cynthia had suffered at the hands of a boyfriend, a psychopathic fighter back in the days Meyers had been training Willette. The boyfriend had dislocated her jaw, and whoever had fixed it hadn't set it right, with the result that it clicked sometimes when she spoke. If it hurt, she never said. Meyers had been on hand the night the boyfriend had tried to murder his opponent in the ring, and the opponent's trainer had taken a three-legged stool to him. One leg had driven right into his brain, almost immediately making the world a significantly better place. Somehow, Cynthia had ended up going home with Meyers that night. She'd stayed till morning. Mostly, they'd gotten drunk while she tried to figure out why she was crying her eyes out over "a rotten dead bastard," and Meyers had insisted on paying her like any john. It was some strange matter of protocol and respect that made sense only to him. In the end as a compromise she'd charged him for an hour of her time. He still didn't know what to call what had happened between them.

He said, "You gotta talk to me a little bit. You were with Kid."

She flicked the cigarette away and lit another. "I didn't think this was no social call."

"Who did it, Cyn?"

"Jesus, Meyers." She drew herself up and for a moment he felt like she was bigger than he was. "Do you know, I got bounced to three different cells in three different station houses last night? Wasn't allowed to sleep and damn near not to take a piss, and they just asked and asked and asked, but they got nothing for their trouble. Ten dollar bill buys you the same as they got, but it's your money, honey." She snatched it from between his fingers.

"Well, at least tell me the way it happened. I know you liked Willette."

She took a deep drag. The dog pulled her a couple of feet along the sidewalk so that he could sniff around a skinny tree. "Yeah, he was nice for a handsome boy with a wad of bills and no sense." The dog whimpered then and she said, "Come on, Johnny, I gotta walk."

They strolled side by side, like two old friends in no hurry to get anywhere. "What happened is, I don't know what happened. They was three back rooms made up that suite—suite, like they's a big luxury hotel and not a hole you could raise pigs in. I was, you know, doing Kid. And then all of a sudden, somebody's scream-ing, and I mean screaming like their legs was being sawed off. It was Cody. Kid pushed me off him, snapped up his braces and charged right outten that room. No shirt, and he was stuffin' him-self back in his trousers with one hand and picking up his gun with the other."

"He had a gun?"

"They all had guns, honey. Anyway, he charged out of that room like a bull, and the screaming, it stopped just for a second. Couple of doors slammed. And then it was back, but it was some other voice, and some shots, and then even more screaming. Kid that time. You got no idea how awful it was. I crawled under the bed with the cockroaches and the condoms and the mouseshit, and I stayed there.

"And then it just stopped, ya know? Everything went quiet. Some time passed, I got up and put on Kid's jacket and snuck out to see. I woulda bolted, but Dottie come out of the next room. She'd been with both of Cody's other guys, and I don't know whose turn it was, so don't ask. You probably know Dottie. She stayed home tonight like I shoulda."

"What about the third girl?"

"Her." She shook her head at some memory. "Cody had her with him already. She just got off the boat. Acted like she only spoke enough English to order a sandwich maybe."

"Off the boat from where?"

"Estonia—is that a place?"

"Yeah."

"Okay, then."

The dog wrapped himself around a light pole. Meyers asked, "What are you not saying here, Cyn?"

She pulled the dog backwards to untangle him. "Dunno what. You'd seen her, you'd understand. Big shiny eyes. Crazy eyes. 'Course we all had 'em right about then, didn't we?" She met his gaze as if his calm perplexity could answer for everything. "Cody said her name was Yuliya, like Julia but with a 'Y'. He was gonna hand her over to Mr. Drozdov later."

"Cody pimping for the boss?"

She shrugged. "Hey, it's a business, isn't it? You get paid and go where you go, same as a cabbie." He ignored that. "And maybe with Drozdov's reputation, ya gotta go all the way to Estonia to find somebody who don't know any better."

He chewed on that. "So she was with Cody the whole time?"

"Me and Dottie found her sprawled in a chair, covered in blood. Didn't have a stitch on."

"Then *she* saw what happened."

Cynthia waved one hand around in a little circle. "What she told the cops was, the two of them was playing, you know, the way Cody liked it."

"What's that supposed to mean?"

"He'd tied her to the chair. I been with him once or twice. It's like he's tryin' it out 'cause the boss does it. Only nobody's afraid of being tied up by *Cody*, ya know?"

Meyers knew. Drozdov had dipped into the fight game awhile, hadn't he, and more people seemed to get hurt on those occasions. Somehow Drozdov and the mob accommodated each other, kept to their respective territories. He must have had connections they appreciated. There were stories about how Drozdov liked to inflict pain, in particular how he liked to play with a boy's wood burning set. He'd been arrested two years back after a couple of mutilated hookers had been fished out of the Delaware. They'd been tortured, burned and scarred with an iron of some kind, and somebody had fingered Drozdov, or maybe the cops had just heard the same stories as everybody else; and either nothing could be proven or he'd bought the right people to make the charges go away. Hookers and hired muscle—nobody cared about either one.

Meyers shook himself back to the present. "Okay, so Cody tied up this dame."

"Said he blindfolded her and the second she tugged it off, she was hit in the face with blood like out of a fire hose—and that's how it looked, all right. Feet was still tied to the chair. We seen her and we ran into the room before we knew what was . . . what all the lumps on the floor was." Her chin trembled and she clamped her lips together and shot him an accusatory glance. After a minute she went on. "Dottie started screaming and then this doll comes around, and she starts screaming, too."

"You were in shock, all three of you."

"Sure." In the streetlight glow he watched her revisit the moment, watched her face pulled by awful currents of memory. "There was four bodies in there, John. The stink. And you couldn't look anywhere at all. You just . . ."

He tried but could not fathom how it had happened. How could nobody have witnessed Kid Willette's demise?

"I'm cold," Cynthia said abruptly. "I think I'm sick, you know? Probably oughta go home, like Dottie. Stay in bed."

"I'll give you a lift," he said. "On the house."

"You let Snuffles in there, too?"

Meyers and the weepy-eyed dog considered each other. "So long as he's done his business," he said. They walked over to his cab.

Somewhere around Fifteenth and Walnut, Cynthia suddenly spoke out of the back. "I know where she is, you wanna talk with her."

He glanced in the mirror, realizing what she was saying. "Where?"

"Cost you another ten."

He laughed that she'd got her nerve back. "And here I am giving you and your mutt a free ride."

"Fine, take it outta my fare. You got a pen?" she asked. "I'll write it down for you."

He took out the pocket notebook he used as a log and opened it to the back page, handed her a pencil.

While she wrote, she said, "Cops interviewed the three of us in the same room. She gave up an address. Might be phony, but it's up in the Fairmount. Brown Street."

In the mirror he watched her scribble in the notebook. "Why in the name of God did Kid go to work for him?" he asked.

She looked up at the gaze of his reflection, her eyes bright and wet. "If you don't know, then nobody does, honey. Didn't tell me nothin'."

He focused on the street again. Yeah, he knew. A lot of dollars and no sense.

Fifteen minutes later Meyers pulled the cab into a space on Aspen Street, then strode on up the hill to Brown at the top of the ridge. This woman lived within spitting distance of Eastern State, and he wondered if she had maybe some relationship to the prison. Or maybe it was just cheap rent.

Kennealy's Bar stood on the corner of 22nd and Brown, and as he rounded the corner, a couple of women came out of the Ladies Entrance at the back. They were babbling happily at each other in Polish. He'd worked with enough Polish fighters in his time to know the sound of it; but he slowed his pace and strolled up beside them. "Evening, ladies," he said, "How are you this fine night?"

The duo laughed a little nervously, and Meyers smiled. He chatted about nothing, and they kept walking. They soon passed the address Cynthia had given him. Without appearing to look, he noticed the glow of a cigarette in a doorway across the street.

Meyers walked another block with the women, then tipped his cap and turned away. He crossed the street. After a minute he started back the way he'd come, but at double the pace now, feet hitting the pavement with the sound of someone in a hurry. The doorway lay just ahead.

He barreled along and at the last instant as he was passing the door he pivoted on one foot and punched a short jab straight into a solar plexus. The man in the shadows didn't even have time to raise his hands in defense. He folded around the fist, spitting the cigarette past Meyers, who swung his right into the man's jaw so hard that the body bounced off the door and against the brick around it. Meyers was ready to hit him again if necessary, but he slid down onto the step and tipped onto his side. Meyers yanked him upright and pushed his legs back into the shadows. He patted the body down, and reached into the coat. He drew out a wallet, and a badge.

This was not good.

He stuffed the possessions back inside the jacket. The cop groaned. Meyers turned and walked quickly across the street.

Beside the door was a panel with three buttons, no doubt one apartment for each floor of the rowhouse. The first two had names beside them. The third floor label was blank. He pressed the button. Even as he did he realized how stupid this was. She had no reason to let him in, and if she was hiding from trouble, she wasn't going to let anybody in at all. To his surprise, though, the door buzzed, and clicked on its latch, and he pushed inside before she could change her mind. He took the stairs two at a time.

The door at the top hung ajar, and he hesitated then, feeling a little too much like a fly visiting a spider. He looked at the name Cynthia had written down. "Miss Luka . . . chova?" he called.

"Come," she answered as if granting him an audience.

The apartment had a short narrow foyer that opened on a living room, with a kitchen off to the right and another doorway, presumably the bedroom, at the back. One low-wattage wall sconce—a fake candle under a little paper shade—lit the room a diseased yellow.

The woman was sitting on a ragged love seat against the wall. Her legs were crossed at the knee. She had long black hair and wore a gray dress and jacket that had an almost military cut to it. She was smoking a long, odd-shaped cigarette and her large eyes glittered behind the stream of smoke. She leaned forward and tapped her ash against a glass ashtray on the small white coffee table in front of her. A scattering of tarnished coins or buttons lay strewn across the tabletop. They had an oily sheen. Meyers stayed in the doorway, his hands balled into fists in his pockets, but nothing else in the place seemed to be moving.

"Who are you?" she asked in a voice that sounded like it didn't much care. "You are not from Drozdov."

"You're right on that score. My name's John Meyers. I was a friend of Kid Willette's."

"Who?" She seemed genuinely perplexed. What she didn't seem was frightened. Cynthia, out in the open, had been more edgy than this. The woman seemed tired, as if she'd run out of gas well back down the road.

"He was one of the boys who worked for Cody Aldred."

"Cody, yes. He was blond man?"

"Yeah. He was a blond man."

"Ah. I am sorry for your loss. I did not have opportunity to know him."

"What happened, Miss Luka . . . What happened at the roadhouse?"

"You are not policeman?"

"No. I drive a cab. Willette used to be a boxer. I used to be a trainer."

"Like father and son, no?"

Meyers leaned against the jamb. "Not really, no."

She nodded solemnly. "But you feel you have duty to his memory."

"Something like that, I suppose."

"I understand. I even share your sentiment. If you would like a drink, I have vodka in icebox."

He shook off her invitation. "How'd you end up at the roadhouse?" he wanted to know.

She hissed smoke. "Circumstance. I am wanting to meet a man I've heard of, but to do so I find I must first entertain this Cody."

She didn't look at him, but off across the room as she spoke.

He decided Cynthia was right—something boiled just beneath this dame's cold surface; and she spoke more English than she'd pretended, too. "So you came all the way from Estonia to work for Drozdov?"

Her look stabbed him, but just as quickly she covered herself by leaning down and tapping her cigarette on the ashtray again. "Mr. Drozdov, he promises to help young women to escape Eastern bloc. Promises job. Promises life."

"You know he's selling you into prostitution, right?"

Her lips curled. "Oh, yes, I know. I have no illusions." Again she stared at him. "None. My sister, however, she did not understand this." This time when she leaned forward, she smashed the gray cigarette into a blob.

Hair prickled on the back of Meyer's neck. All of a sudden, he knew she'd killed Cody Aldred. Killed all of them. She must have accomplices, must have let someone in—he couldn't figure it any other way. He also had a pretty good idea what had happened to her sister. Glancing into the doorways again, he tried to figure how it was she'd been left by herself. Maybe her pals couldn't get near her now. "You know the police are watching your house?"

"What? They mustn't. They mustn't interfere!" She got to her feet. She was tall as a coat rack.

Bingo, he thought. He replied, "Interfere with what?"

A buzzer went off beside the kitchen doorway. Meyers saw the metal switchplate on the wall, but the woman walked to it and pushed the black button on the plate before he had time to react. That would be the cops, and they would not be enthusiastic about his presence. In fact, chances were, he was in trouble. "Maybe I will have that vodka," he said and pushed past her into the kitchen. A big tin icebox stood beside the doorway. He found the vodka on its side in a small compartment directly below the half-melted block of ice. He grabbed it by the neck, hefting it. Just in case.

Footsteps came up the stairs and into the apartment. Meyers leaned back against the kitchen wall, listening. The woman said something and then a man answered, but he wasn't speaking English. His voice sounded pleasant, even friendly. Not cops then. He had a pretty good idea who it was instead.

There was a back door to the apartment off the kitchen, and

as the voice got louder, coming deeper into the apartment, Meyers crept around the icebox and very cautiously opened the door.

A man was standing there. He and Meyers looked at each other. The man's hands were deep in his coat pockets, and he smiled as Meyers took this in, said, "How about we go back inside, pally. Nothing down in this alley but rats."

Meyers nodded and closed the door. When he turned around, two other men stood in the kitchen doorway. He walked back to them, and set the vodka onto the counter next to the fridge.

In the other room a third man, with thick features and a large mustache, stood beside the woman. He beamed at Meyers. "Very nice work on that copper—you have excellent skills," he said, his accent subtle. "All we had to do was tap him to keep him dreaming a little longer."

"Sounds like it's not his night."

"Indeed. Now, you will please accompany us and Yuliya."

"Why?" she said sharply. "He's nobody to do with this. He is wanting to buy my time."

The man glowered at her. "You know that is a lie, my dear. What casual john eliminates police officers for a trick? Mr. Drozdov will want to hear what he says, as do I, even now." His eyes slid back to Meyers, who tipped his head as if to say that it was all fine with him. The mustachioed man held Yuliya Lukachova's coat for her. Then two of the men led the way out and down the stairs with Meyers and her sandwiched in between.

The Packard drove into a loading bay in a warehouse on Front Street. The air reeked of sour refinery, so the wind must have been blowing in from the west. At least it masked the fish stink of the Delaware, which wasn't more than a quarter mile away past the warehouses. They walked by shredded cardboard cartons, broken pallets, and piles of newspaper that were probably used as packing material. Meyers wondered what they manufactured and shipped out of here.

The first time he'd ever seen Pankrat Drozdov was the night he'd fought Mickey Darren at Convention Hall. It was one of Herman Taylor's bouts, a clean fight. He'd KO'ed Darren in the seventh. At the time he didn't know he just had three fights left before his inner ear went. That night he had only the memory of a dark-haired man with the face of a shark and an entourage of six, which included a woman on each arm. Drozdov had stood out, as he intended.

The next time was after Kid had thrown his fight. Meyers knew the Ruskie had been behind it—some kind of bet had been placed. He supposed he should have credited Drozdov for picking the kid up afterwards and giving him the job with Cody. Except Drozdov was the reason Kid needed the job, and the job was the reason Kid was dead.

Drozdov had some gray at his temples now, but he was still lean and hatchet faced. This close to him, Meyers realized it was the eyes that made him like a shark. They were black and empty, eyes that calculated how you were going to taste.

He sat at the end of a large, scarred wooden table surrounded by oak chairs, the kind Meyers remembered from high school. The table had leather straps nailed to the side of it at all four corners. The men sat the woman down beside Drozdov. One of them walked off into the back. The other two flanked her. Meyers wasn't offered a seat. A new man, nibbling a toothpick, sidled up out of the shadows and stood next to him.

"Well, well," Drozdov said. "A long time it's been since Darren went down. How have you been, Gospodin Meyers?"

"Well enough."

"Vasily here tells me you've taken up our cause against the police." Meyers shrugged. Drozdov leaned forward and took hold of Yuliya's chin. His fingers closed on her jaw like a vise. "What is it you want with our lovely sister here?"

"Sister?"

Drozdov chuckled. "Oh, not *my* sister, Meyers."

The look in her eyes wasn't just from pain, but fearful recognition. Drozdov was letting her know that he knew everything. He drew his hand back. She reached up to rub her face.

"I was asking her about Kid," Meyers said. "Because she was with Cody at the roadhouse."

"You see?" Drozdov waved at Vasily. "A simple explanation. And it's true. You can tell when someone's telling the *truth*, you know?"

Vassily's gaze shifted to Meyers noncommittally.

The man who'd walked into the back returned carrying a large wooden box. An electric trouble light hung off the side, the cord slithering along behind it. The flat blade of a large wood-burning iron also poked up above the side of the box, looking like the tip of an enormous screwdriver. Meyers tensed. He thought of the hookers fished out of the river.

"So," Drozdov said, "I'm inclined to send you home. Unless you would like to stay. I hope to learn something about the fate of Cody and Kid Willette, myself." His thug set two of the irons, one small like a pencil and the larger one the size of a leek, down on the table beside him.

Yuliya Lukachova implored Meyers with her eyes and shook her head. He read the look as a plea: She must be shaking her head no, that she didn't want him to leave her here. He couldn't see a way out for her, though, and much as he wanted to, he couldn't walk away. Maybe he could help her; but maybe—and the thought unsettled him—he would hear finally what he wanted to know. "Yeah," he said, "I'll stick around."

"No!" she barked. Everyone looked at her but she stared at Meyers. "You leave here. Now." Turning to Drozdov, she said, "Get rid of him and I tell you what you want."

Drozdov casually picked up the smaller burner, touched it to the table. After a moment a tiny curl of smoke rose from the tip. "Not ready," he said to no one and put it down. "Yuliya, believe me when I tell you, you're going to give me everything anyway. I have found out some interesting facts about you since my dear friend Cody Aldred met you and his fate. And you know what I'm talking about." He waited then, to see how she would answer.

Her eyes closed as if she'd dozed off. But then she drew a deep breath, and quietly said, "Liisu."

"There. That's what I like, when you tell me things."

Still not looking at him, she replied flatly, "You killed her."

Drozdov's bonhomie peeled away like a mask; the face of the shark returned. "Actually, I didn't." He raised the large iron. "This did. Would you like to know where I applied it? Ah, you know, I think I won't tell you. But I will let you find out."

Meyers body was pumping adrenaline. Unable to act, he flexed his muscles, shifted his feet. The guy next to him eyed him sidelong, alert to the pent-up energy.

Yuliya Lukachova bowed her head, and her lips moved as in prayer. Drozdov frowned with disgust. Her breathy syllables grew slowly, steadily into words, phrases, all of them alien to Meyers. Drozdov's brow creased. The words perplexed him as well. He looked as if he had run out of patience with her, and his hand closed around the larger iron. She snarled strange words at him and her hand came out of her pocket and flung blackness into his face. Small objects struck him and rained down onto the table, rolling, some of them, onto the floor. Meyers recognized the odd oily coins he'd seen in her apartment.

Drozdov began to laugh. One coin had stuck to his face and he flicked it away.

The woman started to rise and the goons behind her grabbed her by the arms. Drozdov sneered at her and picked up the iron.

The spill of coins didn't settle. They jittered and rolled, off the table, across the floor as if downhill. In seconds they'd collected in a single spot and begun to spin in place. Only Meyers and his guard seemed to notice. Everyone else was watching the red-hot iron.

Drozdov plucked hairs from her head and touched them to the iron's tip. They vanished in a puff of smoke. "She wants to be on the table now," he told the men.

A breeze erupted through the huge space. From all around, loose objects started to skitter across the floor. They flew to where the black lump spun—broken splinters from the pallets, broken glass, papers, empty bottles, cardboard and tape, baling wire, and small stones, mousetraps drawn out of corners, bricks that crumbled as they reached the spot. The box on the table flipped and the tools in it shot away from Drozdov. A trash container crashed. Its contents sailed across the floor. The air howled like something alive. The cage of the trouble light collapsed and it whipped across the room. Drozdov reacted an instant too late, and the iron snapped from his grasp and flew behind it. The cord on the light whipped like a tail, and by the time the irons joined it, the thing had formed.

It stood like a man. For hands and fingers it had pliers, screwdrivers, nails, and the wood-burning irons that smoked and glowed. Black buttons punched the crumpled material of its face into eye sockets. The woman growled, "Nuku-surnud," and the thing lunged at the table.

Vassily had his gun out. He fired repeatedly at the creature. It rammed its arm ending in the large iron straight into his skull. Flesh and brain sizzled. Its other arm buried in the chest of the second man holding Yuliya Lukachova, spinning, bursting out the back of him. It cut up and down, splitting him in half, and then went for Drozdov. He squealed and dodged aside. Meyers' guard had run forward to help, and Drozdov grabbed him and threw him in the creature's path, then barreled around the table.

The creature tore the man apart like it was opening an envelope.

Yuliya Lukachova screamed at Meyers. "Get out of here, idiot!" she yelled. "It won't stop now. Run from here!" She stood proud, tall, as pitiless as stone.

Drozdov clawed at him and Meyers punched him, smashing his nose. Drozdov fell against the table. He lunged for Meyers again, but jerked back so fiercely that his neck cracked. The creature had caught his collar. It slammed him onto the table. The large iron swept once around his throat, and suddenly his head was flying back into the depths of the warehouse while the body kicked and spasmed.

Meyers ran.

He dodged past the car and down the ramp to the open lot. He hesitated for only a second before racing toward the river—long enough to glance back and see the thing wedge itself around the Packard. It left a wet smear on the car.

He bolted across the open lot. The thing lumbered after him undeterred.

Soon he was in the grass, up a gravel slope and over the rails of the tracks that ran past the warehouses. When he looked back next he could feel the creeping edge of vertigo from his ear injury. He listened instead of looking back then, sure that swinging his head once more would tip the world over on him and for certain if he fell the dingus would catch him.

It crashed noisily through the brush behind him and that propelled him ahead. He thundered out onto the disused loading dock made of old wooden ties as the creature crossed the tracks and descended the bed.

Reaching the edge, Meyers dove into the blackness of the Delaware. Ships had taken on cargo here. It had to be deep enough to dive. He was depending on it.

He hit the icy water and swam for his life. The current clutched at him but he kicked furiously out into the river, refusing to be dragged under. He thought of the girls Drozdov had tortured and dumped, their corpses down below. He swam harder.

The creation of wood and glass and paper and metal leaped in after him. He heard the splash, dared a look back as it vanished into the black water. It surged up once, thrashed like a crazed animal at the surface, and then sank. This time it did not reappear, but Meyers turned and kept going, driven by the fear that any second monstrous hands would snag him from below and pull him to his death.

He didn't stop until he'd crawled up on the rocky Camden side. He was shivering. His breath steamed. He made himself get to his feet and go on, up and into the weeds. He stumbled and shuffled and kept moving, and maybe half a mile up found a service station by the side of the highway that was open and pumping gas, and went inside, pulled out a sodden five dollar bill and begged the most expensive cup of coffee he'd ever had. The attendant eyed him as if debating whether to call the cops, but Meyers told him to keep the bill, and that settled that.

He held the stained mug in both shaking hands as he drank. Two other men, truck drivers, stared at him as they might have stared at raccoon that had wandered in for a pack of Luckies. Nobody asked him what had happened, as if they knew the answer would be impossible to reconcile.

He drank a second cup before he set down the mug and headed out. The Delaware River Bridge wasn't far. He took the footpath up alongside the cars passing from New Jersey to Pennsylvania. Every few feet he was compelled to glance back to confirm that the dingus wasn't pursuing him. *Dingus. That's right.* He laughed at the word, making a joke of the horror, and at the fact that he'd escaped it.

The events rolled around in his head like marbles. The woman had created it, called it into being somehow. He'd seen it with his own eyes. Some kind of witch. She would've done the same at the roadhouse. Those coins, buttons, whatever they were. How many did she throw at Cody? Why was he wondering this? It was crazy. Coins that brought trash to life.

He was cold and tired, and he'd just escaped from a goddam dingus that nobody was ever going to believe in.

Back in Philly, he rode the 3rd Street Trolley to Fairmount Avenue and caught the Fairmount trolley up past the prison. He sat away at the back of both by himself. It was coming up on seven in the morning. He smelled like the river, his clothes were damp, his hair was crazy. He looked like someone who'd gotten falling down drunk in a fountain.

He was never so happy to see his cab as that morning. Tumbling into it, he spent a moment breathing in the stale wonderful smell of Rosario's cigars. A fit of laughter burst from him. He pounded the steering wheel and yelled and yelled until he'd worn out the terror. Then he started the cab, drove back to the depot and parked.

Rosie would be showing up any minute for the day shift, but Meyers didn't wait. He walked the few blocks home, stripped out of the wet clothes, and in dry shorts and undershirt he opened a tin of beans that he heated up on the stove, ate ravenously out of the pan, mopping the red sauce up with a hunk of bread. He wanted a pot of coffee and a steak.

The night's events were bending into some warped dream. Meyers furiously scratched his cheek. He kept turning it all over in his head. Had everyone been killed? He tried to remember, but he wasn't sure. Maybe one of the goons had escaped into the warehouse. And the woman, the witch, she'd gotten away, oh, yeah.

Getting away seemed like a very good idea. If any of Drozdov's guys were still loose, they'd come after him to find her. Or maybe think he was part of it, in with her from the beginning. Sure. He'd been out for revenge for Kid. They'd think that, wouldn't they? And what about the cops? The one he'd punched. He couldn't be sure he hadn't been recognized. And Bulbitch—imagine trying to sell him this story: a dingus that killed four armed men? Twice? Bulbitch had warned him to stay out of it, and unless the cops could buy into witches and papier-mâché monsters conjured from coins and buttons and crap, they'd hang this on him. If he hadn't been there, hadn't seen it himself . . .

San Francisco sounded awfully good. Bound to be a morning bus—get him as far as Pittsburgh anyway before anyone knew to look for him. Arnie Slocum had moved out to Frisco to train fighters two years ago. Arnie would hand him a job right away.

As he collected his whirling thoughts, he moved about the apartment, got out his suitcase, filled it with clothes. He needed a bath but maybe not right now. Some clothes, some cash from the bank on the way. He grabbed his tip box out of the back of the closet and tossed two rolls of bills into the suitcase under the clothes. He'd call Rosie from the bus depot, tell him to hang onto the cab, he'd be in touch to work out the details later. Rosie'd find somebody to take the night shift for now.

Winter in California, that wasn't such a bad fate. Let everything blow over and all the monsters wash out to sea.

That was the plan congealing as he hauled the suitcase into the foyer. He paused to pull on his pea jacket, then grabbed the door handle in the same moment he heard his feet splash, and looked down to see dark dirty river water pooling as it trickled in over the threshold. Meyers thought of Red in his roadhouse reaching for a brass knob, blood soaking into the sawdust below him, as the door of the apartment came off the latch.

SO COLDLY SWEET,
SO DEADLY FAIR

Letter from Abraham Van Helsing
to David Ashfort, dated 4 September

My dear friend,

I sit in the house on Keisers-Gracht, late in the afternoon. The canal is silent outside, the walk empty. No one passes, as if they fear this wretched house. I dread much the short journey to the Amstel market and the view of the Oude-Kerk that Willem loved. I can't bear anymore to set eyes on that spire. We would have moved this season our lodgings, you know, to another house on the Kloveniersburgwal, and so I wonder, had we done so in the spring, would none of this have happened? It is the metaphysician's nature to speculate whether changing a single and seemingly unrelated event would alter everything that follows. It is the sort of thing you fix upon: What could I have done differently? Could I have known the outcome of events in time to prevent them? We pray for guidance, but often I think we are praying for prescience. It is why some believe in prognosticators. Forgive me, I am not accounting for myself as I should, and you've waited so long for a reply to your letter—I am rambling. I know this. Let me infuse my narrative with reason henceforth, or at the very least, composure. I must awhile sit first and compose myself. Please do not inform our friend and former student John

Seward, for he would abandon his clinic and rush to my aid, when there is no aid to be offered. Let me write more tomorrow, then.

Excerpt from the diary of Sonja Van Helsing, July 8.

Abraham has made arrangements for us to travel along the Vecht this summer, to escape from this dreadful heat. Already there are people ill from it. He has secured for us a cottage near Loenen. Willem will have his birthday away from home for the first time in his life. He won't go willingly with us, however. He and his friend, Adriaan, are too inseparable. It's unhealthy, this bond between these boys. His father doesn't recognize it, but that's good, finally, for the child will have no compelling argument for being left here while we escape to the cooler countryside. We will all benefit from a holiday.

Announcement posted on various boards in the town of Loenen:

The household of Ludolf Bicker requests information concerning anyone in the village who might be suffering from nocturnal delusions, or sudden weakness, or of any rabid or wild animal seen in the district. It is a matter of some urgency.

From a letter of Abraham Van Helsing to David Ashfort

A barge carried us from the Amstel to the Vecht. Willem brooded a good deal of the time. He had not desired this journey—that was evident. He wanted a friend to accompany us, but his mother had forbidden this, and rightly so. This is our retreat as a family. In time, of course, he brightened, as all children do when finally they realize they will not be allowed their way no matter how surly they become. Then he sat beside me and watched the land slide slowly past. All along the river's course we saw the shapes of windmills. Some were silhouettes on the land, others close enough that we could spy the ribbing of their sails. There is something so oddly human about their shape—like an owlish faced woman waving her arms at you.

It was late in the afternoon when the boat let us off in Loenen— very warm, but much more comfortable than Amsterdam. I left Sonja and Willem with our belongings while I walked into the town to inquire of the postmaster about the cottage, for I did not know with absolute certainty if my representative, Tulp, had secured it for us as promised, but he had done, and all was well.

On the wall in the postal office I saw a petition in the name of Ludolf Bicker. An important name, a famous one. I asked the postal agent what it meant, this strange petition. He gestured helplessly. "It was put up," he told me, "yesterday by Herr Bicker's servant without explanation. Already a family have responded. Their child, of seven years, was very ill and they took her to the estate but she died this morning all the same. Ludolf Bicker himself has agreed to pay all the funeral arrangements. It is a mystery, Herr doctor."

I was surprised that he used this title. Tulp had told him a good deal, it seemed. Dear Tulp is loquacious when drinking, which he does too often for his health.

As I walked back to the river, a small gilded cart was approaching, pulled by a piebald pony. The man leading the horse was a Romany. He had a short beard and a kerchief around his throat. We hadn't seen a camp, but where there is one gypsy, there are many. They only travel in groups. He was looking at me curiously, and as I drew abreast, asked if I needed a cart for our belongings. For a moment, I wondered how he knew this, but of course he had come from the river. I thanked him for the offer, but said no, I could manage without. He gave a tilt of his head as if to say "if you think so" and continued on the path to town. I could have made use of such a cart; but to invite one of these Romany to your house is to invite them all, and I did not care to have a flock of begging children outside my door come morning. That's what I thought of them. In the city, that's what you see—children trained as thieves, as liars and tricksters to surround you like screeching birds while one of them lifts your money or your watch.

When I mentioned the man to Willem and Sonja, she said,

"How does God allow such evil on the earth?"

And so as we walked to the cottage, I explained St. Augustine's opinion that evil exists as a result of a permissive act on God's part, one of toleration, and that evil exists because of the imperfections in man, but that such imperfections are necessary to the harmony and the variety of our world. Evil is here to show us the good. She shook her head with her eyes closed and mouth pinched, as she always does at fine points of philosophy that elude her. "Evil," she said, "should be erased before it can make more evil."

"So evil, then, is like rabbits," I commented.

Willem snorted, which only teased his mother into smoldering silence the rest of our journey.

The cottage was lovely. The walls were half-logs and inside there was one large room plus a small pantry with a cast-iron stove. A loft accessed by ladder contained two beds, one large enough for Sonja and myself, the other for Willem. He did not like to be sharing sleeping quarters with us. Sonja told him he should be glad to have a *bed* here. He threw down his satchel and stormed from the cottage. I restrained the desire to chastise her for this provocation, knowing that I would succeed only in having the cottage to myself.

Willem went as far as the nearest tree. I watched him as I was unpacking my clothes and papers. Perhaps half an hour later I realized he hadn't returned and went outside, to find him chatting with a stranger.

They both turned at my approach, Willem with a sheepish sort of look, as if I'd caught him misbehaving.

"Father," he said, then faltered.

The stranger spoke into the silence and came forward. "Herr doctor," he said, "I am Peter Bicker. My father owns the estate there." He turned to point to where the line of a rooftop appeared above the trees. "We—forgive me, I am intruding, but we were told you'd arrived here and wished, that is, my father wishes to speak with you."

"Your father?"

"Ludolf Bicker?"

"Yes, I know your father's name," I said. "I meant by the question that I can't imagine the reason."

"It is—" he hesitated, glanced at Willem, then back to me "—a private matter, and Herr Tulp has assured us of your knowledge and discretion."

Tulp again. I would have to find him. "Discretion?"

With an air of disdain, he answered, "Regarding my brother. He has been a very bad boy."

"I don't understand."

"Of course not. I daresay, you'll understand even less in a little while. If you would accompany me, that is."

His flair for theatricality and mystery I found rather annoying. But his family was a noble one, and I admit to being curious. I agreed to go, and Willem asked to come along. I sent him back to the cottage to tell his mother that we would be off together. Then the two of us followed Peter Bicker into the trees.

It was not a terribly long walk—the house was perhaps a mile distant from our cottage. The path we traveled crossed a larger track rutted on either side of a grassy stripe, which appeared to lead to the house. Our guide had a more direct route, through a gate in the wall that bounded the estate.

The house itself was of brownish brick, not unlike many houses in Amsterdam. Columns bordered the entrance, supporting a portico roof. A liveried servant waited at the entrance. He bowed and opened the door and kept his head down as we entered.

Another servant met us inside, a man wearing a white handkerchief over the lower part of his face. Upon seeing Peter Bicker, he immediately turned and walked off.

Moments later the patriarch himself appeared at the top of the stairs. The masked servant walked behind him. There must have been servants' stairs in the back. A household so stratified that servants were dissuaded even from using the main staircase? I thought. How archaic. I had no time to dwell on it, as the patriarch extended his—I would have to say delicate—hand and took mine. "I am Ludolf Bicker, Dr. Van Helsing. I am pleased that Peter was able to persuade you to accompany him."

"He portrayed something of a mystery in inviting me."

"Did he?" He seemed to consider whether that was an excusable offense. His face, I must say, looked haggard, as if he had just come through some ordeal. His chin wasn't shaved, his collar soiled. A white cloth similar to the mask worn by the servant dangled from his throat. He was otherwise well and properly dressed, yet clearly the normal course of the household had been shattered. He finally said, "So there *is* a mystery here. And you must wonder what it's true nature might be."

"Sir, indeed," I replied.

"Then come with me, doctor. Peter, will you please entertain the doctor's son while we look in upon Ralf?"

I was torn between trying to explain that I was not a medical practitioner and telling Willem to be on good behavior. As a result I said neither, giving my son a sharp glance and hurrying to follow Ludolf Bicker, who despite his squat appearance, took the stairs two at a time.

Upon reaching the second floor, it became obvious where we were going. Halfway along, on the righthand side, chairs had been drawn up outside a door, and upon seeing the patriarch, one of the servants sitting in the chairs snapped to attention. He wore a white mask over his nose and mouth. The heavyset maid next to him did not; she also did not meet our gaze as we arrived. Pitchers and basins stood on the floor beside her. Like their master, these two servants looked weary and unkempt.

Ludolf Bicker raised a finger to stop the servant who had his hand on the handle of the door. To me he said, "I pray to God you will be able to assist us, doctor. Would you like a mask?"

He made no move to put his own on, so I said, "No, I shall be fine. But tell me—"

He turned away before I could finish, and the servant threw open the door.

The room inside was darker than the hall. The curtains were closed, and the only light came from candles in the corners. The room smelled vaguely foul, as if it housed too many people. A woman—the patriarch's wife—sat beside a bed. And in the bed . . . I remember thinking at that moment, "I'm too late. They've come for me too late." There was no doubt I was looking upon the corpse of a young man who had wasted away.

The face was yellowish, discernable even in the candlelight. The skin seemed translucent and hard, revealing the veins in the taut forehead. The eyes had fallen into bruised sockets. My surmise was that he'd died of consumption, for the face had that ethereal and false glow of health that accompanies this affliction.

I understood why the room smelled as it did now. He could not have been dead more than a day or two.

"This is Ralf," said Ludolf Bicker, "My elder son."

I looked from him to the red and watery eyes of his wife and felt terrible pity for these people in denial of their son's state. Surely there could be no doubt.

"Sir," I said, "Your son . . . what is it you wish of me?"

"Help him," he implored. "Help *us*."

"But I, that is, how shall I advise you?"

"Advise? I don't want advice. I want an answer, a cure, a *reason*!" His wife reached out and took his hand, squeezing to stop him before his anger took over.

"Of course," I said, trying to calm him, "a reason." Here was a father whose son had died and who could not accept the conclusion that was death. He demanded another answer; he was entitled to it and was used to getting his way. I tried to place myself there, with Willem dead instead of his son, but I could not. Still, I couldn't shatter their illusory hope, either. I would give a diagnosis and leave them to their grief. "A reason," I repeated. "I must make examination to do so." I walked to the curtained windows across from the bed and threw the curtains back.

From the bed arose the most horrible scream. I turned to find the corpse of Ralf sitting up, one arm across his face. He flung himself out of the light, off the bed. His soiled nightshirt flapped in the air as he fell to the floor.

"The curtain, doctor! Close it!"

I admit I stood in shock and did nothing despite his command. "Doctor!" he yelled again. I blinked, came to my senses, and drew the curtains together.

Mrs. Bicker hurried around the bed. A hand shot up, fingers splayed wide, as if warding her off. I heard a low keening, as from an animal whose leg had been caught in a trap, and who knew he was doomed. She took the hand and knelt there. Her body shook.

Ludolf Bicker stared across the bed, his hand over his mouth. Only as he faced me again did he lower it. I thought he might be angry at me for causing this terrible scene, but he said only, "You see?"

"He fears the light?"

"It pains him," Bicker replied. "Sunlight hurts him. Three

days ago I myself opened the blinds, because I thought he was malingering after some debauch."

Eventually, Mrs. Bicker arose and her husband and I picked up the unfortunate Ralf and set him on the bed. His head dangled back as though his neck were broken. On his throat were two terrible wounds, two infected punctures, red and purulent.

"What is this?" I asked.

"We don't know. Nor when they first appeared."

"But surely *this* is the cause of his affliction, there's no need for masks." I thought of course that he knew this, too, else he would have insisted I wear one, and he and his wife would be wearing theirs, too. "Something has bitten him." I thought immediately of rabies. "Some animal, a dog."

"But there is no dog, no animal terrifying the town, the outlying areas. We've asked, we've put up notices."

"Yes, I saw one upon arriving. I was told there was a child brought to you." I held Ralf Bicker's wrist and felt his slow and tenuous pulse.

"A girl, yes. She died shortly after being brought here." He shook his head. "It was nothing to do with . . . with this. She had a fever, hallucinations. It was all for nothing. I paid for her funeral out of courtesy."

His wife spoke up. "But Ludolf, the faceless man—"

"Hush with that."

"What is your wife talking about, Herr Bicker?"

He glowered at her, then turned and marched from the room. Frau Bicker settled beside her son, whose head was now rocking from side to side though his eyes hadn't opened yet. His lips curled back and I saw his teeth, the canines abnormally long.

"What were you saying?" I ventured to ask her, but at that moment the door to the room opened, and the patriarch returned, dragging behind him the rotund young serving woman who'd been seated outside. She wore a small cap tied on the back of her head.

"This," said Bicker, "is Juliana. Juliana, this is Doctor Van Helsing. You will please tell him about last night." She shot him a look of alarm, and he said, "Everything. He wishes to know."

She accepted her fate, I thought, forlornly. Head bowed, her hands clutched in front of her apron, she told her unlikely story.

Juliana had been on duty, tending Ralf Bicker. Someone had been with him at all times since he turned sickly. During the night, she fell asleep. From her expression, I inferred she was supposed to stay awake. The night was warm. The windows were open to allow a breeze. At some point she awoke. All save the candle beside her had gone out. In the center of the room someone was standing. She described a blacker shadow within the darkness. Of course, she had just awakened and it was some moments before she realized that the shadow was moving—gliding—to the bed. She started to cry out, but the shadow suddenly pointed at her and she froze as if she'd been turned to stone. She couldn't speak or move. She could only watch. The man—for now she was convinced of the figure's sex—had no face, no features. He was darkness itself. Now he changed his direction and approached her. Her terror grew so intense that she fainted dead away before he reached her. She awoke to find the candles all lit, and Ralf sleeping. Of the faceless man there was no sign, and so she thought it must have been a dream.

I agreed, but Herr Bicker said, "Go on."

Juliana squirmed in place, and her eyes teared. Finally she confessed, "I got up to see that he was all right. The dressing had been removed from his throat, and the throat was scratched. He—he must have torn it off in his sleep. Then as I bent over him to reapply it, his eyes opened. Oh, sir, the look, the look in his eyes." She wept now and I patted her arm to sympathize, but she flinched at the touch. "He glared at me and then he snarled, like a mad dog, and jumped, his arms around my throat, his teeth . . ." She couldn't finish, but buried her face behind her hands.

I reached carefully to her neck and folded down the collar of her uniform. The puncture wounds were quite clear inside an oval bruise where the rest of his teeth had bitten into her. Never had I seen anything like this. No, this was not rabies, not at least as I understood it.

I thanked her for relating this difficult story. Bicker escorted her out and returned immediately. "Nonsense about a faceless man—she fell asleep, she had a nightmare, it's as simple as that."

"Very likely," I agreed, "but the bite at her throat is real enough. If he weren't so weak, your son might have opened her jugular. Can you tell me, sir, where had your son been lately? Who has he associated with?"

"Ah, you think contagion."

"I think nothing," I replied. "I must know more facts, more information. To know the reality we must learn the essence. Tell me all that you know. Your wife, and your other son, Peter. Whoever knows where this boy has been must tell it to me. Else we can only watch him die. He is desperately weak."

I did think of the new technique of transfusing blood, but hesitated to recommend it. In truth, I did not imagine the boy had more than hours to live; perversely, I tell you that I was much more interested in what the girl, Juliana, had dreamt.

Diary of Sonja Van Helsing, July 10th

By the time Abraham and Willem returned, it was past midnight. Both of them seemed to have been treated roughly. I did not restrain my fury with them—how *little* they consider me! Then our son said, "It's because of the gypsies!" Abraham looked at him heavily, then sighed, "Yes, we were with the gypsies."

"I thought you'd gone to the home of Peter Bicker."

"So, and we did. It's quite a terrible situation, too. Their other son is gravely ill, in all likelihood dying. The gypsies, they awaited us when we set out for home. They stopped us and insisted we go with them."

"Those foul creatures? Did they rob you?"

No, said Abraham, they hadn't been interested in robbing anyone. "And they are not foul, Sonja." His tone was sharp with me for saying so.

Then he described everything.

The gypsies had barred his way, four of them—making it plain there was no alternative but to accompany them to the camp.

This comprised five wagons drawn together. Abraham was taken to their leader, their *ataman*, whose name was Costel—a big man with a wide black mustache. Abraham said that the people, these Romany creatures, all came out to see him. The children ran up, calling him "gorgio" and holding out their hands. It is what they are like: They entreat and beg even their prisoners.

There was an awning on poles, and the *ataman* Costel sat beneath that with six or seven others. When Abraham arrived, he dismissed all but three of them, then invited his guests to sit opposite, Someone brought roast chicken and poured wine from the bottle they had on the table. He said the wine was surprisingly good. No doubt they'd stolen it elsewhere.

Costel told Abraham he knew why he'd come, knew even what had transpired inside the house.

"Do you know what afflicts that boy?" Costel asked him.

Abraham told him the truth—that he'd never seen its like before, terrible wounds on the throat as if some animal were loose in the house.

Costel nodded. "An animal, yes, but like none you've heard of, doctor. Some of my people, especially the Sinti, they call it *mamioro*—the spirit that brings sickness."

Abraham replied that he didn't believe in evil spirits.

"No?" said Costel. "Neither do I. This creature is more flesh than the name implies. And we Kalderash have a name for it, too: *nosferatu*."

I knew nothing of this word. Abraham had to explain it to me. It refers to a night-creature that is neither dead nor alive, but in some state of existence between both, and that spreads a plague where it goes. The gypsies claimed to be hunting it. They had traveled across half of Europe in pursuit. The *nosferatu*, however, is cunning, and it had eluded them every time. Abraham asked why they pursued it.

Costel answered him, "Because it took my daughter." Abraham thought he meant that it had kidnapped her. Not so, replied Costel. It took her from *life*. It bled her to death. Then it replaced her life with its own. It made her one of its kind. It took, he said, a pure, sweet child and poured corruption into her very *essence*.

Even as I write this, diary, my hand trembles, for I know what this dark man says—it's what *I've* felt and not been able to describe. But now—now I understand what's been done, what's happened. I understand corruption of innocence.

"Can you imagine what it's like to find your child made monstrous?" Costel asked him. "What it's like to have to destroy her?" He had slain her himself, found her lair and put a stake through her. As proof of what he said, he had one of those with him, a young man, show Abraham his throat. It had scars from wounds like those on the throat of Ralf Bicker. Exactly the same. This young man was betrothed to Costel's daughter. She'd appeared to him after she was buried. He'd thought it a vision. She feasted upon him, only he cried out in his wagon, and someone came and stopped her. She broke the arm of that man before vanishing into the night like smoke off a fire.

Abraham said the gypsies want his help in finding the monster responsible for Costel's daughter and Bicker's son. They advised him to surround this boy with cloves of garlic, to place it like mistletoe over the windows and the door. Garlic. Abraham had to fight not to laugh: A boy was dying and they wished to hang garlic in his room, not even feed it to him.

Costel must have sensed his skepticism, for he said then, "Our Reason strives to know all of the world, Dr. Van Helsing, but theoretical reason tells us we can never know all." This, Abraham explained, was a quote from Kant, and it revealed the *ataman* to be learned in his metaphysics. I will never grasp, no matter how often he tries to explain to me, this foolish philosophy of his. I know evil. I don't need these finer debates on its many facets.

We have come to the devil's own village. Brought our son to it.

I told Abraham that this other boy, this Peter, should be watched, kept away from our Willem. "He's infected, too," I told him. "This I'm certain of." But he, so sure of himself, said that no, Peter Bicker is not a danger. He's not like his brother at all. "They are just boys," he said. "Let them be," he said. His mind was elsewhere. *Let them be?* What sort of parent am I to follow such instruction? Oh, he is lost in his clouds of philosophy. I know what these "just boys" are doing. I see how they communicate in looks so sly and cunning; just as with Adriaan. I know what I am saying. My husband's intellect blinds him to matters not of intellect. He is more interested in what gypsies tell him than what his wife knows.

from a letter of Abraham Van Helsing to David Ashfort

The following morning I walked into Loenen. I had no trouble finding Tulp. He was in the tavern having a breakfast of beer soup with eggs. He offered me the same but I refused. I was content to drink tea. Although I'd wanted to chide him earlier, now I had far more pressing matters to discuss, and wished this

time to gain from his loquaciousness. I asked what he knew of
the Bicker family.

He tore a lump from a piece of bread dipped it in his beer
broth, then chewed it as he replied. "Rich is what they are. The
boys are trouble, as boys tend to be. A couple of little Til Eulen-
spiegels."

"How did this one, Ralf, fall ill?"

"Initially? Walking home from this very tavern. I know because I was here. And he was in his cups."

"He was attacked by something while walking?"

"Attacked by the demons of gin, more like. It didn't kill him,
did it? He came to his senses and made his way home at the dawn,
and he's not left it since."

"He's the only one been bitten?"

"Bitten, heh?"

"His throat." I tapped two fingers against mine.

"The little girl they brought to the estate?"

"No," I told him. "She had a fever. Different."

"Pity." He slurped more of his beer. "Bitten . . . there were
some animals—that happened before Ralf Bicker. Not in Loenen,
but on a farm to the northeast."

"Animals?"

"Some pigs with their throats slashed. Most everyone suspects
the damned gypsies, because, you know, they're always stealing
pigs. They even have a trick they call 'drab the bawlo' where they
feed the pig a sponge soaked with lard, and the sponge swells up
and kills the animal, and then the gypsies buy it from the poor
farmer for a pittance as no one wants it anymore." I must have
given him an odd look, because he quickly added, "I've traded
with them now and again. A little commerce, that's all."

Tulp blushed so that I suspected they'd paid him to tell them
where the largest pigs could be found.

He changed the subject. "Oh, yes. There's a farm girl there,
too. She and her boyfriend were . . . you know . . . in a field. The
boyfriend attacked her and ran off."

"I fail to see what that has to do with it."

"You said 'bitten.' The girl was bitten. She claims her boyfriend didn't do it, but, after all, what's she going to say?"

"What *does* she say?"

"A crazy story, that a man made out of shadows attacked them both."

Diary of Sonja Van Helsing, July 11

Abraham went off today, leaving us here. Our family holiday has turned into an adventure for him. All exists just to intrigue him. Willem doesn't want to spend time with me nor even remain in the house. Wanders off. For all I knew he went to that camp of gypsies. Abraham investigates a dying boy and leaves his own son to fester with notions he dare not speak to his mother.

Left alone, I went to the river to think. I didn't intend to dwell upon evil, but it finds me. This plague I see in Willem, though I cannot describe to Abraham's satisfaction. The philosopher demands concrete examples, evidence from me while he describes airy, empty notions upon no evidence. Surely God led me along the river today, to the small pool, the stream that broke away.

I heard their laughter first, and crept through the trees. The stream is shrouded in forest. Thus it was easy for me to look down at the pool without being seen.

There lay Willem, floating on his back, naked. Beside him that other boy, Peter. The water wasn't deep for he was standing. I heard him say, "And then the creature fell upon him thus!" and he leapt at Willem, sliding over him, and sank his face into Willem's throat. My son struggled but as play, he did not actually fight to keep this other boy from the attack, and he was . . . oh, I cannot bear to say this. Only with women should a man be so. This word, *nosferatu*, is what this boy, this Bicker, is. He infects my son, as Adriaan did. Does.

I should have stepped out, let them see me, shown them I *knew*. I'm ashamed I fled, but I could not bear witness to their unnatural caresses. Oh, Abraham, you leave your son to monsters!

from a letter of Abraham Van Helsing to David Ashcroft

When Tulp told me the girl's story, I insisted he take me to her farm immediately. We rented a cart and set off, Tulp driving and asking questions that I dismissed and deflected.

The farm proved far enough away that I knew this tale of the shadow man hadn't been traded between the girl in Bicker's house and the farmgirl.

She turned out to be a plump and rosy-cheeked child, whose whole face burned red when she heard what I wanted.

We found her resting in the field after her morning's labors. A flour mill stood nearby, its arms revolving slowly as harvested grain was crushed. Other workers saw us and started over. I sent Tulp to keep them at bay, that we might not be interrupted. It would be difficult enough, I thought, to get her to tell me what had happened; indeed, the first thing she proclaimed was, "Papa says I'm not to speak of it."

"Oh? Why is that?"

"He's angry with me. With Claes."

"Your father believes this Claes fellow hurt you?"

"No one believes me," she blurted, and her face crumpled up. She was about to cry.

"*I* believe you," I said.

Her tears were forestalled, but she looked at me in confusion, not sure if she should be happy at this turn or not, not sure if she could trust an unshaven academic from Amsterdam.

I told her that someone else had described this man she had seen.

"Oh, thank God," she said, but then caught herself and asked, "But, was anyone harmed? Was Claes with him?"

"I think no one has seen your friend. But you must tell me the way it happened."

She lowered her eyes. "We were in the field over there." She pointed to where the tall wheat waved in the breeze. "There's a clearing back in the center of the field, with trees and soft ground." Realizing the implication of that statement, she blushed again.

"You love Claes. So, you and he were expressing your affection, heh?"

She nodded. "It was just sunset. I had my eyes closed. Then I opened them and I saw this . . . this impossible thing. Dust and chaff from the wheat was swirling and swirling in place. I thought I must be dreaming. I could feel a breeze off it. The swirl grew tighter, and became a shadow, as of a man but upright."

"And Claes?"

"He was not looking that way." She almost smiled. "He couldn't see. But I think I made a sound and then he turned his head and he saw it, too. He jumped to his feet, to protect me. But the shadow knocked him aside and came at me."

"What happened?"

"I don't know. All I remember is the face, because I couldn't see one. He was like a ghost, a dark ghost."

She had a kerchief around her throat, and I now cautiously reached over and hooked my finger in it to draw it down. She let me do this, her eyes brimming again with tears. Her throat had been bitten. Bruised from a set of sharp teeth, with two punctures into the skin. Unlike Ralf Bicker, the wounds did not look infected.

"I woke up and it was dark, and Claes was gone. No one has seen him. No one has seen anything. My family were furious with me for letting Claes . . . but it's my wish, too, and they—" She stopped herself, realizing that she was telling a perfect stranger things far too intimate.

I patted her hand and repeated that I knew she was telling the truth and that she should not worry, although I was certain her lover was dead, or worse.

Before we left, we purchased from her father a bag of garlic.

Tulp told me that the others were afraid. They believed her story in spite of her father's insisting that Claes was responsible. His anger blinded him so that the boy was hiding from *him*.

Diary of Sonja Van Helsing, undated

Abraham returned late. He had been to a farm, met a girl who'd been attacked by the creature that attacked Ralf Bicker. When I said, "That would be Peter," he glared at me. I tried to tell him what I'd seen—the boys in the pool, and Peter biting Willem just as Abraham says this phantom does. He became agitated. "For the last time, Sonja, Peter is *not* the issue," he said. "This is *evil*. It defies God's laws! A perversion of His balance. Life must have death, harmony *must* be there—it is how it is for all the world. Instead, we encounter something defiant of the rules, not *exanimus* but *exponaevum*. It beggars belief. *How* does it survive?" What I said was dismissed, and he would not hear more.

In the evening, he returned to Bicker's estate with his stupid bag of garlic. Insisted on putting some around the room, over doors, windows, even placing a clove on the afflicted brother's forehead. The boy went wild at the touch of it, and took two people to be held down afterwards. The garlic left a terrible mark on his skin, as if he'd been burned. The elder Bicker was furious but also terrified. Abraham admits he had doubts before, but no longer. From Bicker's he raced to the gypsy camp. Their *ataman* believed him, because when he came home, he carried not only garlic but also three large wooden stakes. Was upset that I waited for him. He did not, he said, wish for me to be a part of this awful business. *He* would protect us. He wouldn't let it into our house. I wanted to shout at him that he was too late, it was here already, but I knew his reaction. Instead, I asked him to tell me about the stakes, what they were for. He sighed, and said, "For finishing what the garlic begins." When he refused to elaborate, I withdrew and went to bed.

He placed garlic around the house then, in windowsills and in front of the door—I stepped on some this morning. Then he came up the ladder. I kept my eyes closed until I heard him move to Willem's side, then watched him place cloves around him on the pillow. So, I thought, he harbors suspicions, too. Willem sat up immediately and asked what this was about. Abraham told him something—I could only hear the words "in the name of God" as he raised his voice, and even that was whispered. He glanced over his shoulder at me and I closed my eyes again until the lamp light was blown out.

I think we were not asleep four hours when there came rapping upon the door. Abraham got from bed and in his nightshirt descended the ladder.

After a few minutes, he came back and began to dress. I whispered, "What is it?"

"They've found him," he told me. "I must go. I must see this through."

I lay then, unable to return to sleep. I realized I am fearful of being alone with Willem. But he arose soon after his father and left the house. Once he'd closed the door, I crept down to watch him cross the yard. Saw the shadow beneath the large oak tree. Watched them embrace. God sees this, too.

His bedding revealed none of the garlic Abraham had left. Where did it go?

Willem is informing on Abraham's every move. I know. They collude. He will destroy his own father. I cannot allow—

Perversion, it's *perversion*.

I can save their souls, Abraham. I will.

from a letter of Abraham Van Helsing to David Ashfort

The Romany had tracked the fiend down. Costel clapped me on the back and said, "It's your doing, Herr Doctor. We would not have found him were it not for you." Something in the farmgirl's story had helped them. I asked him what, and he said, "Be patient, it's but a little ways."

Costel carried a lantern through the dark. We might have been going anywhere. "You brought your weapons?"

I held up a stake. "Only this," I said. "And some garlic. I haven't had time to go to the church for the crucifix. I left the other stakes behind."

"It's all right," Costel assured me. "One will do." His free hand fell upon the hilt of a small scimitar by his hip.

With the barest hint of dawn on the horizon, we arrived at our destination—an old dilapidated windmill by the Vecht. Something moved outside of it, which proved to be one of Costel's people, the young man I'd met. He hissed something in their language. Costel said to me, "Someone is inside already."

I stared fearfully at the mill, afraid for the first time.

Soon there were six of us. "We go in," said Costel. The one who had been on guard nodded and drew a large knife. The others, too, had knives. With my wooden stake, I felt inadequately armed.

The man nearest the door carefully lifted the latch on the tip of his knife and eased the old door open. We moved inside like shadows ourselves. It smelled of hay. The bit of moonlight that entered through the tiny windows described beams overhead but little else. Something clomped across the ceiling above us.

We located the steps up, then one by one made the ascent.

The boards creaked—there was no avoiding it. I heard a shout and a crash, then a snarl, as if they'd cornered a beast. I stood fairly helplessly on the stairs as the gypsies fought him. Costel lit a candle. What its light revealed stunned me.

The gypsies had caught a boy, a feral savage. He wore ragged clothes and was as filthy as a dog that had rolled in mud. His eyes were red, inhuman. I said, "Is this—" but Costel stopped me.

"No. This, I expect, is your missing farmboy. What was his name?"

"Claes," I said, and the boy faced me when I said it. So, it was he. "He has been turned, then."

"Yes, but not as you think. He has been made to drink his master's blood and in this way has been contaminated with his master's power. He's become a slave to the fiend."

"Why?"

"In the daylight, our prey is weak. He requires a human servant to watch over him then. Such is their way when they plan to remain awhile in a place. The servants are tied to them, always hungry for more of their tainted blood. It's all they can think of." He turned, barked a command in his Romany tongue. "Quick now. The fiend will return with the dawn."

The others stripped the snarling boy. The curly-headed guard also stripped, then put on the boy's clothes. They trussed Claes and carried him off, back down the stairs. Costel went with them. His candle revealed bales of straw and a broken-down wagon with three wheels. The gypsies clubbed the boy with the hilts of their knives, struck him again and again until he was unconscious. Then one of them took off his scarf and gagged him, and they tossed his body behind the straw, covering him with it.

They came up the steps quickly and Costel told me, "He's not dead, but he mustn't awaken for a while. And, anyway, if he should survive this ordeal, he will thank us."

"If?"

He grinned in a way that told me the worst was yet to come. "We must find our adversary's resting place." Clearly he did not think it was on this floor.

We climbed a ladder to the next level above. A trap door had to be pushed back to access a claustrophobic storage space with a low ceiling. In one spot the thatch had been replaced by winged doors as on a stable loft. There was nothing here but the gray remains of old flour ground into the boards. From there a few steps led to the level where lay the mechanism of the windmill. A central pole projected from the ceiling. Gears and ball governors on either side of the pole turned two millstones for the grinding of the grain. One of the gypsies pointed. There, behind the millstones and next to a trough stood a flat open box. Although it was shallow, its interior was dark. It was full of dirt.

"Here is his spoor," said Costel.

"But why if he's weak in the light does he come up so high? Why not use the stables at the bottom?"

"Look around you, doctor. No windows here. A little light falls from the opening in the ceiling, around the windshaft. There's a window in the thatch up there, but not here. See? His servant has stuffed all the holes. Quickly now, up the ladder to the cap. Someone go and close that trap door."

And so we climbed once more, into the small cramped room at the top of the mill. Something burst from the thatch at our arrival—we'd startled an owl from its resting place. One of the gypsies muttered "*Ja Develesa*" and gestured after it. Droppings—from the owl or from bats—spattered the floor. The owl had perched on the great wheel to which the sails were attached. It creaked as the anchored sails shifted and tried to turn in the morning breeze.

We waited. All of us, sitting there, looking at each other's eyes. Light was leaking in around the wheel. I wondered how the gypsy who had replaced poor Claes would fare. The two of them looked nothing alike. Wouldn't the fiend recognize this? I wanted to ask Costel but before I could speak there was noise below. The trap door into the storage room was thrown back. Footsteps came up the ladder to the room below. We sat pressed to the walls, for the light up here would have revealed our presence to anyone in the dimness below if we'd dared look down.

We waited and listened. There was little to listen for, not so much as a breath—a wooden creak. That would be the box of dirt.

I began to wonder when we would move, what we were waiting for. Then I heard the trap door shut below. Costel nodded, and we went down.

It was fast. There was no point in trying to sneak into the

chamber. The first man dropped most of the way down the ladder. The second one came right behind him. Something hissed loudly, horribly, like a snake imitating speech. The thing—still no more than a shape—flew at the first man as if on wings. The second one took his great knife and plunged it—not into the attacker but into the thatch. He cut a gash that spilled in light. Now our third man dropped, his knife raised, and he plunged it into the back of the monster, which shrieked, twisted, and slapped him aside. The first man had fallen. But Costel was on the ladder, and for one moment I glimpsed past the gypsy the face of our enemy staring up at us.

I tell you, my blood ceased to flow for that moment. The eyes were blackened with blood, and its teeth were like spikes lining its gums, two of them like curved needles. The lips were drawn back, but as it identified Costel, I swear I saw fear cloud its expression. It recognized him. Even as he descended, the thing dove for escape. It went headfirst down the ladder to the storage room, Costel right behind it, and I behind him, the others pressing me. The fiend banged upon the trap door. It shouted in a voice like shattering glass: "Claes!" The trap had been locked from below and wouldn't open. We crowded into the storage room with it. I could smell it so close, the sickly smell of putrefaction. Pressed against the roof, the creature cowered, then lashed out. One of the men behind me turned and threw open the shutter in the side of the thatch, and pink sunlight splashed us. The cornered predator howled and tried to shield itself, pressing closer against the thatch. It began to change shape, sprouting wings, and Costel yelled at me, "Now! Abraham, now!" And as if by instinct, as if I'd known all along what I must do, I raised that wooden stake over my head and drove it straight into the creature's throat.

Black blood spurted at me. The birdshape collapsed back into the creature so like a man but not one. It stumbled and pulled at the stake, but I held on. Costel drew cloves of garlic from his pockets. He grabbed the creature by the hair and twisted back the head. The mouth opened, displaying those horrible teeth, and he shoved the garlic into its maw. The teeth must have cut him, but he didn't stop. His whole fist was jammed into that mouth. Then the thing tore free of our grip and I thought it would escape; but it only spun about, and clawed at itself, lurching, stumbling. It fell to the floor.

Each of the gypsies drew garlic bulbs from their clothing, and with the thing still aware they, one after the other, stuffed another bulb into its mouth. The jaw must have broken, it was open so wide. I stood there, with the dripping stake in my hands, with the gore of the vampire's last feast on my face and clothes.

Costel drew his scimitar. He knelt beside the vampire and said, "This, for my daughter. For all our daughters." He raised the blade and swung it in an arc that severed the head from the body.

As I watched, the creature's clawlike hands transformed into human ones which withered and curled. The face darkened, and the mouth blistered as if burning from the inside.

One of the men stamped on the trap door three times, and after a moment it was flung open. The other fellow stuck his head up and surveyed the room. He had smeared himself with dirt and matted his hair. Costel handed him the head, and grinning he shook it a moment, then jumped down the ladder, crying out: "*Opre! Opre, Detlene!*"

"What is he saying?" I asked.

"He's calling the spirits of the dead children this thing has killed to rise up, to go up to God now that the demon is slain."

"*Ja Develesa,*" said the man behind me, as he had at the owl.

On the ground floor we found the real Claes still unconscious but alive. One of the men went out and returned with a bucket and threw water on him. He came to slowly, confusedly, then began to weep. I accompanied Costel outside to watch a hole dug and the head thrown into it.

"Now we can rest. Or, rather, I can. You, doctor, still have a patient. This won't save *him*."

So I set off across the open fields to the estate of Ludolf Bicker. My legs trembled, and halfway there I had to stop and lean against a tree. I felt as though I'd battled an army. I had experienced something I would have deemed impossible, fantastic, even a week ago. Metaphysics is a study of that which transcends the physical, yet nowhere is there explanation of creatures who defied the limits of life itself. Vampire. The evil of fallen angels, of demons and devils. It was the simplicity of good versus evil, which I've dismissed because I believe that none of us is pure evil. None of *us*.

I thought matters would be resolved easily now. Yet upon reaching the estate, I found the servants running about, and the one on the door would not let me in until Ludolf Bicker himself had been called, though surely he remembered me.

Bicker looked deranged. His hair stood in wild disarray, his eyes red, chin stubbled. In his dressing gown and barefoot, he waved me inside. "What has happened to you, doctor?" he asked.

I then realized why the servant refused me entry. Blood was on my shirt, my hands. "We've stopped the fiend," I said, "the one who plagued your son."

"Stopped him?"

"Yes," I said carefully. "Driven it away."

"Ah." His eyes pinched. "Too late."

"What? Why?"

"My son is dead."

"But that can't be, we—" I stopped myself. I recalled the vampire's state as the stake pierced him, the blood that burst out of him, blood from a feeding. "How did it get inside? The garlic should have . . ."

"Peter."

"Peter removed it? Why, in heaven's name?"

"Who *knows* why?" he cried. "They competed for attention, they fought always. They—" He wiped a trembling hand over his mouth. "This battle was nearly our undoing. Ralf's mother was attacked. This demon passed through the window unhindered. She saw it but couldn't cry out, couldn't move, as Julianna described."

"It will have no power over her anymore," I promised. Then I stiffened with awakening fear. "You must let me see your son's body."

"Is that necessary now?"

"Herr Bicker, I fear it may be imperative. I am only now realizing the full repercussions this night might bring."

He looked upon me as if he wanted nothing more than to dismiss me, but turned and led the way upstairs. Other servants saw me, lowered their gaze, shuffled aside.

The body was in the same room, covered by a sheet. I reached into my pants pocket and pulled out my remaining clove of garlic. Before Bicker could stop me, I drew down the sheet, opened the corpse's mouth and stuck the garlic in between its teeth.

Bicker shouted, outraged: "Van Helsing!" at which moment the corpse of Ralf Bicker began to thrash madly upon the bed.

Its eyes opened, suffused with blood. It sprang up. I fell back, but Bicker did not. Ralf spit out the clove of garlic and leapt upon his father, who screamed.

I ran to the heavy curtains and threw them open. Daylight burst upon us, and the revenant Ralf Bicker shrieked and fell against the wall. His hands tried to block the light, unsuccessfully. He collapsed in a heap and whimpered.

The patriarch clutched his own throat, stared aghast. I said, "Listen, Ludolf Bicker. This isn't your son. Your son *is* dead. You understand?"

"Peter—"

"Yes, and you still have Peter."

"No, he's gone, too. We can't find him all night." He shook with great sobs. "The fiend *took* him."

"All night?" I cried. And if the vampire had taken him, then . . . Willem. Sonja.

I ran from the room.

Daylight would keep Ralf Bicker from harming anyone. Later, we would have to take up the gory work, or beg the gypsies to do what we could not.

My dread increased as I neared the cottage. I called out, "Willem, Sonja!" No one answered.

The door hung open as if to say I was too late.

Inside, my wife sat on the floor. If my dishevelment was cause for concern, Sonja's was cause for terror. Blood had run in streaks down her face; her hands were red as paint. The front of her night-dress was drenched as if her heart had burst. She seemed unaware of me. I lifted her hands, squeezed them. "Sonja," I said. She raised her eyes and held me with a glance as the vampire did his victims.

Then she laughed.

It was the most horrible sound I've ever heard, so terrible that I can hear it just by writing this; and I, unaware at first, joined her, laughing and wailing simultaneously. It is the sound of King Laugh, laughter that comes because the horror inside is too great to be contained, and this contortion of hysteria is all we can manage. I knelt and gripped her shoulders to embrace her, but her laugh turned to a screech, and she tore free of me, scrabbling back against the cupboard.

There is a moment that no one should ever have to face,

when you know that everything which has been your life, your commonplace life, is gone. In a moment and forever after. That epiphany sobered me. King Laugh evaporated. I said, "Where is Willem?"

She looked at the floor, then off to the left, toward the east side of the house. I rose and walked back outside. The wind was blowing a bit of rain, a spray that wouldn't last but a few minutes, for the sun was out, still. One large cloud rolled over me.

I walked but saw nothing. I called, but no answer. He had been discrete you see, retreated far from the house for his liaisons with Peter Bicker. They had recognized each other, as I refused to. Yet I'd known, as I'd known about Adriaan.

Augustine's metaphysics tell us that all things were created in the beginning—the physical, material beings and the immaterial ones, the angels. Regarding souls—our essence—he couldn't say with absolute certainty, proposing that either they come into being with our bodies, or that we are products of our parents' souls, by which the parent is complicit in the sin of the child. Does that mean that Sonja could not bear her part or my own? But how could I condemn that which is of me?

The boys lay together, their blood mixed with the earth, bodies silver pale in the sunlight. Bicker was face-down and likely hadn't suspected anything. Willem must have seen and known what she intended. Had he laughed at her, making light of her fury? I expect he did.

She had staked them both with those two sticks I'd left behind. I could have applied the garlic but I knew already that they weren't vampires. They were just children.

Only you and I know this, friend David. For Ludolf Bicker's family, it was better to believe that one son had infected the other, and that both perished from the one cause. Better for Sonja, though it's of no consequence to her. In the asylum all are innocent. Madness cleanses their souls with its purifying fires, burning away their guilt along with their reason. They cannot be evil for they know nothing of it. Evil is for the rest of us to see.

THE PROWL

P *lateye*: **A ghost or spirit that can assume many shapes** from animal to human to monster. Believed by some Gullah people to be the incarnation of spirits of dead pirates, killed to protect the location of buried treasure, the plateye is retributive and mischievous. It is particularly fond of whiskey.

Sure, I know what you want to hear about. You want to hear about the Civil War. I've already been interviewed, and that's all anybody wants recollected. Yes, I know, I *do* look too young to have seen it. I suppose now that there's been this so-called "Great War," people think they need to hear about others, to acquire some perspective. Me, I've seen enough to tell you there's no such thing as a *great* war. They're all ugly, stupid things, and I could relate far more interesting stories on other topics if you cared to listen.

You want to know what? How I learned to speak so eloquently? Hunh. You expected something a little less educated from an ex-slave, is that it? Well, as it happens, my speech is one of those more interesting stories—part of the best story of all, if I may?

Young man, do you know what a *haant* is? Well, it's a Gullah word. They're my people, the Gullah, live on the coast down south below Charleston. No, I don't mean I was born in South Carolina. I wasn't. I was born in Africa. And I was a free man until . . . Tell me, what are you? Maybe twenty-two, twenty-three? Unh-huh. Try to imagine that, at twenty-three, you'd been robbed of your future.

I was sixteen when they captured me. No, not whites. Not my

own people, either, but other black men, who swept down upon us. They took me and some of my friends. They set fire to my village, and I don't know who lived or died that day. Those of us they kept were put in chains and marched to the coast and sold to the white men with ships. I didn't know the name of my country then—it was just home. I know now that the world calls it Angola.

The blacks who sold us got a pittance for us compared to what we were worth at this end of the journey. They sold us for silver, for guns, for rum, for beads, and even for pots and pans. While they negotiated with the ships, they locked us up in big cages on the shore called *barracoons*. People were jammed up together, pushed against each other's stink, but it was heaven compared with what awaited us. There were people from all over, and half of 'em spoke languages I didn't know. Almost everybody was naked. The slavers preferred us that way. We were nothing but beasts to them, and you don't put clothes on a mule, do you? We were there not even a full day before we were purchased and dragged up on a ship.

The captain, he barked at us like a hyena. None among us knew his language, but we understood him well enough, since failing to do so meant you got beat with a rope end till you figured it out. People wonder why we didn't do anything, why we didn't fight. After all, there were hundreds of us and hardly anything at all of them. But they had us terrified. We didn't know where we were. We were hungry and exhausted. I think we all believed that if we were just good and quiet, we wouldn't be harmed. If we'd known the truth. . . There *were* some ships where the slaves mutinied, but not many.

Crewmen came along and pulled some of us out of the crowd and stood us in a line. There was a redheaded fellow who, if anybody was too slow to move, lashed them across the face, and he was smirking all the time and shouting at us. He liked for us to be too slow.

The tall ones like me, we were all lined up together. Then the middle heights and the shortest. Men and women were separated, too.

Then they drove us down into the belly of that ship. They'd fixed it up special for their cargo. Made three tiers of what could be called pigeon holes, but what were more like coffins stacked on top of each other. You climbed in at the foot and dragged your-self up inside it, trying not to lie on the chains that shackled you there, 'cause you were going to lie on them for a long time if you did. The bottom tier was the biggest, which is to say, the longest, for the tallest of us. The first man in line, he didn't want to go in, and that red-headed bastard beat him unconscious with the rope. The man had to be picked up and shoved into his hole. He became the first to die on the voyage, but not the last. The rest of us saw how it was, and most crawled into their coffins willingly. We had no more than fifteen inches across in those holes. There was hardly room above to lie on your side. If you could turn over. Take you half an hour to turn over in that space, and you had to hunch your shoulders and wriggle like a tadpole. You'd end up with splinters in the meat of your arm, and if you weren't careful you could strangle in your chains.

It stank like no pigstye you've ever known, too. But we were property, and worth a good deal, and they didn't want us get-ting sick. They could lose thousands of dollars if some fever swept through their cargo, so they hosed us down regularly.

I had big wrists then, too big for the shackles they supplied, so that the skin was rubbed raw on me in no time. To either side there were uprights, supporting the second and third tiers, which was all that kept us from being squished. During the day enough light got in that we could see the fear in one another's eyes. They wanted us to see that. They wanted us to pass our fear around. I guess you boys who fought in the 'Great War,' you had it bad in the trenches, with mud and mustard gas and all. But you haven't been anywhere as near hell as I have. You never lived three weeks in a coffin narrower than your shoulders. If the person on the upper tier above you got scared and pissed him-self, it dripped down on you and there was nothing you could do about it till they next hosed you off with sea water, and then a soup of human waste from above came raining down between the boards.

They stuffed in a man beside me who had been beaten all over. His eye was swelled up, and his head was bloody, crusted. The flies were at him, but he was smiling, like he felt nothing at all, and even over the stench of that place I smelled him, smelled the booze on him, for he was drunker than a man can get. I think they could have beaten him to death and he wouldn't have noticed for a week.

They locked us all in, then hoisted their sails. People soon started to moaning, some grew seasick and threw up—yet another stench in which to lie. A couple of people went crazy the first days in those tiny stinking holes. I expect I should have. I'd never been confined in my life till then.

That evening they fed us. We could smell the cooking and most of us hadn't eaten in days. It was gruel, thick and nasty, but it was enough to keep a body alive. Of course, when you eat, you shit, and some there were couldn't help themselves, couldn't wait till the next time they were danced up on deck.

That's what they called it when they let us walk around—*dancing* us. One group at a time, they led us up on the deck, letting us wander about, tasting fresh air and exercise, every day, for maybe an hour before they put us back down in those coffin holes. Dancing, I guess, 'cause some began to sing and some swayed to the singing, their bodies taking them home. It was the only means they had to escape. Then and after.

The second night aboard, the thing happened that changed my life. That beat-up drunk beside me, he made this quiet sound, like a gas jet. It wouldn't have wakened me, but I was lying on my back and barely asleep. I was looking at the boards above my nose, so close that my breath came back on me. I turned my head to see, but it was black as a coal mine.

I heard a slithery sound, like a big snake twisting, and more hissing. The chain rattled just the tiniest bit. My hair started creeping up on my head. Bristling like a dog. After a time there was only the absence of sound. I knew that hole beside me was empty and that man had gotten free somehow.

I couldn't see as far as my feet even. Couldn't turn my head to know where he'd gone or what he purposed to do. There was no escape from that place for anyone.

An hour maybe went by like that before he came back. There wasn't a sound until he was slithering into that hole again. I stared so hard into that dark that it burned, but all I could make out was a general shape, twisted up like something made of molasses. Then of a sudden two eyes glistened there, looking right back at me, and a voice said, "Best git ta sleep now, friend." Then he gave this big sigh and his eyes closed into the darkness. He fell asleep, which was more than I did the rest of the night.

Next day they hauled us out for our dance on the deck, and I had a good look at him in the light. All his contusions were gone like they never had been, and he looked like he'd eaten about forty bowls of gruel, instead of the one. The crew hardly paid us any mind. Something had happened but I couldn't tell what because I couldn't understand what they said. That strange fella was kind of tilting his head as if listening, and damn me if he wasn't smiling to himself like he knew a big secret. He noticed me looking and gave me a wink and talked to me, as a Gullah would say, all *sweetmout*. "They lost that red-head lasher," he said. "He just up and disappeared last night and nobody kin find him." I asked myself how he knew their language. Right then I almost guessed the truth about him. But I kept my own counsel on it, as he'd only have to slide over a foot or two in the night to silence me for good.

What was the truth about him? Just wait a bit and you'll see.

After that, he would talk to me while we lay side by side. Most everyone else was wailing or moaning, but he hardly seemed bothered by the inconvenience of being chained up. He told me things I couldn't figure how he knew 'em. Said some of the women were being led off by crewmen, to be used, and then locked back up at night. Some of the small boys, too. "We lucky we's so tall," he said. "They's afraid of us, don't think they're not. They keep you skayred so's you won't git a notion of fighting back. Don't give you 'nuf food to do much more than lie here in your own stink."

I asked how he knew so much, and he replied, "I listen to 'em talk." So I asked how he'd come to know their speech. He chuckled and answered that he knew *everybody's* speech. He asked if I wanted to know their speech, too. I said I did, and he just nodded, then seemed to doze off.

I guess it must have been a week later that fella got into trouble. The ship was riding calm. He'd slipped out again without waking me, and for all I know he did that every night. Anyway, I woke to shouting and feet thundering across the decks. I heard him beside me, scrambling into place. His chains rattled and he grunted and cursed under his breath—nothing quiet and careful this time.

They came down with torches, shouting at all of us, screaming, and I still didn't know a word of it but I knew what it meant same as I knew what it meant when they raised a whip.

Next thing we were dragged out of our holes, kicked and flogged with ropes and pushed up the steps to the deck. It was a perfect night and I stared at the clear sky, the stars strung up there, the moon off the horizon, the breeze so cool and salty-sweet. They lined us up as on that first day, and I glanced at that fella'—his mouth was all sticky dark. He wiped his hands over his face, and his eyes stared at me above them. He said, "You want to know? This is as good a time as any." And he reached over with one of his bloody hands and grabbed my shoulder.

It was as if lightning struck me from all directions. The deck lit up bright white for an instant. I could still see everybody but they were hollow, just outlines against the whiteness. He let go, saying, "There," and went back to wiping his hands down his thighs.

They got us all out finally. Then I saw the body. It lay in the middle of the deck, and it was something to see. The head had been almost chewed right off at the throat, and hung sideways. It was a white man, too, one of *them*.

The captain marched back and forth in front of us, with a long leather cat that he thrashed in the air. He bellowed, "You foul black beasts, I'm gonna whip each 'n' ever' one of you till I find out who did this! Who got free! Mr. Johnson?" he screamed to one of the others.

"All present, sir. No one's missing."

"Damn me, sir, that means one of these vermin is getting' loose and then back again."

"Sir."

"Well, dammit, man, get a torch and inspect them. Whoever did *that*, he gonna have blood all over hisself."

That Mr. Johnson picked up a torch and come over and began to inspect us, holding the torch close in one hand, keeping a wood truncheon in the other. I hardly noticed, for all at once I realized that I'd understood every word they spoke, and I stared at the fella next to me, and he just made a face that told me to keep quiet.

When Mr. Johnson come to him, he says, "Captain, this one's got blood on him." He grabbed the fella's arm and held it up, seeing the blood on the hand.

"Let me see that," the captain answered and started over.

I did something then I can't account for. I stepped in between the two men. I shook my head. I tried to say to Johnson that this man hadn't done anything. But even though I could *understand* his speech, I couldn't talk it. So I held up my own hands, and pointed at my wrists where I'd worked the skin raw on their too-small shackles. There were plenty of us had done that.

Johnson looked at me, then with a snarl raised up that truncheon, and I slunk back out of the way before he could hit me. Of course, the fella had no torn wrists, and in a moment they would have known that. But providence saved him—probably saved us both.

One of the shortest men, on the far side of the deck, suddenly cried out, "No more, I can't go down there no more! You can't put me back. Let me go!" He knocked down two of the crew and ran right up and sprang over the rail, and dropped into the night sea.

It wasn't long before we heard his screams. They only lasted a moment.

You see, sharks followed the slave ships. When one of us died, they just pitched the body overboard, and the sharks found out about this and took to trailing slave ships all the way across the Atlantic.

None of the crew understood what the man had shouted. The captain said, "Well, sir, I guess we found our villain. Mr. Johnson, get 'em all stowed again."

"Yessir!" Johnson snapped. He gave me a funny, suspicious look and muttered, "Stupid nigra." Of course, he didn't know I understood him. I was just a dumb beast that had risked my life over nothing.

They herded us back into the belly of that ship. Had to hose us down again, so many had thought they were going to die.

In the darkness, the fella said, "Pleased to make your acquaintance." Then he said my name, which I was sure I hadn't told him.

That's how I met the *palatyi*.

I'd heard of him—the old people around my home used to tell us stories about him, stories to scare us children. He was a shape-changer, could turn into anything he liked, which seems a mighty powerful skill to have. His only problem was he liked his drink too much, and when he was drunk, he lost his skill. And, son, the *palatyi* liked to drink more than you like to breathe.

The ship arrived in Charles Town—it's called Charleston nowadays. Back then it was a center for slaving. Ships that didn't go to the Caribbean sailed into the bay there direct. Charles Town had a big market square for slave auctions, and people gathered from all over. We were sold off almost the moment we arrived.

They drug us up on a platform a dozen at a time, almost all of us stark naked. The men who bid would climb up and pull back our lips, look at our teeth like we were horses, squeeze our muscles.

Most of us men were bought for field work. Some of the bigger women, too. The lighter-skinned girls, though, got bought up by madams, to work in whorehouses all over.

Me and the *palatyi* got bought by a plantation owner named McTeer. He grew rice down on St. Helena Island. The cypress swamps and the marsh lands there were fertile ground for rice, but you had to dig canals and grub out the stumps and build little dikes to control the water so's you could flood things when you wanted. They grew cotton elsewhere, too, but we worked the rice.

Bunch of slaves he had already came from Madagascar, and they knew how to cultivate rice. Since I could understand what they said, I picked up their skills fast, same as the *palatyi*.

We were branded with an "M" and they gave us all new names. I got called "John Brown," just like the abolitionist. They named the *palatyi* George Wellington.

McTeer called his place Hampton House. The whites around there, you see, had decided they were some kind of aristocracy. Like McTeer, they'd arrived from England with indentured servants already—mostly poor Irish who'd gotten arrested for stealing bread or something else innocuous, and who'd chosen to be slaves rather than get hanged back home. These Irish were mostly house servants, a few were slave drivers. Their masters—our masters—believed themselves to be the swells of the world; here, whatever they'd been back home didn't matter. They put on grand airs. George Wellington relished every opportunity to play on their snobbery.

At first, I couldn't figure him out. He could have escaped anytime, I thought, but he stayed and worked. One reason, I found out, was that he was sneaking out of the shack at night and into McTeer's storehouse, where there were kegs of liquor. He got into the whiskey pretty good; after a month or so they discovered that their supply was disappearing and put a guard named Landis on it. That didn't suit George Wellington at all. One night, I woke up to a gunshot and a lot of yelling, and everybody came stumbling out from Hampton House. We all ran outside, too. I knew it was the *palatyi*, 'cause he was missing in the crowd.

Landis came running past us, two or three other men on his heels, the bunch of them with rifles. He was shouting, "It had to come this way, boys! Wait till you see it!"

When I turned around, George Wellington was standing right behind me, just grinning.

"I s'posed they'd shot you sure," I told him. Back then, I spoke like everybody else round that place, and so did he.

"Those fellers is dainjus," he answered, chuckling. "But mos'ly to demself." Then he rubbed his belly and said, "I jis' had me some buckruhbittle, an' it was mighty good. I b'leew I'm developin' a taste for it."

Buckruhbittle was the word Gullah slaves used to distinguish white man's food from what they fed us. When they'd locked him out of the whiskey supply, George had switched to the kitchen in the bighouse. Tonight Landis had caught him leaving, and George, quick as a wink, had transformed. Landis had seen a monstrous baylynx, a wildcat. He'd shot at it, but missed. I'm not sure it was possible to hit it.

The next day Landis showed everyone the cat's prints in the dirt. Otherwise, I think they would have adjudged he'd been into the whiskey himself. The cat, though, didn't explain the disappearing food. McTeer blamed the Irish house-slaves, but just to be thorough they chained us up at night, too. It didn't bother George, of course, as it didn't bother him what happened to us. He just liked his mischief.

He might have kept stealing their food, but he was bored with that jape already. After a while, things went back to normal. George snuck off at night and I didn't know where he went now. But I found out. One night he woke me and said, "John, you come wid me, we going to have some fun."

I wasn't sure I wanted to, but he insisted it would be good for my education: "Gib' you a chance to sample the pledjuhs of life."

Now, they didn't guard us much, 'cause there was nowhere to run to. It was an island, so they didn't need to keep an eye on us. George and me walked right to the road and inland. I'm not really certain how we got to Beaufort, but we did. Seems like one minute we were on the road with the lights of Jack Mullaters bobbing in the swamps, and the next we were coming up on the lights of a town. In my astonishment, I looked to George, and my heart nearly jumped out of my breast. I was walking along beside a white gentleman wearing a fine coat. He had a grand ginger mustache. He gave me a slantendicular glance, then smiled that wide grin, and I knew it was still George. I started to babble, but he shushed me and took my hand and held it up for me to see. My hand was white, too, and there was brocade at my wrist. I could even *feel* it. He'd changed us both. I still don't know how. He told me, "Now, you let me do the talking, 'cause no matter how you look, you gwine talk the same's you always do. You hab no skill yet."

And I thought, well, neither did he, seeing as how he talked like any Gullah, but I was happy to keep quiet—I was too scared to do anything else.

He led us right down the main street of that town. People nodded to us, said, "'evenin', gen'mun," and didn't give us a second glance. My terror turned to sly relish.

So we arrived in front of this house with balconies and open windows and lights burning bright. He knocked on the door and this big woman opened it. She smiled, then went all quizzical. "Why, sir," she said, "do I know you?" George, he took her hand and kissed it.

"Not yet," he told her, and she giggled like a child half her age and moved aside to let us in.

Then I swear he talked to her just like any white man would, without a trace of the Gullah he talked to me and others. He sounded every note. Reached into his coat and took out a handful of gold coins and closed her hand around them. She giggled some more and led us into a parlor. George whispered to me, "Remember, you say as little as you can. Don't speak to your girl, and keep the lights off once you're in her room. Let her think it's some kind of ritual."

That was what I did. A black-haired girl took me by the hand and led me into a private room. She'd disrobed down to her corset before I blew out the candles. "Shy, are you?" she said, her voice full of laughter.

"Yess'm," I answered, softly. Carefully. She didn't seem to mind.

I guess I tumbled her a couple of times before George knocked at the door and stuck his head in to say, "John, it's time to go."

I dressed hastily, pulling on my work clothes in the dark. He gave me some coins and I set them beside the bed. The girl said, "You pass this way again, John, you look me up," and I answered, "Ma'am, I surely will."

We returned to the shack before daylight. I can't even tell you what moment I changed back again to myself. George, he just thought it was the funniest thing in the world, but I was too exhausted to laugh.

I guess I went with him two or three more times. The money, he was stealing from the bighouse, but he couldn't do that too often.

I stopped accompanying him, though, after a while, 'cause I fell in love with a girl named Alike. That means "the girl who drives away beautiful women." They didn't call her that, though, here. They called her Annie. She was an Ibo woman, tall and sharp-boned and beautiful, and we kind of took up together. You have to understand, in that shack, you had no privacy. You had sex with everybody watching, everybody knowing.

The *palatyi* took me aside and told me not to fall in love with her. He said, "No good gwine come of it. In this here land there's no room for love. Them Hampton House people will see it and use that love as a weapon 'gense you." I didn't listen to that talk. Alike gave me a son, and she named him Orji, a name from her people that meant "great tree." He was a big child. For two years we were as happy as you could be, living like that.

Then one night the *palatyi* came lurching into the shack, falling down, laughing and snorting. Everyone woke up. Outside there were dogs barking and lots of yelling. He crawled into his bed and flopped down drunk. I didn't have to smell him to know it. What had happened was that he'd gotten liquored up in town and forgotten his shape. He said later that he'd been with two whores and all of a sudden they'd begun screaming, because the man entertaining them had turned into something else.

He'd escaped, but with a makeshift posse on his tail, that followed him back to the plantation. The damned fool led them right to our shack. Men with torches burst in. Everybody was screeching, wailing. Alike cringed on our bed with Orji, and I shielded her from whatever was coming. The men knocked people aside. They had no idea who they were looking for, however. George was too drunk to stand. They might have figured him out, I suppose, but they were hungry to punish someone quick.

They grabbed hold of one of the men nearest and hauled him outside, tied him up and whipped him near to death. We stood and watched, not daring to intercede for fear of being whipped to death ourselves. McTeer, when he got there, was none too happy and he made them stop. They were killing his property and they didn't have a story that made a lick of sense to anybody.

Landis came forward with his gun and drove them off. But the next night, we were all shackled again.

When George sobered up, I cussed him a blue streak. He'd inflicted harm on someone else for his amusement. It wasn't funny anymore, his mischief.

He got all peculiar then and withdrew from everybody. They knew he was strange, but they didn't know what he was. That poor other fella suffered awfully. They'd about stripped the skin from his back. He couldn't work, and he rocked on his belly, delirious.

The second morning he was dead. It looked as if the blood had leaked right out of him. The women wailed like Sirens. Landis and the drivers came, carried him off and buried him.

We went back to work, went out to thresh the rice. George walked beside me and after a time he said, "I couldn't help him. He was sufferin', gwine to die. Alls I could do was make it quick for him."

Afterward, he seemed to be more cautious about what he did. He didn't talk to any of us much, even me, and I wondered again why he stayed on.

Maybe two weeks after that incident, with the rice harvested, another group of whites showed up at Hampton House. They were traders. McTeer had us all line up outside the shack. We could see that he was edgy and unhappy about something, but we couldn't imagine what he was about to do. He'd decided he had too many slaves, and was determined to sell some of us off.

The traders wandered back and forth, looking us over. They preferred to acquire slaves who'd been born into slavery, as such slaves wouldn't know anything else and would be easy to handle. They liked in particular to buy children. I didn't appreciate what that meant until one of them grabbed Alike and Orji and pulled them out of line. I jumped after them, got one hand on the man's shoulder, and then something smashed into the side of my head. I stumbled, fell. I could hear Alike crying my name, but when I tried to get up, something hit me again. I didn't pass out exactly, but the whole world spun 'round my head, and somewhere my baby was crying, far away.

When I came to my senses it was night, and George Wellington was sitting beside me. He looked into my eyes and said, "I tol' you not to fall in love. It only sump'n' they kin tek away from you." I understood then that I would never see my wife and son again. I started to cry. George leaned down and shushed me. "Listen up. I'm gwine go now. You wunt see me again. I got no ansuhs for you, but I do owe you sump'n." He touched me, and the world lit up all white as it had on board ship. When it turned dark again, he was gone.

Before the sun came up the next morning, there was a great alarm from the bighouse. We got up, huddling, clutching at each other. We'd already seen loved ones dragged off, and we were sure now it was our turn coming. People began to pray to Jesus, some who'd never been Christians till then. But it wasn't anything to do with us.

Someone had broken into the bighouse and killed McTeer's wife and children. Torn them to shreds. Landis had heard a terrible wail and come out in time to see a white man run off into the woods. He'd recognized the man, too, as one of the slave traders from the day before. The man had stolen McTeer's money, Landis said. Mrs. McTeer must have caught him in the act.

They left us—the entire pack of white drivers and servants. They set off after that group of slavers. We could have fled, but we didn't. Some of us did enter the house, though. We found the family. It was horrible to see, but I'd seen that kind of slashing before, and I knew who'd killed them. I knew he'd done it for me, out of revenge. McTeer had robbed me of my family. And so the *palatyi* had robbed him of his. We didn't expect McTeer to be alive, but he was. The *palatyi* had slashed his hamstrings so that he couldn't walk, but had left him alive, if demented beyond words. I was cold then. I didn't mind what had been done to him.

They caught up with the slavers in Beaufort, Landis and his men. They hung the lot of them for the crime they hadn't committed, but that was good enough justice and all we could hope for, who'd watched our loved ones legally taken away.

The plantation went up for sale, but it was a tainted place. I think people believed it was haunted, which might have been George's doing. None of us saw him, though. We were all auctioned off, separated.

I ended up on a big spread outside Charles Town, met a woman there named Kaya and married her. Her name meant "stay here and don't die." But after our third child, she did die, of a fever. Me, I never got sick at all. Other women 'round the place took care of my babies and helped raise them up. By the time they were young men, I was past fifty, but I didn't look a day older than them. I knew the *palatyi* had done something new to me. Folks pretended I was just aging gracefully.

I developed my gift for language, and learned to speak as well as my masters, better in fact, although I was careful not to let on how well. I taught my sons how to speak proper English, too. I gained a position in the house, put in charge of other houseslaves, and I did what I could for them. Our owners were decent enough people, I suppose, if you didn't mind that you belonged to them. I kept expecting George to turn up again, but he didn't. Eventually, I'd worked and saved enough to buy my freedom and that of my boys, and I took 'em north to Boston. I enrolled in a university there, and put the boys in, too. We caused something of a stir, the four of us like four brothers. Nobody believed I was their father. The boys almost didn't believe it, either.

I took a law degree and set up practice there. I met your Mr. Lincoln once, some years before the war.

Eventually, though, I had to go back to South Carolina. A newspaper article was what finally drew me. From the city of Charleston. People told of being haunted and stalked by a spirit— a *haant*, you see, which they called the Plateye, or sometimes the Plateye Prowl, 'cause of the way the thing seemed to select people to terrify. It would come to the back door of white people's houses and scratch like some pet to be let in. If they were fool enough to let it in, they didn't live to tell about it. It seemed to appear in various shapes, and I suspected it had to be George. I didn't go right away. None of my sons was still in Boston. One moved to Chicago. Another had gone off to France, and the third had made his way to San Francisco. They were in their thirties, one of them turned forty, and it had become increasingly difficult for me to pretend to be their elder. In fact, I'm sure they put distance between us because of it.

I saw to my affairs, settled some things. I didn't know exactly what I was going to do afterward, you see—just that I was going to vanish.

After the war, I took a train south. I made sure I had papers defining who I was. Reconstruction was under way, for the few years that it was allowed to work.

I kicked around that town a bit, asking people about the Plateye. Everybody had a story about it, and a couple people claimed they'd heard it scratching at their door but they'd had the sense not to let it in.

Finally, I found one old Gullah fellow, who talked just like George, and put me onto him, although he did ask, "Whyfore you wanna go and meet the Plateye? He jist tear you open if he don' tek a likin' to you. You go, jist be sutt'n you armed with w'iskey." He told me there was a peach grove the Plateye supposedly frequented, on the edge of the town. I purchased a bottle of bourbon and carried it with me. I set it under one of the bigger trees, then I sat down a ways off and waited.

Sometime around midnight, a big baylynx came slinking across the road and into the grove. Even though I knew what it was, I found the hair standing up on the back of my neck just like when I was in that coffin hole the first time I'd met him. The cat looked around suspiciously, sniffing the bottle. Then he took it and clambered up the tree. No cat ever moved like that. But that was the restraint on the *palatyi*. He could *look* like an animal, but he was still him—whatever he was. Humanlike, but not human.

The cat sat on a low limb, dangling his legs like a kid fishin' off a dock. I got up and walked out into view. He kept right on drinking while I approached.

"Evening," I said.

The cat licked his lips awhile. Then he answered me. "You lookin' purdy good, John."

"You never came back."

"Didn't I? Well, shuh! It's early still. There plenny more time."

"Not for me. I'm more than eighty years old now, George."

The cat shrugged. "You don' look a day over twenty." He took another pull from the bottle.

"And how is that?"

He didn't answer directly, but when he did, he'd dropped the Gullah façade in his speech. "*George*," he mused, "nobody's called me that in a very long time. Guess it *has* been awhile, hasn't it?" He set down the bottle. "You stuck up for me once. You shielded me when there was nowhere for me to go but into the belly of a shark. And all my shape-changing wouldn't have meant a thing to a shark—dinner is dinner for all God's creatures. You risked your life. You forced me to recognize something decent in a human being. Something worth saving, and something I don't have in me at all." He tilted his head a bit. "About the only real power I have is to protect myself so's no one'll know me as different. I blend. *You* know. But I got a little bit to spare, and so I gave that to you. Might be a blessing, might be a curse. I can't say. Ain't gonna make you last forever. But you'll sure last a sight more than eighty."

I said, "What about you? You could find a ship, go home now, back to where we came from."

He chuckled. "I got dropped here against my will, and I have to say, I'm not much persuaded to board another ship with these people. Besides, there's just a whole lotta folk in Charles Town I ain't scared yet." That cat face split as wide as a barn with the biggest grin you ever saw. Then he disappeared out of that tree just like that. The bottle came rolling down the trunk, empty. He'd drunk a fifth of bourbon in as many minutes.

I never saw George Wellington again. I suppose he's still there, having his mischief. I came up here to Canada and started over, but someone spoke erroneously of the Civil War and I corrected him, and had to admit to having lived through it, and the next thing I know, you journalists show up to write your articles. It's hard to stay anonymous.

Anyway, that's the story of how the Plateye Prowl of Caro-

lina came to be, and how I learned to speak—as you say—so gra-
ciously.

You're confused as to the time frame of these events? I'm not
surprised. Near as I can figure, it was 1783 the year I was captured
and brought to this continent.

That's right, that *does* make me a hundred and thirty eight
years old. But between you and me, I don't feel a day over sixty.

THE FINAL ACT

McGowren caught up with him in the lobby amid the end-of-the-day exodus. One moment Leonard was heading through the gray granite lobby by himself, the next the person he least wanted to see was striding along beside him as if no bad blood lay between them.

Leonard pulled away as if from a foul odor, then set his jaw and kept walking at the same pace, refusing to be rattled or to acknowledge the intrusion beyond a sidewise glance.

McGowren's chinos were stained, his shirttail hung out on one side, he seemed to have lost his tie, and he had a heavy enough five o'clock shadow that he must have shaved the night before. Leonard, unconsciously smoothing down his own tie, wondered if the schmuck had met any clients like that. Had any of the partners on the fifth floor seen him in this shape? Maybe he'd been sacked already, he sure looked the part. But no, Len would have heard. Too many people knew he'd have liked nothing more than to hear that about McGowren, and someone would have called or even ridden up to tell him. Almost to himself he said, "You look like you slept under a bar."

"Nice to see you, too, Len."

"And unless you're here to beg forgiveness, you can fuck off." Then Leonard was in the revolving door, pushing his way to the sidewalk, ditching McGowren and merging into the departing throng. However, before he'd reached the corner, McGowren reappeared beside him. "Leonard, bro, I need to talk to you."

"Don't call me 'bro.' Or buddy or pal or anything else."

"Len—"

"I don't have time tonight. I have to pick up my car." At least he didn't have to fabricate an excuse.

"Geez, man, I was hoping you'd give me a ride."

"You take the train, asshole," he replied. He maneuvered around a light pole and then walked on the narrow strip outside the parking meters, passing most of the crowd and temporarily outstripping McGowren again. He heard behind him the words, "I don't have my pass on me. I lost it. I need a *ride*, man."

Leonard nodded his head. It might have meant he'd heard or it might have signaled that he would agree to help. He wasn't sure which, either.

It had been five months since he'd spoken to Gary McGowren—not since the Christmas party where he'd caught McGowren and Laurel in the coat closet, about two items of clothing away from a full-on fuck. The closet was the size of a meat locker and could have contained an orgy, but there were just the two of them, his wife and Gary. Idiots. At least Laurel looked horrified as she snatched up her clothes and ran past him. He stood his ground. McGowren raised a hand in pathetic imitation of an apology, shambled forward and slurred, "Don' be mad, Len, I'm sorry, just too much punch at the watering hole is all, 'm sorry." He pawed, clutched Len's arm. "Listen, Laurel's just—" was all he got to say before Leonard shoved him sprawling into the coats, that clutching hand grabbing for purchase, catching hold of the rod as his forehead hit it and he fell, his weight snapping it out of the wall and dragging coats and furs down on top of him. With a displaced calm, Leonard collected his own and Laurel's coats from the other side of the closet. Why hadn't he done something? Why hadn't he stomped the bastard to death? But even there in that moment of fury he was afraid of violence, scared of acting out. He could stand in a courtroom and gloatingly reduce people to self-contradicting imbeciles, but he couldn't deck McGowren. Just couldn't touch him. He hated himself for it, and McGowren as the proof.

Laurel had cried all the way home except for the few moments she spent vomiting out the window. She hadn't meant—hadn't known—what she was doing. All the excuses failing to explain why, of all the people she could have drunkenly pursued, she'd picked McGowren. He was good looking, okay, but come on, the guy had the verbal skills of an ape. It was why he'd been passed over for promotions, never offered even a junior partnership, just maintained his position, handling work injury cases that he had next to no business pursuing, billing enough hours to get by but not much else. If they'd worked in the same department, crossed paths at all, Len would have had him fired. Instead, roiling in his own sense of inadequacy and failure, he'd just let him be, hoping McGowren would go away and die on his own. Laurel had seen a counselor and then she had insisted they see a counselor together, as if her indiscretion was somehow his fault as well, and he'd gone, he'd borne it. In five months they'd attained a kind of stability, forbearance moving toward acceptance, maybe some kind of forgiveness. Over and over she had told him how good he was, how kind, but he wasn't sure kindness wasn't just weakness. He doubted he would trust anything or anyone ever again.

At the corner of 12th and Locust, Leonard waited for the light and McGowren slid up beside him. The bastard did look pretty banged up. Maybe he *had* been sacked. Maybe he *was* sleeping under a bar. Good.

Leonard had told no one about the coat closet, but someone must have come upon McGowren, and it was only a few days before Debbie, his secretary, had stepped into his office and just said, "I'm really sorry." He'd looked in her eyes and known what she was saying, known that his co-workers all knew. McGowren had stayed away, the one smart thing he'd done. So what was this appeal all about? What did he want, sympathy? Forgiveness? Those ships had sailed.

They'd known each other since high school, and McGowren had been an ape then, too, a running back on the football team who was always playing pranks: convincing someone to climb out on the cafeteria roof and then locking the windows to keep them out there till some outraged faculty or staff member let them back in; turning a firehose on the cheerleaders just before they ran outside, where it was 45°; filling a water bottle in chemistry class with mustard and spraying his chem partner with it. Mostly he started fights. The trouble was, for some perverse reason he wanted to hang around with Leonard's group. They weren't nerds exactly, but they weren't the popular kids, either, and they foolishly thought a football player in their midst could open a door into the world of girls. Instead, McGowren had only managed to get them in trouble by association so that they were drawn into every fracas, often in defense of the schmuck. Leonard had steered clear of him as much as possible. Even then he was petrified of confrontations, of violence, of being hit. So when McGowren had applied for a position at the law firm and given Leonard as a reference, it was an act of pure stupidity to have hoped he'd grown up.

Without looking at him, as if it was hard to express, McGowren said, "Listen, Len, we have history, okay? I just need a ride. I don't want your forgiveness. I don't expect it." The light changed. He finally glanced cautiously at Leonard. "So, can you?"

"Fine, I'll give you a ride, all right," he replied, amazed to hear the words, as if his mouth had answered without consulting him. He knew he didn't mean it, knew that he had reached the end with this jerk who'd followed him like a slug's smear from high school to the law firm. He didn't know what he was going to do yet, but it was time to get rid of Gary McGowren once and for all.

He paid the bill for the lube job and oil change, and got in. Then he remembered his passenger and unlocked the doors. Where had McGowren got to while he'd looked over the bill and paid up? Restroom probably. For an instant he considered driving off without him. Then the door opened and McGowren folded into the seat. He sat in a forward hunch as if intrigued by the Infiniti's dashboard. "Put your seatbelt on, Gary."

"I hate 'em."

"Yeah? Well do it anyway. I'm not going to be liable when you go through the windshield."

As with obvious reluctance he clipped in, McGowren asked, "You remember that water balloon fight where I filled one with tempera paint and nailed you coming around the corner?"

Leonard pulled into traffic. "I caught hell for that prank. The red never came out of my shirt. My mom bleached it till the fabric disintegrated and it was still pink. So was one side of my face for like a week."

"It was pretty damned amazing. You dripped like some kind of swamp thing."

"Yeah, real fucking amazing. Thanks. What are you, still fifteen? You're an idiot, McGowren. You always were. You want a ride, then shut up."

In silence Leonard drove awhile, stuck in the jam to get onto the parkway. This was all a mistake. He wasn't going to do anything to McGowren—what *could* he do, push him out of the car at 80 mph? It would be just one more thing for him to stew over, one more imagined act that wasn't going to happen.

Then down the ramp and merging onto the faster parkway, he reached for the radio knob, and McGowren spoke up. "You never did get the dynamic, did you, Len?"

"What dynamic?"

"Us. You and me. Even in high school. You got this image of it being like we were buddies or something. Like I was the person you'd call if you wanted to do something."

"I don't think so." Where was *this* coming from?

"Oh, yes you do, and it was never like that. You didn't want me joining the firm, you don't want me in the car now—"

"Gee, I can't imagine why I don't feel much like doing you favors anymore."

"Anymore? When did you do me favors?"

"I could have shit-canned you when you put me down as a reference. I should have. But I thought, 'hey, maybe he's grown up, maybe he turned into an adult.'"

"You're a snob, Len. You and your little pals, all you wanted from me was to score some girls, you didn't give a rat's ass about me otherwise."

Leonard looked out his side window. The driver passing stared back at him. "Jesus, it was high school, Gary." He turned to face him. "And you know, I'll tell you what I remember. I remember a dumbass jock who pissed off even the other jocks. Who managed to implicate everybody he was with so that they either had to fight on his behalf or else got hauled into the vice principal's office along with him. A guy who is so terminally fucked in the head he doesn't even know why maybe I'm less than enthused to be in his company right now, even though he's tried to screw my wife. Christ. Why am I trying to talk to you?"

"Maybe you want to know."

"What do I want to know?"

"Everything. Why you're the way you are. Why I'm talking to you, despite your rejecting—"

"We're not in high school, you asshole. What, you've been waiting for twelve *years* to get back at me for trying to convince the rest of our crew to get rid of you?"

McGowren glanced at him and smiled.

Leonard couldn't stop the laugh of disdain. "Are you serious? Never mind that this is all in your head, how long can you maintain a grudge? You put me down on your job application! And I let you pass when I could easily have told them not to hire you. *God.*"

McGowren said nothing.

"So, what, the thing in the coat closet was just you getting back at me through Laurel?"

"That was the first part of it."

"The first part? How many parts will we have? Two acts or three? I can stop at a bar so you can get tanked and recreate the night in the coats." He pushed his hand through his thinning hair. "Man, here I am, giving you a ride home because you lost your pass. And I'm the bad guy because I didn't like you in high school. You're really a piece of work."

Everything had changed now. Leonard could see that so long as McGowren was around, there would *always* be another prank, another act of eternal escalation. He had to get rid of him, there was no choice. The question was *how*? How to make him disappear for good and not pay for it? He flipped through scenarios: sledge-hammer McGowren's skull and then the floor in the basement and stick the body under that, except he didn't have the concrete; okay, in the back yard then, hit him with a shovel and then dig a hole in the garden and plant the bastard under the roses; or better still, drive twenty miles to the state park and dump his corpse in the woods, let him rot outdoors where nobody would ever connect them.

"You know what, Gary. I should just bring you to my place. We'll have a drink or two and straighten this out between us once and for all. You can even talk to Laurel if she can stomach being in the same room with you."

"Fine. That's where I need to go, anyway."

The way he said it, Leonard knew even through the heat of

his own anger that something had already happened. The second act of the revenge fantasy had already begun. The train pass, the ride home—he reached into his suit and drew out his cell phone, flipped it open. Before he could even thumb a number he saw that the battery was out of juice. The car charger was dangling out of the cigarette lighter but he couldn't plug the phone in on the parkway. He flipped it closed.

"Change your mind?" McGowren asked.

It seemed that maybe he didn't know the phone was dead. Leonard saw no reason to disabuse him of this idea. "Yeah. That's what you want me to do—call home."

He closed his eyes, still smiling carelessly. "Right." He brushed the hair down the back of his head, in the process pushing his collar down. Leonard saw scratch marks on the back of his neck. He forgot himself momentarily, and his foot backed off the gas pedal until the BMW behind him honked. He jerked up as if he'd fallen asleep, and accelerated. The next exit was his anyway, and he hit his blinker and edged off to the right. The BMW zoomed past, honking again to make sure he got the message. McGowren snorted.

"Anyway," he muttered, his eyes still closed, "you'd just get a busy signal."

"Really, how do you know that?"

"Because it's off the hook. The way I left it."

Leonard's desire to dispense with McGowren evaporated, replaced by sickening uncertainty. "*You* left it?"

"Yeah. Right after I killed Laurel."

He heard the words, so impossible they didn't make sense, like he'd heard them out of order and needed to rearrange them to make a sentence he understood. But McGowren wouldn't give him time.

"No, you know, we had quite a thing going. That night in the coats, that wasn't exactly the first, and, man, she wanted more than just a taste. I thought it was over the second you walked in, you know, but she called me—I mean, right at the office, right underneath you. Said you were none too spectacular in the sack and that she was gonna stay on the prowl and I could either get it on or get lost. How's your sex life been since Christmas, Len, hmm?"

Leonard's brain ran through images, memories, doubts: guilty red-eyed looks from Laurel, withheld responses in therapy—even the therapist had complained that she wasn't engaged—dinners shared in unbroken silences as she made eye-contact only with her plate. Silences were gaps and he could fill them with anything he chose. He sought and created hidden meanings everywhere. At the same time his body drove on auto-pilot, zooming past the speed limit, braking, turning, the car's air gone stale, dead. He needed to open a window. His mouth said, "No."

McGowren now looked straight at him and all but sneered. There was a bruise over McGowren's right eye now that hadn't been obvious before. It must have been recent, forming, hours old.

"You're bound to say no, Len. But it's yes. Yes, you've seen the signs. We've been meeting for months. Remember when they sent you to Boston? Oh, that was a night. Didn't know she liked that kinky shit. Did you?"

"We were . . . she was seeing a counselor because of you," he answered, but his mind had flown away back to a night last winter where she'd bound him with his ties and then teased him, tormented him, made him beg for her to sit on him. He'd loved it. *Kinky shit.*

"Counseling, yeah, right. She needed counseling." Laughing.

He swallowed the metallic thickness in his mouth. "Get out of my car."

"You kidding?"

"Get out—out of my car, out of my life, out of my *head*!"

"See what I mean, Len? Total prick. Here I am confessing to you, turning myself in to you and you're telling me to get lost. I'm filling in the blanks for you, dude. But if you want me out—" He started to open the door.

Leonard grabbed at him, but swung the wheel at the same time and the car veered. He screamed and slapped both hands on the wheel again, and narrowly failed to smack into the car in the right lane. Horns blared around him.

McGowren chuckled. He hadn't opened the door, hadn't gotten out. He was looking straight at the road. "You should have taken care of me at the Christmas party, Len. You should have kicked my head in through the coats. Shoulda woulda coulda. Now you won't ever know, will you? Am I lying or telling the truth about Laurel? You just won't ever be sure because a little worm's gone crawling right up inside your head. The night in the closet—oh, that's real. You can still feel the moment, it's so raw. You can box it off, put police tape around it. Isolate it. Sure, but the rest is going to run around and around the squeaky hamster wheel in your head, eeky-eeky." He laughed again.

Even as he made the final frenzied turn onto his street, Leonard saw the police cars—two on his front lawn—and the EMT wagon backed into the driveway. Neighbors outside, Monroe, the stockbroker across the street, standing idiotically beside his mailbox, envelopes in his hand.

McGowren leaned back and let go a deep sigh as if finally drained of all taunts.

Leonard slammed the car against the curb. The tire thumped, bounced. He fumbled, flung the door open before the car had stopped, snatching the keys, staring at his apparently dozing passenger one last time, then running, up the sidewalk, across the lawn. A cop at the front door put out a hand, but responded to the look of him and drew aside, saying, "Husband?"

He nodded as he pushed past, into his house, calling over his shoulder, "He's in the car, I left him in the car."

"Huh?" said the cop, but Leonard was already crossing the living room toward the hall. A flash went off in the kitchen, past the wall of live bodies. It seemed like a crowd, but it was no more than five: uniforms, plain clothes, medical, standing, gathered, starting to turn at his approach.

Between them as they parted, creating a sliver of an opening, he finally glimpsed his wife.

She was in the tall chair at the breakfast bar, her head hanging down. He thought again of the dinner plate. He should have made her talk, demanded to know why she wouldn't look at him. Below her now on the floor was a little card with a metallic strip across it. Her blouse was torn at the shoulder, the bra strap broken beneath it, her shoulder red, cut with parallel gashes—fingernails had done that. What had McGowren's fingertips looked like? Then, ever so slightly, she raised her bruised and swollen face, and saw him as he froze. She burst into tears. She sprang from the chair, reaching, reaching with red fingers. Everyone looked his way now, and he felt the impact of her against him, heard her wail, but he had come unmoored from the moment, from the world. The card on the floor, it was a train pass. And beside it . . . He stared into the half-lidded eyes watching him—the body on its back, scratched, battered, one arm flung out, fingers curled into a claw, the brown belt undone and chinos half down. The black handle of a German carving knife stuck out of the center of his chest like a flag planted on a hill. McGowren's head rested on its crown. His mouth was open as if in the middle of a word, a sentence, a laugh.

You won't ever know, will you?

Laurel had stepped back, sensing the wrongness of him, the immobility and hardness. He gazed from McGowren's dead eyes into hers. Was there guilt there? Something more than relief? Leonard could hear her story already—she would tell him McGowren had shown up drunk and attacked, wanting to finish what they'd started in the closet, would never let it go because there was so much more to destroy yet, the same as in high school, and even in the car. He wouldn't stop until he'd pulled everyone down along with him, that was McGowren. She was only act two. What was the last?

He pushed Laurel away, backed and then turned from the hall and ran out of the house, down the drive behind the EMT van. His car, parked askew with one wheel up over the curb. Empty. Empty. He'd told the cop, he'd said . . .

He shuffled his feet, unable to go in any direction, unable to get away to anywhere. He heard his name, and sure it was McGowren, he spun around. Two officers had pursued him, and the nearer one spoke his name again.

Up past the drive, Laurel stood at the front door, a million miles away across the lawn. She was calling to him, too, but her voice, his name, seemed to break apart beneath a crackling in his brain, the noise of something awful burrowing in for a long, long stay.

NO OTHERS ARE GENUINE

Something had happened to Miss Comuzzi and no one in Mrs. Claymore's boarding house would tell Eustace what it was. Eustace overheard Mrs. Claymore whisper to Mr. Vanderhoff, "who could imagine something so terrible?" Then they'd caught sight of him crouched on the landing above, and clammed right up. Mr. Vanderhoff might have told him later, but he'd gone out on the road again, selling his catalogue merchandise. The adults all knew, but they weren't about to share it with a ten-year-old boy in knickerbockers.

None of them knew that Eustace was in love with Miss Comuzzi and was pretty sure she was in love with him, or would have been eventually—after all, by the time he turned twenty, she would only be thirty, and hadn't Father been almost that much older than Mother?

As if that wasn't bad enough, not a day later, Mrs. Claymore had rented out Miss Comuzzi's room to the awful Mr. Schulde. Tonight, the house was filled with music from his Edison wax cylinder player, a marching band's brisk rendition of "The Girl I Left Behind Me." Miss Comuzzi had liked to hum and sing that song sometimes when she had been in that same room, across from his and Mother's. Hearing even the scratchy rendition of it, he could almost smell her wonderful rosewater scent again.

But two nights earlier he *had* smelled it, so strongly that he'd opened the door, expecting to find her in the hallway. Except that, the hall lay empty. Mother was dozing, and he'd crept across and tried to steal into Miss Comuzzi's room, certain he would find her inside, a captive. He imagined discovering her tied up, and then rescuing her from her oily captor, Mr. Schulde. But Mr. Schulde had locked the door as if he'd known Eustace might come looking. The scent of rosewater was overpowering; he wasn't imagining it. He resolved then and there to get into her room. To that end, he formulated a plan.

The first time he'd ever heard music on wax cylinders was back in February, one unseasonably warm afternoon when his mother had met him at the end of a school day. Back then she'd been studying at the YMCA to learn to be a stenographer and typist, and some days she finished early enough to accompany Eustace home. Now that she was employed, those times together happened rarely. But on that afternoon, they had strolled up West Ohio Street and come upon a shop that had its doors open. Just inside, on a table, was a big box with a funnel sticking out the front. Half a dozen people stood on the sidewalk, as posed as mannequins. Even as he peered between them at the source of the music, they remained still. A polished wooden box sat on a table a few feet inside. One small piece of it—a shiny, yellowish cylinder—spun in place, but what drew his attention more was the huge cyclopean eye of the horn out of which the sound poured. It was glossy indigo, decorated with red radiating lines, and so large that a supporting stick propped it up. There for a moment he fell under the same spell that had captured the adults. Those red lines seemed to pull him out of his body and into the dark empty hole at the center, into the tune.

Then Mother broke the spell, identifying it to herself. "'By the Light of the Silvery Moon,'" she muttered, and suddenly there was movement. Heads swiveled to look at her. Someone else concurred. "Yes," they said. Then they all listened again.

After a minute the tune ended, and a man who had been standing beside the box all along stepped forward and pushed a knob on its side. The cylinder stopped rotating. "Next performance in half an hour," he announced. "We have a wide assortment of songs in here, enough to entertain for hours and hours."

A few people stepped through the doorway. The rest walked off or peered into the shop window, where another of the devices was displayed on a stand, flanked by a trumpet and a viola.

As Mother took his hand again, Eustace heard the man explain, "Why, you can play a cylinder up to a hundred times. And buy the shaver and recording accessory and you can make your own recordings again and again. Imagine it!"

After that, Eustace meandered to the music store frequently. For a time, he just remained in the crowd—there was always a cluster of listeners on the sidewalk. Then one day he entered the store and discovered that the beautiful young woman who lived across the hall, Miss Comuzzi, worked there. She played piano in between performances of the "amazing Edison phonograph," and also gave lessons, which were often sold with a piano purchase. Miss Comuzzi recognized Eustace. She let him sit beside her while she played sonatas and nocturnes—never the contemporary pieces that might have put her in competition with the phonograph. Unlike Mr. Righter (another tenant of the boarding house, who smelled overly of Bay Rum), she smelled wonderful, like roses.

Occasionally, when the store was deserted, she would teach him keys and chords, or even a simple tune that he could practice. The salesman encouraged it. "The picture of domestic bliss," he said. Sometimes she brought home sheet music and presented it to Eustace after dinner, and though he couldn't yet read it, he would sit and stare at the arcane lines and shapes while he invented a tune to match. She bought him chocolates and penny candies, including candy corn, which he'd never seen before. Mother liked her, too. Despite their age difference, he decided that one day they would be married and she would play for him whatever she liked.

When one afternoon his worshipful presence beside Miss Comuzzi convinced a customer to buy a piano for his daughter, the owner, a round-faced little man, declared that he wanted Eustace there every day.

He taught him to stand on a box beside the phonograph and load a cylinder on the player. Eustace learned to balance the yellowish wax along two fingers and, pushing only against the end of it, slide it onto the mandrel, after which he locked it into place. He pulled the lever that started the cylinder turning, and carefully lowered the arm of the reproducer. While he diligently performed this task, a salesman exhorted the crowd on the ease of using the Edison machine. Why, look, even a *child* could enjoy the pleasures of this musical wonder.

Late in April, an Edison machine was set up beside the piano, and Eustace was allowed to direct the recording horn to capture Miss Comuzzi's performance of a Chopin Prelude, which she played faster than she had previously to make it fit onto the two-minute cylinder. Some in the crowd actually gasped when it was played back. The small spectacle generated a buzz, and soon Eustace was daily shaving cylinders and recording Miss Comuzzi, or her accompaniment of someone in the crowd who sang.

Sales of the $20 machines jumped. The happy store owner gave Miss Comuzzi a raise, and even paid Eustace a small consideration for his assistance, by arrangement with her. At first he spent all the money, but then he began saving it with the intention of buying something nice for Mother. For two years, since the day his father had been killed in a rail yard accident, Mother had worked tirelessly to take care of them both.

In the end Miss Comuzzi helped him pick out a necklace with a teardrop moonstone cabochon, and Mother loved it so much she wore it all the time, which made Eustace feel warm and grown up and wonderful.

A few times in those last weeks, the owner had handed Miss Comuzzi small notes, which she opened only after he went away; and then she made a small laugh and hugged Eustace as if *he* had done something clever, which made him wish he had. Those days she finished her shift but did not walk home with him. Instead she hurried off down Desplaines Street, and did not appear at the boarding house until late in the evening.

Then, abruptly and unexpectedly, it all ended and the whispering among the adults began.

One day Miss Comuzzi did not show up at the music store. That morning before leaving the boarding house, she'd promised him a big surprise when he got to the store after school. She was so elated that he'd thought maybe . . . well, it was silly but he'd thought it.

When he got there, the owner was furious. Miss Comuzzi had appointed lessons to give. The little man glared at Eustace as if he must know where she'd gone, and he ran home to the boarding house and rapped hard on her door. She wasn't there. It seemed she wasn't anywhere at all.

Two days later, when he came home from school, he saw that her room was open. He looked in to find that her belongings had been removed. A policeman had come, Mrs. Claymore told Mother. The news was . . . but she had seen him watching and instead of speaking only shook her head. A dark fog of silence clogged the boarding house that night.

Yet by the time they'd all been seated for supper the following day, the room was rented out to a new boarder, a Mr. Schulde. Mrs. Claymore announced it with delight as she set down the bowl of whipped potatoes. "Why, I hadn't even hung the sign out," she said. "It's kismet is what it is."

Eustace didn't know that word, but he decided it meant *unfair*.

He took an immediate dislike to the new tenant, the interloper in Miss Comuzzi's room. Mr. Schulde was tall and slim, and his hair was black, oiled until it was as smooth as glass. He sported a waxed mustache that looked to Eustace like two scorpions. Behind the mustache, his face was smooth; Mother remarked upon how young he appeared for someone with such a palpable presence.

The first night that he sat at dinner with everyone, Mr. Schulde asked their permission to indulge in his particular musical vice. Mr. Vanderhoff was there that night, home from the road. His appearance at the dinner table was inconstant, but Eustace liked him a lot, and he seemed fond of Mother. After one of his long absences he'd brought her a box of Whitman's chocolates "all the way from Philadelphia." Eustace and Mr. Vanderhoff shared a secret that he swore never to tell Mother—that Mr. Vanderhoff carried a gun in his valise when he traveled. He'd even let Eustace hold it once on the back porch when no one was about.

Vanderhoff asked, "You have one of those contraptions in your room, do you?"

Mr. Schulde looked up from his plate. "I do. And I would be *pleased* to demonstrate it for you." Mr. Schulde smiled at Mother as he made the offer.

Mrs. Claymore clasped her hands upon the promontory of her bosom. "Oh," she said, "I love that someone *cultured* is among us."

Mr. Righter spluttered at her insult. Mr. Righter spent much of his time pontificating on virtually any subject from automobile manufacture to glider flight (all advancements happening in Germany instead of here in our great nation, according to him). He had what mother called a *goiter*. Eustace thought he looked like a frog.

Mrs. Claymore remained oblivious of her gaffe, all her attention focused on Mr. Schulde. "Oh, come, sir. Show us, please."

With a magnanimous air, Mr. Schulde led them all up to the second floor, where they crowded into his doorway. Eustace wriggled between them to stand at the front. Mother politely eased in beside him.

It was still Miss Comuzzi's room, Eustace saw. Hardly anything looked different. Even the bed quilt was the same, the one he'd sat on any number of times. The room bore the hint of rose petals still, as if she had departed only hours before they'd entered. It was more spacious than his and Mother's room, too, and Eustace added to his list of objections that they had not been allowed an opportunity to move in here before this man intruded.

For a moment Eustace didn't realize that Mr. Schulde was standing beside the player—it looked so different than those the music store had sold—but when he unlatched and lifted away the wood cover, revealing the mechanism, Eustace quickly identified the mandrel, the circular reproducer, and the knob that set the cylinder in motion or stopped it. But these features were part of a larger apparatus than any he'd encountered. They sat atop a cabinet more than half the height of Mr. Schulde, resting upon four knurled feet. The cabinet face bore an odd rectangular opening, something like a baffle fronted by numerous uprights. It made the cabinet appear to be grinning.

He expected the horn to appear. Instead Mr. Schulde opened a door in the lower part of the cabinet and removed a pale cylinder, lifting it upon two extended fingers as Eustace knew was the proper procedure; then slid it onto the mandrel, locked it into place, and pushed the release. Delicately, he lowered the reproducer.

The song emerged from the rectangular mouth of the cabinet— "Alexander's Ragtime Band."

"Oh, my," said Mrs. Claymore, and she touched one hand just below her throat. Everyone else stood silent until it was over, very like the crowd at the music store.

When it ended, they clapped, as though Mr. Schulde had performed some magic trick. Eustace crossed his arms and pushed out his lip. *He* had done more than that just helping to sell phonographs.

Mr. Schulde put the cylinder away and lowered the cover over the mechanism again.

"Can you record on it?" Eustace asked, and sensed everyone looking at him, including Mr. Schulde, who seemed surprised that he could speak.

"As a matter of fact, dear boy, I can . . . though I shan't demonstrate *that* for you now." He bowed to Mother, standing beside Eustace. "I assure you, I'll be discreet in playing my cylinders, and not at all late at night, as I know that some of us" —and now he speared Eustace with a look— "need to go to bed earlier than others."

Mrs. Claymore answered, "Oh, we're all great lovers of music here, sir, and poor Miss Comuzzi, who occupied this very room—I was just saying—was the music performer among us, and I'm sure she would delight that it's in her room." She sought approval from her tenants. Mr. Righter nodded with enthusiasm. Mr. Vanderhoff looked troubled, as if unhappy to be in Miss Comuzzi's room.

Then Mr. Righter began one of his speeches about progress and invention, and everyone dispersed. As they were turning away, Mr. Schulde came up to Mother. "You are my direct neighbor, Mrs. Lutts, so you will tell me if ever I am an annoyance, won't you?"

Eustace wanted to tell him he was *that* already.

Mother smiled demurely and dropped her gaze. "I surely will, Mr. Schulde."

He stepped nearer. "Please. We're going to be close neighbors. You must call me Franklin."

The look on Mr. Vanderhoff's face expressed Eustace's own animus. He dove around Mrs. Claymore and fled down the stairs. Mother called after him but he pretended he didn't hear, and did not stop until he was outside in the twilight.

It was too awful: Miss Comuzzi was lost to him in some way only the adults knew, this hideous man had taken her place across the hall, and no one else saw how repulsive he was.

He could not explain to Mother his need to enter Miss Co-muzzi's room (he refused to think of it as anything else). No one else knew about her promise of a surprise for him. Whether she had left something behind—a final sheet of music, a farewell letter, a valentine—or not, it didn't matter, though he truly believed the two of them had been too close for there to be nothing. She had promised.

Plus, that man, *Franklin*, was now clearly courting mother. He was thus the enemy of *everything*.

Schulde went off each morning at seven to his job—which was to do with what he called *phosphorescent lighting*, at the Columbian Exhibition that had just opened in Jackson Park. He returned each afternoon after three. His routine was established.

Eustace awoke the next day and pretended to be sick—not so sick that mother needed to remain with him, but just sick enough to warrant a day at home in bed. A prepared hot water bottle provided his "fever." In secret he laid it across his forehead so that when Mother placed her hand there, she agreed that he felt warm.

The door to Miss Comuzzi's room was of course locked, but Eustace had prepared for that. One of the curious benefits of being a child was that adults often disregarded your presence while they performed some private act, which was how he knew where Mrs. Claymore hung the spare keys, and by pretending to mope about the house, he had already secured the one he needed.

However, Mrs. Claymore had promised to look in on him throughout the day, and that presented him with an unforeseen impediment to his plans. All he could do was lie in bed and wait.

It wasn't long before she checked up on him. Providently, she apologized that she needed to go out—a visit to the butcher in order to make their dinner. She wouldn't be long, an hour perhaps. He assured her he would be fine, with a whole volume of Stevenson to read.

The moment the front door closed, he was out of the bed and across the hall. There was no one else about. Mr. Vanderhoff was traveling, Mr. Righter at his accounting job.

Eustace unlocked and entered the room. Everything stood immaculate.

Carefully, he searched for anything from Miss Comuzzi--at

the very least, the rosewater that he'd smelled. The narrow closet held two suits, one formal black suit and one brown tweed, and two pairs of shoes, one with spats. He felt under the mattress, looked beneath the bed, but found nothing, no secret message nor forgotten item of hers. Yet he had smelled her rosewater. He was sure of it. There must be a handkerchief, a stocking, or a bottle of perfume hidden somewhere. Eventually he had investigated every place but the phonograph cabinet.

It stood beside a hard-backed chair that he climbed up on in order to remove the cover; but standing there, with the latches thrown, he balked at touching it. He must, he knew. There might never be another opportunity. He lifted off the lid, climbed down and placed it carefully on the bed, then got up on the chair again.

Close up, the mechanism looked far more complicated than the Edison players in the store, even the one that had recorded Miss Comuzzi at the piano. For one thing, a cluster of copper tubing ran behind the mandrel and down into the cabinet. The tubes were almost as thin as Mother's bone crochet hooks. They emerged out of a steel block with a row of fins along the back. Below the fins was a bank of switches that he could not comprehend, and what looked like two receptacles where something might be fitted in. The reproducer itself lay tilted back on its articulated arm, revealing the sharpest stylus he had ever seen. It shone like glass. He extended a finger, but hesitated to touch the tip. The extra elements of the phonograph presented a mystery all their own.

He climbed down to the front of the cabinet, opened both the doors. Inside were shelves of cylinder records in their cartons. He drew one out. The label proclaimed "Edison Records" and as he rolled it, showed a photograph of Edison himself and the words "No Others Are Genuine." On the end cap, it said "4035 Original Lauterbach". He worked off the cardboard cap and carefully slid the cylinder out. It was brown just like the ones in the music store, made of carnauba wax, and he could see that it had been played many times. The grooves were worn. He recapped and put it away. He didn't need to hear it. More than likely he *had* heard it. He squatted down and looked at the lowest shelf. Only more cardboard cylinders. He finally closed the doors and reached to get the lid off the bed.

And that was when he saw the other door. It had been assembled into the side of the cabinet so that it looked like nothing more than a split panel—except that near the top and bottom lay two tiny brass hinges. There were no knobs to pull like on the front, but when he pushed, the panel moved a little and clicked outward. He drew it open.

The cylinder cartons here were like nothing he'd ever seen, of shiny black leather. He drew one all the way out. It bore no label at all, and the cap had an unbroken wax seal around it. Eustace replaced it, tried another, and then another until he pulled out one that had been unsealed. Carefully he worked off the cap. There was a cylinder inside and, as he had been taught to do, he inserted two fingers into it and tilted the carton to slide it out.

The cylinder was blood red. Eustace stared at it in awe.

It bore not a trace of writing, no etched words and no label on the inside either; but it was grooved all around, not a blank.

What was it was made of? He knew from the music store salesman that Edison was perfecting better cylinders.

Now curiosity took over. There was still plenty of time before anyone would return to the house.

With great care he again climbed up on the chair, slid the red cylinder onto the mandrel, locked it in place. Then, gathering a deep breath, he drew the knob and let the cylinder spin up to speed. He lowered the glittering reproducer.

The cabinet hissed with a sound like an exhalation that rose and fell, and then within it a single small, helpless moan. There was no music at all. And then quite suddenly *she* was in the room with him. His whole body sensed her nearness. Roses were everywhere.

The air grew charged. It sizzled against him, making the hairs on his arms jump up. Sparks danced before his eyes, swirled into a vision, ghostly as a visitation but visible, transparent before him. It was her shape. It stood stiffly, like someone reciting or singing in a choir, but only the breathing emerged. The crackling of the cylinder matched the shimmering aura she threw off, of tiny sparks that stung his skin. A swell of energy thrummed through him. He might have flown around the room on it if he hadn't been rooted to that chair, absorbing it. Miss Comuzzi was inside him, her skin slipping along his own like oil. He shook, and sweat popped out upon his forehead, trickled down from his hair. His eyes closed and he was about to swoon in a fever no longer contrived.

Then all at once it stopped. The stylus had come to the end of the groove and only the crackling remained as it rode around and around in place. With trembling fingers he drew the reproducer away the way he knew he should; but his fingertips were moist, and it slipped in his grasp. Terrified, he clutched and pulled it back. It took all his will to slide the knob and stop the spinning. He collapsed in the chair like a rag doll.

Sweat stung his eyes. He wiped his hands over them. Time must have passed. He shivered not from fever but from energy that he could barely contain. It was as if his muscles wanted to swell and burst through his skin. *She's still inside me*, he thought. His legs jittered. He couldn't sit any longer.

Put the lid on and get away—that's what he had to do. But the cylinder! He couldn't leave that there. He got onto his knees, pulled away the locking arm and then carefully pushed the cylinder onto two fingers. As he returned it to its sleeve, he saw the damage the reproducer had done when it slipped—the stylus had cut a gouge across the middle of the delicate grooving. His fingers hovered over it. Was there some way to smooth it out? But he dared not touch it and finally put the leather case away, closed the secret compartment. Then with a strength he had never before possessed, he lifted the lid and held it in one hand while he climbed back up on the chair. Lowered the lid. Snapped the latches.

Jumping down, he scanned the room to make sure it looked undisturbed. He ran to the door, listened with his ear pressed against it, uncannily able to hear the emptiness of the whole boarding house. He locked the door and stole across the hall to his own room.

He tried to sit but seconds later jumped up, paced, sat again shaking, and finally, madly, rushed out and down the stairs, outside, across the walk and down the street.

The sun was so warm, the colors so bright. Passing voices assailed him. He winced at their sharpness. Buildings, shadows, the stink of sweat, of fresh laundry drying on lines strung across the alley overhead—he could *smell* it up there. He walked and walked until he came to rails, and his attention was pulled along them by the smell of a train that had passed by within the hour, a stink of stockyards, blood and offal, though the yards lay nowhere near here. By then he'd crossed the tracks, walking in whatever direction, it didn't matter, but finally east toward the lake, which lay flat and blue across the horizon; and it wasn't until he'd jumped down from the boardwalk and waded into the coldness that his driving fever abated. The welter of sensations and limitless energy resolved and was at last contained within him.

Ten years old again, covered in icy water and muck, he climbed out upon the rocky bank, where he collapsed. The sun whirled in the heavens. He lay panting as if he'd run the whole length of Chicago.

He came to inside a large looming shadow. Sure that Mr. Schulde had caught up with him, he thrashed about until a voice he didn't know said, "Lad. There now, relax." He focused on brass buttons, a leather belt and holster, finally upon the badge.

The policeman put a cool hand to his forehead and brushed back his hair. "I feared you was drowned, boy. If you can sit up, I'll take you home. Where is it you live?"

Eustace and the policeman walked back toward Princeton Avenue, and it was only then that he appreciated how far he had gone. The energy of Miss Comuzzi still thrummed within him, but had settled now like a low wood fire in the belly of a stove.

The policeman asked casually what he'd been doing. He didn't know how to answer. "Were you sick?" Eustace nodded, tense. "I see. And does your mother—"

"There was a lady named Miss Comuzzi, she disappeared and then . . . but then she was in the room."

The policeman stopped, leaned toward him. "*What* was her name?"

The intensity of the policeman's stare unnerved him. He answered softly, "Miss Comuzzi."

"You say she was in a room with you? When was that?"

He wanted to explain or confess, but his every instinct rebelled—there was something wrong with the questions—and he said nothing.

When they finally arrived at the Claymore Boarding House, the policeman tried again to ask about Miss Comuzzi, and Eustace might have told then, only the front door opened and Mother ran onto the porch and swept him up in her arms, saying, "My baby, oh, Eustace, what did you do?" She hugged him tightly. He might have told then, but in the shadows of the doorway behind her, with eyes drilling into him, stood Mr. Schulde. His slight smile bore no trace of humor, and his eyes conveyed his message so loudly that Eustace heard the words *I know what you did*, and those eyes shifted to his mother and then back again. Did he understand the threat? Oh, yes, he did. No word to the policeman, nor anybody.

"I'm sure he's all right, missus," the policeman was saying. He'd taken off his helmet. "But you might want to keep a tighter rein on the lad. My name's Gallagher. Can I ask—"

Whatever question he'd been about to ask, he never finished it as Mr. Schulde strode across the porch and to Eustace's horror placed one hand tenderly upon Mother's back. "Officer Gallagher," he said, "We thank you. He's a good boy, but like all boys he does get into mischief." This close to him, Eustace noticed the touch of gray at his temples.

"Surely, I know that. I've two of my own," the policeman replied. He tipped his cap to Mother. "I'll bid you good afternoon, then." He gave Eustace a smile still edged in concern, then walked back to the street and was gone.

"My dear," said Mr. Schulde. "You see? All that worry was unnecessary. He's a rambunctious boy on an adventure and unconcerned for the feelings of others."

Mother set him down. "Eustace," she scolded, "You must never do that again." He wanted to explain that he'd run off because of the energy burning inside him, Miss Comuzzi's life whirling inside him; but Mother continued. "You must never go into other people's rooms when they aren't at home. Why, Mrs. Claymore will evict us, d'you see? If Franklin" —and she turned her head and actually smiled to the villain— "weren't so kind, why, he could've had that policeman arrest you."

"I didn't—"

"Eustace, don't compound it with a lie. I *found* the key you stole, on a chair in our room."

He couldn't remember where he'd left it. It must have fallen from his pocket.

Mr. Schulde's hand slid from her back to her shoulder, snaked along her arm. "Miriam," he said, "I would never have him arrested."

Eustace stared at Mother in horror. How could she? Only Father had called her by her *private* name. How could she reveal it to this awful man with his scorpion mustache?

"No," he said, and he stepped away from the intimacy.

"It's all right," assured Mr. Schulde. "No harm done. But you must obey your mother, boy. If you wish to listen to my music, you may always ask. It would be my *pleasure* to have you as a guest in my rooms, any time at all."

"There, Eustace, you see? You must thank Franklin for his kindness."

Franklin again! He squirmed, but there was no way out of it. He had to agree, or at least pretend to agree. "Thank you," he said, staring at their feet with miserable eyes.

Mr. Schulde placed both hands upon his shoulders. "Excellent."

It wasn't until Mother had him standing in his nightshirt in a basin to wash the mud off his legs before putting him to bed that she noticed some part of his transformation. She was talking to him about his behavior, when all of a sudden she fell silent.

Then she said, "Why, Eustace, your cheeks and forehead have never been so pink and shiny since you were a baby. You should spend more time out in the sun and less in this house by yourself up to mischief." She gave him a towel and got up.

He looked at his arm, his hand. *He* didn't see any change, but he knew what it was, and blurted, "Don't tell Mr. Schulde."

"What?"

He saw in her perplexity that he could not stop her—that the bigger he made the issue of his luster, the more certainly she would relate it.

In the end, it didn't matter. As Eustace was toweling his legs dry, a howl of inhuman fury roared through the house, and something shattered in the room across the hall. Mother ran out and knocked on Miss Comuzzi's door. "Franklin?" she called. "Franklin, are you all right?"

It was some moments before the door opened. Schulde stood there, his hair for once pushed into disarray. He looked drawn, even stricken as he faced Mother, but then he stepped forward, and his focus shifted past her to Eustace. She couldn't see his face, but for a split-second a look of hatred flashed at Eustace like a lighthouse beam, so stunning that he leaned away. He comprehended that his enemy had not previously discovered the damaged red cylinder.

Whatever détente had been arrived at on the porch, it no longer applied.

Mr. Schulde drew back to smile sheepishly at Mother. "Forgive me, dearest," he said, "I didn't mean to startle you. It's just that I . . . I slammed my hand in the cabinet lid." He took it in his other hand as if only now discovering the injury.

"Oh, let me see," she sympathized, and stepped out of sight into his room, propriety overcome by compassion.

Eustace didn't dare follow, and could only wait in the hall.

A minute or two passed before Mother emerged. She tossed a laugh after her like a girl, saying, "Oh, Franklin, I couldn't possibly. You soak that hand now, and goodnight." His reply slid murmurously through the gap before she closed the door after her.

Mother saw his look. "Why, darling, what's the matter? Mr. Schulde's hand is fine."

"I know."

"Well, then, you'd no cause to wait out here—"

"What did he ask you?"

She blinked at him, blushed. "Oh, it's silly. He offered to record me singing one day—me, can you imagine? He has no idea how awful that would be. Why, I expect his whole contraption would seize up at the sound." She laughed again, a mixture of elation and embarrassment.

"You can't," he said. "Ever."

"Well, my goodness, the least you could do was *pretend* I have a nice voice."

He took her hand—the same one Schulde had held—in both of his. "You have to promise me you won't."

"Eustace, whatever has gotten into you?"

"Promise!"

But Mother refused to be serious. "Well, I don't know--what if he placed me with a twelve-piece band? Maybe I *would* sing."

He sagged with exasperation.

"Really, stop being surly with me. You're the one of us who misbehaved today. In any case, you may stop crushing my hand.

I'm not about to put my voice on one of those crazy things for all the world to hear."

He wanted to believe her.

He didn't understand what he knew, but he knew with utter certainty that the man who'd taken Miss Comuzzi's room had also stolen her life. She *was* dead—that was what they had all refused to tell him. But how ever would he prove what he knew to Mother?

The next day Eustace watched Mr. Schulde as surreptitiously as possible. He tried to seem disinterested. Over the dinner table, his enemy behaved as if Eustace didn't exist, but made a point of sitting at the far end of the table, where he spoke in somber tones to Mr. Righter. He appeared drawn and tired as if he had not slept well. His hair looked more gray.

Eustace kept the door off the latch, too, and when later that evening he overheard Mother in Mr. Schulde's company, he charged out of the room and interrupted them with a request that she look over his arithmetic homework before he went to sleep. She was terrible at numbers, but she capitulated, giving Schulde an apologetic smile. "Perhaps I should turn in, too," she said. Mr. Schulde nodded, but his black gaze fell upon Eustace as he passed by, leaving no doubt that he understood the request.

The next night, before Schulde even had a chance to make his overtures, Eustace insisted that Mother stroll with him to the soda fountain at Toliver's Drug Emporium, where they both ordered egg creams the way they had last summer.

It was a pleasant night with a breeze, and they sat outside at a small wire table that trembled if either of them touched it. Mother wore her straw boater and bolero jacket. They discussed the Columbian Exhibition, and when they would go take it in now that it was open. Granted, they had the whole summer, but Mother commented that she would like to see "where Franklin works." She fell silent then. He asked what was wrong, but she waved off the question.

When they returned to the boarding house, Mr. Schulde was absent.

Much later, the snap of a key in a keyhole awoke Eustace. The door across the hall quietly closed and the key turned again.

Mother didn't stir. She could sleep so deeply that even thunderstorms wouldn't wake her.

Eustace arose and sneaked out into the hallway. In the narrow slit beneath the door opposite, light flashed for an instant, followed by a gasp. There wasn't a hint of music, and afterwards only silence.

If Mr. Vanderhoff had been there, Eustace would have gotten him to come and see. Instead, he must undertake the investigation alone. Very carefully, he went down the stairs.

Mr. Schulde's room overlooked the side yard, where two sturdy trellises enclosed the end of the porch where Mrs. Claymore was attempting in vain to train vines up their latticework. Eustace carefully climbed the trellis onto the porch roof. The moon shone at the other end of the roof. It cast his shadow down across the yard. He eased himself over the wood shingles and into the darkness beneath Schulde's open window.

The queer copper-tubed back side of the cabinet faced the window. On the chair beside it, a kerosene lamp burned, the wick high and smoking.

One of the red cylinders had been fitted onto the mandrel of the phonograph. Eustace knew which it must be.

Schulde was rotating the mandrel by hand, slowly, while he squinted at the stylus of the reproducer and with great care pressed one finger against it for a moment with each turn. He was sweating, his face drawn tight. The stylus tracked around and then, where he pressed, recut the groove across the gouge. Even from the window, Eustace could make out the scar in the cylinder.

Then Schulde leaned back, and wiped a hand over his face. He tilted the reproducer up and away, flicked the glass tip clean, and pushed the knob that started the mandrel spinning. With teeth gritted fearfully, he lowered the reproducer to the cylinder, then reached and turned the lamp down to a low glow.

The sound crackled. Schulde stood up and spread his arms as if for an embrace. His smile was expectant and terrible. Light flickered around him, flashes like dandelion puffs. Eustace wondered if the air had looked like that as he'd stood upon the chair and absorbed Miss Comuzzi. In the flutter of lights, Schulde's body seemed to contract and expand. One second he was strong and sleek. The next he looked ancient and bloodless.

All at once the sparkling air around him snapped and sizzled. A thread of blue lightning leapt from the reproducer and struck him. His arms wrapped tight around his vest and he bent double. He collapsed onto his knees.

When he raised his head next, he looked as if he'd aged another twenty years. His hands, balled into fists, pressed to his eyes and a sob escaped him. He writhed from side to side like some enormous snake and at last slumped to the floor.

Two minutes he just lay there. The crackling continued. Another thread of blue electricity jumped from the machine to him, but he might have been dead for all the effect it had. Sparks danced like motes upon the air, but there was no hiss of breath, nothing like what Eustace had experienced. She wasn't there anymore.

Finally, the stylus circled the end of the cylinder, and Schulde climbed wearily to his feet.

He lurched to the player, tore the cylinder from the mandrel and crushed it in his trembling fist. Eustace gasped.

Schulde stiffened, stared straight at the window. He snatched the lamp and thrust it out.

Desperately, Eustace scrabbled backwards down the shingles. Splinters stabbed his arms and knees but he ignored them. The lamp flared in the window above him. His toes poked the trellis holes for purchase as he heard the window open wide and a footstep thump on the roof. He slid over the edge, then hung by his fingers.

The roof creaked.

Eustace dropped the rest of the way to the lawn and rolled beneath the porch.

He stared out at the porch roof shadow stretched across the lawn as another shadow grew upon it, tall and spindly as bones.

A scratchy whisper reached him, like from an Edison cylinder: "Eustace. I know you're out there in the dark. Where *are* you, Eustace?"

He didn't dare breathe.

After a minute, the shadow withdrew back up the roof, and the window rumbled shut.

Eustace put his head down and whimpered.

An hour must have passed before he dared to crab his way

out from beneath the porch and steal back up the stairs. His pajamas were smudged with dirt. As he climbed he placed his feet close to the wall to keep the treads from creaking, painstakingly managed to turn the knob of the door and slip back into his room without a sound, but though he turned the key gingerly, the noise of the lock catching seemed as loud as an explosion.

He hid in his bed until he fell asleep.

A new tenant moved in the next day, a small, dark-haired woman older than Mother who called herself Miss Mary Owens. She said she worked at the Marshall Fields Wholesale store. Mr. Schulde barely acknowledged her. She was friendly to Eustace, and even to Schulde despite his rudeness.

When that evening Mr. Schulde didn't show up for the meal, Mr. Righter commented that "something seems to be wearing the poor fella down." Miss Owens asked him what was wrong, but Mr. Righter only shrugged.

After the meal, Mrs. Claymore and Mother prepared a plate of food that Mother carried upstairs. Eustace wanted to follow but Mrs. Claymore held him back. He sat unhappily, listening to Miss Owens and Mr. Righter discussing Mr. Vanderhoff, who was still on the road. "Indiana, I think," Mr. Righter told her. She wanted to know about everyone.

Eustace couldn't stand it. He got up, but as if hearing him Mrs. Claymore stuck her head out of the kitchen and called, "Eustace, don't interfere." Wiping her hands on her apron, she herded him up the stairs and into his own room. Across the hall, the door was closed.

Mrs. Claymore had just gone back down the stairs when Mother burst into their room, sobbing and clutching at her handkerchief.

"Franklin," she said, sinking down beside Eustace, "is gravely ill. He's seeking treatment, but refuses to allow me to help. It's all so terrible. Oh, Eustace, the *change* in him. He's withering away."

Eustace said nothing but stroked her hair.

The next morning, Eustace noticed that Mr. Schulde had bruised pouches beneath his eyes, crow's-feet and lines in his face. He'd brilliantined his hair, but looked almost as old as Mr.

Righter for all that. He was gone before the other boarders had sat down to breakfast. He didn't seem able to spare enough energy even to glower at Eustace. Eustace smirked at his bowl of oatmeal. Mother was safe. His enemy was dying.

That afternoon, walking home from his last week of school, Eustace decided to detour to the music store. He hadn't visited it since Miss Comuzzi's disappearance. He wondered if someone else played the piano for them now.

He was still a few blocks from the store when, just ahead, Mr. Schulde walked straight across his path.

Eustace stopped dead. Mr. Schulde didn't see him because he had his arm linked with that of a woman younger than Mother, with golden hair. On her shoulder, above the big leg-of-mutton sleeve of her dress, rested a lavender parasol that she twirled as they strolled. Mr. Schulde looked like her weary uncle, he'd aged so.

They crossed the street. Eustace followed them. He kept behind others, but Mr. Schulde didn't look around even once. It soon became clear that they were headed for the boarding house.

Eustace worked his way nearer, and strained to hear them. Mr. Schulde said, "I'm sure your voice is as lovely as the rest of you," and the woman tittered. She squeezed his arm with hers and said, "Don't you worry, I'll do whatever makes you happy, Harry."

That was strange enough that Eustace slowed down. Then, all at once the people in front of him were stepping aside and Mr. Schulde and the woman had stopped. Eustace hastily scurried into a shop doorway and sat on the step. He kept his head bowed as he looked up the street at the couple.

A police officer had stepped in front of them. It was Gallagher, the policeman who'd found him at the lake. Gallagher's arms were crossed and he held a nightstick in one hand. He tapped it rhythmically against his upper arm. From that far away, whatever he said wasn't audible, but all of a sudden, Mr. Schulde took a step back as if slapped. The woman stared at him like he was a troll that had crawled out from under a bridge. She sidled away, unfolded her parasol, and then hurried back past Eustace, hiding her face as much as possible from passers-by.

Mr. Schulde glared miserably at Gallagher, who now prodded the nightstick at him and said, "Sooner or later, you understand?"

Mr. Schulde backed up. He looked around as if to see where

the woman had gone and his eyes fell on Eustace. For that instant they were locked, neither one able to break away. Then Gallagher came toward him and Schulde fled into the street.

Eustace didn't go to the music store. He went home, comforted in the knowledge that he might have an ally in his war against Mr. Schulde.

The next morning Mr. Schulde remained in his room, which was just fine by Eustace. His place was set at the table, but he hadn't come down by the time Eustace left.

After school he went straight home, where he found Mrs. Claymore descending the stairs. She held a tray with a plate and utensils. "The poor man," she said as if he'd asked. "It's all he can do to sit up and listen to his music." And indeed, when Eustace got to the top of the stairs, a song was playing behind the door opposite. He listened to its refrain: "Every little bit added to what you've got makes just a little bit more." It sounded cheery. After a minute the same song started over again.

About an hour later Mother arrived. She didn't come up the stairs, but he heard her voice and he crept down a few stairs to peer through the balusters. She stood in the dining room speaking to Mrs. Claymore. She was still wearing her straw boater. Mother had two fingers pressed to her lips and her eyes were wide and worried. He heard the landlady say, "Give you a little time together." Mother nodded.

Eustace made his entrance then, thumping down the stairs. Mother came up to him, ruffled his hair. She unpinned her hat, revealing the curled fringe of hair over her forehead. She linked arms with him and they went up the stairs again to their room. More music was coming from behind the closed door across the hall, a tinkling banjo version of "Alexander's Ragtime Band."

Mother sat in the large cushioned easy chair in the corner, unbuttoned the stand collar of her blue striped dress, and then pulled off her one-strap pumps. Her feet looked sore. Mother leaned against the winged back of the chair with a sigh. "Oh, Eustace," she said, "Why is nothing simple?" He didn't know how to answer, but she didn't seem to expect one. She held her hand out to him, and he came to her, knelt and put his head in her lap. The music ended.

There was a rap at the door. Eustace got up and opened it. Mr. Righter stood there, wearing a cloth cap. He beamed at Eustace. "Well, there, son," he began, "ready for a little adventure?" His eyes shifted to Mother.

"Darling," she said, "Mr. Righter wants to take you to the Columbian Exhibition for the evening."

"What? No, *we're* supposed to go, you and me."

"Yes, and we will, Eustace, before summer's over, I promise. You can show me everything there is to see, because you'll know what's wonderful then. Tonight's the spectacle of lights, and we wanted you to see it, and I can't go, my feet ache so."

"Absolutely right," Mr. Righter agreed. "Tesla's spectacle. Aw, it's the future, just like I said to you, yours, my boy, and full of miracles, yessir." While he spoke he came into the room and patted Eustace on the shoulder. "If that ain't enough for you, why, Buffalo Bill's set up his Wild West Show right next door." He gave the shoulder a friendly squeeze.

Mother's eyes were wet. It wasn't tears, not yet, but he recognized that she needed him to do this.

He bent over and tugged at his knickerbockers to disguise his unhappiness. "All right," he said.

"Let's go then. Trolley's not going to wait."

Eustace looked again at Mother.

"I'll be fine," she said.

He followed Mr. Righter into the hall. The door across the hall remained closed.

Mr. Vanderhoff was just coming in as they left. He looked tired, his eyes red like he'd been staring into the sun all day. "Eustace, old buddy," he said, and patted him on the shoulder the way Mr. Righter had, but Mr. Righter guided him out and down the porch steps. Reaching the street, Eustace glanced back. Vanderhoff was still watching in perplexity. Miss Owens stood behind him in the shadows.

They took a trolley a few blocks, then switched to one of the new Calumet Electric Street Railway cars, which rolled south along Indiana. Eustace stood and Mr. Righter sat. Admiring the new car, he began to wax enthusiastically about electricity and the glories of the "White City" as folks were calling it. "Why," he said, "you know you can't lay *hands* on these tickets. Everyone wants these. If it weren't for poor old Schulde and his kindness toward you—why, sick as he is, he got hold of a couple tickets just for you. That's a generous and thoughtful man. Shame what's happened to him."

"But he was laid up all day." *We*, he thought, Mother had said *We wanted you to see it.*

"Oh, well, probably intended to bring you along hisself. I bet that's right. He's real sweet on your ma."

The truth was obvious and awful.

The car stopped, and a dozen people climbed aboard. Eustace moved aside for them, out of Mr. Righter's sight, and quickly jumped off before the electric car started up again.

He heard no cry of alarm as he raced away. He ran for a few blocks, until he was walking across Washington Park. On one hillock there, he looked toward the lake and spied the shape of the enormous Ferris wheel in the late sunlight. The buildings near it flew pennants. They waved in the dying breeze.

Eustace had no money for another trolley, and he'd been taken miles out of his way; but he knew where he was now, and hurried on, moving north and west. That took him near the stockyards. He veered from the stink and continued north, crossing the Chicago River again.

On Ohio Street the music store remained open on this balmy evening. The Edison machine stood playing a jaunty tune just inside the doorway, but nobody was listening. It was as if the machine was running on its own.

By the time he reached his own street again, it was twilight. A horse-drawn wagon stood out front of the boarding house. The driver looked to be catching a nap.

On the walk in the front, Mrs. Claymore stood conversing with Mr. Righter, who'd obviously ridden home on another trolley. They were watching for him. They didn't understand. Nobody did.

He circled behind the houses opposite, cut across the empty lot where he'd played stickball last summer, and approached the boarding house from the side. He scurried to the narrow back porch and entered through the kitchen, hurried up the back stairs.

Along the second floor hall all the doors were closed and the place stood silent. As quietly as he could, Eustace crept to Mr. Vanderhoff's door and knocked. A murmured reply answered, the word indistinct. Then the door opened and in trousers and braces over an undershirt, Mr. Vanderhoff blinked down at him. He or his room smelled of spirits.

"Why, Eustace, I thought—what's the matter?"

"Mr. Schulde got rid of me so he could get Mother in his room and have her all to himself. There was another woman, but the policeman stopped him before he could use her. And none of you would tell me what happened to Miss Comuzzi, but I know he killed her, and her soul—" He stopped before he had to try explaining the cylinders and the rest that nobody would believe.

"I knew that bird was bad news first time I clapped eyes on him. Holding Miriam 'gainst her will, is he?" He stepped away from the door, but reappeared almost immediately with his revolver. "We'll show him," he said, and marched past Eustace.

He pounded on the door with the butt of his gun. Eustace scurried around him to see. The door was flung back, and a shot fired, but it wasn't Vanderhoff's gun. Eyes disbelieving, Vanderhoff pressed against the jamb and clutched at his belly. Blood flowed out between his fingers.

Eustace edged toward the stairs as Mr. Schulde entered the doorway. He stepped impassively over Vanderhoff's legs and into the hall. He held a valise in one hand, a pistol in the other. His gaze swiveled to Eustace. He wasn't sick anymore. Though not as immaculate as before, his hair was black, his face smooth. "You," he snarled. "You meddling little brat." He strode for the stairs. The top of a black cylindrical case poked up out of his coat pocket.

Eustace backed down the stairs on all fours. The smoking barrel of the gun tracked him. Then from behind Mr. Schulde came a loud "bang!" and he stumbled against the wall, then blindly fired back at Vanderhoff. Seemingly more furious than injured, he plunged headlong down the stairs to the landing, forcing Eustace to flee to the front door where he ran up against Mr. Righter and Mrs. Claymore. They stood together, horrified.

"Get out of my way!" Schulde commanded them. His gun swung to show them where to move, revealing a bloody stain on the side of his jacket. "Now!" They scrambled for the dining room, dragging Eustace with them. Mr. Schulde stared daggers at him. Clearly he wanted to shoot, but instead he bounded out across the porch and down the front steps. "You! Teamster! " he called. "Wake the hell up, go up to my room and get the box under the canvas! Go on, hurry up!"

Eustace tore out of Mr. Righter's grasp and ran onto the porch.

The driver had jumped from his seat and across the walk, but drew up at the sight of Mr. Schulde's gun.

And then came another shot, from the side yard that Eustace had crossed only minutes before, and Mr. Schulde abruptly pitched sideways. He nearly went to one knee, but came up again and swung about to face his enemy. He brought his gun to bear. A second shot went off and Mr. Schulde tripped and went down on his knees, then collapsed back into a sitting position, like a rag-doll in the grass. He gazed down at himself in confusion. His whole shirt was dark with blood now.

Raising his head again, he saw Eustace. His face was gray and creased. It seemed to be pulling tight over his bones. Beneath the scorpion mustache his lip curled, and he tried to lift the revolver once more. A third shot smacked his forehead and he flopped back.

Officer Gallagher strode out of the side yard, followed by Miss Owens. He held a small caliber gun that still bore down on Mr. Schulde. They would reach him in a moment.

Eustace sprang down the steps and ran. He heard Miss Owens call him to stop.

To his amazement, Mr. Schulde was still alive. Breath wheezed out of him. His cloudy eyes were sinking into his skull, his dry skin cracking like old leather even as Eustace snatched the cylinder from his pocket and ran back to the house.

Gallagher called out, "Lad!" but he ignored him and dodged past Mr. Righter, who'd finally emerged from inside. He heard Miss Owens say, "We're the police, Mr. Righter." Then Eustace was on the stairs.

Mr. Vanderhoff had somehow reached the landing, and Mrs. Claymore knelt, ministering to his wound. "I got him, didn't I?" he asked as Eustace leaped past them.

He charged up and through the bloody doorway into Miss Comuzzi's room. A stained canvas tarp covered the phonograph, tied around with rope.

For a moment it looked like she wasn't there after all; his heart seized upon the idea that she was in their room, safe, and he nearly called to her before he saw in the heaped bedclothes the bit of striped blue fabric—the color, the braided hem of her dress.

Beside the bed he stared, paralyzed, unable to act, until finally, hesitantly, he clutched a corner of the bedding and drew it aside.

He'd expected—dreaded—to find her dead, but this was so impossible that his brain denied it was she. Within the dress there was only a husk. In the gray dimming light it looked like something made out of spun cotton candy. Her feet that had been red and tired were brown, mummified, the toes curled. It couldn't be Mother. Yet over the unfastened collar there lay the necklace with the moonstone cabochon he'd bought, that Miss Comuzzi had helped him pick out. It rested upon her crossed hands, the fingers sharp and brittle as wishbones.

Downstairs Miss Owens called his name. He came to himself. The leather case was in his other hand.

He ran to the door, closed it, and turned the key to lock them out. Then he went to the machine. Putting the black leather case on the bed, he undid the ropes and hauled the canvas off. He got up on the chair, unlatched the lid, and stepped down to place it on the floor. Then he retrieved the case and got back up.

As carefully as if it was crystal, he slid the blood red cylinder out onto his two straightened fingers. It shone in the twilight as he held it up. He slipped the cylinder onto the mandrel, and started the motor spinning. Mr. Righter rattled the doorknob, called his name.

Eustace eased the reproducer against the start of the cylinder. He stepped across to the bed, and then lay down beside Mother. He put his arms around her, and with eyes closed tight, he waited for the sound of her breath.

RUBBISH

Phil Rizuti had disappeared.

Watching the police walk past his townhouse to the one next door, Cal Thigpen lowered his number 3 flat from the canvas and stared out his sliding glass doors. He had the A/C off, one door open, and could hear them knock on Rizuti's door.

A moment later there came the sound of a door opening followed by the voice of Carol Rizuti, but quavery and hysterically high. Only bits of the conversation at the door drifted to Thigpen inside what had been intended as his dining room. He put the brush in a tomato soup can full of turpentine, lifted one of the crimped-paint-tube littered folding trays out of the way, and opened the screen.

Thigpen had known Carol and Phil for almost three years, nearly as long as his stay here. They alone among all the tenants in this block of townhomes had befriended the painter upon his arrival. He saw them socially maybe twice a month at most, but still considered them true friends. Phil worked for the Police Department in Internal Affairs; even so, Carol had once confessed to Thigpen that she feared the "official visit" like any other cop's wife.

Before the two "uniforms" had gotten inside, he reached the doorstep and caught Carol's attention. She was a short, soft brunette who always meant to exercise but never seemed to find the time. He saw worry in her blue eyes—and not about her physique.

"What's the trouble, Carol?" he asked.

The two officers glanced back at him. He got the idea they wanted him gone right now. Later he could come back, but at the moment he was screwing up their business.

Rather than cause trouble, Thigpen let Carol know that he would be around later if she wanted him, then went back inside his own place.

He sat again before his easel, stared at the three-foot square canvas, but could not think of what he wanted to do with the half-finished painting just now. He still had some late afternoon light, enough to work with, but had lost the intensity that accompanied his work. The cops had interrupted him, broken the flow by stepping between him and his vision.

It was just as well. Within half an hour one of the cops had stopped outside his screen and asked to come in. The young man, looking freshly poured out of an Aqua Velva commercial, gave his painting a once over, then scanned the others that hung on the walls or stood in stacks around the room. Thigpen got the feeling the cop actually appreciated some of the abstracts, but he said nothing about them. He returned his attention to Thigpen with a half-smile.

"You know Phil Rizuti and his wife."

"Yeah, a few years. Something happen to him?"

"We're not sure yet. He's disappeared, according to his wife. I noticed you're situated in a position to notice who comes and goes along this walk."

"Yeah, if I pay attention."

"When was the last time you saw Mr. Rizuti?"

"About four."

"Coming in or going out, Mr.—"

"Thigpen comma Calvin. Coming in. On schedule. He normally arrives about that time every day, Monday through Friday. You're telling me that he isn't there now?"

"That's right." He looked at a little notebook in his hand. "But you didn't see him leave."

"Nope."

"And you were sitting here painting."

"That's right. I use this room for the light. Wouldn't have moved in here without it, as a matter of fact. But, uh," he gestured at the two folding trays, one of which held an empty plate and a glass, "I got up and made a sandwich at one point, although that would have been before four o'clock. And I went to the bathroom at one point."

"When?"

Thigpen shrugged. "I don't check my watch when I go. Maybe an hour ago, but if you're trying to narrow down the time he went out, that doesn't necessarily mean anything. See, when I'm in the middle of something and the canvas is opening up for me, I tend to erase the rest of the world. It just goes away. He could have danced bare-assed in front of the window at some point and I never would have noticed, unless he blocked the light. Then, I would have seen his shadow. Other than that, I'd never know. I mean, I didn't even notice when Carol got home. You see what I'm saying?"

The young officer closed the notebook with a sigh and put it in his hip pocket. "Okay. Um, if anyone else needs to talk to you—"

"This is where I'll be from one to six seven days a week."

The young man noted that and went back out the screen, but peeked in before closing it and said, "I like the balance in that one." He pointed to the unframed painting Thigpen had on the wall behind the easel—one of blues and greens evoking a rainfall deep within some Smoky Mountain forest.

"Me, too," said the artist.

As the cop closed the sliding door, there came a knock at the front door. Thigpen went to it, half-expecting to find Carol there; instead, he opened the door on the complex's maintenance man, an old oriental gentleman with whom Thigpen had had very few dealings over the past four years.

"You got toilet problem?" asked the maintenance man, whose shirt had the name "Chuck" emblazoned on the pocket in red thread.

"Was I supposed to have?"

"Chuck" looked exasperated. "Places at other end of row have flooding in downstairs toilet. Maybe you, too."

Thigpen let him in and waited in the hall while the man checked out his commode. It took "Chuck" only a minute. "Nope," he said. "You water level down, but no flood." He made a "tchick" with his tongue. "Somepin' fouled up the sewer line, way down under the hill. Time for snake." He gave Thigpen a meaningless smile and left.

After closing the door, Cal Thigpen went back to his easel, but the light had gone now, the very last of it being useless to him. He picked up his plate and glass and carried then into the kitchen. His stomach rumbled, wanting dinner. Another sandwich would not satisfy that hunger. He wished silently for the thousandth time that he had learned how to cook before Nan had divorced him. He decided to go out for a pizza.

For a moment he considered changing out of his paint-stained jeans and T-shirt, but the muggy Carolina heat coming through the screen made him exhausted just thinking about it. Let 'em smell paint. He grabbed his wallet and headed out.

She must have heard the slam of his front door. Before Thigpen had taken half a dozen steps along the sidewalk, her door opened, the knocker rattling, and she called to him to wait. He looked back at her and knew he could not leave without reassuring her.

Maybe he would *order* a pizza instead.

Carol had a glass of white wine in her hand. She asked him if he wanted a drink, too, and from her tone he understood that she needed him to drink with her. He let her fix a gin and tonic while he called in to have a pizza delivered. She sliced a fresh lime and polished off a bottle of tonic in making his drink. Thigpen watched her, marveling at her ability to assemble something as simple as a drink without making a mess—something he could never do. In fact he was constantly amazed at how tidy she kept this overstocked and gadgeted kitchen. She opened the pantry door, put a new plastic trash bag in the trash container, and dropped the empty bottle and the heel of the lime into it. Then she mopped off the counter with a sponge and only then handed him his drink and led him from the kitchen.

Compared to the sparseness of his own apartment, the Rizuti's lived in opulence. Carol was a decorator with very definite ideas. Paintings and prints lined the walls, most of them from the Metropolitan collection; Carol had even honored him by selecting and displaying one of his.

The living room couch was composed of four square beige blocks and two smaller, rectangular footstools arranged around a glass and silver coffee-table. A huge bulb lamp hung over them like a microphone on the end of an arcing boom. The stereo system was not too big for the room and had been placed out of the way, carefully, among small glass-fronted bookcases. Phil and Carol Rizuti were, to Thigpen's mind, people born to apartment life. He, on the other hand, longed for a big old house with high ceilings and wooden floors: a place where he could work on huge canvases. Sometimes he could almost smell the oil paint wafting through the rooms.

"So tell me what's going on, Carol," Thigpen said. "Did Phil walk off with a kilo of Exhibit A?"

He had tried to keep it light, but Carol's expression became hard and tight, and she stared down into her wine. "He's gone," she replied, so softly that he nearly missed it. "He must have come home, because his clothes are upstairs—the suit he wore this morning, his shoes."

"He changed clothes."

"Right."

He waited, expecting her to continue. When she remained silent, he prompted her. "Then what?"

"Well, I don't know. He was gone at five when I got home. No note, no sign of him."

He understood then that the department had come out here at *her* insistence. He tried to control his voice, but it got away from him. "Carol, you called the cops after only *two* hours without Phil? What if the guy went to the store, fer Chrissake?"

She looked at him with a glint of anger. No doubt the police had treated her in much the same tone; normally, they would not have responded to a Missing Persons call for 24 hours, but Thigpen felt sure she knew someone who could pull strings for her, though surely with no less skepticism than he had. "He couldn't very well go to the store," she said, "when he left behind his wallet, his checkbook, and the keys to both the apartment and the car."

Thigpen thought that over. "Was the house unlocked when you got home?"

"It was."

"Well, wherever he went, he meant to come back. There you are—maybe he's out jogging."

"Phil?" she asked incredulously.

"Yeah, okay. Dumb idea." At forty-seven, Phil Rizuti was

evolving into a human pear. "Well, what about the pool, then? He might have gone swimming."

"He would have waited for me to get home, or left a note telling me to come on down to the clubhouse when I got in."

"True," he said, giving in to her. "I don't know a more conscientious man than Phil. Especially when it comes to you, dear." He smiled at her, but could find little reason to offer hope. Still, the fact that her husband had been missing for only two and a half hours made the whole matter seem utterly absurd, and he *knew* how Phil doted on Carol. The one thing that came into his head he kept to himself. It seemed impossible to consider and was certainly nothing to voice to a friend's wife; besides, he could not make himself believe for a minute that Phil might be having an affair with someone in the complex. And even if by some outrageous circumstance that were possible, then Phil had the brains not to advertise it like this. No, Thigpen decided, out of the question. Incomprehensible. He sipped his drink in silence and studied his painting.

Someone knocked on the front door.

"That'll be my pizza," Thigpen said. He jumped up, adding, "I'll get it, stay put," and went down the hall, pulling wadded-up bills out of his wallet and hoping that it would, in fact, not be his pizza, but rather Phil instead.

It was neither.

At the door stood a tall, wiry man with reddish hair going to gray and a face that had creased deeply with age. The skin under his chin had softened into two pleats. It was a face that Thigpen could have found interesting enough to paint. The man wore a dark suit that did not fit him quite right in the shoulders. After looking him over, the man said hopefully, "Phillip Rizuti?"

"Nope."

"Is he here?"

"Nope. Why?"

The man studied him all over again with a different look, of curiosity and formulation. He held up a wallet that was not a wallet—Thigpen saw that it was a black case containing a badge.

"I'm Lieutenant Painter," the man drawled.

"You're kidding."

"What's that s'posed to mean?" He had the accent of a natural-born Carolina boy.

"Nothing. You want to talk with Mrs. Rizuti?"

"Who are you?"

"Nobody. I mean, my name's Cal Thigpen. I live next door."

"Oh, yeah. One of the boys interviewed you earlier. Didn't have much to say. You're the painter." The explanation of Thigpen's earlier remark overtook him quite suddenly. For a second his eyes crinkled. "Okay."

"Something new turn up?"

"Wal, I was hoping not. But maybe, since you say Mr. Rizuti isn't back yet."

"What's going on?'

Both men turned and saw Carol Rizuti at the end of the hallway. Cal Thigpen stepped out of the way and let the Lieutenant enter. The policeman explained who he was again, then explained as delicately as he could that there had been a traffic accident with an unidentified male in it who might be Phillip Rizuti, but they would like a positive ID from her. She made him repeat that the man was dead.

"Wait a minute," Thigpen interjected. "The guy's from your office, fer Chrissake. Surely somebody down there could identify him, couldn't they?"

"They all went home hours ago. Internal works reg'lar hours, Mr. Thigpen," Painter explained. "Mrs. Rizuti?"

Shaken and pale, Carol Rizuti agreed to go see the body. She went upstairs to get her things.

While she was gone, there was a second knock on the door. Thigpen's pizza had arrived. He paid the delivery girl and set it on the dining room table. The smell of it nearly drove him crazy, but the idea of eating at this time struck him as blasphemous.

"You always get your food delivered here?" asked Painter.

"Who's going to answer my door if I have it sent over there? Or is there supposed to be more meaning in that question."

"No, just wondering."

"Sure you were."

Painter scanned the kitchen briefly, then clucked his tongue. "My, my, if she doesn't have one of everything in there. Bet she makes her own ketchup." He stared sternly at Thigpen. "I was just amazed that anyone would be eating at a time like this."

Thigpen felt himself getting hot. With great control, he kept his voice level, and quiet enough that Carol wouldn't hear: "Dammit, the guy has only been gone about three hours."

Painter nodded, one corner of his mouth turned up in what might have been the hint of a smile. "I know." He reached into his inside suit pocket, removed a pair of heavy-black-frame glasses, which he put on with one hand while scooping up a stack of unopened mail from the dining room table. He noted the return addresses on each and that each was postmarked. Thigpen watched him with growing annoyance, but kept silent, supposing that this was part of the job. He listened to Carol moving around upstairs.

She came back down carrying her purse and car keys. She had put on makeup and brushed her hair. That seemed incongruous to Thigpen at first, but he realized that shock might actually make people like Carol more meticulous that normal. It was her defense.

She turned to him before leaving. "Please stay until I get back. He might call or . . ."

"Sure, Carol." He patted her arm. "I'll just nibble on the pizza and watch TV or something."

Left alone, Cal Thigpen went over to the dining room table and considered the flat cardboard box that dared him to confront the treasures hidden within. He still thought it improper to eat but knew better than to argue with his stomach. As he stood there, he found himself drawn to the same unopened mail Painter had looked at; with a slight flush of guilt, he started looking through it.

He left her some pizza, but she did not want any when she returned. He told her to keep it for later, when the shock wore off and she found herself hungry.

The body had not been Phillip Rizuti. And he had not checked back in since she'd left.

Thigpen started to clean up, but she stopped him. "I don't feel like going to sleep just now," she told him. "I'll probably clean the house or something until I'm too tired to see straight. Then I'll go to bed. I don't want to take any pills. If he calls, I want to be awake."

"Sure. You know where I am if you need me. I'll be home all

day tomorrow, too. I have Susanah coming in for another book cover piece. We'll be at it all morning."

"Painting?"

He grinned. "Well, at least you haven't lost your sense of humor."

"Look, why don't you bring her over here for dinner tomorrow night."

"You going in to work tomorrow?"

"I don't know. I don't think so."

"Okay." He started to turn away, then paused and looked back at her. "Better still, why don't you come over for dinner. Phil would know to call you there."

She agreed and he left her standing in her kitchen looking lost and empty. At least, he thought, Phil Rizuti was still alive. Theoretically.

"**G**od, I *really* need a cigarette."

"I'm almost finished, Suse, just sit there a few more minutes, will you?"

He had her kneeling on one knee and holding up his fishing rod which, in the final painting, would become a wicked trident. For the pastel sketch he was doing as a preliminary, it was a single straight line.

Susanah was his favorite model of all he had ever worked with. He figured once that he could have painted her body a thousand times and never gotten bored with it. That she already adorned well over a dozen paperbacks of various sorts only substantiated this belief. Her dark blonde hair hung to the middle of her back. She had been a gymnast in high school and college, and her body remained remarkably firm from a daily regimen of exercises. Artists did not generally get involved with models who answered ads in the paper—the models usually had a private life of an entirely different sort already carved out—but Susanah and he had practically fallen in love before the first sketch had been completed.

"Please, Calvin, I'm goin' nuts," she begged.

"Smoking's bad for you."

"That kind of talk'll get you tarred and feathered in this state, honey."

"Think what you're doing to your body."

"What's wrong with my body?"

Exasperated, Thigpen set down the cray-pas stick and wiped his fingers on a rag. "All right. Five minutes. Smoke 'em if you got 'em."

Susanah stood up and flexed her legs, then walked boldly over to her purse.

"You know," mused Thigpen, "they can see you from across the road over there."

"Really?" She stood up with her cigarette dangling from between her lips. After lighting it, she placed both hands on her hips and took a defiant pose in front of the glass doors. "Let 'em drool." Then the Chinese maintenance man appeared at the bottom of the hill, wrestling with what looked like a long metal tapeworm. She stepped back from the window, turned away, blowing smoke out her nostrils. She took the cigarette out of her mouth and grinned at Thigpen. "Let me see what you've done."

He had placed her at the foot of a massive throne on which sat a lizard king—a figure he had borrowed from sketches done a year before for a romance novel. The area around her had been sketched to suggest strange creatures emerging from mist at the borders.

"Do I get this one when you've done?"

"As always," he answered. She pressed up against him, her arms snaking around his shoulders. Smoke curled out from behind his head. He pretended to cough. "Dear, you know the smell of your cigarette is enough to take the sex drive out of the most virile male."

"Cal," she said with a trace of annoyance.

"All right, all right. Your five minutes are up. Give yourself another puff and put it out."

"Oh, come on."

"I mean it. I want to get this done before Carol arrives." He had told Susanah about Phil Rizuti's strange disappearance. "I don't want her seeing all these naked women running around my place."

She pulled back his head. "What d'you mean, *all* these naked women? What others?" She glared down at him.

"I was referring to you and your multiple personalities." He reached up and grabbed some of her hair and drew her face down to his.

When he released her she returned to her pose.

"The cigarette is not part of the setting—lizards don't smoke." He waited impatiently until she had stubbed it out in an ashtray. "Grand."

A half hour later he had finished the sketch and decided that they had enough time before dinner to disappear upstairs for a while.

Cal had the fire going in the grill out back and Susanah was making hamburgers in the kitchen. After satisfying himself that the coals would do just fine, Thigpen carried the plastic container of lighter fluid back inside.

"Did you see Carol?" Susanah asked over her shoulder.

He set the fluid down on the counter beside her pack of cigarettes and lighter. "No, I didn't. She may have taken a sleeping pill after all. Now that you mention it, maybe I'd better go over and make sure she hasn't forgotten. It's not like she hasn't more than one thing on her mind."

"Mmm."

Thigpen went out through the sliding door. The townhouse next door was closed up and he wondered as he reached the door if Carol had not perhaps fled from her trouble. This nagged him enough to step back on the sidewalk and look down at the cars parked in the lot beyond and down the hill from his own place. Carol's Toyota was there, right next to Phil's Colt.

Thigpen's neck tingled with apprehension. He went up to the Rizutis' front door and rapped with the knocker. The door yielded slightly: it had been ajar.

He stuck his head inside and called out, but received no answer. The place smelled as if it had been closed up all day, which was odd, because Carol would never have allowed mustiness if she were home. It went against her fundamental beliefs.

He left the door and wandered inside. The dining room table was bare; no trace remained of last night's pizza. He went down the hall to the living room and found it the same as it had been last night, save that the drink glasses were gone. Returning down the hall, he decided to go upstairs, still hopeful that she had simply conked out after a fitful night.

The bed was made and no one lay upon it. But Phil's suit still lay at the foot, probably as they had been left. He could imagine Carol playing a sort of mental game that if everything remained the same, her husband would come walking back in normally, time truncating so that all the nasty business with police and identifying corpses would never have occurred.

He checked the bathrooms and the guest bedroom. No one was there.

Back downstairs, he considered that she might have left a note for him on the bulletin board beside the phone and went into the kitchen to see.

The kitchen had been cleaned, too: dishes put away, all the parts of their drinks restored to cabinets. The closet door stood open. Inside it, he saw that the previous night's trash had been taken out—namely, his pizza box. Yes, that fit. She would not have been able to tolerate the idea of that smelly cardboard container sticking up out of the bag. Carol was, as he and Phil had joked on more than one occasion, a true anal retentive. Her world required immaculacy—which included being forever on time.

So, where the hell was she?

The little bulletin board revealed nothing. All the messages were to herself about shopping or future dinner engagements and the like. No note to him.

Flustered, he turned around to leave.

He screamed at the sight of the figure in the kitchen door-way. In that split-second he recognized Lieutenant Painter, but he could not calm down that fast.

"Jesus, Mary and Joseph! Did you find that entertaining?"

"Cheapest thrill I know." The lieutenant stepped further into the room. "Might I ask what you're doing in this apartment *this* time?"

"Trying to find an explanation. Haven't had much luck."

"Explanation to what? Where's Mrs. Rizuti?"

"That's what I'd like to know."

The amusement vanished from the policeman's face as if it had never been there. Thigpen went on to tell him about the in-vitation to dinner and Carol's non-appearance at the appointed time. He told Painter what he had found in the rest of the house. "You didn't touch anything, I hope?" asked Painter.

"Nope. Just the front door. What is going on here?"

"Damned if I know."

"What did you come back for? Internal Affairs raising hell at his disappearance?"

Painter shook his head. "Nope, I was in the next block of apartments and decided I'd stop in to see if the lady's husband had turned up."

"The next block of apartments?"

"Yup," replied Painter, and Thigpen could see that he did not want to explain himself, but he let Painter know that he would have to. Reluctantly, the lieutenant added, "Someone else has disappeared."

"Jesus. Who?"

"Single male named Halliwell. Had a one-bedroom over in the next bunch of apartments like I said. Hasn't been to work for the past two days. His office finally called the management here to have the place checked, thinking very wisely that their office manager might have had a heart attack or somethin' of the kind."

"And?"

"That about wraps it up. The office sent somebody over to check. They went in, found nobody home and most of the lights on. Near as we can tell, everything was there. Makes no sense."

"Can there be a connection?"

"Seems like there oughta be. They didn't disappear at the same time, but it's pretty unusual as the crow flies. Did you know him, Halliwell?"

"Me? No, I didn't know him. Why would that make a difference? I haven't disappeared."

"You're about the only one here who hasn't." There was a malicious glint in his eye. "As of last night, too, I would have bet fifty-fifty that you and Mrs. Rizuti had offed her hubby."

"You son of a bitch."

"Sorry. Comes with the territory."

"You're going to be around awhile, aren't you?" asked Thigpen.

"I will now. We're gonna have to go over this whole place."

"Then I want you to come next door with me. I want to introduce you to living proof why I wouldn't run off with Carol Rizuti."

They went back outside but left the door open.

The sun had set behind the trees on the hill across the street. Painter directed a handful of people to the various tasks he wanted done in the Rizuti apartment.

Thigpen came over after a few minutes and found Painter sitting at the dining room table, filling out some form.

"How's your girlfriend?" the policeman asked without looking up.

"She's okay."

"Sorry 'bout catching her like that. Never saw a woman exercise in the nude before."

"Yeah, well, I paint her in the nude, you see, so she generally doesn't bring a lot of clothes with her. And she's sort of spontaneous."

Painter looked at him then. "That's a better word for it than I could have thought up."

"How's it coming?" He indicated the others with his head.

"Nothing, which is about all I expected. Same's the other place. Won't take 'em more than a half hour here, though, 'cause everything's so tidy."

Thigpen scratched his head. "Look, um, for what it's worth I was wondering if I could have a look at what's-his-name's place."

"Why? I thought you didn't know him?"

"I don't. I just feel—well, it's stupid—but I feel involved. And maybe I'll see something that clicks, you know, between the two apartments. Something I'm looking at here that should hold the answer for me but doesn't."

"Oh, you got that feeling like the answer's here in front of you but you can't see it?"

"No." Thigpen shrugged. "It was just a thought."

"I s'pose it can't hurt." He stood, looking very tired. Then he went up to one of the other men and retrieved a key. As he led Thigpen out of the apartment, he said, "There's nothin' in the world I hate more'n a mystery."

"Yeah," Thigpen agreed, "I have a similar regard for a blank canvas."

Outside, a wind had come up, but the heat of the day had not lessened. In the north, distant thunder rumbled. A line of clouds stretched the length of that horizon, and both men knew the storm would soon be here.

Thigpen stuck his head inside his apartment and called out to Susanah that he could be right back. "What about the burgers?" she yelled back. He promised he would throw on some more coals when he returned and cook by flashlight.

The two men went up the sidewalk then turned right and headed across the hill to a block of apartments set on the next higher plateau and surrounded by oak trees swishing and hissing in the wind, leaves twisted upside down. Painter said nothing the whole walk. Thigpen wondered what he was thinking but decided not to ask.

He had never been inside one of the apartments in the complex. Halliwell had been a fairly unkempt sort of person. His clothes lay strewn over half the apartment furniture although a pressed suit still in its dry-cleaning bag hung over the back of the bedroom door.

The small kitchen reflected much the same lifestyle, with dishes stacked out of the sink and dollops of food on the counter tops. The pantry closet hung open, showing itself to be well-stocked. The floor hid beneath an uneven layer of folded brown grocery bags, one of which carried a dark rectangular impression where another bag had apparently sat and leaked through onto it.

Thigpen went back into the combined living/dining room section and studied the debris throughout. The furniture looked cheap, but that was about the only conclusion he could draw.

Painter followed him from room to room, switching lights on and off, allowing him complete freedom. The policeman watched everything he did, still allowing for the slight possibility that Thigpen was the link between the disappearances. But when at last the artist sank down on the couch, the exasperation on his face declared his innocence and his total discouragement. "No luck, huh?" asked Painter.

"I don't know what I expected to find."

"Me, neither." Painter sat on the arm of the couch and looked the place over in silence for a time. Then he said, "Maybe you can still help, though, Thigpen. What do these places have in common with yours?"

Thigpen looked up. "What, you mean structurally?"

"Maybe. But I was thinkin' like what do they share?"

After a moment, Thigpen started to list what he knew. "There's the parking lot—they park down the hill there, which is why that trail exists down to the sidewalk. Maybe they're supposed to park elsewhere, but *some* of them use it.

"And, uh, the mailbox up the street. That's for the whole complex. So is the pool and clubhouse."

"What's there?" he asked, though he had already checked it out. No one at the pool had seen either Rizuti or Halliwell, neither of whom had been frequenters of the poolside social gathering. But he listened while Thigpen listed the sauna, weight room, coke machine, ping-pong table, and shower stalls. "Presumably that goes for the women's side, too."

Having completed this inventory, Thigpen searched Painter's face for some positive feedback, but he could see immediately that he had added nothing new.

They went back to the townhouses in silent frustration. In the north, lightning flickered across the sky. Thigpen paused at his door to say, "I'll see you—let me know, will you?" to Painter, who nodded his assurances.

Susanah stood in the kitchen. She had just taken the bag of charcoal out of the pantry closet and handed it to him as he entered the room. "Here, and you better get them started quick, because it's gonna rain inside a half hour."

He stared down at the bag glumly, then finally turned around and grabbed the plastic container of lighter fluid and her lighter from the counter, absently, not even considering whether or not he needed them. "I'll come back for the burgers," he promised.

"Okay. I'm gonna take your garbage down before it climbs out of the closet. You know, you've got stuff in this bag I helped you eat two weeks ago? And the cans of turpentine—ech!"

"Yeah, well, it's a big bag, Suse." He walked on down the hall and out the back to the patio. Vaguely, he heard the front door slam.

The coals in the grill were shrunken to white-hot cores, way too hot for hamburgers. He used a pair of tongs to lift off the cooking grille, then started to layer in fresh coals. This completed, he replaced the grille and picked up the fluid bottle and lighter. He stopped. The answer rushed in unbidden, pushing all other thoughts from his mind.

He saw again the interiors of the two apartments: Halliwell's, with the big dark stain on the brown bag where another, a trash bag, had squatted; then Carol's kitchen, the pantry door open, the pizza box and bag gone from the rectangular plastic bucket that held her trash; and last, the same kitchen on the night Phil had disappeared, as he watched Carol have to take out a new trash bag and fit it into the container. And, over this, Painter's voice: "What do they *share*?"

The trash bin, the huge green trash bin. He had forgotten that. Susanah!

Thigpen ran back inside, shouting her name but recalling the slam of the front door. The kitchen was empty, and he was already turning away. He shoved back the screen door and shouted her name into the deep twilight, then charged down the sidewalk. Behind him, someone called to him, but he did not pay attention. "Susanah!" he yelled again. She should have heard him, even above the wind. Why didn't she answer?

From the top of the steps he could see the three-sided fence enclosing the trash bin, enfolding it in complete shadow. The opening was on the opposite side—a sliding door at waist level—out of his view. He leaped the steps in two bounds, stumbled as he hit the bottom, scraping his knee, leaning his weight on the container in his hand—he still carried the fluid and lighter.

His ankle hurt as he rose up, but he ignored the pain and ran between the cars, across the lot. The bin rang with a deep boom, like a gong in a cavern.

She was doubled over the edge of the little door, and Thigpen saw her legs rising up from the ground and sliding into the filthy recesses inside the bin. Her bare feet thumped against the wooden fence once.

He made a weird sound in his throat and ran forward. Half-consciously he pried loose the cap of the fluid bottle with his thumb.

Her knees jerked over the rim. He grabbed her ankle and pulled as hard as he could. Susanah came halfway out of the trash container. Inside it, something growled in angry surprise —something inhuman. Thigpen had expected a rapist, a crazy killer; he was unprepared for this.

Feral eyes glowed out of the darkness. A huge webbed and taloned hand swung at him out of the opening. He jumped back but fell against Susanah and the fence. The tip of one talon reached him, slit open his cheek.

He hastily aimed and squeezed the lighter fluid, spraying it at the glowing eyes. The thing in the trash bin howled. For an instant, lightning lit up the interior of the bin, and Thigpen glimpsed an erect serpentine body with sausage-like sinewy arms. Still in darkness, the eyes seemed to flare, to mirror the threat of lightning.

He quickly grabbed hold of Susanah again and pulled her the rest of the way out. Blood coated her neck and shoulders. He prayed she was not dead as he dropped her in the grass beside the fence. A first drop of rain splashed in his eye. He leaned shakily for the fence and stumbled back on his bad ankle.

Something grabbed his hair, tugged sharply enough to jerk him off his feet. He slammed into the trash bin just below the little door. A second set of claws stretched down for his shoulder.

Thigpen flicked the lighter and held it up at the arm over his head. The other leathery hand found his collarbone and grabbed hold. He spasmed as the talons pierced him. The thing stank of wet earth, a smell like worms.

"Thigpen!" someone shouted.

The lighter had gone out! He hurriedly adjusted the flame with his thumb, then sprayed fluid on the hand beside his face. With a sudden twist, he flicked the lighter and set the hand on fire.

The creature shrieked and released him. His shirt burst into a small circle of flame. He rolled over to put it out, nudged against the ground like a dog. His shoulder stung as if a nest of hornets had converged upon him. He could smell the singe on his hair.

Something smothered him and he fought it wildly until he realized it was a jacket. It stank of cigars. The jacket came away and Painter was kneeling over him. "I'm all right," he groaned, tried to say Susanah's name and failed.

Inside the trash bin the thing was screaming and thrashing hard enough to actually rock the whole bin.

Painter stood slowly, taking out his revolver. He looked in just as the thing—now a black shape wreathed in flames—dropped from sight. Painter leaned over the edge, ready to shoot, and saw the last of the thing kicking up dirt with hugely taloned feet as it scrambled back into a wide hole. The bottom plate of the trash bin had been removed, it seemed, though he could not be positive; too much burning debris blocked his view. He turned back toward Thigpen a moment before the turpentine in the trash erupted with a "Whump!"

For a moment Painter leaned against the fence. Something spawned of nightmares had come up out of the earth; now, hopefully, Thigpen had sent it back there to die. Painter knew he would have to assemble a team to go into the sewers underneath this hill. His glance strayed out to the manhole cover in the middle of the street. How many? he wondered.

Thigpen had crawled over to Susanah. Under the smear of blood on her neck, there had been no wounds—the blood had run from her shoulders where the thing had picked her up. She was breathing rapidly, but steadily. He hugged her to him until Painter shook him out of his blind and thoughtless state. Rain was starting to fall. The trash bin, he could see, glowed red in places. The howling from inside it had stopped. He looked up at Painter and the sky and said, "I think we need a hospital."

He sat cradling Susanah as the downpour broke over them. Painter went to get a car.

THAT BLISSFUL HEIGHT

"Populus vult decipi...decipiatur!"

I. POST TRANCE

Think of me," the child's voice fades, "as you do a gentle moonbeam. . . ." The medium's arms spread as wide as her dark hoop skirt and she sinks down until her head presses against the rosewood breakfast table. Its tip-up top wobbles slightly from palm to palm as if the securing bolt has loosened and is about to flip it vertically. Mercifully—not for the woman, but for the couple who hang upon her every gesture—it does not.

They are young, early in their twenties, still struggling to make their way in the world of 1850. The loss of their six-year-old daughter has been as cruel as anything can be; as cruel, thinks Robert Hare, as the loss of his own sister so long ago. Their misery has driven the poor couple, named Howitt, out of the objective sphere: their need to believe become their universe. Is it truly the voice of their daughter that has emerged from the seemingly unconscious medium? How can anyone be certain when the girl has been dead so many months?

Hare recalls the words of the great Scottish philosopher Sir William Hamilton: "Is it unreasonable to confess that we believe in God, not by reason of Nature which conceals Him, but by reason of the supernatural in Man which alone reveals and proves Him to exist?"

If that question needs proving, here the proof lies. The weeping wife supplicating the Deity while her husband, pale and teary-eyed but determined to be the rock against which she can lean, gathers her up. The shoulder seam of his coat has begun to unthread.

At the sound of rustling skirts, the medium stirs. Her hands slide together and she pushes herself upright, disheveled hair wisping her forehead, her eyes shifting as if to re-establish her surroundings. Hare watches her with a skeptical eye. She composes herself in time to collect her fee from the dazed Mr. Howitt before he can maneuver his wife through the door.

Once she has led the couple from the room, Hare glances at his friend, Joseph Hazard, positioned opposite him on the far side of the table in order to have a clearer view of the medium during the performance. Hazard cocks an eyebrow and shakes his head sadly as if to say, "Those pitiable people."

Hare rises from the mahogany side chair, what they call a wheelback chair, although the design it has pressed into his frock coat looks more like a spider's web than a wheel. All the chairs in the room bear this design.

The medium, Margaret Fox, returns from the foyer. She's a small woman, of shy and genteel character—not a low-class trickster as many of her peers seem to be. Because of this alone he finds it hard to dismiss her. Her color has lost its flush. She is composed as she takes her seat at the table, and smiles to both men with a sympathetic serenity. "They know now," she says, "that their girl is well and they need not be concerned." She clasps her hands, "Praise God, and it's as much as I ever hope for."

"You've helped them, you mean," says Hare.

"Can I do less, Professor Hare?" Her blue eyes sparkle.

"Retired, ma'am, near six years," he corrects her, although it's nice to hear the title now and again.

"I think it a good thing that such as yourself—a scientist, one who seeks for great truths—should open yourself to our small society."

"The society of spirits? Well, and I wish to believe, Miss Fox, that all this which Mr. Hazard and I have witnessed *is* real."

Her brow creases for a moment, no more. "You entertain doubts even now."

He bows slightly, his knees stiff from so long being seated. He is over seventy. "As you say, Miss Fox, I'm a scientist. For me there can be no absolutes."

"What about death, sir? Is that not an absolute—the certainty of death?"

"Yet," interjects Hazard, "while he must play the skeptic, I know he was moved, as was I, Miss Fox, and I'm certain he will return for another session with you."

"As will you?" she asks, a hint of coquetry beneath the words, so slight as to be disregarded given the absolute decorum she has maintained. She is so young, her gentle tease is but a trick played upon old men's vanities.

"Mayhaps, ma'am, another day." He adds, "Alas, *I* am not retired, and still must perform."

For an instant Hare stands apart from these two, and seems to hear them speaking some cloaked language, full of amatory import; but he knows better than to act on such indistinct supposition. He wouldn't even ask. Hazard would be shocked, and what can Hare know but that what he has inferred comes from within himself and not without? No, he can say nothing.

"Robert, come, I've my afternoon appointments yet to keep." Hazard turns.

The two men are shown out onto Arch Street. It's warm in the sun, positively an August heat on this late April day in Philadelphia. The door closes behind them and they climb down the five steps to the walk, as a carriage passes. Hazard signals to one further up the street and its reins flash. He won't allow Hare to walk anywhere, so concerned is he over his friend's condition. He is, Hare thinks, more like a mother hen than a lawyer.

Hazard turns to him. "Now you must tell me, you suspect what of Miss Fox?"

"Everything. The spiritualist is artful, perhaps by nature. Whether or not deceitful has yet to be established, but when I witness such a performance, when I see her come to her senses before her clients can elude her in their misery, what am I to make of it? I cannot *help* but suspect. There's not enough here to trust."

Hazard nods. "I tell you, Robert, I have seen tables caper, and ghosts display impossible knowledge through the use of alphabetic cards such as she manipulates, but in the face of it all remains the niggling doubt that some cunning is at work. I can prove nothing. Nothing in Margaret Fox's actions evinced deception. How, other than by supernatural means, *did* she know so much about the daughter, when I could find nothing near as much about the child through legal process? Yet I began to wonder in the midst of the child's appearance if those people would have confirmed anything she said, however far it might be from true. Out of their suffering. And so—"

Hare takes hold of his arm. "Precisely, Joseph. What can you know from a woman pointing her fingers at a card full of letters?" He smiles conspiratorially. "To which end I have ordered materials for construction."

The carriage rolls to a stop before them. Hazard turns to help his friend, but Hare grabs hold of the splashboard rail and pulls himself up. "Materials? What would you do, Robert—box in your spirits?"

Hare takes his seat. "What would I do? Know absolutely the fate of—" his smile falls slack "—of them all." The carriage jerks forward and Hazard drops into the seat beside him.

It's the age of the supernatural. Ever since Walpole's *Otranto* ninety years earlier, Gothic subjects have freighted the literature, and matters wholly fantastic have been embraced by the greatest minds. Hare knows well that he's in good company.

As Man is enveloped in systems of weather, he may also be surrounded by invisible and wondrous forces, most as yet undetermined save that their presence is detected. Mesmer's magnetic fluid, Franklin and Kinnersley's electricities; somnambulism, clairvoyance, mediumship—all are squintings into the inexpressible. Hare's own concentration—chemistry—promises similar revelations one day, and perhaps will tie the disparate elements of mind, body and energies together. Not simple-minded alchemical transubstantiation, no. More remarkable discoveries, which a generation other than his will behold—energies he can but imagine. And who knows but that a doorway will open between the corporeal and spirit realms? Are they alive who have gone before? Is his sister there, waiting for him? Dear, dear Anna—he must know.

He thinks: *As Mrs. Crowe argued in her wonderful book,* The Night Side of Nature—*all phenomena must be open to the proofs of science, even if the means to prove do not yet exist. Not yet. But I have within me the capacity to change that. When I return to the world of the spiritualists, I will shake that world till the truth falls out. One way or the other, I will know.*

Enquiries thus far have already estranged former colleagues from the University of Pennsylvania, where he once chaired the School of Chemistry. What he proposes to investigate is deemed unworthy of serious contemplation. Not, mind you, blind acceptance; on the contrary, the mere contemplation of *possibility*.

When he plunged concentric coils of copper and zinc into troughs of muriatic acid, producing not only electricity but a heat intense enough to consume charcoal, they were not shocked, although the specifics of what was happening and why were not immediately known. Yet, when he turns to something that may be no less explicable, they turn their backs. Well, he's old, and has pried at one time or other into everything from chemistry to meteorology to banking, and don't forget the brewing of porter. He'll address former colleagues as he does the Christians, who have no trouble swallowing the camels of Scripture, yet dismiss Spiritualism, about which they know nothing. In the end, in print he'll declare his findings and let the findings speak. Proof he will offer, the requirement of science.

Of those scientists who once called him friend, only Seybert and Silliman remain allies. Seybert inadvertently pushed him in this direction years ago with questions regarding the afterlife. To the extent that Hare refuses to countenance divine revelation, he has regrettably alienated Silliman: How can anyone—Silliman in particular—accept on blind faith the validity of his religious inclinations while demanding absolute proofs about everything else? There can be no dichotomy of thought. *Everything* must submit to testing. Still, for all that they differ and will neither yield, he loves and respects Silliman. Though they don't speak any longer, it's to Silliman that his proof will be, however obliquely, proffered. Whatever the outcome, he must sway *someone*.

In the carriage, he surprises Joseph Hazard as he suddenly blurts out, "It's precisely as you say: The cards by which these guides communicate with their audience are unreliable under the best of conditions. Pushing a finger from letter to letter to spell out any word one chooses—how can rational men such as we countenance that? It requires a leap of faith across too vast a chasm.

No more defensible than Bechworth's absurd argument that six to eight people gathered around a table produce an electric current capable of causing everything that's attributable to spirit phenomena." He laughs. "Do you think Bechworth ever in his life *beheld* an electric current? 'A dry wooden table,' I responded in my letter in the *Inquirer*, 'is very nearly a perfect non-conductor.' That fool."

Hazard agrees, somewhat edgily.

"You mention table motion—I'll tell you the substance of table motion: accumulated muscular force. It's as Faraday suggests: The hands upon the table do the actual moving. So long as there are hands upon the table, you and I and the rest will harbor doubts. I say: No hands upon the table then, no fingers upon a card." He waggles his own finger to emphasize.

Hazard ponders, lulled by the clopping of the horse's hooves. He remarks, "You would think, on the face of it, that Christians would *wish* the afterlife legitimized, wouldn't you?"

"Fah. The truth is they only want it to conform to what, without a shred of evidence, they already hold that it is. If anything, the Christians are worse than Bechworth. *They* ascribe all these goings on to Old Nick. If there is anything imaginary in the whole of these proceedings, it is the supposition that the phenomena are brought on by the interference of the devil. That—*that* is the sage opinion of a church that extirpated the Canaanites, the Albigenses, that created the auto da fé, the inquisition, the massacre of St. Bartholemew, set the fires of Smithfield, roasted Servetus, and have persecuted even here Quakers and witches!" He could list many more examples, but speaks to the point: What could be more devilish than for God the creator to have created the Devil? The Devil is nothing more than a means for small men to disavow their own evil passions and disguise their own villainous handiwork."

Jumping from thought to thought like a child leaping stones to ford a stream, he then abruptly announces, "Comté is a fool to think that reliance upon scripture will magically shrink as science grows. Science would have developed already on this ghostly front and resolved it had not the entanglements of Biblical intolerance confounded every effort." He falls then into silence, his features apoplectic.

Hazard keeps still, but gives his friend a sidelong glance.

Hare's keen dark eyes smolder with the inner fire of his contemplation. His chin juts, the jaw clenches. It's a formidable profile—one befitting a Roman statue—and that has kept more than a few men from voicing unworthy opinions. Hazard knows him well enough to know such fear is groundless.

He has been friends with Robert Hare for many years. No less hostile or arrogant man exists. Hare has always been so vivacious and agreeable in his conversation that he willingly gives opponents any opportunity for rebuttal while he soundly defeats their every objection as though he had run through it all before them. After which the opponent is respected for his attempt to scale the heights. There seems to be no subject with which he is unacquainted; but this one is different. This dark investigation stirs the old man's blood in ways that voltaic chemistry does not.

Hare has had his enemies—the early ones, like the Englishmen Clarke and Maugham, who tried to appropriate credit for his oxyhydrogen blowpipe, were thieves and ultimately revealed as such. Hare had only to hold his ground and let others vindicate him. That won't work here, Hazard knows.

This time, the people on his side are the ones about whom there are questions.

II. The First Device

On a hot June morning two men unload from the back of their wagon a canvas-draped object that ends in four beautifully turned table legs. Unlike a table it bulges on one side, where the canvas is pushed up in an off-center hump. A woman holds open the door at 178 North Tenth Street to let them carry it up the steps and into the rowhouse.

Mrs. Margaret B. Gourlay is of medium height, with dark hair pulled back into a large bun. She has a broad, handsome face just beginning to lose its definition. Her eyes are brown and warm: gentle and honest eyes. She is dressed very plainly in dark green, although the fullness of her brown skirt over cage-crinoline requires her to retreat from the door far enough to let the freightmen inside. They carry their burden into the parlor where her clients come.

Her husband, Dr. Gourlay, stands in the doorway from the dining room and looks on in some bewilderment as the twine is untied and the canvas lifted, revealing an arcanely cobbled device. He watches the men tie a sinker weight to a vertical cord so that it hangs a few inches above the floor. A second, larger weight they tie to the end of a second line and set forward of the table like a small iron doorstop, the line stretched taut.

Finished, the men gather up the canvas and ropes, then wait for money, although Hare has paid them at the loading. Dr. Gourlay reluctantly tips them, not generously by any means, and, feigning indignation, they depart. His wife's voice echoes from the foyer.

He approaches the device with grave caution.

It is a lovely satinwood needlework table—or once was. Now, attached to the top, marring more than half of the veneer, sits a tall metal box with a steeply angled lid, a kind of enormous bread box. From the back of this emerges the cord on which the sinker weight ultimately dangles, but first the cord wraps around the spindle of a large wheel. The wheel hangs off the side of the table. It has letters inscribed around its rim: ZJWKERUCFH&ALUSMOP around the top half, GTNXOBIVD around the bottom. Where the spindle protrudes through the center of the wheel, the line from the iron counterweight attaches. There is also a thin metal rod that sticks up to mark which letter is to be read. At the moment it rests upon the letter "F".

The doctor circles the table. Around behind the wheel, the metal box is open. Inside it is some sort of lever. Gourlay leans on the table, bending slightly, and reaches to put his hand in the box and press the lever.

From the doorway, his wife says, "Don't."

The doctor straightens. "I was going to—" He stops, for he does not know what he intended. "Did you know of this . . . this contraption of his? How it works?"

"No," she replies. "I've put my trust in Professor Hare as he has in me."

Her husband brushes his hand across the table as if in defiance of her. He turns smartly on his heel, sweeps up his gray stovepipe hat from the chairback settee where his wife's clients usually sit, and marches out of the parlor. "I shall refrain from interfering, of course, in *spiritual* matters," he tells her, then leaves the house. Mrs. Gourlay waits until the vibrations of the front door have ceased reverberating before she sets foot in the parlor.

When Hare arrives some hours later, Mrs. Gourlay meets him at the door in an excited state. "She's spoken to me," she tells him. "Come see, come see." And she leads him by the hand into the parlor. She has drawn a dining room chair to the table, on which she settles, her skirts billowing around her. "Look," she says. Hare takes a seat where he can read the wheel and watch the medium.

For a time she sits in seeming contemplation, her gaze unfixed. Then her eyelids flutter and close. She leans forward as her hands, within the box, begin to press upon the lever. The wheel answers her pressure, rolling clockwise in sluggish rotation. Around and around on its axle the wheel spins, stopping briefly, sometimes with difficulty, upon each letter in sequence, having to rotate around a full turn to spell the same letter twice. By then he knows; a cold apprehension suffuses him like a chemical reaction overflowing a flask. The medium doesn't seem to be aware. Her head is down. He can't see her eyes at all. She cannot be watching the wheel, and couldn't see the letters on its face in any instance.

The wheel spells out the fourth letter, the name ANNA. His sister's name. Mrs. Gourlay's head remains lowered.

The wheel continues to spin another quarter hour, until he has recorded the message: ROBERT WELCOME. At that point, Mrs. Gourlay exhales sharply and draws back from the device. Her head circles, coming upright. She opens her eyes and looks at him. "It is so difficult, so draining, to use this machine. But she came, did she not?"

"Who?"

"Your sister, Professor Hare."

"My sister?" He tries to seem unenthusiastic.

"Yes, that was her relation to you, I'm sure of it. A sister." She glances at the wheel. "You hadn't told me of your sister."

Had he though? No, he's quite certain he withheld everything. He replies, "I hadn't thought—" He had not dared hope.

"Your device is a most cumbersome thing to use. Levers and wheels."

Here's something he can speak to. "Cumbersome, yes. And yet you succeed in demonstrating its merit, Mrs. Gourlay. More than that, I believe you've made a case here for the truth of your claims and those of other mediums. This is a great stride forward, do you have any idea? The first scientific validation of your craft, Mrs. Gourlay. Exhausting or not, please apply yourself again to the spiritoscope, if you would be so kind."

"Spiritoscope." She stares apprehensively at the thing before replying. "I must tell you, sir, that it takes *all* my energy to maneuver it."

"*Your* energy?"

"Indeed, sir. 'tis after all mine that the spirits utilize. Look how quickly I was drained. How quickly she withdrew from me—one message and no more. A card is very easy for them, as you can imagine. It takes but a finger." As she says this, she raises her index finger.

Precisely. That was the point. But now the point impedes. He wants only to hear from Anna again. He contemplates the machine awhile in silence.

Mrs. Gourlay doesn't begin, and instead pushes her chair back from the table. "Might I offer you some tea, Doctor? I'm, myself, quite thirsty just now."

"Please," is all he says. His gaze does not shift from the table, even after she has risen and gone away.

He reconsiders the design of his spiritoscope. He has re-engineered everything he ever constructed—he modified the oxyhydrogen blowpipe a dozen times in twenty years to make it more efficient, even though the original was already the hottest heat source in the world. Nothing that is humanly engineered cannot be improved upon.

His father, the senior Robert Hare, was a brewer. *Hare's American Porter* was a superb ale, the most popular in Philadelphia at the turn of the century; yet he was forever working with the formula, experimenting with different roasts of malt the further to enhance the flavor. His son, apprenticed to him, assisted in much of the experimentation, from whence came his fascination with chemistry but also with sources of heat, with all that heat could

do. The slightest increase or decrease in the temperature or dura-
tion of roasting of the malt changed the characteristics of the finished porter significantly—in many instances beyond drinking.
The younger Hare's mind raced along as it contemplated variables
and cobbled a device to roast the malt faster, thus enabling his
father to increase his output. The process existed; he refined it. As
he will do here.

The problem served up by Mrs. Gourlay is how to make
working the spiritoscope easier without sacrificing the safeguards
built into it. He can't communicate in two-word dribs and drabs
like this. He dwells upon it to such an extent that he barely notices
her return, doesn't see the china cup and saucer set before him,
hardly recollects the tea, and only returns to his senses when she
says to him, "You know, Professor Hare, I must tell you a thing
I've sensed about you since first Miss Fox introduced us."

He finds he's perched on the edge of his chair. Tea steams out
of his cup. "What you sense about me," he repeats, as if the repeti-
tion will explain what she has said.

"Yes, sir."

He regards the tea as a fortune teller might before sipping it,
as if it might yield a secret, and compresses his lips as he swallows
the bitterness. "What would that be, ma'am?"

"Why, that you share the spiritualist's gift."

Whatever he thought she might say, this isn't it. "I'm sorry, I
don't know that I understand you. Do you mean to imply I should
be able to speak to them?"

"And they to you."

"How, then, do you explain that I have never in my life received any communication whatsoever from the spirit world?
Even as I would have hoped and prayed to hear of the continuance of my sister, there was no rapping on walls, no shifting of
furnishings." He abhors the suggestion. Hands trembling, he sets
aside the cup. "Indeed, it is outrageous, madam."

"Oh, but, *sir*, you would not be aware. You have no training
in the spiritualist's art. Your faculties lie dormant, untapped and
untried. I and my spirit guide do both sense about you such powers, restrained, awaiting release, that with training—"

"Please, Mrs. Gourlay, *no more!*" He waves her to silence. "I
have in my time been a brewer, a chemist, a professor, an econo-

mist, and an inventor in all of these rôles." The thought slides in below his words: *And a neglecter of her in all of them.* "I believe I have quite enough talents for a lifetime without adding spiritualism to the list. Especially—" he hesitates, wrestling his ire under control "—especially as the city is quite well populated with such like already. Inventors seem far less procurable." He stands, leaning upon the table for support. "And now, as the demonstration has exhausted you, Mrs. Gourlay, I will be on my way. You've set me a fine challenge, to improve upon my invention. I'll consider it. But, I would like you to utilize the spiritoscope as much as possible. You may find it easier to maneuver as time goes on. Also, as I intend to publish my findings, you will likely find yourself with a clientele desirous to witness its demonstration."

Her smile as she sees him off is stiff—no doubt, he thinks, as a result of what he has said of her spiritualist compeers. But it's true: Philadelphia is a haven for spiritualists. There must be one for every street in the city. Mrs. Gourlay has a reputation as one of the more upright of her kind ... which is to say that no one has ever caught her in a deception. That's why he chose her to receive the first machine. It was to be Margaret Fox, whom he no longer entirely trusts. But to suggest that he ought to practice spiritualism himself is—

Is what? he asks himself.

By the time he has been coached safely home, he has the answer.

Terrifying. It is terrifying.

III. Expansionism

He has dreams after his meeting with Mrs. Gourlay in which his sister visits him. In one, she divides like a cell, becoming three of herself, in wide-striped skirts and puff-sleeved blouses, her long chestnut hair crimped and coiffured into chains encircling each of her heads. The nineteen-year-old sisters knock wooden balls across the lawn of the chemistry building with croquet mallets. He has a mallet, too, but the multiplicity of sisters play their game around him, never offering him a turn, as though they don't notice him in their midst. Annas enclose him; the wickets trip him up and like bear traps catch his ankles. The mallets clack familiarly as they strike. The croquet balls roll up against the posts and stop; there are three posts, and he thinks that this is wrong, there should be only two. The sisters pause over the balls, leaning on their mallets as they stare straight through him to one another in silent communion. If he could only move, if he could reach one and warn her, protect her. The wickets are driven through his legs, and when he tries for her, he totters and falls.

The instant he hits the ground he opens his eyes. His heartbeat hammers, his nightshirt is stuck, twisted, to him. He wipes spittle from his cheek, and sits up in the darkness.

She was so close that he heard her skirt swishing as she strode about. What if she is always as near as that? He has no way to know.

For days and weeks afterward, intense dreams interrupt his cerebration and render him incapable of invention. He broods upon her, turns her over like a coin, each turn a painful remembrance.

She grew up a tomboy, fearlessly investigating what she was not supposed to see, what girls were supposed to stay out of. She made him teach her conkers, a game that only boys ever played. They picked out chestnuts together, he advising her on the quality of each one she brought to him. He took the acceptable chestnuts, soaked them in vinegar awhile, and then nailed a hole through the light caps of six of them. After tying a bootlace through each, he left them dangling from a clothes peg beside her bed. Then he waited. The thrill of her squeal as she discovered what he had made for her still sped his heart. She came out of her room, the conkers clacking together, and she kissed him. With that kiss she transformed from the tomboy sister into Anna. Anna, the perfect jewel. Who married late and died young; who survived the yellow fever plague of 1793, only to surrender to consumption before she had even borne a child of her own. When he thinks of her, he thinks of those clacking chestnuts swinging like simple pendulums on their laces—a moment suspended in time to which all other memories lead . . . because he, from the moment he began to help their father at the brewery, became so bound up in his researches that he barely noticed her, eventually losing sight of her. He thought she would always be there. As if, had he paid her more attention, she would have lived. His guilt coils into a wall of thorns around the spiritoscope.

He turns to other, less cumbered fronts.

There are some improvements he has wanted to make to his deflagrator, and another paper to deliver upon the caloric properties of weather systems: For some years he has studied the possibility that warm water from the Gulf of Mexico charges the air above it with such heat that, as the heat meets the cooler inland air above the mountains, it produces violent weather such as tornadoes, which are themselves—so he has determined—comprised of electrical currents of air. That study returns him to his calorimotor, and its production of heat in tandem with electricity. The circle of phenomena with which he's familiar ever expands, ever merges.

Through the sciences he finds he can approach the subject of spirits again. Might the realm of the spirits incorporate such things as electricity and heat? Are spirits cold? Mediums often describe a chill that settles upon them, and he once gripped a medium's hand that had gone ice cold in an instant, but that is hardly the sort of proof he can use. Are they electrical in nature, the souls that guide Mrs. Gourlay's hands? It seems fitting that they should be—they would add another layer to what he already knows of electricity. Why shouldn't it be the unifying principle? All the world and all the energies, driven by electrical forces.

Hare recalls when he was twenty-two and fused strontianite for the first time with his oxyhydrogen blowpipe. Silliman assisted. Woodhouse and Seybert were practically beside themselves with excitement and wasted no time pushing through his election to the Chemical Society. He remembers thinking that his future would be like this. He would continue to invent, continue to win praise. Nothing could stop him. He had no inkling then of spiritualism—Seybert's fascination was not expressed until so much later—or that he would run up against such ignorance and prejudice within his own society. They forget that it's he who first fused heavy spar and threw platinum, gold and silver into a state of ebullition. He whose process, under names such as Drummond light and Calcium light, illuminate lighthouses the world over. He whose Compendium of Chemical Instruction is the standard text to which all chemistry students are referred. He who possesses the Rumford Medal for his discoveries. He who is a life member of the Academy of Natural Sciences. It isn't arrogance. He *has* accomplished all these things. And he's not done yet.

With renewed purpose, he completely redesigns his spiritoscope.

Invited to speak in New York, he loads the new version onto a wagon and has it carted there.

He's allowed to choose the nature of his talk in New York—they know how broad is his range; nevertheless, the audience of professional and amateur scientists gathers in anticipation of a discourse related to chemistry.

Instead, Hare pounces upon the infinite chimeras of scripture, blasting the Bible, and then describes the possibilities of spirit communication. Finally, like a stage magician who has saved his best trick for last, he offers a brief demonstration of the new, improved spiritoscope. He wants them to appreciate the mechanics of the machine.

It's a rectangular dining table now. The same revolving wheel hangs off one of the long sides of the table, facing the audience. He, as acting operator, sits across from them. On his left the two table legs end in small truckles, whereas on the right they're fitted with larger wheels connected by an axle. Rolling the table back and forth turns the axle, which drives the lettered wheel. His maxim remaining "no hands upon the table," he has placed a small wooden tray on casters of its own. The operator moves the table by rolling the tray back and forth upon it. Cumbersome once again, but less so, he feels, than the earlier version Mrs. Gourlay is mastering; and if it works it removes the medium even further from direct contact with the wheel.

But when Hare attempts to demonstrate it for the audience, he can't move the table at all. Discouraged, he finally sets the tray aside and pushes the table back and forth manually. The wheel turns, but spins without any inclination to stop. He can spell out nothing. So much, he thinks, for his latent powers. So much for the proof of his claims. Even though the presence of a medium would have given his audience an easy excuse to dismiss him, he sees he has been stupid not to bring one. Something remarkable might have happened. He can see that the people don't care what he's doing. They can't wait to get out of the hall.

His reputation saves him from direct humiliation. So exhausted is he from trying to wrestle the table back and forth that he disregards the disappointment in the voice of the professor who arranged the talk—"that was a most singular performance, Doctor Hare"—and falls asleep in the carriage that takes him to his hotel.

Within the month of his appearance a letter arrives from a man named Isaac T. Pease of Thompsonville, Connecticut. Pease has learned of the spiritoscope. Perhaps he attended the New York lecture or knew someone who did. In ingratiating language he explains that he has experimented with a similar device at the urgings of local spiritualists and redesigned it on a much smaller scale than Hare's grand spiritoscope. He includes schematics of his devices, which he has dubbed "Pease's Dials." Looking them over, Hare doesn't know whether to be pleased or furious, remembering how the British attempted to steal his credit for the blowpipe.

He admits that Pease has made one or two improvements: rather than the wheel, he has the index needle spin, which seems much easier to accomplish once considered; the activator operates by a spring rather than a system of cables and weights and axles, and directly affects the index. The smaller disks, which can be adjusted for the medium to see, incorporate phrases as well as letters. The needle can point to "Think So" or "Must Go", "Yes" or "Doubtful", "I'll Spell it Over", "Done", "I'll Come Again", and even "Good-bye"—all spread around the wheel, written as if along the spokes. Ultimately, Hare is too impressed at the ingenuity to be angry. He admires invention too much to discount it even when accompanied by apparent hubris: "Pease's Dials" indeed. He'll catalogue them in his book, but otherwise, with their simple mechanisms, they return too much control to the medium for his necessary proof.

For the summer Robert Hare departs Philadelphia and travels with his household staff to the Atlantic Hotel on Cape May Island. The New York spiritoscope makes the journey with him, to be set up in the salon of his suite where he essays it from time to time in solitude. For all that he denies it, Mrs. Gourlay's pronouncement on his powers has burrowed into him. Silently, he turns over and over the question: where does the supernatural mechanism dwell? And is it likely we all possess it?

Throughout the month of June he sits before the table at night, often with a cellar-chilled pint of Hare's American Porter—his private stock—and rests his fingers upon the sliding tray. Night after night, when he lets his thoughts drift, the back and forth pushing of the small board on casters begins to move the table and the wheel. He can't see the face, but what the wheel is spelling doesn't matter. It's moving now under his impetus, if not control.

Finally, he watches in awe as the table rolls from side to side as if loose upon the deck of a rocking ship and the wheel stops, moves, stops, reverses. The back of his neck prickles with the electricity of terror.

"I cannot be doing this," he says to the empty room. Therefore he is not. Something else—unseen—is there with him. The table stops.

He retracts his hands from the tray and retreats to his bed, where he lies for hours, alone, nervous and awake. Night surf on the cape roars in the distance and salty ocean breezes swirl through the stuffy room. Trees outside the windows hiss. The moonlit shadows of their dancing branches anthropomorphize the wallpaper and furnishings. The branches slap together: "clack, clack, clack." Dark ghosts whirl about him. The whole room tilts and spins. "Anna," he sobs, and drifts into a fitful sleep.

He meets at the hotel a number of people, including a Dr. Thomas Bell from Somerville, Massachusetts, who will later contribute much information to his book. Bell, a thin, dark man, is a head taller than everyone around him and speaks with a twisted curve to his words somewhere between Cockney and Bostonian English. He asks, then wheedles, and finally demands to see the spiritoscope and, when Hare takes him to the salon, insists on a demonstration. Other men and women present in the public dining room drift after Bell, coming to see, spilling in through the foyer past Hare's surprised servant, Gilhay. They hang in the doorway. Some have snifters in their hands, and cigars, and whisper to one another. This is so casual for them, a lark to pass the evening.

He determinedly takes his place, ponders for a moment, then closes his eyes. His fingers begin to push the tray on casters back and forth, and even forward. Sluggishly, the table begins to roll, the wheel to rotate.

"It's spellin' out something," whispers a woman, and he opens his eyes. She's a large, fish-faced creature, but he tries not to see, not to think.

Bell has his note pad out and a stub of a pencil. It takes ages for each roll of the table, for the wheel to stop on each letter. The crowd stands silent, motionless, until the sixth letter, and the table comes to a stop. "W-A-R," says Bell, "U-E-N. What's that, then, Dr. Hare? Waruen?"

Hare settles his hands palm up in his lap. He stares at them uncomfortably. "Warren," he replies, "the U and R are side by side, it was supposed to be another R, I'm sure."

"Who might 'e be?"

Hare's eyes glitter bright. "Mr. Warren was my father's partner in business before I was born. He left Philadelphia and sided with the British in the war—that's who he is."

Bell and the others seem unable to put this together with anything—their expressions betray what's missing from his answer.

He explains, "I was asking, don't you see. Asking the spirits to give me some information only *I* knew. And they spelled out his name, didn't they?"

"I suppose," says the fish-faced woman, and she glances sidelong at others. Gilhay, his manservant standing beside the door, looks no less troubled by this revelation.

Hare wants them all gone now. "Well, thank you. I didn't know what was being spelled out, if it was an answer to anything. I've no idea when it works, if it works. That's the way I've designed it."

"Oh, continue, please, sir," Bell insists. "Let *us* ask something."

Hare dismissively waves his hand and falls back on Mrs. Gourlay's excuse. "It's too enervating. One answer—a single word—exhausts me. I'm not a skilled practitioner." He can see it in their faces—the same look he has given to spiritualists, to Margaret Fox—skeptical smiles, the identical doubts expressed by the look of the audience in New York and by the look in Gilhay's eyes, embarrassed on his behalf. Oddly, the doubt is harder to take from strangers. But there's nothing like doubt on Bell's face. Bell is thrilled.

Seeing that the performance is truly over, people begin to withdraw, all save Dr. Bell.

Gilhay lingers uncertainly behind him. He's an Irishman. His people know about spirits and demons, ghosts and *ban sidhes*, know the treacheries they can perform. Even dead friends will play tricks upon the living now and again—Hare's heard countless supernatural tales from him since undertaking this project. Also, it might be that Gilhay despises Bell as an Englishman. That would be enough to set him scowling at the intruder's back. He looks to Hare for a signal to eject Bell, but Hare shakes his head and Gilhay finally abandons the open door and retreats to his own small quarters.

Bell says, "Doctor, I'd like to contribute to your investigations. Already, I've looked into the matter substantially on me own. In Boston there are practitioners of remarkable skill who I've met. Once I stood at the end of a ten-foot table and watched a small woman sitting beside it put out her hands above without touching it, like someone working a puppet, and make it move, glide a foot or two at a time, this way and that. We set an iron rod in between folding doors at the bottom, and the table clambered over the rod into another room. Then it come back, right over the rod again. I noted in me journal that if the medium raised her hands above two foot from the table, all movement ceased. Whatever it was driving that thing, it was coming through her. I'm a tall man, you'll mark, and I could see down the whole length of the table that nobody was touching it. Not a soul—well, not a corporal one." He smiles. "There's much more that I could describe for you if you'd let me further my investigations and add them to the weight of your own."

Hare sits dumbfounded. A colleague in this business? "Dr. Bell, I should be most honored," he hears himself say, as if listening to the conversation from another room. "I'm compiling proofs to present to the scientific community. I would well appreciate yours, if they're objective."

Bell smiles once more. His teeth aren't very good. "I understand too well the rejection of traditionalists. No imagination in 'em. Have you read Poe, sir? *There's* a soul who understood the nature of life beyond death."

"Poe, yes." He recalls that name vaguely: he doesn't follow the careers of sensationalist writers. "Very good, Dr. Bell," he says, and moves forward, effectively urging Bell out the door. "Compile all you like. I'll certainly consider whatever you have to show. And of course we'll talk again here at the hotel."

"Of course, sir." He steps back into the hallway, bows formally. "I bid you good night then."

"Good night." Hare shuts the door. He turns, leans against it and stares at the spiritoscope, expecting almost to see it rear up on its hind legs and caper through the salon. The table remains at rest.

Thereafter Hare takes his meals in his rooms or at off-hours to avoid Bell's company. He can't say why exactly, but he doesn't want to share his work with Bell. Maybe not with anyone else. Having accepted the role of iconoclast he's unwilling to part with it. He is his own hair shirt, he thinks, and chuffs at the inadvertent pun.

By the end of June he has improved his skill upon the spiritoscope. His mind drifts, the wheel spins freely.

He has established communication with Anna. It's as if she sits out of sight in another room, listening to his questions and writing him notes in response. If only it were true and he could look round the corner and find her.

Gilhay transcribes what the wheel dictates. One time he writes down a slightly misspelled "pulsatque versatque," and Hare snatches his hands off the tray in amazement. "My *father* is with us! That was one of his favorite phrases. It referred to the beating Entellus gave Dares in the *Aeneid*, beating him so that he spun. My father used to recite it to me to warn me what I was about to get if I didn't behave. It can't be anyone else! Who else would know?" Gilhay glances around the room uncomfortably.

Although the manifestations of Anna and his father delight him, Hare comes to realize that he must produce something more by way of proof for others, else he is no different than any performing medium. The truth of what passes through him to operate the wheel can't be determined by this exercise. It has meaning for him alone. Spirits come and talk to him, but who else would recognize them?

He would dearly like to speak with Franklin and Washington, both of whom he admires so, if only he could draw them about himself like some great incorporeal cloak.

A few weeks later he's taking a late supper of cold chicken and leeks in the dining room when Dr. Bell appears, towing behind him a severe blonde woman named Miss Julia Hayden. She's from New York, and wears a dull black dress as if in mourning. Bell says, "She was 'ere on holiday. A remarkable medium, you must let her try your device." And so, pressed to it, he has to yield. They let him finish his meal, then he leads them up to the salon and the spiritoscope.

To his surprise (and delight), Julia Hayden is incapable of using the thing. The wood tray rolls back and forth on its casters. The table budges not an inch.

Eyes closed, she grimaces, twists her features, contorts her lips in a gruesome spectacle. Her face fades the color of a winding sheet. Her hands tremble on the tray, slide off and lie slack upon the table surface. Her head lolls, her expression gone loose. With a sharp breath, she opens her lips and the words commence: "Brother beloved, I am here."

It is not Miss Hayden's normal voice, but creaky and burbling. His sister died with her lungs full of liquid. The sound puts him back beside her as she failed, his hands wrapped tightly around hers as he desperately, uselessly, willed his life into her weak body. He doesn't want to hear this.

"Please," he indicates the table. That's how she's supposed to communicate.

The medium's head shakes as if someone is clutching the back of her neck and twisting. "Not physical . . . vocal. She has no skill here," she says, nodding at the wheel.

"Who are you?"

"You have to ask?" The words come slow as molasses dripping from a jar. A small bright drop of blood appears on her lip.

A sudden frost coats his lungs.

"Robert. You seek a proof you cannot receive from the table. I'm present to deliver it."

"Deliver? How do you intend?"

"Give me a message."

"A message for whom? I don't—"

"To Gourlay."

His jaw stiffens. He peers at Bell, at the medium, as if betrayed. How could her name be known to them? He hasn't mentioned it. She never came up in his brief conversations with Bell. No, this must be real.

What sort of message will do then? Something involving other people, not Mrs. Gourlay alone. Proof beyond the medium and the devices, that's what he requires, his spirit sister is right about that. He must involve someone who doesn't believe. He casts about and the answer comes of its own free will.

"Go to her, then, and tell her to instruct her husband to proceed to the bank at 1:00 p.m. tomorrow, find out when the note is due on the brewery property and report what he has found to me at home at 3:30." This will prove everything. There's no telegraph between Cape Island and Philadelphia, no way for the message to make the journey any quicker than he can.

There comes no reply, no confirmation. The medium suddenly draws a breath, sits stiffly upright, then sags. Within a minute, color floods her cheeks as if she has just performed something strenuous. She raises her head. He is amazed at this transformation. It isn't something she could induce—the suffusion of blood into her cheeks. Eyes enclosed in sickly darkness, she glances from Bell to Hare, blankly. Then at the spiritoscope. "Did I . . ." she begins, removes her fingers from the tabletop, folding her hands before her throat.

She glances at Bell for confirmation. He leans solemnly forward. "You were directed, ma'am, by someone else."

Hare remains silent, looking for any hidden messages passing between these two. He finds himself asking how he can continue to suspect them when he has been operated by the same unseen forces in that very chair and endured the same suspicions from others.

He thinks, *We are all of us in uncharted waters.*

When no one speaks or moves for an interminable moment, Hare asks, "Do you know if she received my message, Miss Hayden?"

The woman—strange how severe she first appeared and how timid, helpless and confused she now seems—replies with her own question: "Message? For whom?"

Hare asks nothing more. The medium wishes to retire and Bell escorts her out of the apartments. He turns back at the door to offer an apologetic, "I hope this hasn't proved an intrusion, Dr. Hare. I sensed immediately you'd want to meet her. We strive to maintain open minds about all forms of spirit communication, do we not, sir? We must consider the non-physical a legitimate expression, too, and this clever proof you've devised will establish her defense as well as yours. Please do contact me at your earliest convenience as to its outcome."

"Of course. Another time, Dr. Bell. I will have to leave early on the morrow." Hare nods to Miss Hayden beyond Bell, who rewards him with a weary smile. "Rest, ma'am."

Bell gives him a final, troubled glance, as if sure he's going to miss a critical event here.

As he closes the door, Hare hears behind him Gilhay's door bump closed. Hare smiles to himself. The ever-protective retainer.

Although he will eventually use much material uncovered by Bell in his book, he never meets with him again. They communicate thereafter through the mail.

IV. PROOFS

Upon his return to Philadelphia, Robert Hare sits through an edgy, sweltering hour and a half of waiting until the appointed time. 3:30 arrives. His appointment does not. He has failed, his communication was not received. He rises from the French settee. The clothing that he has worn for the hasty journey from Cape May sticks to him everywhere like a wet sausage skin and is discolored by large patches of perspiration. Sweat from his brow stings his eyes. He looks out upon the tree-lined street where no breeze blows. Below him, roses stand, dappled with sunlight through the maple tree across the way. He hears the hooves of horses on the stones of nearby Chestnut Street. The carriages rarely come past the front of the house, situated as it is on a close.

A woman's figure passes by. It looks—but she has turned into his yard, and he leaves the window, nearly runs out of the room as the knocker raps like a musket shot through the front hall. He opens the door upon Mrs. Gourlay.

The look on his face must perplex her. She says, "But surely you were expecting me."

"I did so, but—well, please come in. I despaired as the time passed."

"Oh, it has? Our mantle clock is not reliable. It runs both fast and slow, and the doctor takes his continental watch with him."

He seats her on the red Empire sofa there in the entrance hall below the stairs. "Tell me," he says.

She does. She had been working with his device when her contact was interrupted by an errant spirit, his sister, with an urgent message. Receiving it, she sent her brother to find her husband, and the two men went to the bank together. They determined that the note was not due for more than a year—which Hare knew already but anticipated no one else would, as it was so far outside the range of what anyone—even someone who had researched his family—would investigate. But there is more. She unfurls a piece of paper on which she has scrawled a poem in stiff handwriting.

"Brother beloved," it begins, "of ardent soul,

Striving to reach a heavenly goal;

Wouldst thou attain the blissful height

Where wisdom purifies the light . . ."

He folds the sheet of foolscap and lowers his moist gaze. He has never seen the poem before, but its authorship is clear; nor can he can read further just now. His joy is inexpressible. "Thank you, Mrs. Gourlay. More than you realize, you've sped away the clouds of my doubt. I must now endeavor to show the world what you and I recognize in our hearts."

"Let me help," the medium says.

"I shall. Believe me, I'll require all your assistance. We've much to undertake now."

He begins work on his book in earnest as accounts come trickling in. Bell reports that entities who've spoken to him through verbal mediums are able to read his thoughts and see what he can see, yet lose their knowledge when answering what he and the medium do not know, a supposition he tests by asking them to duplicate a signature in a folded letter that he hasn't seen. They can't. But the moment he opens the letter and looks upon it, the medium's hand begins to write in imitation of what he beholds. Bell proposes that what he has uncovered is more than mere spirit communication, but a form of clairvoyance. He writes: "What the questioner knows, the spirit knows; what the questioner does not know, the spirits are entirely ignorant of." It's a provocative observation, one for which Hare has no answer.

Inquiries made earlier to acquaintances on the continent have also begun to bear fruit.

He receives a report that the Archbishop of Paris attended a seance and witnessed communication via rappings on a table. The spirit identified itself as Soeur Francoise, deceased the week before in a Paris convent. And when an abbot present demanded in the name of Christ the woman manifest, she did appear to them and answered questions. All the participants were afterward several days indisposed, as if the spirit had drawn upon them for her energy.

From Germany a Dr. Geib communicates to him about table moving phenomena, giving a name to the spirits responsible: *klopferle*, for "rapping specter."

It's generally believed, says another correspondent, that this phenomenon has arrived, like some plague, off ship from America. One day there's nothing, the next, with an American medium present, tables turn, hats swivel on heads, and chairs spin on one leg. The news agencies, fearing for their reputations, refuse to report on these initial events. Even Hare has to wonder at what sounds on the face of it like a great fraud.

To his amusement, French scientists attempt to explain it with no more logic than Bechworth applied. They claim electricity is the culprit, or imperceptible muscular action, moving the tables. "Humidity of the palms" is responsible asserts another expert, an explanation that takes its place beside magnetisms and polarities, and even "two interacting nervous atmospheres." However perversely, the press now turn their sights not on the phenomena but on the accepted theorists. In response to the comment about nervous atmospheres, one French journal suggests that, given the dullness of the theoretician, "the nervous system of the table (disgueridon) must be *very* sensitive." The journal later describes an episode where French scientists attempted to move a table by use of those proposed magnetisms while a spiritualist sat aside and watched in bewilderment. When they failed utterly and retreated outside, the table, left alone, began to buck.

From England, a Mr. Robert Owen writes to him of an apron untied from a woman and passed around a group at seance, and which was then ripped away from them by invisible hands. These same hands passed Owen a flower. His handkerchief was snatched from his pocket and formed into a hat. One spirit shook his hand, "and, sir, I could feel the individual fingers." In a passing remark, Owen's report mentions a spirit stating what Owen believes to be true but which later proves to be false—information which seems to have come from his own thoughts, much as Bell has suggested. Both observations he will include in the book. Let readers draw their own conclusions.

Hare has become a magnet for spiritualist data. Every day brings more letters, many impossible to use, some impossible to comprehend. Meanwhile, he routinely visits a coterie of spiritualists to whom he has been introduced by Mrs. Gourlay.

In the presence of local medium Henry Gordon, he watches a table float into the air.

When he takes his seat in the salon of Mrs. Ann Leah Brown, he finds his name written on a scrap of paper lying beside him on the carpet. Mrs. Brown denies all knowledge of it and, when she applies herself to one of Pease's Dials, through her a spirit explains that an old friend, William Blodget, has written it. Blodget is some six years deceased.

While Mrs. Brown communicates, a table against the wainscoted wall over a foot away from her begins to slide back and forth on the floor like one of his trays on casters. Both he and the medium sit in stupefaction.

"I've never seen the like," she confesses to him when the activity has stopped. "It is you, sir, causing this." And though he doesn't express it to her, he does feel uncanny energy pervading the air, like a huge bubble filling the room.

Phenomena spring up on all sides, as if casting him headlong toward some explosive event. Darkness is at his back. Friends have fallen away. In his absence he's either pitied or scorned, but he notices none of it. His whole world has become the spirit one.

In January Joseph Hazard returns from Rhode Island. His reason for visiting: "I have to check up on my old friend now and again, and business at present is sluggish." Hare refrains from admitting that just now he finds Hazard's appearance intrusive, like a distraction concocted by his enemies to slow him down, just as Hazard refrains from confessing that mutual friends whom Hare might currently consider enemies have urged him to come.

Hazard intrudes further when he insists on accompanying Robert Hare to spirit meetings, two or three a week.

In various parlors they sit apart as they did with Margaret Fox. With Hazard present tables don't dance and caper but rattle only mildly in corners or shift under the spiritualist's hands. If Hazard spots trickery or harbors doubts, he says nothing, only watches. His presence acts as a damper to Hare's elation as well as to the proceedings themselves, wherever they go. Yet Hare can't bring himself to ask his old friend to leave. Silliman's an abstraction, Hazard concrete; and if he can convert Hazard, the exemplar of a rational mind, that may silence the naysayers once and for all.

The first week of February of 1855, Hare goes to a sitting alone, returning late in the evening. Gilhay lets him in.

Hazard awaits in the dining room, and pours a mug of hot buttery cider to warm him. Two other mugs on the table indicate that Gilhay and Hazard have been sitting together awhile.

Still wrapped his heavy coat, Hare sits heavily and sips the steaming cider. A few minutes pass in uncomfortable silence. Then he says, "There is to be a convocation of spirits at the home of Mrs. Gourlay. This is what I've been flung toward, Joseph, and could not see in advance—all the strange events that have led me this far—*this* is where they were leading."

"To a gathering of the tribes," Hazard comments, then apologizes. "I don't mean to make it sound trivial. But how else does one describe it?"

Hare waves at the air. "Describe it however you choose. But this event *you* must attend. Many from her group will be there, adding the strength of their energies to Mrs. Gourlay's, calling upon the spirit world to come and speak and inform. They're about to reveal everything of the afterlife to us. Everything, Joseph! Say you'll accompany me. I need you to transcribe for me. My hands shake too much in the presence of the spirits. And there must be more than one witness to so incomparable an event. It might never happen again."

"Of course, of course I will," Hazard assures him. He would have it no other way.

After finishing his cider, Hare retires to his study and writes furiously for two hours as he does each day, compiling his notes, his arguments, his proofs, his rebuttals into what he has now titled *Experimental Investigation of the Spirit Manifestations*. The gathering of the tribes, as Joseph put it, will be the climax.

V. THE CONVOCATION OF SPIRITS

At 9:00 a.m. on February 18, Hare and Hazard sit in Mrs. Gourlay's parlor, surrounded by mediums and believers. Word has gotten out. There is Miss Fox, who breaks into a demure smile each time Hazard glances her way; Mrs. Brown, solemn and nervous; Henry Gordon, who looks to have steadied himself with drink for the event; Julia Hayden, sent by Dr. Bell. There are even people such as the Howitts.

As Mrs. Gourlay lowers her head and rolls the tray upon the table, the dial spins and spins, and Hazard writes down each name as it is spelled out. More spirits than corporeal forms surround the two men at the center. The spirits sign in: George Washington, John Quincy Adams, William H. Harrison, W.E. Channing, H.K. White, Isaac Newton, Andrew Jackson, Henry Clay, Benjamin Franklin, Lord Byron, Martha Washington—the list goes on and on, like the signatories of the Declaration of Independence coming forward one by one to take up the quill. The cataloguing seems to last for hours. Hazard fills two entire pages with names, having written too large at first. He couldn't have known.

When the wheel does finally come to rest, the entire room seems to sigh as one. Hazard sits back from his writing board and flexes his hand awhile before taking up the steel-point pen again.

After first offering a welcome to the invisible guests, Hare begins the questioning. "How do we arrive where you are?" he asks.

The wheel spins, and with it the story.

After death, the soul awakens from a profound sleep into a state of consciousness very like dreaming. Bright and shadowy forms appear to it, as does the body it has left. These forms soon solidify into spirits, usually those of departed friends. They greet the nascent spirit with affection and conduct it to a celestial abode in accordance with its moral state at the time of death.

He ponders briefly, then asks, "How is the spirit world composed?"

The answer comes: Between Earth and moon lie seven concentric rings, the regions of the spirit world. These have terrestrial scenery—mountains, streams, plains, rivers, birds, beasts, but all of greater beauty, and at each successive, ascending level, more lovely. The last is so glorious, it cannot be described.

Then, as if someone else of a slightly different opinion has wrested control, the answer is revised. Earth is the first level. The remaining six spheres compose the spirit plane. They commence about sixty miles up, rising out into space.

"The sun, then, illuminates your world as it does ours."

No, comes the answer. A black sun shines upon the spirit world, although its nature cannot be satisfactorily explained to mortals. Its rays consist of an all-pervading ethereal fluid. *We live in a realm of perpetual day, full of aromatic flowers, herbs, fountains and rushing water underfoot. And singing floats through the air.*

"Then how do you see yourselves? What are you like, how do you appear differently that you make a distinction from the body cast off?" he asks. Hazard nods encouragingly as he writes. He was wondering the same thing.

The reply: *We are luminiferous. Like lightning bugs we glow.* Each spirit has a circumambient halo passing from dimness to effulgence as the spirit moves to higher planes.

"These spheres. How do you move to higher ones?" he asks, trying to grasp this. Is it fair? Does it seem reasonable? It sounds upon the face of it like a caste system, which is not how he wants heaven to be. Underneath his questions, he wonders, too, which of the great and famous men is speaking to him.

Each ascends as he or she improves in purity. Purity, which can take two forms: love, and love/wisdom.

George Washington resides already in the seventh sphere, as Hare anticipated. Infants—which are considered blessed in their untimely death—ascend directly to that sphere, where they're instructed and grow up. They then return to earth to watch events unfold. He recalls the Howitt child whose spirit told its parents to think of it as a "gentle moonbeam," and glances over his shoulder at them. The husband nods to him, a painful joy inscribing his features.

"Angels," remarks Hazard as he writes this down.

Hare turns around. "Just so, Joseph, angels."

Hazard looks at Mrs. Gourlay with her head bowed. "But I'm troubled," he says before Hare can think of another question. "What of those who aren't in the seventh level?"

Degradation, the wheel spells out, *is an inevitable consequence of vice.* Not punishment—there's no punishment necessary, for God is all-love. The afterlife follows the apostles' injunction: Hold fast that which is good. They exist in what can only be called a republican order.

Too, some crimes occur in the lower spheres, and punishments are meted out in accord with these.

Hazard's brow knits as he writes this seeming contradiction down.

Hare, too, tries to understand. "How can one expect to rise in such a place?"

Love is the simplest way. Those who know unfettered love rise immediately. For the rest there are teachers on each level who impart wisdom to those who seek it—wisdom that, conjoined with love, advances them.

"Can we not see anything of your world?" Hare asks. "We're here to establish proof that we can show to anyone, so that they'll understand without having to come as far as I've done to arrive at enlightenment."

The wheel falls silent for so long that Hare fears contact has been broken. When it moves again, he leans forward as if to hear more clearly that which is said in silence.

The wheel spells out J-U-P-I-T-E-R.

The spectators exchange confounded glances. Hare, who has seen the night sky through a reflecting telescope, suspects he's hearing now from Isaac Newton. He says, "Please explain further, sir."

The wheel tells him: *The bands that can be seen around Jupiter are the spirit spheres of that world. Look upon Jupiter for evidence of our realm.*

Hare nods, slowly at first but with increasing effusiveness.

Hazard, who also has astronomical knowledge and has many times looked upon the Jovian sphere, raises his head sharply from the page and asks, "How then do you account for the changes in the appearance of those bands? For they do change. I know."

The wheel hangs, then spells out simply: *optical delusions.*

Hazard sits grim-faced for a moment before he dips the pen and writes down these two words. He is unaware of shaking his head as he does so.

Late that same night, in the dining room of Hare's home, the two men sit divided by the dark table. Steam from a bowl of hot cider and their individual mugs floats between them. They're bundled up, though they returned nearly an hour earlier. The fire in the hearth softens the edge of the cold but not its heart.

Hazard has done little more than murmur since the convocation ended. He took copious notes—Hare rejoices at the precision of the transcription. But a chasm has opened between them that was not apparent even as the event began—broader than the chasm between the living and the dead.

Hare takes the transcript between his hands and straightens it, tapping the sheaf against the table. "It's marvelous, Joseph, it truly is. I need add nothing to your words."

"Not mine," mutters Hazard, not looking at him.

Hare hesitates, almost asks what he means, but thinks better of it. Hazard won't meet his gaze however hard he stares. "Mmm," he adds finally, a non-committal assent, but he must say something more than that. They ought to be celebrating. "Still marvelous, whoever's words—"

"Good Christ, Robert! Whose do you think they were? Monsieur Valdemar's?"

Hare doesn't know the name, but it doesn't matter. The doubt he's cast off threatens to ignite and consume everything.

Hazard continues to stare at the surface of the table, where his hands lie flat. "You genuinely believe you sat in the presence of Washington and Franklin and Newton," he says, and glances up finally, his eyes squinched with the pain of awareness. "You know what you've done? You've become the Howitts. You're as possessed as any medium ever claimed."

"Joseph, stop this."

"Because you'll lose Anna if you admit it? Robert, you lost her decades ago."

Hare's jaw sets and his brown eyes catch fire. "And I found her again."

"Where, in the bands of Jupiter?"

"And I am to gather you know for a fact what those bands are?"

"No, of course I don't know. No one knows. That's beside the point."

"I thought, Joseph, you weren't like the others, that you were capable of contemplating things considered unnatural, that you could see through their fog of superstition and religious eyewash. I hoped . . ." He breaks off.

Hazard leans closer. "Old friend, you say yourself that I copied the details of the dialogue perfectly. That being the case, look at the descriptions both of the spirit realm here and there. Seven concentric rings or spheres rising into space with the Earth at their core—the physical realm at the bottom. That's how the spirit world was described. Not as latitudinal bands, do you understand? The two explanations are contradictory. They look nothing alike at all." Hare seems puzzled, doubtful. "Oh, think, Robert. Look at it, read it."

"No." He slaps down the pages. "I've thought everything through, eliminated all possibility of treachery. The spirits are confused, nothing more. Or we are. I've spoken to Anna, I've used the spiritoscope, I know. Who's to say that the spirit world here wouldn't look the same to someone on Jupiter as theirs does to us. We can't be sure."

Hazard stops arguing. Anna occupies the heart of him; he can't win against her. Robert Hare created the perfect device to defeat spiritualist trickery, and so of course what comes pouring out of it must be true. Confused, misunderstood perhaps by the very audience of experts gathered round, but not an outright lie. Anna could never lie.

He might have thought as much himself had they not hauled in the planet and violated their own definitions. Optical delusions, indeed. The bands of Jupiter do change form. It's well enough documented, and a scientist would know that. Hazard can no longer pretend to believe, as he can do nothing for his old friend. He climbs to his feet and says, "Good night."

Hare sits awhile longer, wounded, confused, and angry. Then he gets up and retires to his study to write up the convocation while it's still fresh in his mind. The work is what matters.

When Hazard departs the following morning, Hare is lying asleep at his desk upon the document.

Five months later, Hare has assembled all his notes into a coherent volume and threaded throughout it his opinions on the unreliability of scripture.

He points out for instance that we have only Moses' testimony of his communication with God—a report that has God slaying three thousand who were led astray but sparing Moses' brother, who *made* the golden calf. Hare calls the Old Testament a "pernicious idol" that patronizes men of a chosen seed, though they are guilty of robbery, fraud and murder, and quotes St. Jerome's preface to the gospels wherein the saint complained that no one copy resembled another, the translations were so poor.

His final act is to attach a preface including a letter from his spirit father that he receives only days before he turns in the manuscript. The spirit says: "Ask yourself how much happiness you have found in the contemplation of the fact which has been demonstrated, not only to your wishes but to your senses, that the thinking mind *never dies* . . . that it lives on, lives ever, and must throughout the ceaseless ages of eternity continue to unfold its power."

With the book at the publishers, he offers to exhibit his spiritoscope to a convention of his own clergymen and is rebuffed. In November, invited again to New York, he gives a lecture on the evidence he has compiled. It's well attended, if only by those already converted.

After the book comes out, there follows no upheaval, no slanderous assault, no clear enemy at which to take aim. He's not vilified, he's disavowed.

Not one to sit idle even then, he turns his attentions to other subjects. Spirits continue to warn him to prepare himself, and he continues secretly to await the attack, but it never comes.

In 1857, not long before his death, he exhibits at the Franklin

Institute an apparatus for determining whether phenomena at-
tending the attrition of pieces of quartz, when rubbed briskly together, have anything to do with the new substance described by
Schönbein as "ozone." His reception is cool. Some noise is made
about the apparatus, but most of the dialogue is traded as if he
were not in the room among them, or they cannot see him. For-
lorn, he goes home.

Maple leaves blow in through the door before he can close it.
He drops his cloak upon the Empire sofa in the entrance hall, and
drifts to his study through the silent house. He stokes red embers
in the hearth and adds new wood to the fire, then takes his seat
before one of Pease's Dials he has set upon his desk.

He opens his glass inkwell and places beside it a steel-nibbed
pen, inadvertently bumping a large anomalous chestnut he uses
as a paperweight—actually two grown together into a single
mass—hard enough that it tumbles off the side of the desk and
rolls beneath his feet, where he can't reach it.

With a resigned sigh he lets it go and turns to the device. He
adjusts the wheel so that he can see clearly anything spelled out
there.

He presses his fingertips to the sprung plate that operates the
machine and, thus poised, awaits his Anna.

VI. Epilogue: The Seybert Commission

In 1883, Henry Seybert, a descendent of the same Seybert
who once urged a young Robert Hare to consider the afterlife, en-
dows a chair of Philosophy upon the University of Pennsylvania,
conditional on the university investigating the truth of modern
spiritualism. A commission is assembled, including William Pep-
per, Provost of the University, and Joseph Leidy, the anatomist.
Horace Howard Furness chairs the committee and writes up its
findings. His wife died relatively young and he has good reason to
want the continuance of the soul proved true.

Seybert himself dies before the commission can even begin
its investigation, but the money is set aside and the work goes
forward. The commission examines the subject for three years,
inviting the most prominent mediums to conduct seances before

it. Those who accept include one Mrs. Margaret Fox Kane, who is truly celebrated within her ranks. Furness finds her small and genteel, and so unassertive that she immediately wins him over. Yet, as the evening progresses, he slides into doubt.

She communicates with spirits through raps on the table. The spirits, while appearing to have intimate acquaintance with family affairs of some of those present, send Furness's brother a message from his spirit father. Except that his father is still alive. Later, the rapping is determined to be the product of Mrs. Kane's ankle striking the table while she seems to sit away from it, her hands in plain sight. She is, it would appear, usefully double-jointed.

The devices of Robert Hare are neither used nor mentioned, nor is his work cited. His work, in this arena, is forgotten.

The commission's report, published in 1887, causes a great stir in that it finds not a single fact upon which to base any belief in spiritualism. In summing up, Furness reports that no truth could be established because the whole business is so clouded with trickery that no phenomenon can be trusted. Filled with regret, for now he can know nothing of his wife's continuance, he confesses how desperately he wished to be converted by "these shabby charlatans."

ILL-MET IN ILIUM

Bitten—**Goddess sing of how the rescuing hand**
was bitten by the radiant one it had rescued.
Taken from that son of Atreus who'd nursed and encouraged
her strangeness—
one belonging to the hidden face of Apollo—
his aspect called Smintheus, bringer of plagues,
lover of vermin, mice and rats.
Out of love and affection Paris mistook
Helen's unnatural beauty as would anyone have done.
                                        Unwitting Paris allowed
that undisclosed unsavory characteristic to fester.
It flowered, swelled, consumed and conquered.
Had he known this, would Menelaus have sailed forth
to the beach before Ilium to confront
those unyielding Trojans behind their walls?
Would he have understood the cost of success?
The Gods, even they saw not the thing that grew
in the dark of a hold, where it claimed, one
after the other, the will of many among
Paris' crew, while the young prince, himself a moon-calf,
saw none of it. The ship sailed home.

                                        It was Thersites
That hideous warrior, shamed by Odysseus
for his effrontery and foul language,
who first of all the armies fell victim
through his treasonous rage.
Wandering from the camp in the night, he

met the Spectre—
she who'd called Lacedaemon home
and until recently been locked
in the bowels of the city, its victim
now turned victimizer while Apollo,
their immortal guardian, slept.
Revenge, she would have it upon both sides.
Thersites recognized her not at all, having never set eyes
upon her till then. He drew his sword against
the shape, as it drifted nearer.
Close-up, like Paris he was smitten—
he, club-footed and double-humped,
had little experience with the fair sex,
alive or undead.
                              "You," she called him,
ghostly pale as a living moon. She hovered nearer.
"I sense your contention, your leashed anger toward
the leader of your band," she whispered, and
Thersites trembled at her iced touch,
and swallowed hard his words.
        This apparition then opened the brooch upon her shoulder
and let the cloth covering her breasts drop.
For all her paleness, the tips of her breasts shown
ebony in the moon's light. She, with a finger,
drew a curve above one nipple, and a black line
flowed behind it as if she'd painted upon herself.
                              "Drink your fill, oh, man,"
she said. And Thersites, quivering, dropped his blade
and bent his head to the wet rivulet. Feasted long.
A taste he wanted, a taste that any man
would have desired. And little would
they or he have realized that the liquor
of a plague now flowed past their lips.
So was Thersites changed
while all attention lingered elsewhere,
upon the warring Agamemnon as he abused
the prize he'd stolen from that
swift runner, Achilles.

                                            Gods and men alike
watched the rage unfurl, the heated words
dividing them as the walls of Troy separated
their armies from the transformed goal.
"Dog-face!" Achilles named Agamemnon
and thereafter turned his back on war.
Scant secret and less shadow was necessary
for the theft of Thersites' will by
the highborn revenant, that beauteous Helen.
    Then as Dawn spread rosy fingers over the sea,
the apparition evaporated with her power implanted
in the hunchback. When the time came,
he would do her bidding.

The battles raged, the daily slaughter
for one king's greed and another's honor.
Truces struck served to delay
the challenges. The Atrides' hot words
betrayed their promises, until a Son of Priam
slew Odysseus' brave comrade Leucus
and the battle lust burst again.
Spears through temples, groin
and back. Jaws unhinged and blood
erupting like a fountain's deadly art.
Idomeneus' men slew and stripped
the corpses. Days of battle, bloodied sand.
    Then came Night who makes even lofty Zeus
tremble, and the Achaeans granted Ilium
the claim upon its fallen heroes, so that
the absence of the corpses come morning
did not seem to them odd at first, but of a process,
of honorable retrieval, while those of the city
assumed their enemies were playing cruelly
upon their grief in stealing the bodies.
Only after the second or third time
that the same warrior, killed in previous battle,
was felled in a late skirmish, did the rumors spread
of something unnatural.

And did they, behind those wide gates,
know what plague lurked in their own midst?
It is spoke how Paris burst into action at the death
of his friend Harpalion, but not that the act
took place by torchlight, as night drew a blanket
over the sandy plain; or that Paris dropped
upon the soldier, Euchenor, whose prophet father
had offered him a choice—to die of plague in his
own halls or at the hands of Trojans.
The old seer had got it right twice over.
Paris drained the life from Euchenor
without the need of lance or arrow's tip.
He had been turned sometime before.

    All this while Hector slept, as others did,
safe from one death, prey to another.
How quickly it did move no one can say,
although each day warriors aplenty
faced Ajax and Idomeneus,
charged the ships and beat the Argives
back. Time and again they struck,
and their ranks hardly dwindled, never
were exhausted. Thus cautiously did the revenants ensure
their own continuance.

    Patroclus, disguised, fell to Hector, else the
wretched contests might not have changed.
Hector, he the stallion-breaker, died
from Achilles' spear, went down in the dust
and had to be ransomed back.

    Epeus boxed for a mule and Cassandra stood
upon the battlements at dusk, most lovely daughter
of Priam, and foresaw the death of her city.
She laughed and fairly dared those princes and kings
spread out across the blood-drenched plain to
prove themselves better men. She was by then
already turned as well. She had witnessed her fate
and embraced it willingly, inviting Helen to her bed
where she bared herself for that most painful pleasure.

    The two of them next approached Hector's

wailing widow, and fed upon her in her grief, these two
sisters. Engaged in their lurid business,
they failed to detect innocent Aeneas, himself whisked
from Achilles' wrath by the god of earthquakes.
Aeneas saw it all, that poor innocent, and his
martial will left him.

    Weak with horror he withdrew to his family,
gathered them up and crept through the shrouded city.
At fires he saw others whom he knew. The first few
rejected his pleas, his seemingly mad warnings
of doom at the hands of the fanged Harpies.
Inured to fantastical notions after years of war,
of ceaseless slaughter, they laughed.
                          He saw that he would
never convince good friends of this and, instead,
proclaimed the city certain to fall now
that its towering hero, Hector, had been brought down
by swift Achilles. Upon those words his number
grew, and swelling, drew the attention of Helen's
undead league. In the end, unwittingly, his followers
carried the plague to their new land.

                          Through a hidden exit—
the very one that Helen had used to prey upon the
wounded and the dead upon the field—the swelling cluster
escaped the city's fate. When was brave Aeneas' wife
stolen from him? Snatched certainly by those who
wrapped themselves in darkness. The moment passed
in utter silence, so that he, brave man, didn't notice.
He led his people, his children, only to discover, finally,
her absence. Then he left his followers and raced
back into the city. There he encountered her shade,
both hungry for him and gifted now with profound sight.
"You will be great," she said, "and found a new city in
a foreign land. I cannot touch you else unmake this
vision." He could not raise his blade to her,
his wife, no matter what she had become.
He retreated from the horror, his only course.
                          Again, upon the beach,

he and his people eluded the Achaeans. They were themselves
too busy, engaged in erecting the scheme set in motion
by Helen through her abject slave, Thersites.
He, like a grotesque gnat, had buzzed into the ear
of clever Odysseus a scheme of great daring—
and in pretend penance, he gave credit
for the idea to that skillful one.

                   Thus it was that Aeneas and
most of his followers alone escaped the plague
delivered by Helen and her sisters
upon Priam's city and citadel.
                   The corpse of that great hero,
Hector, lay twelve days in Achilles' care
without decay nor any sign of death's embrace,
so that when Priam kissed the hand of Achilles and begged
for the body, both of them thought only that Apollo,
Troy's protector, had preserved it until its return.

                   On this point the blind poet
ended his story, knowing full well that what followed
was too horrible to relate. He left it
to others to tell—and those, coming so much later,
received and related only spoils,
replacing what was too impossible to state
with clever tales more likely to gain acceptance.
                   But here is how it went,
and how the blood-leeching creatures blended
into history.

                   The next day
only those in thrall like Thersites
roamed the streets, pushed back the broad Scaean Gates,
and strode out upon the deserted plain
haunted as it was by the ghosts of so many comrades,
to where the Argives had left their "gift."
                   These servile citizens
of Ilium knew what to do, guided as they were
by the mind of Helen, her body

somnolent in the heat of day.
With ropes and tackle they hauled
the monstrous horse through the gates,
into the city. As if dazzled by the offering,
by its vanished creators, they left the gates unbarred.
                              Even ensorcelled by the blood
they had supped, these minions found it
difficult not to laugh at the wooden horse,
at the occasional sandal, the flash of breastplate,
which showed between its ribs.

        Odysseus and his small army waited through
the warm afternoon, sealed in their own
stink till it was time. Then in the darkest
of the night, they would open the trap and descend,
just as Odysseus had described to them,
as Thersites had whispered it,
as most diabolical Helen had planned it.
                              Philoctetes, who'd arrived at the war
last of all, lay among them in the equine belly.
He shared his hydra-venomed arrows with that other
skillful archer, Odysseus, little knowing,
either of them, how Hercules' weapons would save them.
The poison in those shafts, expertly shot,
exploded every fiend it touched.
The revenant horror called Hector died again thus impaled.
Where most of the horse's band fell to the guzzling monsters,
the two brave archers fought back to back,
till Agamemnon's army burst the gate to find them,
and upon Odysseus's cry, set the torch to the enemy.
They overcame Helen's horde while Apollo,
Sungod, slept in ignorance.

                        Afterward, Odysseus paid the price
as angry Apollo blotted out the day of his homecoming
for ten years. Many others, bitten by Ilium's undead
yet seemingly alive, burst into flames aboard their ships
where there were few places to hide from the golden sun.
        Only Agamemnon, because he was a king, was

able to remain in the shadows once he was turned.
It was Cassandra who drained him.
She had locked herself in a cell
and pretended to be a poor victim of her father,
instead of one of the chief plague-bearers.

    Agamemnon, foolish man, carried her off as a trophy,
leaving it to his wife, Clytemnestra, to discover
what he'd become. She had taken a lover, but even
he doubted her story of her husband's unnaturalness
and abandoned her to her fate.
                For nights she kept him at bay.
But finally her husband fell upon the queen
and tore at her throat.
He would have drained her dry had not the god Apollo
flung his rays just then upon the undead king,
driving him underground. She lived but would not
another morning survive without cunning and resolve.
          When Agamemnon awoke that next night
he found his wife at her bath. She stood
and welcomed him, her fine body so slick with oil
that he could not find purchase,
his fingers slipping as she sank back,
his hunger growing at her enticement as she drew him.
He did not see the spike she brought up
out of the frothy bath and plunged
through his chest. He toppled into the bath,
his body melting away like a taper. After that,
Cassandra met the same swift fate, for no one there
cared for her cries or pitied her.

    And Philoctetes, whose venomed points had
saved them all—he roamed ever after across
the wine-dark Aegean in search of those monsters
who had escaped the fire and death, and who spread
the plague of their kind into his world.
He came to rest years later in Sybaris,
after leaving his vampire-slaying missiles
with the Sungod Apollo in his temple at Krimissa,
where the fiends dared not seek them,
and where they await the next archer even now.

THE BANK JOB

I ancu Svekis sat in the chair beside the bank manager's
desk. He sat still, his outward calm belying the turmoil of
impatience within. He awaited word that the transfer of
funds from Rumania had gone through as it should have done by
now; he awaited also the return of his passport. While Pascu had
confirmed in a phone call that he would have as much money as
he needed to continue his quest here, the bank manager—Erica
Langdon was the name on her cubicle plaque—had explained
that with all the anti-terrorist checks and verifications nowadays,
things like this took much longer than in the past. He ought to
have been gone by now, and with a full wallet. Instead, tired and
unshaven and hardly presentable so far as he was concerned, he
was sitting unattended when the robbers showed up.

There were three of them, and one—a blonde woman—must
have been in the bank awhile, in plain sight. He had no doubt
looked right at her earlier. Now she wore a Wonder Woman mask
and pressed a gun to the neck of the guard while her crew strode
in carrying two canvas satchels and waving their weapons as if
no one would notice them otherwise. One had an autoloader, a
carbine with a profile that reminded Svekis of a shark. "Hands up!
Everybody move!" shouted the taller robber. He sported a George
Bush mask.

The guard went to his knees compliantly, but one of the tellers
reacted by hitting an alarm button in her cage, and George Bush
shot her. The low plexiglass barrier on the front of her counter
splintered and she fell.

People screamed then. Seventeen customers and three tellers hit the floor. Erica Langdon ran to the fallen teller, and the

killer might have shot her if Wonder Woman hadn't spun him around and punched him in the chest. "What in *hell* are you doing?" she yelled.

"She hit the button!"

"Yeah, and?"

When he didn't respond, she shoved him backwards. "I wanted her to do that, you stupid shit. I *told* you someone would."

She swung about, faced the robber with the carbine. He had on an imitation hockey goalie's mask. "You and your fucking brother!" She thrust a finger at the guard. "Let's try not to shoot the damn cop at least, okay? Just stand over him!" He nodded and took his place. "Jesus," she snarled. She shoved a satchel into the hands of George Bush. "Go collect their cells from them." She walked into the midst of the crouching customers. "All right, who's the manager? Who's in charge here?"

In the distance sirens sounded.

Svekis continued to sit, to observe, as motionless as the furniture, amazed at how quickly a plan could unravel. The thought made him wince. His wife was dead because of an unpredictable unraveling. Nothing he could have done about that, but he was here for this one.

Erica arose from behind the teller's cage. "I'm the manager," she answered the robber. Her terror and anger had her trembling.

"Great. Buzz me into the back now. How's your girl?"

"Unconscious, but—but not dead. The barrier . . ."

"That's good. No one needs to get hurt here, okay? But you get it that we mean business, right?"

Erica nodded.

"Buzz me in and get the rest of your people out of there. I want 'em on the floor out here like everybody else." She took one empty satchel the others had brought. Erica released the electronic lock, and Wonder Woman went through the doorway. The vault stood wide open, and the robber led Erica inside. Svekis studied the other two.

Beside the kneeling guard, Hockey Mask shifted back and forth on his feet, anxious. Bush the Idiot strode up and down through the trembling crowd of hostages, collecting cell phones in his bag like an oversized trick-or-treater. It wasn't until he was walking back toward his brother that he looked at Svekis.

"Hey! Hey, you. What the hell are you doing?"

Svekis looked around himself. "Nothing," he replied.

"Yeah? Well, you better do your nothin' over here on the floor." When Svekis didn't move, he pointed his gun. "Now!"

Wonder Woman had come out of the vault. "What's the problem, dickhead?"

Bush pointed at Svekis. "Him."

She set the satchel on the counter. "Here, get the drawer money."

She unlocked the door and came out from the back, but left the door ajar. Behind her, Erica stood in the vault doorway. She stared at him fearfully. He smiled to her.

"We got cops!" shouted Hockey Mask. Flashing, colored lights striped the side of him.

"Good, that's what I want, you stand right there and let them see you, the guard, and that gun, so they don't think they can rush in here," she answered. She walked over to Svekis. "You got some nerves, Pops."

He lowered his head. "Not really. I am too tired to react to anything today."

"Bad week, was it?"

He thought of the *strigoi* he'd battled, the child and mother who would go on living because of him, the horror of that unbridled hunger he'd slain. "You would not believe."

"Yeah, I'm sure. You want to sit here, that's okay with me, but you don't try to call anybody, okay?"

"Yes."

"What's your name, in case I have to yell at you all by yourself over here."

"Iancu." When she continued to stare, unmoving, he added, "In your language, it's 'John.'"

"John." She repeated it as if doubting it. "You give him your phone, John?"

He dug into the pocket of his raincoat and handed her his phone. "He did not ask me for it," he said.

"Thank you." She turned and carried his phone away, but hadn't gone ten steps when the desk phone beside Svekis rang. She turned back to answer it. He pretended not to notice her, but he had already satisfied himself that her clothing was bulky and ill-fitting as if she was wearing extra layers against the cold.

Except, it wasn't all that cold outside.

"That's right," she said into the phone and gestured at Bush Mask. He went through the open security door and then walked down the line, pulling cash out of the teller drawers. "We got twenty people in here, and we want twenty people to go home tonight, right? One of them's hurt already so we're going to send her out. Play nice and she'll be the only one. No. I'll tell you what. You get us a touring bus. You know, something a rock band would like. You get the bus and you bring it up outside. Then you call us back. Bye."

She nodded to herself, and headed back across the lobby. In the middle she stopped and asked, "What's that smell?" She looked over the customers huddled below. "Somebody here shit himself?"

Finally, and with great hesitation, one man raised his hand. He kept his head bowed.

"Great. Well, we're gonna be here awhile, folks, so maybe you need to go take care of your mess. And the rest of you, too. You need to pee, don't leave it till you're pissin' on the floor." She snatched the satchel from Bush. "Go out there and lead them to the bathroom," she told him. "One at a time, got that? And don't shoot anybody else, for Christ's sake."

The embarrassed man got up and walked uncomfortably across the lobby to a set of restrooms. They were locked but Erica was already holding out the keys. "They're for employees," she explained.

Bush Mask and the man went into the nearer bathroom. Wonder Woman went back into the vault.

When the bathroom door opened again, the man emerged first. He was wiping his sleeve across his face. It was clear that he'd broken down. He quickly sat and grabbed his knees as if he could hide from everybody. A few others raised their hands to be allowed into the bathroom. Bush Mask surveyed them all. Svekis raised his hand, too. The mask twitched, and Svekis heard him snort, no doubt amused that the old man he'd intimidated had finally broken. Thus it was that he let one woman into the ladies room and came back for Svekis while Wonder Woman returned to the vault and Hockey Mask watched the cops outside. "Come on, geezer," he said and all but prodded him with the nose of the automatic.

Svekis got up heavily. He drew a deep breath, but kept his shoulders hunched, his head down. His rumpled London Fog disguised the solidity of him. He walked ahead of his captor, waited while the door was unlocked, then let himself be shoved inside. "Try not to mess the place any worse, huh?" Bush Mask said.

Inside were two urinals and a single stall. Polished chocolate brown tiles covered the walls and floor. The room reeked, the smell coming from the trash bin. No doubt the frightened customer had thrown out his soiled underwear. The window of frosted glass was wired inside and out. There was a vent in the wall past the sinks, perhaps the size of a notebook, and a narrow closet door behind which would be shelves of toilet paper, cleaners, and mops.

Svekis went to the stall and closed the door. He took off his coat and hung it on the door hook, then followed with his shirt and trousers. Even as he stripped down, the roar of transformation filled his ears and a redness rose behind his eyes, blood becoming like acid in his veins. His body creaked like a tree about to snap in a high wind, but distantly. He was falling away from it, into pure white pain. Ribs flexed and curved in, his muscles following, reshaping. It took every last shred of conscious control not to cry out. He doubled over in the narrow space, pawing at the metal wall. His senses plunged into shadow. In shadow he was reborn.

The tall old man hadn't come out after ten minutes. Bush Mask figured he'd had a stroke or something, and stuck his head into the restroom. "Hey, let's go!" he shouted.

When nobody answered, he went in. He had the good sense to keep his gun leveled at the stall. Nobody stood in front of the urinal or at the sink. Except for the broom closet, there was nowhere else. He walked to the closet and checked the handle. It was locked. He turned, and saw that the slats had been removed from the air vent high up in the wall, but the hole was so small that nothing bigger than somebody's head could have fit through it.

Under the door of the nearer stall, he could see the tips of the old guy's shoes on the floor. "Goddamit! Whadja do, have a coronary on me? She's gonna blame me for it, you bastard." He kicked at the stall door. It wasn't latched, and banged wide open, revealing an undershirt, boxer shorts, and socks beside the shoes on the floor.

For a brief instant he imagined that the old man had somehow flushed himself down the toilet. Instinctively he looked behind the door and found that the rest of the old man's clothes were hung on the hook there. "What the hell?" he said. Where could the guy have gone, naked?

The wall switch by the door clicked. The lights went out. Fear drove him then. He backed out of the stall and up against the sink. Wan light came in through the frosted glass of the window, showing the darker wire within like strands of spider webbing. He held his gun ready. He sensed movement, started to turn, came up against orange eyes glowing in the dark, and a solid form surrounding them that was furred blue-gray in the light from the window, a snout against his cheek, the smell of its furious breath like a color. Bright red.

He opened his mouth to scream, but a sharp crack resounded off the tiles and amid searing pain he felt himself flying through the air.

One of the women finally went to Wonder Woman and said, "Please, I've *got* to use the bathroom!"

"Well, then—" She turned about, realized that Andy's idiot brother was nowhere in sight. "Great," she said. She went over to Andy in his hockey mask, setting the second satchel—the one full of cash—down beside the guard. "Your brother's screwing up again. *Deal* with him. Now."

Shaking his head, Andy crossed the lobby in strides of anger. She was half-hoping he'd just shoot the idiot.

He skidded at the men's room door, slipped and fell onto one elbow. Scrambling up, gun in hand, he shouted, "Jesus!"

Gun at the ready, he shouldered open the door to the bathroom. She could see how dark it was, but instead of going in, he backed away, all the way to the wall. The hostages were all staring. She could not let this happen.

She hauled the guard to his feet, pushed her pistol to his cheek, then walked him to the restroom.

One side of Andy's clothes was smeared in blood. On the floor lay a puddle of it that had leaked from under the door. She cautiously nudged the door open again. Lobby light slashed across the dark room, across the simian Halloween mask of George Bush.

"God *damn* it," she said. She let go of the guard and reached cautiously around the wall until her fingers found the light switch. She held her gun ready to shoot. "I told him not to . . ." The overhead light fluttered on. A headless torso lay in the middle of the room. There was blood in sprays across the stall, all the way to the ceiling. The mask, she saw now, was still attached to the head. The gun lay in the middle of the floor.

Andy started to babble. "That's Markie, that's—he's dead, oh, Christ, what the hell, what the hell—"

She backed out into him, then grabbed onto him as much to hold herself up as to shut him up. "I don't know what the hell. Who'd he take in here, who was the last to use the bathroom?"

They turned and looked at the crowd that was looking back at them. The horrified guard gaped, too. She turned and faced the manager's cubicle.

The old gent, John, sat exactly as before. If anything he looked more rumpled, pale, and exhausted than half an hour ago. His head hung low, but he seemed to be watching from beneath his brows, as if too tired to face things head on.

The phone beside him began to ring then, and she made herself walk calmly over to the cubicle to answer it. She stared down at him while she talked, until he finally glanced up. He wasn't as old as all that, she decided, just thin and weather-beaten, like a cowboy, someone who lived hard. It was the white hair that made him seem older.

"Glad to hear it," she told the cop on the phone. "Outside in ten minutes. We bring out the hostages with us, so no Annie Oakley shit. I'll tell your driver where we're going. You don't need to know, and you don't follow. Anybody follows and nobody gets off the bus, understand?" Oh, he understood, all right. She hung up.

Andy came over. She told him, "The bus is ready. Pick out your group and let's get the hell out of here. Whatever happened in there, I don't know, okay? I'm sorry. Your brother was a dickhead but whatever's in there is staying the hell in there. We're not going to go in after it. Nobody else gets to go to the bathroom, period." Andy moved off shakily.

"What happened to your friend?" John asked her. He had an accent she couldn't place.

She faced him, stared into nearly golden irises. Something in his gaze closed around her like a steel trap, pinning her. The moment passed, and she threw off a shiver, blinked, and took a step back. Instead of answering, she found herself telling him, "You'll be joining us on the bus."

"Yes," he answered, "of course."

The transfer of hostages went smoothly. Svekis could appreciate that they'd given this a lot of thought.

The robbers split the hostages into two groups. The only one left behind was the guard, trussed up in the vault. Everybody got a Halloween mask, and each group was bound by a clothesline rope looped around their wrists and held by the robber in the middle of the group. The groups shuffled out to the bus like two bent, ungainly centipedes. They clambered up the steps and past the driver—no doubt a cop—and through a privacy curtain into the back. Wonder Woman told the driver to turn off the interior lights. Then she assigned everybody their seats. She put Svekis at the back.

Hockey Mask, meanwhile, had pulled out a knife and was cutting the rope between the rows and using each length to tie the duos together. He pushed their masks up, too, to make it harder for them to see, but Svekis couldn't tell if that actually had a purpose or if he just enjoyed it.

The woman returned to the front and sat down behind the driver and quietly gave him orders.

The bus lurched into gear.

She got up and walked up the aisle again. A speaker crackled to life. The woman counted off the rows as she passed them, touching the people in the aisle seats as she said their number. She came to Svekis as she said, "Eleven." Then she passed him and said, "Twelve." Turning back, she headed toward the front again, passing her partner as he finished tying up their hands.

Her voice blared like that of a tour guide. "You all sit in your seats, and when you're told to get off—when I call your number—you get up and get out. The bus will slow down enough for you to jump, but we're not stopping. So try not to break something. What you do after you get out, I don't care, but if you want to live, you'll follow my orders. I told you your numbers. You don't get up unless you're called."

The bus rolled along through the city. After ten minutes the speaker crackled again and she called out, "Three!" Two people scrambled up and ran clumsily, strung together, to the front of the bus. He heard her say to the driver, "Just slow enough that they can jump." Svekis looked out the window. The area was deserted, full of warehouses. It would be awhile before they found anyone to help them. Alternatively, they might be mugged. He sat back and waited his turn.

The bus rolled along out of the city proper and toward the western suburbs. They entered an area of tenement rowhouses, and two more were let go.

Hockey Mask had passed by him after tying his hands, and now Wonder Woman followed, into the very back of the bus. He listened to the rustle of her clothes, to the sound of a zipper, to other noises. He had a good idea what they were up to.

The speaker crackled again, and the woman called out, "Twelve. Get up, get out. Now."

Svekis watched a fashionable pair of slacks, a turquoise blouse, and dark hair pass him. The mask was different, too. She carried a small, full backpack over one shoulder. No doubt it was loaded with the contents of one satchel. She held her hands out in front of her, rope looped around her wrists and connected to the man behind her in the jeans, windbreaker, and another backpack. They walked down the aisle and through the curtain. The door hissed open and the bus slowed for a moment.

Then, over the speakers, she said, "Go on," as if she was still inside the bus. Svekis smiled. It was a clever trick.

The bus picked up speed. He tore off his mask. He'd already made one hand transform so that he could slip it out of the ropes. Standing, he glanced to the rear where her and her partner's clothes lay in heaps beside both discarded satchels. He knelt and rifled through both bags. He found his cell phone, but that was all.

He rose and walked down the aisle. Passengers lifted their heads at his passing, instinctively fearful. Most of them had left their masks askew. They kept their tied hands in their laps, too.

Even as he reached the curtain the woman's voice blared over the intercom: "Take your next right and drive for two miles until you go under the interstate."

Svekis stepped up beside driver. "How is the door opened?" he asked. The driver glanced up in astonishment.

"But she said—"

"I must insist." He placed his hand on the driver's shoulder, and the driver pointed to the handle that operated the door. "Thank you. Now, please, don't slow down any further. Do exactly as you were instructed." The door opened with a hiss, and Svekis sprang into the night like a man jumping off a cliff.

They'd parked the Toyota on a tree-lined street a block from the nearest regional train stop. The plan had been for her and Andy to take the car, and for Markie to jump on the next train back into the city. Nobody would expect that. She changed the plan now. She would take the train and he could drive off alone. That way they wouldn't match anything anyone was looking for; but with Markie dead, they needed to get out of town soon.

They stood on the sidewalk beside the car. A man was walking his dog, a white terrier, in their direction. She stepped up to Andy and said loudly, "I'll see you when you get back, sweetheart," then gave him a big kiss. "Drive safely. Don't *speed*."

The dog-walker looked away, a shy smile on his face. Just what she'd hoped. They stood together, waiting while he rounded the corner and went on up the street. She pulled away. "I mean it about the speed," she said.

"Yeah, I got it in one."

Around the corner, the terrier started barking. She took that as her cue and started up the street. She heard the car door open. She was thinking about how they'd actually pulled it off—her plan so carefully worked out. By now the bus had reached the interstate and was waiting for her to tell them to let the next passengers go. She switched on the walkie-talkie and said, "Okay, six, get up and get out." The thing was supposed to have a ten mile range.

If it did, they'd go awhile longer, and she would broadcast one more set of orders, send the bus out into the 'burbs for another half hour. If not, they'd shortly be looking for a man and woman in masks. She was halfway up the street before she realized that the car door had never closed.

She turned around, walking backwards. The Toyota sat there against the curb. The driver's door hung open wide. She couldn't see if Andy was in the car or not. What the hell could he be doing, putting his bag of loot in the trunk? Idiot. For a second she considered going back, and she slowed her pace. Something was wrong back there. Instinct compelled her to move, to get off the street. She turned and picked up speed.

The thing came out of the darkness beside her, a moon-colored blur moving in swift smears across the night, across a lawn from shadow to shadow, and then suddenly right before her. Golden feral eyes met hers. She ought to have been terrified but it was as if she'd expected this, as if someone had told her it was coming. The rich, dark voice—real or imagined—said, "You've borrowed something of mine, I'm afraid, that you should not have."

She thought of words to say but couldn't find them before the eyes swelled like twin suns and drank her down.

"It was terrible," said the branch manager. Iancu Svekis nodded.

"A tragedy, I'm sure," he said.

"They *could* have killed them. You know, that's what everybody's scared will happen in a robbery. That one girl—the one they shot—she's going to be okay."

"That's good to hear."

"But you were there, right? I had to call Erica, because she'd put through your wire transfer and she knew what was going on with it—"

"Yes," he said heavily, "I was there."

"That thing in the bathroom—she said even the cops can't figure it out. They think maybe it was a gang thing, but nobody saw any gang, did they?" Svekis said nothing, but she went right on. "Of course, finding the bodies in that car trunk along with the money—that's got everyone thinking it's a gang thing, too. It's so *weird*." When he only sighed, she seemed to understand that he didn't want to talk about this any further.

"Anyway," she said, and handed him back his passport, "everything's fine, your money was transferred from overseas into your new account. Here's the documentation and the number. You can draw on that at any of our branches anywhere from here to Boston—there's a list of addresses in here, too. But you should get your ATM card in about ten days."

"Thank you." He took the envelope she held out and started to get up.

"I was wondering," she said. "Can I ask you one more thing?"

"Yes?"

"Um, Erica wanted to know how you got your passport back. She said she was sure they scooped it up when they were cleaning out the tellers."

He looked at her with some concern. "Oh, no," he assured her. "They left it on her desk and I took it back when they weren't watching."

"Wow. That was pretty brave."

"I did not, you know, think of it that way. Perhaps brave, perhaps foolish. But then stealing is foolish." He tucked the envelope into his jacket and reached out. "Thank you," he repeated, and she shook his hand. No one was watching, and he only needed to hold onto her for a few moments.

He left her sitting, staring off into space. Someone would notice eventually and shake her back into the here and now, but she would remain vaguely confused as to what had occurred and to whom she'd been speaking just before she dozed off.

Svekis pushed open the door and walked out into the light.

TRAVELING ON

Three days after the Rapture the kitchen faucet starts dripping again. From where I sleep on the couch the steady *ploik ploik ploik* might as well be right over my head.

I call up Bynum, the plumber we've always used, but he must be one of them was taken up, because instead of his usual voice mail I get that rising and falling wind howl the news people talk about, that you can almost hear a voice in—dial tone of the dearly departed.

I was asleep when it happened, on the couch where Sally Ann insisted so that she didn't have to hear me snoring. C-PAP's busted a month now and without it when I get going I can probably pull the curtains off the windows. Ought to have got it replaced, but I never remembered to call the Sleep Center because if I did and they swapped me out a new one, she'd have to give the real reason she didn't want me in her bed, namely the stink of booze leaking out my pores in the heat. It's hot most nights anymore.

7:06 a.m. was when I woke up, the red numbers of the end table clock staring back at me. I thought it peculiar that Sally Ann wasn't already flushing the toilet and running her blow dryer while she got ready for her shift at the nursing home. I climbed up off the couch and, half-awake, shuffled down the hall. The Word-a-Day calendar by the stove was still yesterday's word: *enumerate*: "to mention (list) one by one." The carpeted plywood creaked underfoot like always.

She'd forgot to set her alarm on other occasions and I was all prepared to offer her some coffee, get her engine running, only she wasn't there. Her nightgown was, and the sheets lay all tangled and whirled around it in the depression of the mattress where she normally slept.

The spot was moist but cool to the touch, like she'd got out of bed ten minutes ago to take her shower. When I went back along the hall, I couldn't help but glance into the bathroom, though I knew she wasn't there. Really, I'd known it the moment I woke up—just hadn't registered. You can always tell when the single-wide's not occupied. Expect I must have missed the whole thing by like half an hour, and it had to have been damn quiet when it happened. You can't fart in there without it echoing the length of the place.

Three nights later I still hadn't moved back to the bed. Every time I drifted off I thought I'd wake up to her shaking me, giving me hell over my snoring or my drinking like before. I considered I ought to try lying down in there maybe to piss her off enough to come back. But what stopped me was how I could almost see her in that pressed-down spot. Like looking into a grave. Once I knew, I couldn't even touch the sheets.

Not everybody says it's the Rapture, you understand. I mean, two thirds of the world's population is gone. That includes Muslims and Hindus and Chinese. *The Event* is what the CNN people call it, which is I guess their way of including everybody, especially since nobody agrees what it was.

Seems like most of them taken up left notes, like they all had a couple minutes' warning and were okay with it. Charlene, our local newscaster, she's been reading us different ones every night. They mostly say stuff like "I love you but I'm traveling on," which when I heard it made me think of that hymn my mama loved.

Sally Ann didn't leave me any note, although maybe the medical marijuana for her bursitis played a part in that. She might not have been awake—lots of people weren't. I mean, it was the middle of the night some places.

That first morning, when I stumbled outside, the Bethel West Mobile Home Park was full of crying and shouting, enough noise that it didn't seem that empty at all. I even thought right then that Sally Ann might be out there, gone to see what was the matter, which was something she'd have done. I didn't understand yet and just kept walking, drawn by the wrongness of it all.

Some homes stood like always, but some had their doors hanging open. There was music and TVs jabbering loud, but nobody there listening. Around the corner, down the middle of F Street, a few people were on their knees with their arms up. It was sort of biblical. I mean, "wailing and the gnashing of teeth" biblical. I'd heard that phrase since I was a kid, but I'd never seen it in action. Maude Evert knelt bare-ass naked, reaching for the sky like it might pull her up. Her husband and daughter were both gone, I found out later.

F street dead-ends at the sweet-corn field that covers the whole hillside above us. That morning a combine harvester sat in the middle of it, engine off. I guess the combine had cut about a third of the corn, and I wondered if maybe the farmer had been taken up right there, in the cab. Wondered if his family would finish the harvesting. Third morning, when I come out to drive to my meeting, it's in the same spot, which starts me thinking I should go grab some of that corn while it's still good.

Wednesday mornings I go to AA at the Darby Street Methodist Church, in that big room they have in the basement. Usually it's before work, but this Wednesday I'm off. My boss at the Home Depot, McCormick, totally approves of my attendance at those meetings, I guess because it shows I'm on the straight and narrow, which it wouldn't if he knew that some of those "meetings" I spent in Peebles Tavern just up the way, usually for a couple three beers. I guess I'm what they call "high functioning," or at least I don't drink to where I can't go back to work. You know, everybody's got a different tolerance.

Anymore at AA the opiate addicts outnumber the boozers anyway, and I kinda want to see who's left. Wonder if my sponsor, Larry Kanudin, made it. He's about fed up with me, always calling me a recidivist. That came up on Sally Ann's calendar one time. Repeat offender, it means. Well, I can't argue with that.

Going down the steps into the church basement, I can hear some yelling and arguing coming from below. Sounds like maybe more of them than I was expecting.

The card table's set up near the door, with donut balls and

graham crackers, and lemonade and Diet Pepsi and paper cups. The usual twenty folding chairs arranged in a big half circle, but hardly anyone's sitting and there are only six people on hand. Larry isn't one of 'em, and I think, "Well, that's something anyway."

A tall, skinny bozo named Crist is windmilling his arms and dancing back and forth like a prize fighter with no skill. He's going, "Ah-wuh, ah-wuh, come on, you just try for a piece a me, you," at Jamie, who's a druggie working really hard to stay clean, twenty-eight but looks fifty easy, skin all scarred and sunken. Whatever started it, Jamie isn't even trying for Crist, just watching like maybe this isn't really real and he can back out of the room if he goes slow. Nobody's doing anything to stop it, not even Jack Burchfeld, who's always acting like he's the new sheriff in town. He might be as of today since there's no sign of Carlotta or any other senior sponsor.

Jack and the others aren't giving Crist any attention at all because Brenda Towsend's bellowing in that voice of hers that slices steel: "I got me a nine months token even!" She holds it up like a crucifix. "And I wasn't taken, but *Bobby* was, an' he did nothin' with his life."

Brenda's one of those women developed flaps of skin off their upper arms as they got big. Sally Ann worked out with barbells so as not to go that route, called it toning her biceps. The little barbells are still in the bedroom, so I guess she doesn't need them where she's gone. Brenda works at the nursing home with Sally Ann, or did, I mean. Bobby was her older brother, I think.

Skinny Melissa Canto snorts at her. "Maybe if you'd earned a one-year token, you'd have been found worthy, Brenda." Melissa's got a temper, and she's a smart ass, which is maybe why we tend to get along at the meetings.

But Brenda doesn't take it well. "How dare you?" she squawks. "I gone to church every Sunday my whole life. It ain't right, it ain't *fair.*"

The other one, Emily Pernudi, just looks back and forth between them, then at Jack, who's showing enough sense to keep quiet. Emily's kind of like someone's lost box turtle, wide-eyed like always. She testified once that she'd escaped into drink because her father was doing her all through high school and community college. Hell, if anyone deserved being taken to the bosom of the Lord, it was Emily. Brenda's right that nothing about this is fair.

Crist keeps right on threatening and blocking Jamie, so I finally say, "Hey, Christmas, cut it out."

He swings around, fists still up. He's always saying dumbass things. One time I shut him up by telling him how close he'd come to being somebody important, only missing it by one little "h". Took him a whole two minutes to work that out, then he was cursing me like crazy. Carlotta did not put up with "such language" and booted him out for two weeks. Now he lowers his fists and slinks off.

Melissa Canto turns around, and says, "Oh, hey, you." The other three look me up and down like maybe I'm not real. "So, turns out you are not among the selected either, hey?"

"Didn't think I was a contender."

She glances back at Brenda. "Puts you in the minority then. Everybody else is sure there's been some everlasting mistake."

Brenda's chin quivers, then she bursts into tears and goes running out of the room.

"Everlasting," Emily repeats, like she's grabbing the word for herself.

I say, "What you think, Jack? You been sober two whole years longer than I been coming here."

"Oh, I dunno," he blusters, going red-faced on the spot. He tugs at his beard. "God works in mysterious ways, right?"

"That a Baptist or a Methodist explanation?" asks Melissa, annoyed, but he doesn't seem to notice.

"Why, Methodists are just Baptists what learned to read," he replies. It's his favorite slogan. I've heard it three times already since I started here. Helps that we're in a Methodist church.

"Don't you think that's all *insignificante* now? I mean, who cares, Baptists or Methodists?"

"Or Mexicans," adds Crist.

Melissa starts laughing. "Wow. Two-thirds of everybody gone, and you're still a dickhead."

Crist glares, mouth gone tight. Well, he asked for it.

Jack's gone pale. "Is that the number were taken?"

Jamie slides up, munching on a graham cracker. "Man, how can you not know that?" he asks. "It's been, like, on every news show everywhere?"

Jack mutters some non-answer, red-faced again, and Melissa interjects. "Hey, did you hear the president's gone?"

We all look at her. "Gone, as in taken up?"

"No, but his crew on Air Force One was and the jet went down in the Atlantic. Was on CNN just before I drove here."

"Why are we only hearing about this now?" asks Jack.

She gives a shrug. "There is a recording of the pilot's voice, where he announces he has heard the call and has to answer, and the co-pilot or navigator says, yes, him, too, and then they say how much they love their families."

"Are they crying?" It's Brenda, who's come back in to hear this.

"No, they're so so calm, it's—I don't know what to call it. It's creepy, you know? But then they stop, and there is that wind sound, and after that no one answers."

The wind reminds me of Bynum and the faucet, but also that they had time to say goodbye—which bothers me—but not to land, when there's been all sorts of stories of pilots bringing planes in on schedule but then someone checks and there's nobody in the cockpit.

"The president?"

"Huh," I say. "So everybody else was taken up but he went down."

"Hey, I voted for him," Jack says.

"So what?" replies Melissa. "I mean, whatever you were or did before now."

"Before's all gone, man," Jamie puts in.

And before that opinion stands long enough to sound deep, Emily Pernudi in her sing-song voice says, "Today is the first day of the rest of your life."

"Jesus," says Crist, and walks away shaking his head. He plants himself on one of the folding chairs as far from us as he can get.

"So," Melissa asks me, "if this is your first day, what are you going to do with it, you and Sally Ann?"

Brenda gives me a horrified look. *She* knows, but none of the others do. "Well, tonight if Pete's is still in business, I'm gonna order a pepperoni pie, because Sally Ann hated pepperoni, and I haven't tasted one in about three years. Figure I better do it now before she comes back."

"Oh, Earl," Melissa says. "I am sorry."

"You think they're coming back?" Jack gives me this sorta urgent look, like he thinks I've maybe heard something else he hasn't.

"Not really. I think one miracle's the limit. Two would be, I don't know, like me staying sober three weeks straight."

"But you have, right, Earl?" he asks. "Larry and you, it was working, right?"

"Long as you don't count the two weeks in the middle where it wasn't." Trying to sound a little bit ashamed, I tell him, "I'm just a . . . recidivist, Jack."

It's like I let all the air out of him. "You're never going to earn your *first* token, Earl."

"Yeah. Probably get my wings first." He scowls at me, disappointed, and all of a sudden I'm really tired of this "things are gonna get back to normal" horseshit. "Give it a rest, all right? Most of the people in the whole damn world are gone. I work in a big box store that'll go out of business soon since there's hardly anyone to fucking buy anything, and the high point of my week is gonna be the toppings on my pizza. You're goddam *right* I'm gonna drink. What else, huh? Change my life? I think that kinda happened already."

None of them wants to look me in the eye then. I wonder how many people in their lives up and disappeared, but what I know for sure is, right now I don't need to sit and hear any goddam testimonies about it.

"Well, hasn't this been one of our finer meetings?" And I turn and storm out of the empty church. Pack of goddam losers, trying to get straight when there's no one left to get straight for.

Power blips twice during the evening—the second time while cable news is playing a story about how suicides are at an all-time high among survivors. That's what we are now. *Survivors,* as opposed to *the ones left behind.* We're all shell-shocked, like Emily Pernudi except all at once with God instead of over and over with Daddy. It's like the jet we were in crashed and everybody else burned while we got up and walked away. Nobody can tell us why.

Power stays out a good hour. I try eating my pizza by candlelight, but Sally Ann's candles smell like vanilla shit, and pretty soon the pepperoni doesn't taste right anymore. I give up trying, open the windows wide, and stick to beer after that. Anyway, the pizza wasn't all that great. Pete was taken and his two kids don't have the knack yet.

That's one more crazy ass thing we learned the first couple days after the Event. We'd been left with a skeleton crew everywhere, all over the world. Just enough people in every, whatdyacallit, facility to keep things running. Sure, we get brownouts, and cell phones aren't real reliable when you do get someone to answer. Web sites are mostly 404 codes and pages don't update, but who really cares?

Cable news mostly reruns the same stories like 200 times, so that's pretty much the same as it was before. You can get everything anybody has to say in about half an hour.

Our local news out of Waterloo, the one I watch, has just two reporters now: Charlene, who's been there for years, and some bozo they must have hired the day after. I never saw him before that, and tonight I'm guessing he got bombed before airtime. Hey, maybe he'll join us at the church some Wednesday. It's pretty clear Charlene wants to kill him. She's a pro, still made up perfectly, and her clothes all pressed. He stumbles through his first story, and she takes it away from him. Spotlight on him goes out and he just sits in the shadows back there while she rolls on. Maybe I should apply for his job.

The stories are still mostly personal interest ones—tonight it's cars pulled off the road with notes left behind. "My dearest Annabelle, how I wish we could be together one last time but I am called now and there's no turning back." "Dear Bill, I'll be waiting when it's your time, which is not today I know, because I've been shown . . ." Every single one knowing the unknowable and saying so long before they step off the ledge. Charlene runs footage from some Canadian news report, interviews with religious leaders from all over, mostly debating if this is the Rapture or not. One guy says he knows it's UFOs that somehow surrounded the Earth and just zapped everyone at once. Someone else says that's stupid, points out how many planes landed, buses and trains came to a safe stop, hardly any accidents (except, I guess, Air Force One). Just people all gone to a so-called better place.

I find myself muttering that hymn: "My heavenly home is bright and fair. I feel like traveling on." Always sounded strange to me, but not anymore. Even the Pope's gone. He left a note naming a cardinal to succeed him that they're fighting over. Still, how did he know that cardinal wouldn't be taken up, too? That kind of shoots down the UFO theory.

Local news goes for a commercial—bunch of animated bunny rabbits streaming toilet paper over a hillside—and I move on to the vodka. Beer can't fully protect you from bunnies telling you to wipe your ass.

When they come back, the bozo's chair is empty and Charlene's smiling while she tells us about one local family the station's found who survived intact, everybody still here, and maybe it's the vodka, but it's a weird-ass interview, 'cause they don't know if they're happy or screwed. I choke on my drink, and my eyes burn with tears, but from laughing. Don't know what else to do.

I kill half the fifth before I conk out on the couch. First time I haven't polished off a bottle in forever.

Next morning as I'm leaving for work, I see that someone's set up a stand at the entrance to Bethel West with a couple crates and a marker-scrawled sign that reads "Fresh Corn." Well, so I'm not the only one who noticed the combine. I don't see who's manning the stand, though, but I need to remember tonight to go up there and grab me some of that corn before it rots.

At the Home Depot I usually work unloading deliveries, but there aren't many of those just now, so mostly I move pallets around with the forklift, and stock the shelves. It's a "don't interact with the public" job and I can do it even half in the bag. Have yet to drop a pallet. The other stocking staff are cut from the same cloth—I don't mean they're boozers, but none of us is customer-assisting material. We're "dock and stock." That's what McCormick, the manager, calls us.

Thursday morning it's just Gary and me. I haven't been to work since the Event. The Depot was closed the first two days after. Most everything was closed while people tried to make sense of the world. And then it was my day off.

"He fire everybody?" I ask Gary.

"Nope," he says, which doesn't really surprise me. "He tried calling."

"The wind?"

Nods. "You shoulda been here yesterday. Really spooked his ass. Finally got eight of us. He was afraid to call you."

"Yeah, I'm such a likely candidate. Guess that takes care of who to let go, though, huh?"

"He was gonna let somebody go?" Gary gawps at me. Clearly he hadn't worked out that fewer customers require fewer employees.

"Look at it this way, you and I might get promoted out onto the floor awhile."

"Think we'll get a raise?"

"Fuckin' hope so. I got only one income now." Then I think *hang on a second.* "Go back. You telling me that Spoonie's phone blew the wind, too?"

Gary's eyes widen. "I *know.* What the fuck, right?"

Spoonie's real name is Martin Spooner. He's a pedophile who served six years, and got a job in "dock and stock" because there aren't any kids around to tempt him. Part of his parole deal was he had to tell all of us who worked with him that he *was* a convicted pedophile. Not everybody was happy to learn this, and at least a couple of floor help wouldn't even look at him when they wanted something brought up. McCormick told us on the QT to keep an eye on him, but Spoonie never once misbehaved. The pen had beaten that out of him. Word was he'd been shanked once and lost a kidney.

While Gary and I move tubs of pneumatic cement, we try to make sense of this development.

"First thing I thought," he says, "was what in hell did God want with a crumb like him?"

"Beats me. He ever talk about himself, like growing up?"

"I dunno, why?"

"Just thinking," I say. "Lotta people, the stuff they do they learned to do it. Had assholes for parents or friends. I just wondered was Spoonie like that, couldn't help himself."

Gary bobs his head. "Even Jesus got mad at a tree, you know." The way he hauls that out, I can tell he's been waiting for the opportunity to use it.

"So," I suggest, "maybe when he was a kid he did something

nice, like rescued a baby bird."

"Okay, but doesn't that still make you a dick now?"

Gary, man, you're hilarious. "Besides, what could Spoonie have done to cancel out all the kids he damaged." Neither of us has an answer for that. "Yeah, old Spoonie's most likely roasting someplace."

"I wonder if he left a note."

In the breakroom we're still going on about the damn notes and Spoonie. Sarita, one of four remaining checkout people, listens awhile before shutting us both down. "First of all," she says, "it's not two thirds of the world, but two thirds of the *people*."

Gary latches on to that. "Yeah, I saw a story about folks rescuing their neighbors' dogs and cats and stuff."

But Sarita's not done. "The other thing is, this shows us we all have been praying to the same God. Like, everybody, all religions."

Warily, I ask, "What about those of us don't pray to any?"

"What if it's, you know, a test?" says Gary.

"What's being tested?"

"You know, what you can stand. Like Job. Everybody's lost somebody." He nods to me. "Sally Ann's gone, Sarita's got her kid but Enrique's gone. My mama's gone, my sister."

"So, we're tested if we can go on? If we'll feed the neighbor's dog some kibble?"

Thinking fast, he argues, "Well, like, Sarita's kid is safe from Spoonie now."

"Jesus, Gary, *everybody* was safe from Spoonie. Anyway, if he was such a big problem, why not just have a bus hit him? You saying the world's collateral damage to get rid of the pervs?"

"Okay, maybe not."

"We simply do not understand," proclaims Sarita.

"That" —I point at her— "is exactly right."

We go back to work. Around quarter past four the power goes out and when it's obvious it's not coming back on, we clock out, McCormick filling our cards by hand since the time clock's not operating. He gives us our checks, it being the fifteenth and a payday. Beside him's a stack of envelopes he's not going to pass out ever. Maybe they'll get sent to families. We close up but he stays behind, concerned that with the power out, someone needs to be on guard. The front doors are jammed closed, but I suppose the power could come back on at any time. The first twenty-four hours after the Event there was some looting, but way less than anyone expected. Might be because there are plenty of empty houses and apartments where nobody's going to miss anything. Or maybe we're all scared that this *is* some kind of test, like Gary said.

I deposit my pay at the ATM near home, get some cash and go shopping. Not a lot of people in the Hy-Vee, but they all move like zombies in the aisles. I grab some beer, couple enchilada bowls, two bottles of Tito's vodka. I even make it to the sleep clinic before they close to pick up my new C-PAP. Hope the trailer park has power tonight.

The corn stand is still set up at the entrance. Turns out it's Maude Evert in a big floppy weave hat. Got her pants on now. She gives me a wave to stop, and I roll down the window. She hands me two ears of corn. "Free to residents." She grins, showing her nicotine-stained teeth.

"You making much?"

She shrugs. "What's much nowadays?"

"Good question. Stop by for a beer later if you want."

She nods and goes back to her stand.

There's a car parked in the street in front of my place, and when I pull onto the concrete pad beside the trailer, there's Brenda Towsend sitting on the cinder block steps up to my front door. Part of me wishes I'd just driven on by, but it's too late now, so I park it and get out casual-like, lean across the roof of the car.

"Hey, Brenda." I think she's wearing the same print dress she had on at AA yesterday. "I didn't know you knew where I live."

"I work with your wife, Earl. Worked."

"Oh, right." As I come around with the bags of food and booze, she gets off the steps to let me open the door. There's something jerky, off-kilter about her. Not like she's drunk. More like she's afraid I'll touch her. I give her a look, because that sure as hell isn't the usual bellowing Brenda. Her eyes are puffy.

Inside, I set the stuff down on the shaky kitchen table. She's followed me in. I reach into one bag. "Want a beer?" I ask, and immediately remember. "Sorry, wasn't thinking. You mind if I—" and that's as far as I get before she's bawling her head off and wrapping herself around me, face buried in my shirt. I don't know where to stand, where to put my hands, what to do except set down the beer. Finally, I say, "Tell me."

Between sobs and gulps, she answers. "Harvey killed himself."

Now, despite that we both attend the meetings, we don't exactly know each other, and I have to think a minute what I can recall. "Harvey, that's your husband? He's—he's a cop, right?" That makes her wail some more and clutch me.

I remember Sally Ann saying something about them separating—I hadn't paid it close attention. Something about Brenda binge-eating on account of it. No matter what gets said, I'd rather not be hugged anymore, so I quick go over to the couch and strip off the bedding, ditch the pillow. "Why don't you, uh, come take a load off and tell me, Brenda."

She does, sits away from me, stares at her hands or feet while she talks. "His partner was waiting when I got home from work. Wouldn't let me go in. There was a couple other cops there, too, wanted to talk, but he said he wanted me to hear it from him."

"He did it in your place?"

She nods a couple times, still not looking my way.

I'm imagining crime scene tape across a door. "Well," I say, "it's good he had a partner." Don't know why, but my throat knots up and my face is hot all of a sudden. I quick get up and grab that beer I'd started to open, leaving her on the couch.

"It's my fault," Brenda says.

I turn around, beer tab hissing. "What is?" I take a swig and another to wash down the first one. She doesn't seem to have an answer, so I ask, "Harvey leave a note?"

She nods, pulls it out of the pocket at her hip to read it, but all I can think is, *Everybody else in the whole damn world got a note.*

Then she's reading his words about how he'd been broken for a long time but didn't see it till so many of his pals were airlifted. I think about how that's a good word for it. Once he realized he'd been on life support and his support was all gone, Harvey found himself cut loose. Without her he couldn't see the point of going on. And that's why she thinks it's her fault.

I realize I don't know her story, not really, never heard it at

AA, and likely picked up most of it from Sally Ann talking about the nursing home. Still, his excuse for this is he was *broken*? What bullshit. His wife hadn't been taken up. He could have gone home to her if he'd really wanted to. I feel like, if I tell her that, though, she'll go to pieces. So I don't. Maybe we'll argue it at AA, because she'll for sure bring it up next time.

I glance past Brenda at my groceries, some of which are gonna thaw out if I leave them.

"Hey, listen, I bought a couple enchilada bowls if you want to share a meal here. Guaranteed safe, 'cause I ain't doing the cooking."

She gives me a searching sort of look, and I can see how she's trying to figure me, who's never been particularly nice to her in the meetings. I can't exactly say why I am now, either.

She folds Harvey's letter and gets to her feet—I think, to leave. So I stand up, and then she hugs me again. No place for me to go, I just stand like that in silence while the faucet goes *ploik* a couple more times.

We eat at the kitchen table. Sally picked it up at some yard sale right after we moved in. It's like a laminated board stood on four giant clothespins, came with its own ring stains, too, and I doubt I ever once have sat here of a morning without sloshing my coffee. Plenty of times I've blamed my other sloppiness on it, too, which I guess is why I never argued to get rid of it.

I have a second beer with the enchilada bowl. It's damn spicy. But after, I don't go for another as usual. I feel, I don't know, leveled off, and I don't want to be useless right now.

Brenda makes conversation about the trailer park. "All these so-called mobile homes sittin' on foundation blocks and got aluminum or plastic skirts that cover that up. What I can't figure is what makes 'em mobile."

"Tornadoes," I reply without even thinking.

She lets out a belly laugh that could vibrate us right off those foundation blocks. That's the sound of Brenda. By the end of it, she's tearing up again, but slaps the table, saying, "Feels good to laugh at something. I'm afraid even to look in the mirror."

"Why?"

"Afraid I won't see nothin."

"Sure, could be we're all ghosts." I throw that out to make conversation, but it starts something skritching in the back of my mind.

Her chin quivers. "I *shoulda* been taken up, you know. Maybe that would've saved Harvey."

"Brenda, I can't see how that's true. He even said it in his letter—his damage, not yours. Hell, I give him credit, he owned it when he could have blamed you." Talking about his suicide tires me out, and I think we'll get into an argument if we keep worrying it. Don't know what else to do, though, so I turn on the TV. It's about time for the news anyway.

Charlene's got a "big story that's going to affect everybody." The picture cuts away to some pre-recorded footage that has to be from one of the cable channels. A woman wearing businesslike clothes. The screen gives her name and identifies her as a climate scientist from Oxford, which I'm guessing doesn't mean Oxford, Iowa. She's got a British accent, too. She explains how she and a group of her peers who survived "the catastrophe" have run new models based on the reduced population of Earth and all of them predict a "relatively swift" reversal in global warming, starting with a reduction in mean ocean temperature.

"I didn't know temperature could be mean," Brenda says.

I can't be sure if she's serious. "Ever been to Death Valley?"

"Nope."

The scientist keeps talking while a map of the Earth shows all the places where ice is going to come back before the end of the century. Doesn't seem too swift to me, that long. I won't be here, even if there's no second round of airlifts.

"So, the world is going to heal itself?" asks the unseen interviewer.

"That is what we are finding. Provided we maintain something close to ZPG and work at this, we may very well find ourselves, a century from now—and not to overstate it—living in a second Eden."

I shake my head. "She's got a lot more faith in people not messing up than I do." Maybe I do want another beer.

Meanwhile, Charlene's slid from someday-Eden to a batch of reported sightings of Jesus and the Virgin Mary. This includes

"Mary's face" appearing on a slice of challah-bread French toast at the Crabtree Diner in our own town this morning, with video footage of the syrup-drenched toast off somebody's phone, a face that looks to me mostly like Obi-Wan Kenobi with a deformed eye.

Even Brenda, the churchgoer, says, "Has she got a beard there?"

Should have gone for Jesus or John the Baptist. People get desperate, any swirl becomes a sign.

I guess that's when the thing that's been niggling at my brain kicks loose. I mute the TV. "Hey, what do you think the chances are we all been looking at this thing through the wrong end of the telescope?"

Brenda's brow bunches up. "What d'ya mean, Earl?"

"Remember how Melissa said I was in the minority 'cause I didn't think I should be airlifted?"

"I guess." She frowns at being reminded of the meeting.

"So supposing the ones who got airlifted are the ones left behind?"

"Left behind where?" I can see she's trying to work it out.

"Dunno. Suppose they got scraped off the board so the rest of us could have another shot at doing it right." I nod at the TV.

She stares at me while the faucet goes *ploik* three times. Then she says, "You think we'd ever get it right? Isn't this divine retribution?"

"For what? If we're supposed to suffer, how come we got enough people to keep the lights on? Why help us out if it's punishment? I mean, don't get me wrong, we suck as a species. Everybody's just addicts in rehab trying to make sense of things. Take pain-killers when we aren't hurting and booze ourselves so we don't have to listen to the noise. Life's nothing but noise all the damn time, and you can't stop it unless you . . . like Harvey did." I point. "Like that damn faucet over there. That's what I mean. Goes on and on and on."

At Harvey's name she winces like I stung her, but she doesn't blubber about him. She turns it all over in her head, says finally, "I thought you didn't believe in anything."

Can't help but smile a little. "Well, maybe I'm coming around to it."

She looks narrowly at me. "So what would you do different going forward, Earl?"

I stand there. The faucet goes *ploik ploik ploik*. I stare at it like if I had laser eyes I'd melt it.

"Well, I think tomorrow before work I'm gonna go see if the community college has got a UA union course in plumbing certification. I mean, if anybody's left to teach it."

"You gonna go back to school?" Plainly disbelieving me.

"Why not? Learn to be a plumber, so I don't have to listen to that damned sink anymore." And I think, hey, maybe I will. World's got to have plumbers. Also I'm gonna crawl under there and turn that water off tomorrow. Brenda gazes sinkwise and nods a few times like she agrees maybe that's a good idea.

"What about you?"

"Nursing home's still got old folks in it. Ain't gonna run itself."

"Expect that's true."

Seems to me it's about time for her to go—there's nearly nothing we can talk about now that won't bring up Harvey or Sally Ann—when she asks, "Do you think I could maybe stay here for the night? I don't—I can't go home with all that . . ." Her hands try to shape what "all that" means.

I want to say no. I'm all ready to say no, but I hear myself telling her, "Yeah, Brenda, sure. But I gotta clean the place up first. Nobody's been in the bedroom since—you know. Won't be a minute."

I leave her sitting on the couch and march down the hall. What the hell am I doing?

Bed's the same as always. I close the door so I can talk, quietly: "Sally Ann, I know you won't mind Brenda being in here, 'cause she's your friend and you'd want me to help her, wouldn't you." I don't expect any sort of a sign, but I'd take one if it came, which it doesn't. I walk around the bed, like I'm going to figure out the best way to do this. I haven't touched the bedding still. Finally, I just take hold of it, trying not to look at what I'm doing while I'm doing it, and pull the sheets and her nightgown to me, mashing it all up like you might if somebody with the flu had been sleeping there. A piece of paper slips out from somewhere in the bundle and settles on the floor beside my foot. I bend down and pick it up. Was it under her nightgown all this time? I unfold it. It's in pencil.

Earl you fuckhead, I love you.

I think we didn't say that anymore after the first year, did we,

and I'm sorry for my own goddam part in that. No use complain-
ing, and I'm not, but I won't be there to try to fix it neither. You got
to by yourself. Now I gotta go. SA

I'm shaking, holding the note, rereading it and then looking
all around for the pencil—where the hell did she hide the pencil?
She take it with her? Were they allowed to do that? Is there any
other story where people took their pencils?

Then I realize I'm crying, and I press my face into the wad-
ded sheets so's not to make noise when I sob. They smell like Sally
Ann and that's worse. Eventually, Brenda calls my name. Probably
afraid I've been airlifted, too.

I yell back, "Yeah, hang on!" Wipe my eyes and blow my nose
in the sheets, toss 'em in the closet. Don't know as I'll ever wash
them. Then I get new ones out to make the bed. But I've got that
piece of paper tucked in my pocket.

Later, once Brenda's all settled, I take it out and read it again,
and I guess I'm grinning like a dope at the same time that I'm
messed up all over. But after a while I just sit there on the couch
with a cold beer and hold the note like it's some kind of treasure. I
set it beside me where I can see it while I make up my bed.

That night I sleep with my new mask on. The faucet drip fades
behind the C-PAP's fan.

It sounds exactly like the wind.

ELLENDE

essie stares into the front corner of the Packard, at the crank handle for the side window, at the triangular vent window that's pushed open to let in air, at the built-in clock in the polished dash. Her face burns as if she's been slapped on both cheeks. She knew this is what would happen, why did she voice an opinion at all?

Floyd, behind the wheel, comments that he didn't really expect a stupid bitch to grasp the situation—the situation being that he's pulled out a tatty hand-drawn map that belonged to his grandfather, for whom he's named. It's a shortcut map to Lake O_____ that he claims will shave an hour off their trip.

Floyd's people have been coming up here for decades. There used to be a family cabin on the lake but when an uncle got into financial trouble during the war, they had to sell it. This is only the second time he's brought Jessie north in the four years they've been married, the first time to Lake O_____. She has earned it—by being properly obedient—but look how quickly she slips up. That he suddenly brandished this map should have told her the matter of whether or not to take the shortcut was already decided, but her instincts for self-preservation lagged just behind her desire to have a say in what they do. Probably if they weren't so far along, he would have turned the car around to punish her. She hates herself for it at the same time she craves his benediction.

Floyd hasn't hit her, ever. That's not the way of his control. In order to wave the map while he shouts about her stupidity at not seeing immediately the wisdom of his alternate route, he has stuck his large cigar in the ashtray. In a minute, in the sullen aftermath, he will pick up the corona and, waiting for the lighter to heat, renew his disparagement of her for having caused it to go out in the first place. Yes, it's all entirely her fault. *That's* his way of control. He works the details to ensure that she's complicit.

To relight the cigar, he has to put down the map. She hazards a glance over her hunched shoulder, looks at it on the seat. It's a folded piece of paper with pencil lines on it that he hasn't shared with her, which is typical of him. It's a test of her faith in and reliance upon him, hardly the first; and nothing in the world could compel her to question it at this point. She returns to staring into the corner.

The Packard is a handsome car, plush and well-appointed. It's just the sort of car for an important doctor like Floyd. Back when she was a nurse, he'd courted her in it, taking her to dinners, to films, to hospital fêtes. Every day she had observed him with all of those pregnant women whose babies he was about to deliver. His bedside manner was so tender, so compassionate, and that's what she fell in love with. There was no way to recognize then that the caring persona of Doctor Floyd Ensley, like the white coat he wore, was merely veneer, nothing more than the outward expression of a man who knew himself to be of peerless stock, never to be disputed or questioned. If he has in his possession an alternate route, then it is a given that this is the best possible course to their happy holiday cabin.

And so, an hour north of Brainerd, they turn off the two-lane highway and onto a narrow dirt road that has been oiled to keep cars from kicking up dust—at least for the first half mile. After that it abruptly turns to plain dirt with dips and valleys of pure juddering washboard. After that no other cars join or pass them. They would have to negotiate passage with oncoming vehicles, but there are none. The thick pine forest scents their way, deep woods press in from both sides. At one point a string of ancient, seemingly abandoned cabins is visible through the trees on the right. Beyond the cabins she catches glimpses of diamond-bright water—some other lake than theirs; but then Minnesota is the land of a thousand lakes, and most of them seem to have formed in the north.

The press of trees makes it feel as if the day has gone dark and cloudy though Jessie knows it's not. She considers saying as much, as a way back into normalized communication; but then she decides it isn't worth the trouble, for his reply will surely include some carefully clothed derogatory remark, a "See how well we get along when you aren't an idiot" line couched in language that leaves no opening for objection. No, better to sit on the bench seat, watching upside down images scroll over the polished mahogany dash, a flowing terrain dissociated from the one outside; better to remain silent with her arms wrapped around herself until Floyd has traveled as far from that vituperative moment as possible.

She must have fallen asleep because she comes to against the burgundy door panel in time to witness the sign of "Ellende, pop. 268" glide past.

Floyd acknowledges her alertness with, "Town up ahead. We're going to stop and gas up, though the cabin can't be but half an hour now."

She wipes a ghost cobweb off the side of her face.

He says, "This map's not drawn very to scale, is all I can say. It looks like we should have reached it awhile back." His tone holds a breath of apology—not acknowledgement that she was right in anything but that he's conceding his grandfather's unreliability. Nothing to do with him at all of course, just one more person who's disappointed Floyd.

The town of Ellende proves to be a main street and not much else. It has one Sinclair gas station on the far side with one skinny green pump. Nobody is there to operate the pump. Nobody is inside the unlocked station. Floyd walks around behind the place, comes back, finally opens the door and enters. Jessie stands beside the Packard and listens. Towns make noise, even with a population of only 268. Not this one. It's as silent as a snowfall. No pine trees whish, no birds are calling anywhere, no deer flies buzz around. Directly overhead, a sun halo hovers like the eye of God. It's a cool, wispy-clouded day, and there's not a living thing anywhere. *End of the world*, she thinks.

Floyd emerges from the station building. "There's money in the till," he says. "I can't believe they've just gone off." With that he considers the pump hose. She can see that he's trying to recall how the boy does it at the service station where he buys his gas. He lifts the nozzle, inserts it, and then starts filling the Packard's tank.

Jessie wanders out onto the road. Main Street is dirt with some gravel in it. She walks away from town, passing the final side streets, all of which seem to dead end after a block or two.

Just as Floyd calls her name, she comes upon the signs. They're small and weathered, the kind of homemade signs you see for roadside produce stands in northern Iowa. The first says LAKE with an arrow, which strikes her as funny. Wouldn't everybody in town know where the lake is? It isn't as if it can move around. The second sign reads: CARNIVAL. Its arrow points the same way.

Footsteps behind her, then Floyd grabs her by the arm. "Where are you going, Jess?"

She indicates the signs. "That's probably where they all are, don't you think?"

He squints—at her, at the signs, trying to make up his mind if he wants to be vexed or not—then says, "Of course that's where they are, 'course it is." As if the conclusion was his all along. "Come on then. Get back in the car."

Did he pay for the gas he pumped? She cannot be certain. He is both usually honest and ruthlessly cheeseparing. He might easily rationalize that the station owner should have locked up properly if he didn't want to provide free gas.

Jessie finds it interesting that for all that he wants to get to the cabin, after some seven hours of driving he now turns left and heads for the carnival and the lake. Maybe he wants to find the owner of the Sinclair station and pay him, but she suspects that he's as curious as she is about the empty town. Of course, he'll never admit it.

The road here is not oiled either, and the car kicks up a cloud that hangs and slowly drifts behind them. Neither destination seems to be all that close. Enclosed by woods again, they drive up over a rise before they get their first sight of either lake or carnival.

The woods ahead give way to a broad sward on which a half-dozen large tents have been pitched. It looks to have been someone's neglected field on the way down to the lake. The road just runs out, becoming a path well before they reach the first of the tents. Floyd stops the car and shuts off the engine.

The carnival appears as desolated as the town. The tents look as though they were put up twenty years ago. Weather-beaten, mildewed, and trimmed in faded paint, they're the carnival version of Ellende with not a soul in view.

Floyd needs to turn around and go back right now. Jessie no longer cares where the town is lurking, no longer wants to meet them. What's a shortcut if you don't stick to it?—the question rides on her tongue, just inside her lips. But years have taught her not to verbalize it. Silent, she prays hard that he'll be infected by her dread, and act.

Instead, he says, "Let's go see," as if this is a mere detour into rustic tourism, as if the tents promise a bearded lady and a dog-faced boy, a show. He gets out of the car and Jessie thinks *Doesn't he hear them, doesn't he hear the voices?*, which is the point at which she acknowledges that *she* is hearing them, hearing voices like ancient parchment, crumbling and dry, tickling her brain with almost-language, syllables and vowels but in the wrong order, a whispered discordant babble that floats beneath the hissing of the breeze.

Nevertheless, she gets out of the car and sets off after him, calling, "Floyd, wait."

He's entered the nearest tent, the largest one, big enough for a three-ring performance. She reaches the open flap and almost gags from the stench of something rotting inside. It recalls to her the war, triage, and gangrene. She shudders. There's no light within, but enough daylight enters the open flap that her eyes quickly adjust to the dimness as she covers her nose and mouth.

There is something in the center of the tent, weird and sharp, angular and bony like some abstract statue. Only when she draws nearer can Jessie comprehend the shape. It's been assembled tier by tier out of animals that might once have performed in this tent. Somehow, the bones are interlocked, like a cleverly assembled puzzle, stacked and joined into a thing fifteen feet high, with short arms and an antlered skull at the top. It's like a rood but without a Christ.

"Sweet Jesus," says Floyd. He stares transfixed. "Look at this, would you?" Finally, they seem to share the same unease.

"We should go," she urges.

He twists around, gives her *that* look, and she wonders what did she miss? Isn't getting out of here the right answer, the one they just agreed upon?

"Listen," he tells her. "We're not going anyplace until I understand this. This . . . *thing* didn't build itself."

Farther back in the darkness is a mound, source of the terrible stink, that she guesses is the flesh and muscle of the creatures sacrificed to build this freakish totem pole. Terror compels her beyond being further cowed by his bullying. "Who cares who built it?" she says. "Don't you hear the voices, Floyd? In your head?"

"I don't . . . don't care." Even as he says this, they grow louder, as if the mephitic stink of shredded and stripped flesh is wedded to the chant. "It's the call," he says absently as if reminding himself. Then he walks on through the tent as if towards the lure of it.

Jessie runs after him, but not as fast in her bareback pumps and long polka dot skirt that Floyd picked out for her for the trip.

He weaves a path around the next tent and out of sight. Following, she catches up to him, because there on the far side he has stopped dead.

Past a final tent the ground slopes to the lake. Cattails and reeds line most of the bank except where the path arrives at a small beach off which an old rickety dock extends over the water. On the dock stands perhaps a quarter of the populace of Ellende, most of the rest dotting the narrow beach, all softly chanting. Five are standing waist-deep in the lake itself, in a line extending from the dock. Even now, someone else jumps in off the dock and takes a place at the end as someone else wades ashore.

At the head of the line stands a figure in a purple robe with a pointed hood and holding high some sort of oddly shaped iron instrument. This priest slaps his hand upon the forehead of the woman before him and shouts out in the same babbled language that's sliding through Jessie's head, syllables that echo across the lake: "Yhoundeh caireth amach Tsathoggua!" Then he pushes her underwater.

She thinks *Dear God, it's the Klan, we've stumbled into a Ku Klux Klan initiation*, and she hisses, "Floyd! We need to get out of here. Now."

Clouds are amassing over the far shore. If this ritual below isn't unholy enough by itself, a storm looks to be rising in response to it, and something far out is churning the surface of the lake.

Jessie clutches his sleeve. "Floyd." She tugs urgently, trying to turn him, and that's when two more people emerge from the last tent. Also adorned in ritual robes, they gawp at Jessie and Floyd. There's something horribly wrong with them both. Their faces are narrow, as if the sides of their skulls have been pushed together. She thinks of angelfish viewed head-on. Then one of the two cries, "Hey, Rube!" and everyone on the beach and dock below turns and looks up at them.

It isn't just the two nearest creatures. The entire goggling population are the same, mostly chinless, some of them plagued by swellings like goiters at the throat. As a nurse she has seen textbook examples of congenital deformations—enough to know that she's beholding the result of a closed breeding pool that has interrelated for decades if not centuries. She can't be sure of the ones in the water, especially the baptized. The woman has arisen with her features in motion, flowing, gray, wriggling, exactly like the face of the man wading out ahead of her. Her arms, too, but it's a moment before Jessie identifies what she's seeing: Leeches, to which the baptized seem oblivious, have attached to them in. It's not just humans who've heard the call.

The first time she came up north with her husband, a huge leech attached itself to her while she was swimming. It was a gray ribbon of a thing, six inches long, like some grotesque animal's severed tongue, and Floyd had to use ammonia and, finally, his cigar lighter to get it to release. It left a huge bleeding circular pucker on her calf, and they killed it by burying it in the sand. The people dipped in the lake are vampirically infested with them and don't even seem to notice.

The hooded priest shouts more gibberish, a command this time, and the two creatures grab hold of her and Floyd, and drag them down the slope toward the dock.

Floyd doesn't begin to struggle until they're almost on the beach. Then as if coming to his senses, he twists and flails, and bellows, "Take *her*, you idiots, not me! I'm an *Ensley*!" His fury seems to confuse them. The one gripping her relaxes his hold as if he's about to help with Floyd, and Jessie tears herself free, kicks off her bareback shoes and flees back up between the tents, expecting at any second that a hand will grab her, pull her down, her fear so certain that she cries out when she reaches the car. She yanks open the door and dives inside, knocking Floyd's folded shortcut map onto the floor.

The sky above the tents has grown darker, uglier. The thick mass of clouds is shot with lightning and yellowish-green on the underside. She's lived in the Midwest long enough to know the threat of such clouds. It's nature's existential version of the two batrachian creatures that have caught up with her. She locks the doors. One of them reaches his fingers through the vent window, and she grabs the window knob and pushes hard, crushing his fingers between frame and glass. He screeches and tugs to free himself. She only relents when she sees the other one trying to snake his arm all the way in through the passenger vent. The nearest creature tears himself free, stumbling back hard.

Floyd has left the keys in the ignition as he always does. Jessie starts the car. She grinds the gear lever on the column, tries to depress the clutch and shift into reverse. Floyd refused to let her drive. There was in his opinion nothing she needed to do or see on her own, and if she even broached the subject, he would accuse her of planning to meet someone secretly, so she learned not to ask. Thus her experience of driving a car is years' unpracticed at best. But finally the gear catches—not reverse but first— the car lunges forward, dragging along the creature on the passenger side, knocking down the one who's pulled free. The tires thump over him as she steers madly in a circle, digging up the green sward before the right tires find purchase on the dirt path, and the car lurches ahead again. The fingers clinging to the passenger vent window finally slip loose and vanish. In the rearview mirror, everything has darkened, as if storm and roiling lake have converged upon that dock.

She manages to shift into second gear as she plunges along, down the narrow road, the storm lost beyond the woods, until a thread of blackness seems to reach out from the lake and flow after her as though eager to attach to the rear of the Packard. In the mirror it looks to be full of eyes and writhing annelid limbs.

At the "Lake/Carnival" signs she swings right and speeds back through the deserted town, her eyes flicking repeatedly to the mirror where the seemingly conscious darkness surges ever closer. As it rolls through the town after her, the buildings appear to flex and bend in toward its center, then are gone.

She speeds back along a course she mostly slept through, though she wonders how. The wheels thunder over every packed washboard section hard enough to shake her fillings loose. The maw of darkness yawns right behind her now, almost licking the bumper. The rear of the car stretches away from her. Air roars in her ears. She's yelling and doesn't even know it, flooring the accelerator while her hands grip the wheel so tightly it's a wonder she doesn't wrench it loose from the column; and then quite suddenly there's a "pop" as if she's dropped a thousand feet, the sun bursts out, the dirt road is oiled and smooth again, and there's another car coming right at her out of thin air. She cries out, cuts the wheel madly, and the Packard fishtails, sliding off the road and down into the woods, bouncing, bouncing, flinging her forward too fast to recover. She strikes her head once, twice, and the car comes to a rest between two trees with Jessie sprawled along the bench seat.

By the time she sits up, dazed and blinking, the other car has stopped, and the driver, a local man in dungarees, has run over to her. "Miss," he says, "miss, you all right?"

She looks at him as if he's speaking a foreign language. Closes her eyes as she reaches up, touches her head.

"You got a egg-size bump there," he tells her. "Maybe we oughta get you to the ranger station like."

"How'll I get my car out of here?"

"Oh." He assesses the damage. "Well, it don't look too bad. I can maybe back it out for ya."

"That would be . . . I would appreciate it." She opens the door and climbs out, forgetting that she's barefoot until she steps down among the sticks and twigs. Carefully then she makes her way up to the dirt. Her feet sink into it. It feels like she's standing on a cloud.

The motorist starts the engine, and gently shifts into reverse, cautiously backs the Packard up along the ruts it's made in flying off the road. He manages to get the car out of the woods. At that point a local police car arrives. Jessie lets the helpful motorist do most of the talking about what happened. He kindly blames the event on her tires slipping in the oily dirt. They all look back at the ruts of her tires. Impossibly, these only start about twenty feet up the road, as if the car had just been sitting there before leaping forward. It's smooth, oiled dirt beyond that as far as she can see.

The policeman has her perch on the front seat with her legs out the door. He kneels and shines a flashlight at her eyes, seems satisfied by her reaction, but says, "You know, it's against the law to drive barefoot."

"I—no, I didn't, I'm sorry. I'll, uh, get a pair of shoes out of the trunk."

"May I ask where you're coming from?"

"Oh, uh, I was on my way to a rented cabin on Lake O_____. There's this shortcut map." She leans down and picks up the folded map off the floor, opens it up.

The old sheet of paper is blank, not a mark on it beyond dirty smudges, as if it's been carried around in someone's pocket for years.

She masks her dismay, a skill she has long-since mastered in Floyd's company. "Oh, I guess this isn't it after all. I wonder where it got to. In any case, he claimed it would save half an hour off the drive, my husband."

"Well, that might be so, but I would say right now you should stick to the highway. Can't be sure your car hasn't suffered some undercarriage damage and I'd hate to think of you stuck on this dirt road and trying to get a tow truck. Anyways, you're only an hour out even if you stick to the highway."

"What," she asks carefully, "is down this road?"

The motorist chimes in. "A string of cabins, one of 'em's mine. Not on your lake, but on the way there, 'bout five miles along or so."

"Isn't there a town?"

The motorist shakes his head. The policeman adds, "Not for a long while now. Was one, back in the '20s I think it was, that up and vanished."

"It what?"

"Oh, yah, it's near a legend nowadays. Folks figured a twister flattened the place, but ya know there's not a trace of it anywhere, and you'd expect there'd be something left, since tornadoes hardly ever replace a town with woods." He's all but winking at her to let her know he's pulling her leg a little.

The motorist adds, "One of my old neighbors, he says that God went and swallowed up a whole lake to boot, used to be there, too."

"But," adds the policeman, "what's one less lake around here?" He's grinning now. "More likely," he says, "when the highway got put in, it bypassed the town and the place just died. But people like their stories."

She smiles politely. "Well, I promise I'll stick to the highway. But I want to thank both you gentlemen for your assistance. I could have been stuck on this road forever."

The motorist wishes her luck and drives off, heading on to his cabin, back the way she's come. The policeman waits while she gets a pair of shoes out of her luggage. The rear of the car isn't stretched out of shape at all. Already she's telling herself she didn't really see that.

The policeman escorts her back onto the highway. He paces behind her car for about five miles before he turns off with a quick flash of his headlights to say goodbye.

Jessie drives along carefully, not too fast, no cause to hurry. Every time she looks in the rearview mirror, though, she relives that final glimpse she had of the squirming darkness behind her flexing like a cheap pie tin and suddenly snapping back as if reeled in on a line. Floyd's trapped somewhere in there now along with Ellende, and she's probably going to have a hard time finding an explanation to provide folks with, but then she remembers him yelling "Take *her*, you idiots!" and she thinks that she'll find a way.

SWIFT DECLINE

A **back asphalt highway off Route 99 led into the town** of Dogget. It was one of those state roads with a number assigned to it that nobody bothered to use. The kid in the Texaco outside Eccles had just called it *the Dogget Road*.

I rolled in as a beautiful splash of sunset spread across the horizon. Smoke in the atmosphere will give you sunsets like that—after Krakatoa, the whole world was treated to them—but I doubted the effects from underground coal fires made it out of the hills.

Even that sunset couldn't do much for the town. Dogget had passed the "Last Chance" sign and run out of gas. At the city limits a rusting sheet of tin on a pole demanded that I reduce my speed. It looked like the last imposition the town would be making on the world. Obediently, I trolled up Main Street as though I were looking for an address instead of Polly Lutts.

The downtown, such as it was, ran for three abandoned blocks. Buildings on both sides of the street stood boarded over and ramshackle. Some had cardboard "For Sale" signs propped in their dusty windows. They looked like they'd been for sale the day Kennedy was shot. I passed two buildings with big old balconies running the length of them. Might have been hotels back in the '30s; they were flophouses for termites now.

I glanced down a side street, Elm. A faded "Drink Double Cola" was painted on the brick wall there, and beyond it lay more buildings, two, maybe three blocks off the main drag. Past them one plume of smoke hung like a grease stain against the clouds.

I was looking at a rip in the carcass of West Virginia where the cracked and dried–out skin had shrunk back to reveal bones.

Back in the middle of the last century, places like this had movie houses, civic pride and fresh paint. More than a dozen mines in a ten mile radius had coughed up coal. The mines had died fast compared to the towns, but they always did. The populace hung on in blind faith, ignorant of the fact that invisible corporate bodies had already bagged the mineral rights and could strip the rest away any time they pleased. It had been the same up in Pennsylvania--people forced to discover how utterly expendable they were. No, that wasn't quite right. "Expendable" implied somebody still had a use for them.

I counted a barber shop, a grocer's, a filling station that might have been operating in the morning, a Church of God, and, across from it at the end of town, The Meteor Bar. A dozen vehicles surrounded The Meteor like piglets feeding off a sow. Everything else looked closed up, giving the impression that the whole of Dogget had moved in there.

Two stone pillars framed the drive of the church. Grass and weeds grew in its yard and boards "x"ed its skinny windows, but lights were burning on both floors of the rectory house adjoining it. God was hanging on by his fingernails, and He still had power.

I rolled past the bar and then pulled off onto the gravel shoulder. The road curved out of sight ahead behind a mileage sign. Lynchburg was closest. I turned the car around and then backed it into the overgrown church driveway. The pillars and weeds would hide it from anyone passing by—not that there appeared to be anyone left to pass by.

After turning off the engine, I pocketed the keys, got out and crossed the road, armed with a small Maglite. The clear air had gone chilly, the way the cold settles into valleys and drags the dust down with it. I hunched in my jacket as I walked along the row of parked cars in search of a blue plate that said, "You've got a friend in—XPN 885—Pennsylvania": Mrs. Polly Lutts's car. If it had been there, I could have gone back to my motel outside Eccles a happy man and gotten a good night's sleep. Curiously, I found cars with tags from Tennessee, Ohio, even North Dakota—a long way to come to be here—but the errant Mrs. Lutts was absent, or at least she hadn't driven to the bar.

Somewhere up in those black, ominous hills something boomed like a freight train shaking loose its cars. That was probably what it was. The noise reminded me of hanging out the window of my bedroom as a kid and watching the headlamps of trains go flickering through the woods way off down the hill.

I wove between a four by four and a station wagon, noticing at a touch on the hood that both were cold. "Happy Hour" had been going on a while.

I opened the door. Everything stood quiet, absolutely still. It was not the sort of stillness where a lot had been going on before I came in either. There was no music playing. The TV wasn't on.

I looked around at maybe twenty people—the ceiling lights were so dim that the blinking strings of old Christmas lights around the top of the bar were tossing off most of the illumination. I couldn't be certain how many lurked in the booths against the far wall.

They'd raised their heads at the creak of the door but hadn't paused in their conversations, because there weren't any conversations. These people were sitting still as death without saying one word to each other. I turned and dragged the door shut. What the hell had I walked into?

It was a good-sized place, with an old wood dance floor off to the right between me and the other booths. All the bar stools looked taken but there was room to stand at the opposite side, and I headed there, which gave me a closer look at the patrons.

Prominent eyes gave me sidelong glances, a dozen faces that looked deformed by a combination of thyroid imbalance and mongoloidism, half of them under billed caps. People joke about inbreeding in rural populations but this looked like a homologous family reunion. I leaned up to the bar.

The bartender, a wide-eyed chicken ready to be geeked, limped over like it was the last thing on Earth he wanted to do. The leg seemed to pain him a little.

"Beer?" I asked.

"Got *Moose* on tap," he replied, rubbing his thigh.

"That'd be fine."

He nodded and reached without looking for a mug off the shelf. Beside me a tall guy in a short sleeve shirt and dirty trousers got up, saying, "You can have this stool, mister." Looking at him directly I saw that his left cheek seemed corroded, as if by acid. He shuffled behind me to a booth and sat down.

I skooched up on the stool and took out a pack of cigarettes. I didn't know if that was allowed in the Meteor, but even someone telling me I couldn't smoke was the start of a conversation. Not here though. Cigarette in a vacuum here. Nobody said a word or bummed a smoke, but they did watch. They watched me light up as if it was an arcane ritual they'd only heard about.

The bartender set my Moosehead on a coaster, and I paid him. I took a few sips, blew a little smoke, and tried to appear relaxed, which in that atmosphere meant devoid of consciousness. There wasn't a sign of the elusive Polly Lutts.

She'd run away from home, left her teenage son and angry husband. All evidence pointed to this unlikely ghost town as her destination. Their phone bills had revealed that over the past few months she'd placed half a dozen calls to Dogget. Lutts said his wife had a best friend from high school who'd gotten married and moved here, God knew why. He'd given me a snapshot of two high school girls in their blue graduation robes. They were laughing the way you'd expect on so solemn an occasion. "Me 'n Carrie," was scrawled in ballpoint on the back. Big, rounded, childish letters.

The other photo I had of Polly Lutts showed a nice-looking woman with permed sunset-red hair and sad eyes. I had a feeling I knew the source of that sadness, but he'd hired me to find her. I hadn't made any promises to bring her home though. If I did find her, maybe I could get her to seek counseling, or maybe a restraining order. Lutts claimed she was going through some sort of midlife crisis that he didn't understand, and maybe that's all it was. But in that case, had it been me, I'd have fled to South Beach and gotten a tan. I would not have come to Dogget, West Virginia to share the rot with my best friend from high school.

By the time I'd finished half my beer, some of the eyes had stopped watching me, but no one had proffered a conversation, either. They seemed to be waiting for something.

People have a way of assigning a stratification system to themselves. They tend to cluster, to form tightly knit groups within the larger population. They do this in all kinds of situations. Some play pool, others huddle and talk about sports or politics or spouses they'd like to brain. Even in a crowd, if you watch, you can see the individuals connect and divide like cells, spot who thinks he's charge and who's following. In that bar either nobody connected or they were all of the same grim purpose.

I tabulated the oddities around me. In a booth on my right, one woman had gone bald over the crown of her head that her emplastered, bleached hair couldn't hide, while the man across from her had a goiter a bullfrog would have been proud of. Elsewhere, knots of flesh, all those bulging eyes, and one case of mushrooming lip cancer—I couldn't have found this much deformity in a hospital waiting room. I thought of places like Love Canal and Chernobyl, and towns in Poland and Romania where industrial poisons had soaked into the gene pool. Did toxic wastes permeate Dogget? I'd thought coal mining just promoted black lung.

I drank a little more beer. The guy beside me had on a suitcoat, stained and in need of pressing, but probably no dry cleaning service remained in town. He looked like a fat used car salesman, or the mayor. He had a mustache over his pushed out, fishy mouth, and a bulbous nose. In the mirror behind the bar his large eyes seemed periodically to swivel my way, but when I glanced at him he was looking dead ahead, his utter disregard of my existence defying my experience. Nobody was this incurious.

"Cold night," I said.

Slowly, as if pulling against enormous magnetism, his head, then his eyes, swung in my direction. Straight on, he looked even more fishlike. The eyes did shift now, as if searching for the memory of speech. "Cold. Nnnh, cold night, sure is." At once he began turning away.

"Is it always like this in Dogget?"

"Always. And forever. World without end." A slow turn to face me. "You passing through?"

"Yup," I said, "on my way up from Lynchburg."

"Long drive. Out of the way, here." Big pearls of sweat had broken out on his brow, as if it strained him to talk. I could feel other customers looking our way.

"Yeah, some business in Eccles," I said.

"I've made that drive. State Patrol like to pick you up on the road. You prolly shouldn't drink too much."

"Thanks for the advice."

"I'd go."

"Right. Thanks." I squashed my cigarette in a tin ashtray and finished off the beer.

The restrooms were at the far end of the bar. I pushed up and headed that way. As I passed each booth, I glanced in but kept my head down as if looking at the floor. Some of them gazed over, big eyes glistening.

In the fourth booth along the wall I thought I saw a familiar face. Her hair was a tangle of thin blonde strands over darker roots. Askance I was sure it was Polly's friend, Carrie. But straight on, I saw that she had the same vaguely amphibian features as the others, and I thought that while you might put on a lot of pounds, you wouldn't change that much. All the same, I hesitated long enough to look at the other two women in the booth. Neither of them was Polly Lutts. Clearly, I'd made a mistake.

When I opened the restroom door, I found a man inside. Tall and lanky and wearing a billed cap, he stood at the far end, with the tiny window open. It was too high, and so he'd overturned a bucket and was balanced on that. Upon my arrival, he became confused, and dropped down off the bucket, then didn't know what to do with himself. His hands were twitching, his big eyes contemplating the one stall. Finally he gave up all pretense of having a reason to be there and lit out.

I closed the door after him, then made legitimate use of the urinal. The sink was by the window, and after I washed my hands, I stepped up on his bucket. Out the window I could see across the road the lights inside the rectory house. If I looked hard, I could distinguish the glint of metal that was the snout of my car sticking out from between the old pillars of the drive. So much for my cleverness.

Whatever was going on here, I wasn't armed with anything more lethal than a Nikon, a Maglite and two canisters of Mace. This had begun in the category of a simple missing person's case. Most of those, you find out the wife has fled to a boyfriend. You take a few pictures of his trailer and his pickup, of the happy couple on the way to a pancake breakfast, and then you go home, collect your fees and let the husband file for divorce. Later you maybe sit in court and describe what you saw while making eye contact with the adulterers in question. It's no big deal, and no guns, knives, or chainsaws are involved. No idiot car chases through remarkably accommodating traffic. Nobody dies, they just misbehave and get a spanking. Here, I'd thought maybe the runaway had fled an abusive husband—actually, I still thought so. But my inconsiderable case had become entangled in something else, and damned if I could figure out what. Casting call for a Todd Browning film, maybe.

I dried my hands, then eased open the restroom door. The tall guy from the bucket was sitting on my stool. He still had the jitters. I didn't think he would ride that stool for long but I couldn't stay to find out. Heads were turning my way. I pretended not to see, and strode out through the door.

The cold outside air stinking of coal fire crossed me like a slap. I lingered a moment to light up another cigarette, then tromped back across the gravel lot to the road, and edged past my car. I strolled up the driveway toward the rectory. If everyone in the bar was watching it, I might as well find out why.

The man who answered the door showed himself to be confused by my presence, which made sense, given the state of Dogget. His was the first face I'd seen that didn't appear to have a fish in the family tree. Large-jawed and unshaven, he was tall, a little stoop-shouldered, and dressed in a collarless shirt and dungarees held up by old-fashioned braces. It was like encountering a member of the Joad family. His focus flicked past me for an instant, then back again.

"Who you?" he said.

"I'm a fella who's looking for someone." His brows knitted. I took a chance. "Nobody over at the bar could help me, so I thought the town pastor might know the new faces." I handed him the photo of Polly Lutts.

The skin around his eyes tightened as he looked it over. I hoped he wasn't going to lie and tell me he'd never seen her. He swung the door open wider and said, "You'd best come in."

The interior of the house had a grimy antiquity to it—antimacassars on the back of an old worn couch, and lace trimming around the bottom of the rocker. The lamps cast a yellowish low-watt light, and all over the walls hung posters proclaiming "Vita-

Z. The Miracle Drink! Become as Reborn!" "Dr. Hiram Fulgit's Amazing Discovery! God's Waters of Life!" and "Life from the Stars. Cures All Bodily Evils! Vita-Z!" A lot of exclaiming. Assorted blue-glass bottles of every shape lined the shelves and mantle over the fireplace, although in the center of it lay what looked like a baseball sized chunk of dark geode. Some of the old bottles still bore Vita-Z labels.

I stuck a thumb toward one of posters. "Mailbox out by the road says *Fulgit* on it," I told him as if he didn't know.

"My great-grandad. I was named for him." He closed the door. A shotgun, I noticed, was propped against the wall behind it.

"So, he was in the patent medicine business."

Strands of his greasy hair sliced one of his eyes in two, and he pushed them aside with his palm. "Oh, no, sir, not like you think at all. Show you somethin."

"Well, okay, but about the woman in the photo—"

"Oh, she's here," he replied, as if it was nothing. "I'm keepin' her upstairs and away from *them*." His head dipped toward the front door.

"That's why they're watching your house?"

"Are they? Miserable fools, can they not wait? I say to you, we wrestle not against flesh and blood, but against principalities," he proclaimed, as if that clarified something. "I'll take you up to her, but let me show you this here first."

I followed him through his house. Stacks of newspapers, yellow and dry, stood on the floor and shared some of the chairs along with mail that had never been opened. It was the house of a crazy old man, but at least he'd taken in Polly Lutts.

The kitchen gave onto a mud room full of small crates. An open one revealed more blue bottles amid straw packing. These had new labels affixed to them. He snatched up a big flashlight lying across the corner of the crate and led me outside.

We hiked across a deep yard. On my left the church loomed out of the night, and in the light of flashlight I could see that it needed a lot of scraping and new paint.

"The whole town's a cavin' in," he said over his shoulder. "Coal veins run all underneath her. Even here. Some been on fire for decades. Eventually we're all goin' under if we leave things like they are. Can't do that. Here we go."

We walked up a hillock toward what I thought at first was a shrine, like a Catholic grotto. It was a big, open circular structure, and in the middle of it was a boulder, and beneath that a small pool. Hiram stopped in front of the pool and shone the light up above it. I saw that the grotto was made of blackish lumps of rock all cemented together into an arch, a kind of miniature amphitheater.

"'Bout a century ago," he said, "a meteor crashed right here one night. Wasn't no church here at that time, just a piece of land my family farmed and a skinny dirt road out front. Thing came down outen the sky and smacked into the ground here. Old Hiram came running, and stood over it. This one big hunk was bright red and smoking, and the rest had broke into bits spread all over the area. But there was water trickling out from under this one."

"This?" I nodded at the pool. His light sparkled on a thin trickle running from beneath the boulder into it.

"Oh, yeah, hasn't moved." He laughed. "Opened up a natural spring where it hit. Great grandad, he scoured the area and found the other pieces of the thing and built this, like a shrine.

"See, he came with a pail and took some of that water back to the house, and he drank some. He'd been suffering from gout and arthritis something awful. Plagues our whole family, the rheumatism. Anyhows, one sip of the water coming out of the ground here, and he was all but cured of every pain."

"I do see. He built himself this . . . shrine, and started bottling Vita-Z."

"That's right." He swung the light away, and for a moment that trickle of water glowed on its own. I turned to follow him. He waved the light at the church. "Hiram Fulgit had been a man of God, preaching the gospel in tents all around. He saw this as the hand of God touching him, and so he started preachin' here and selling his miracle water, too."

"He didn't give it away?"

Ignoring me, he went on, "By the time my daddy was born, they'd erected a church here." Hiram kept going along the side of it.

"Well, nostrums and the Bible have mixed before."

"No sir, this here's no confidence game. This is water from the stars. Got properties you can't even begin to imagine."

I thought about the people in the bar across the road. "Maybe I'll have to take a bottle home with me," I said.

"Gotta try it soon. Don't know how long it'll be available. Spring dried up back seventy-five years ago and only just reappeared this year again. Been all I can do to keep up for fear it'll stop. You want to try it. Time's coming, and only the chosen shall be saved."

"God says, 'Drink Vita-Z,' huh?"

"God's not what you think." He held the door for me to go back through the mud room.

"Sorry. You keep your beliefs. I just want to see Polly Lutts, and find out if she wants to go home."

"Her husband beats her, did you know that?"

We were back in the parlor among the bottles and bad lighting.

"She told you that?"

He shook his head. "She told Carrie, and Carrie told me. She doesn't want to go back, mister."

Well, he'd confirmed my own misgivings, hadn't he? I said, "I had my suspicions. I'm not here to make her go back, just to establish this is where she's run to. I'll even help her get assistance if that's what she wants. But I do have to see her for myself, you understand."

"You say so. Well-uh, she's up here, come on." He gestured, then led me to the stairs. "You sure you wouldn't want to try some Vita-Z first?"

"Thanks, but the sooner I see Mrs. Lutts, the sooner I'm out of your hair."

Without another word, he led the way up the creaking stairs and into a dim hallway. More yellowish light emerged from beneath one of the doors. He opened that door and stepped back, the light flowing over him like paint.

Tensed against I don't know what, I stepped into the doorway. Polly Lutts lay spreadeagled on a bare mattress on the floor, eyes open, stark naked and chained. A dark lump squatted between her knees—another chunk of that meteorite. Weird symbols covered the floor around her. I saw that she was alive, breathing, but she didn't so much as acknowledge our arrival. Like a dope I said, "What?" and then my head lit up. I have vague recollections of pitching forward on top of her, of chains rattling beside my head, of voices, of being kicked, shoved, rolled over.

I came to on my back on the bare mattress. I tried to sit up and my head thundered with outrage. Concussion. I lay still, groaned, waited for an idea.

A door slammed downstairs. I moved again, slowly this time, but my arm wouldn't play. I'd been chained to the leg of the bed beside me. Glancing at the bed, I saw a shape underneath it, and I rolled to the side and reached under with my free hand. It was that damned lump of ugly meteorite. Up close the outer surface of it looked like armor: Small plates side by side forming a thick convex surface, like rhinoceros hide.

I sat up cautiously. Car doors slammed, engines revved. I glanced over my shoulder to see lights moving outside the window. The chain had been strung through a loop on the cuff around my wrist. They must have been in a hurry not to have done me up as they had Polly. I stared awhile at the chains, the chunk of rock. My brain had trouble coming on line, unable to connect any dots. Finally, enough thought percolated, gathered, that I picked up the rock and brought it down on the chain. The links, I saw, weren't all that strong. Polly Lutts could have broken it if *all* her limbs hadn't been restrained. What had happened in this room?

I banged down the rock again. My brain pounded to get out of my skull, and the rock, that stupid piece of galaxy debris, began to heat up in my hand. I slammed it down again. Now it hurt to hold onto. Screw the concussion. I yelled, "Jesus Christ!" and slammed it down again, hard. The chain link snapped. I tossed the meteorite and began unthreading the chain. Then out of the corner of my eye I thought I saw the chunk of rock move. I stopped. Turned.

The rock flexed, then wobbled. It was swelling, breathing. I tore the chain out of that cuff as fast as I could, and rolled out of the space between those symbols. My foot kicked the rock and it slid toward the window. The last few cars were pulling out, their lights playing across the ceiling.

Something whiplike snaked out of the underside of the rock and slapped the mattress where I'd been. It was slick, greenish, and the ticking hissed, crackled, and tore where it touched.

I scrambled to the door, flung it back, and ran for the stairs.

Nothing came after me.

The shotgun still leaned against the wall behind the door. I grabbed it, snapped open the breech. Both barrels were loaded. I spent a minute then rooting through various drawers and cupboards, finally opening an under-the-stairs closet where I found boxes of shells. My head throbbed like a boombox.

Out the door, I lurched down the drive and into my car. I gunned the engine, backed out in a cloud of dust onto blacktop. Only one car remained at the bar. I saw it in my rearview mirror as I barreled toward Dogget. Wherever they'd gone, they had all gone together. I hit the center of town before I had the sense to turn off my headlights and look around. Through the trees to the left I caught a glimpse of taillights in the darkness, like a Christmas tree string, all red, but traveling in the direction opposite mine. Next chance I had, I turned left and headed after them.

Navigating by parking lights, I had to go slowly. I didn't want the others seeing me, and I didn't want to find myself airborne either.

I reached the gravel road I'd seen them on, turned left again. This road ran along the side of a ridge. Far ahead over a small rise I could see a brief bright glow of someone stepping on their brake lights. There was a lot of dust in the air.

The other cars had driven three sides of a square covering a mile or so. Near the top of the rise I shut off my lights and cautiously rolled forward until I could see over it. Down the road a hundred yards or more, flashlights floated around like fireflies for a few minutes, and then winked out. It was just me and the cloud-covered night.

To be safe I switched off the dome light before easing out of the car. I stuffed my pockets with shotgun shells, drew the gun out after me, eased the door shut, then started up the road. No silent approach on gravel, but I tried to make as little noise as possible.

Beyond the rise cars had been parked every which way across a plateau. It was like a junkyard. The plateau pressed up against a sharp hillside. Off past the cars I could make out Fulgit's church tower against what had to be the lights of the Meteor Bar and the highway. We had looped all the way around behind it.

I wove between cars, shotgun at the ready, but no one had stayed behind. They had no cause to expect any trouble: I was chained up back in the house, prey for their little monster.

The hillside, as I approached it, showed a darker patch in the center. At that point, my toe caught on something immovable and I stumbled. I knelt, patted the ground. My hand wrapped around a cold steel rail. It ran toward the dark patch. I realized I was looking at a mine entrance. No wonder the hillside was so steep; it was artificially so.

Inside the mine entrance it was truly pitch black. It smelled like motor oil out of an old Ford pickup.

I listened but there was nothing, no movement, no one near, so I tucked the shotgun under my arm, took out my Maglite and, with one hand cupped around the lens, twisted it on. My hand abruptly glowed red and slivers of light spilled around my fingers, enough that I could make out the twin rails, wooden ties beneath them, a sheen of creosote or grease. Raising my head, I saw the car.

The cream Toyota had been parked off to the side of the rail, nose-in. The tag, "XPN-885," gleamed dully. Naturally. Who'd ever look for a missing vehicle in a coal mine? Next time I went looking for a chop shop in Pennsylvania coal country, I would have to remember that.

The keys were in it. I supposed there had been no reason to take them. Keep them with the car and then nobody could accidentally leave them lying around for the authorities to find.

Farther down the tunnel, I played my light around for a moment. On a thick beam overhead someone had carved "1924." I played the light across the ground ahead to make sure the way was clear, then shut it off. I kept one foot alongside the rail.

Soon I could see a dim glow ahead, which turned out to be from an adjoining tunnel. This one was newer, and strange. The supports were stone, cut like squat obelisks, and though the ground crunched underfoot, the uneven walls and ceiling looked almost polished, or fused, as if intense heat had melted the surfaces.

The light grew brighter and brought with it voices, joined in a kind of chant. All of a sudden came a yell, Hiram Fulgit, shouting something like "Kaykeebah!" The sound bounced around ahead, coming from somewhere beyond where the tunnel sloped.

Reaching the slope, I pressed back behind a pillar and looked down into a broader cavern. Everybody had gathered there. Flashlights and lanterns, set down or stood on end, surrounded a couple dozen figures. It took me a moment to understand what I was seeing.

They'd all devolved further, into something even less human and more froglike: Hump-backed, their arms shortened, hands splayed, webbed; grotesque faces with thickened snouts and bulging eyes. They stood in a circle around a slab of rock. Hiram Fulgit, unchanged, stood upon the slab, declaiming in some language I couldn't identify. At his feet lay poor Polly Lutts. Fulgit held one of his elixir bottles, which he poured over her body as he shouted.

I raised the shotgun, trying to figure out how I could shoot him and not kill her, seeing myself foolishly wading into their midst where I would be torn apart, unable to reload fast enough to kill all of them. As I tried to sort out my options, Polly suddenly arched her back like in an extreme yoga pose. She screamed. The crowd roared--a burbling, inhuman chorus. Fulgit knelt, opened another bottle of his Vita-Z and poured it into her open mouth. He raised his arms to the ceiling and called out, "Come, Nyarlathotep, black wizard! Come Yog-Sothoth! We open your gate!"

I stopped thinking how I would deal with them. I stopped thinking at all.

Polly's body bent up higher. I heard bones snap, joints crack. Her hands slid beneath her and touched her toes—no, joined them. The flesh of her body twisted. Breasts, arms, head, all flowed like some awful putty. A loop of it snagged Fulgit's wrist and he dropped the bottle. He shrieked, "No!" His hand melted into her, and more strands snaked around his throat, his back. The look on his face just before the thing broke his neck said it all: He'd thought he was in charge of this. His mass joined hers and the fleshy ring expanded. The frog people roared, wriggling, wobbling. The ring thinned as it grew. Out of the dark center of it, something began to emerge. Feelers protruded, twitching and alive, seeking purchase. They lashed to the edge of the stone slab and around the fleshy ring, and pulled. A thing like some enormous deformed squid slowly began to appear. Its bulbous awful head pushed into view, a mouth edged in needle teeth, red eyes on stalks. It moved as if fighting against a relentless current. I turned and ran back up the tunnel.

Skidding into the coal tunnel, I found two more frog things approaching, come late to the party. Waving flashlights at me, they gawped and shook. One of them let loose a wordless bellow. I pulled both triggers on the shotgun, and the things erupted into geysers of blackish goop. The stink was worse than a sewer.

The thunder of the shot echoed everywhere. Now I was for it. The other frogs would come hunting me while their squid god finished oozing into our world.

I reached Polly's Toyota. I popped the breech of the shotgun and reloaded, then laid it down and opened the trunk. Desperate for something I could use, I was rewarded with two oily rags. I took them, tied them together, then pulled off the gas cap and stuffed them down into the throat of the gas tank. I slammed the trunk, grabbed the gun, and got into the car.

The engine turned over, caught. I backed up and headed down the tunnel again, felt and heard the tires squish over the corpses just before I swung it into the new tunnel. The passenger side scraped one of the support pillars, snapping off the side mirror.

A few of the frog things had made it up the incline and now shambled toward me. They raised their stubby arms and yowled, goggle-eyed. I stopped the car, climbed out and shot them. I took my lighter out and lit the oily rag behind me. It caught quickly. I dropped the shotgun, got in again, revved the engine and released the brake. The car lurched forward. I floored the pedal, and the car raced for the top of the slope. The instant before it became airborne, I jumped. I hit sharp stones, slammed against the wall, but made myself get to my knees, then upright, as the Toyota sailed into the cavern. Something beyond it squealed. I started to run back up the tunnel. Behind me, the car exploded, and I fell again, scraping my hands and knees further, got up and reached the shotgun as a second explosion shook the whole place. The end of the tunnel burned brightly with sprayed fuel. A chunk of roof collapsed beside me. I jumped, then watched a fissure split the ceiling all the way from the cavern and past me. I ran for my life then. Everything began falling in around me, and I pressed in against one of the uprights, shielding my face, praying the support would hold. Dust drowned me. The gasoline blaze disappeared behind a solid wall of collapsed rock.

When it was over, I stood in a pocket that hadn't caved in. I was coughing so hard that I doubled over, and each cough was like an ice pick to my brain.

Ahead, part of the tunnel remained open, and by flashlight I made my way to where it was blocked. Took me half an hour to clear a passage through for myself. In that time I re-ran what had happened, what must have happened. Something had crashed here a hundred years ago, something that poisoned the population, maybe altering their DNA. Was it waiting, or not strong enough till now? Or did the mutation have to work through successive generations? When the call had come, they'd all been drawn back to Dogget. It explained the cars, the license plates. I wondered if Hiram would have served as the goat if Polly Lutts hadn't inadvertently wandered into town. She'd fled one horror only to fall victim to another.

Squeezing through the hole I made, I found more collapsed rock beyond it, but that had left a space at the side through which I could drag myself and the shotgun, and which let onto the main tunnel. The 1924 shaft had withstood the explosion intact. I muttered, wheezing, "Just don't build them like they used to." I stumbled up the tunnel and out into the night air. The stink of coal fires in the night was the smell of heaven.

The rolling landscape back toward the bar was now lit by small fires and half a dozen tendrils of smoke. The church tower had canted to the side. The coal tunnel must have collapsed beneath it, too.

I turned away and dragged my feet down the road to my car. My pants were ripped, knees bleeding, palms, too. I hawked and spat some crud from my lungs. I got in. After a minute my head stopped hammering and I started the engine. I would have to take it easy on the way to Eccles, find a hospital there, pray my brain didn't seize up before that. Then, if I lived, I wanted a bath and a smoke and a drink. Only then would I call Albert Lutts and tell him his wife wasn't here anymore, and Dogget . . . Dogget had really gone downhill.

THE SEALS OF NEW R'LYEH

D
id you hear something?" Detwiler asked.
Stipe paused to listen.
Detwiler couldn't help himself; he glanced back down
the tunnel. He could hear blood ringing in his ears; underneath
that he wasn't sure if he heard wind or the "whump-whump" of
leathery wings. It was paranoia. He needed confirmation of that.

"Besides wind, you mean?" Stipe asked.

"Yeah."

"Just them chanting upstairs. But you have to listen hard."

"Fine. Let's hurry up." Detwiler turned his attention back to
his pry bar. He'd already chipped out the mortar around the massive stone block, enough room to wedge the bar in. Whatever else
he had to say about life under Cthulhu, he appreciated the de-
pendability of the architecture—dependable in the sense that it
made the removal of one stone from the foundation wall a simple
matter of physics. Fulcrums, levers, and offset stones. Stipe referred to the form as *Ugaritic*. In the old days, Stipe had read a lot
on the toilet, mostly National Geographics. Detwiler only cared
that he could pull out one stone and not have the whole wall col-
lapse on top of him.

Together they revolved the loosened stone. Then Stipe got a
rope around it, and they pulled it out. It hit the floor of the tunnel
with a boom that must have set off seismographs in Mongolia, assuming either Mongolia or seismographs existed any longer.

They paused to listen again. No wings, no sound beyond the
distant roar of wind. Nobody—more to the point, nothing—was
crawling down the tunnel after them; and now there was a hole in
the wall big enough to climb through.

"This better work," said Detwiler.

"John. If Cthulhu catches you inside the vault, what'll he do to you?"

"Pull me apart like your little brother torturing an insect?"

"And if you go back to living in the rubble of our dying world?"

"The same, I suppose. Just, you know, later on."

"So?"

"Yeah, great." Detwiler flicked on his halogen flashlight and pulled himself halfway into the hole.

Inside lay a vault exactly as Stipe had described, as huge as a cathedral, with twisted columns of stone supports. It was almost how he'd imagined Ali Baba's cave to look back when he was a kid. Ali Baba had been something of a role model. Thieves who rode in, got what they wanted, and rode out again to their secret lair. Detwiler figured a lot of his disappointments as a thief were because nobody rode in on horseback anymore. And that was before Cthulhu had shown up and pretty much flattened civilization. Try to find a horse *now*.

This time, however, things were looking up. The vault abounded with riches, and everywhere golden and silvery objects glinted in the light of his torch. Two enormous soapstone tubs presented heaps of cracked emeralds and what he dared to hope were uncut diamonds, a few as big as his fist. The tubs were covered with carvings, inhuman figures in relief. He wondered who had done the work. Some poor slob enslaved by the hideous Cthulhu, probably destroyed the moment he finished. "There are jewels in here, Stipe!" he called back. "We have to take some jewels. We can't break in here and not take some jewels."

"Okay, we'll get some jewels, but what about the stuff?"

Detwiler waved the flashlight around. Across the chamber, set on clawfooted displays stood five circular seals the size of garbage can lids. "Oh, yeah," he said.

"Let me see!" Stipe pulled him out of the hole. Detwiler handed him the torch, and Stipe leaped into the hole almost froglike. Then, "Oh," he said, as if a woman had just unexpectedly made a pass at him—which for Stipe would have been a life-changing event. He drew himself out. "The seals."

"They're worth a lot, right?" Detwiler asked doubtfully.

"Detwiler. They're so valuable nobody even believes they exist."

He considered that. "Good," he replied. "Then nobody will believe when they aren't there anymore."

Stipe bent down and picked up one of three duffels they'd brought, pushed it into the hole, and climbed in after it. Detwiler sighed. Grabbed the remaining two bags. So typical of Stipe that he had taken only his own duffel. Stipe the solipsist, a curse and a blessing; it meant that he was always looking for a score, but also that once he had had his own, he lost all interest in everybody else's circumstance. This had resulted in Detwiler's one stretch in juvie two decades ago, and five months in Otisville more recently.

Now that Cthulhu had come along and shredded the fabric of society not to mention time and space, everybody he'd known in the joint was free. A lot of them, he thought, probably shouldn't have been. And because of Stipe, Detwiler felt he bore some responsibility for Cthulhu in the first place, an opinion that was not going to make him popular with the remaining clusters of humanity.

Not unless his plan worked.

The cult of Glynn Beckman had caught Stipe's attention for a couple of reasons. First, most of its members were wealthy inbred loons too scabrous even for the Ayn Rand followers to tolerate, but like Rand's thugs, smug in their superiority, so much so that they tended to leave a lot of things unlocked—like for instance the walk-in safe in Beckman's study where the cult's finances and papers were kept—and available, like the valuable artworks decorating Beckman's walls. That appealed to Stipe so much he joined the cult before they'd finished buttering him up. Actually, they didn't know him as Stipe, but as Kellogg, the current and insanely wealthy scion of the cereal empire of the same name.

The cult was far more cautious and guarded about a book that Beckman claimed to have translated. He claimed that his was the only accurate translation anywhere. "All other followers of the mad Alhazred made mistakes. That's why everyone from Whately to Akeley—who refused to act, the fool!—ultimately failed to open the gate. *Yog-Sothoth* is indeed the gate, but it's only the first of six!"

It all had something to do with seals.

"Like at the circus?" Detwiler had asked.

Stipe had replied, "No, I don't think so."

All he expected Detwiler to do was pretend to be a rich refrigerator magnate and a total believer in Beckman's lunacy. "A couple nights in the house, we wait till everybody's asleep, load up all we can carry, and get out of there. By the time they notice we haven't shown up for mimosas, we're like in New Hampshire."

It sounded ridiculously simple, which was probably why Detwiler thought it couldn't possibly work. But once he was inside the house and, dressed in a rented tuxedo, and was given a tour of the place, he had to admit it looked as simple as it sounded. The artwork wasn't wired. The safe was left ajar. And when he mentioned this to Beckman, the answer astounded him. "After we open the gate, my friend, there'll be no need for alarms, security, protection." As Beckman explained, he puffed on a cigar the size of the Hindenberg. "We shall rule the world!"

Yep, Detwiler agreed, nuts. There was no time to waste. The group was preparing for a big ritual the following night. Detwiler worked out the scenario: the two of them would pretend to get drunk while celebrating and pass out downstairs, allowing all others to go to bed. Then they would clean the place out. He determined the fastest route through the house while carrying priceless Miros and Picassos. He'd already gotten the code number that opened the front gate of the estate—the one security element Beckman did rely upon (and which Stipe had missed). All they had to do was join in the group's little event.

Of course things hadn't exactly followed the script. The ceremony with the weird stone seal, which Beckman split in two, had ripped open reality, a horrible, lightning-charged rending that Detwiler still couldn't believe he'd witnessed. From some other foul and pestilent dimension, Cthulhu slithered into this one. Unfortunately, he proved to be about the size of Godzilla, far larger than Beckman's house. The whole place came down, beams and ceilings caving in, circuits bursting into flame. Cultists were crushed left and right, including Beckman himself.

Detwiler hightailed it into the study as the building collapsed around him. He threw open the door of the walk-in safe, at which point something clocked him. Stipe later claimed it was a plumbing fixture from the second floor, just as he claimed that Detwiler had survived only because Stipe had dragged him into the walk-in safe. That had shielded them both. But Detwiler had awakened alone. True to form, Stipe had snatched half the cash from the safe and taken off.

Cash, of course, had already become a useless commodity. Cthulhu and the rest of his loathsome, wet, leathery entourage leveled Maine in an afternoon, and then settled in for a long stay, laying seige to the whole east coast. The next week was like a bad B-monster movie, with various militaries throwing everything at them. Some of the lesser creatures were destroyed, but Cthulhu seemed only to devour the energy flung his way. Even the nuclear option failed, although nobody would be living in Baltimore again before 2400 A.D.

Like cockroaches that had lurked in the woodwork, a network of cults uncannily like Beckman's had emerged across the world, pledging their allegiance to the god. According to stories that he heard later, only some of them survived the contact. "Some people never learn," Detwiler mused. Granted, the ones who did survive had it better than most everyone else. The arrangement reminded him of trustees in Otisville.

Detwiler lived quite some time in the Beckman house safe. It provided protection against the weather, and the location remained undisturbed. Nobody wanted to come near.

From the remains of the house—notably the basement pantry--he managed to retrieve assorted canned goods and jellies. A plethora of jellies. It seemed that Mrs. Beckman had enjoyed canning jalapeño jelly for all occasions. In Detwiler's case, "all occasions" meant just that.

He scrounged boxes of crackers, but really missed not having some cream cheese. Somebody, probably Cthulhu, had stepped directly on the refrigerator.

The next weeks, he pulled up various parts of the house, occasionally finding someone's remains, including Beckman's. The cigar case and lighter from the suit jacket were about all that survived intact. Finally he came upon the broken seal and other objects from the ceremony.

When the food was about to run out, Detwiler gathered up the remaining supplies and recovered items in a large leather laptop satchel and over a period of months worked his way down the coast and back to the Bronx, or what it had become.

The creatures had taken over. They had marshaled the survivors of Beckman's inter-dimensional holocaust into an army of slaves to build monuments to the great Cthulhu, with cultists as their overseers. Already the landscape was starting to look like a representation of ancient Egypt, if the Egyptians had ingested a lot of magic mushrooms before constructing their pyramids. He learned to avoid the barrel-shaped guardians with eyes on tentacles and huge bat wings, and subsisted mostly on canned goods while trying to ascertain what use somebody with his skills was in a world turned so upside down.

He came upon people hiding out in underground garages and former basements and shooting each other over who got to sleep on a dirty piece of cardboard. How good it was to see that we'd all settled our differences in the face of a common enemy.

The general opinion was that over a billion people had perished in the first week alone, but nobody knew what was true. It was merely the prevailing rumor. The future for Detwiler narrowed to encompass how to get food, how to survive the night without being shot, and how to stay warm as the weather turned cool. The last thing he expected ever again was to encounter Stipe.

One afternoon as he was creeping through some rubble, Detwiler came to an oddly fashioned tunnel. It wasn't a sewer tunnel or a subway. It was something that looked freshly carved, and weirdly organic, glowing with an eerie rippling phosphorescence, as if the walls within were pulsating, a kind of living formation that produced patterns as he passed by—at least it seemed organic until he came to a wall of immense, roughly rectangular stones. Those appeared to be the foundation for something aboveground. Detwiler suspected that he'd blundered beneath one of the weird temples. He turned to leave, only to find his way blocked by a Twinkie.

As such creations went, this was the granddaddy of Hostess desserts, a slithering brown, granular lump the size of a Clydesdale that only moved when necessary—and very quietly at that. He was trapped, but instead of crushing him or absorbing him or whatever else he expected it to do, the thing let him sidle past, and then herded him back out of the tunnel and up to the surface, where three more joined it, offering him only one course to take. They drove him across a roughly hewn stalagmitic plaza toward one of the many ugly, off-kilter temples. Well, he thought, he'd had a good run, come about as far as anyone could hope in this twisted world. That's when he heard someone call his name, looked up, and found Stipe striding across the knurled landscape. Stipe, wearing a black suit and white shirt, looking for all the world like a beaming Jehovah's Witness come to lay on him a copy of *The Watchtower*. The twinkie wranglers parted to let Stipe through.

Stipe slapped him on the shoulder, took him by the arm. "Man, I almost didn't recognize you with the beard. Good to see you. I was sure you'd do okay."

"Yeah, I was real safe in that safe."

"Safe in the safe, ha!" Stipe laughed, wiped at his eyes. "That's a good one. Here, come with me."

Detwiler eyed the clustered twinkies.

Stipe insisted, "No, really, it's okay. They know you're one of us."

"Us?"

"You know what I mean. You're a Beckman."

"I'll have nightmares forever."

"Well, I think maybe I can help with that. You need a bath, John. A shave. Come on." They walked off across the plaza toward a group of humans, all dressed in much the same garb as Stipe, even the women. Some of them looked to Detwiler a little peculiar, as if maybe their parents had been spadefoot toads. Stipe explained to them that Detwiler was a surviving member of Beckman's group. The others oohed and aahed as if he was a lost treasure. They welcomed him to New R'lyeh.

Eventually Stipe dragged him off for a tour of the facilities.

"What's New R'lyeh?" Detwiler pronounced.

"It's what Cthulhu renamed New York. The parts he's had rebuilt, anyway."

"What happened to Old R'lyeh?"

"I think it sank into the Pacific. Anyway, this is where we all are now."

"Home, sweet ph'nglui."

Stipe chuckled. "Hey, you remembered some of the words from the ceremony."

"One or two."

As they entered through a gaping doorway, Stipe asked, "So, like, what d'you have in the bag?"

"Toothbrush," replied Detwiler.

"Right."

The inside of the place was just as rough and knurled. No surface was either exactly horizontal or vertical. The light came from more phosphorescence.

"Lichen," Stipe explained.

As they walked, something huge, brown, and repulsive flew by. Its stalked eyes turned to observe them. It's leathery wings flapped heavily. Then it shat something green and noxious. "Oh, great. Can we go another way?" Detwiler asked.

"It's just *fhtagn* poop."

"I'd say this whole *farkakte* setup's *fhtagn*."

"Aw, don't be like that. We're gonna score hugely here, man, now that you're back."

"No kidding," Detwiler replied. "How do we define hugely in the universe of flying tentacled beer barrels?"

Stipe explained that Cthulhu's human followers were already hoarding all kinds of treasures: great works of art, things lifted out of what had been the Met and the MOMA: jewelry, gold, silver, anything that seemed like it might one day represent wealth for a new ruling class.

"Like that cash you made off with."

Stipe shrugged. "Yeah, that didn't play out too well. Why I had to rejoin the overseers."

"So where are they keeping all this wealth-to-be?"

"Inside the monuments. Well, underneath them, really."

"Like the tunnel I just came from?"

Stipe's eyebrows raised. "No wonder they nabbed you. Cthulhu's got a thing for tunnels. Loves 'em."

"Why? He's the size of the moon. He couldn't fit his left nut in one."

"And you know what else?" Stipe confided. "Some of the other groups showed up with more seals."

"Seals like Beckman's, you mean?"

"Absolutely. A shame Beckman's book got smushed."

"How so?"

"Well, see, that's the only translation that was accurate, just like Beckman claimed."

"So nobody can work the seals."

"Nope, and now they're not gonna get the chance."

"Why not?"

"Well, Cthulhu doesn't want anyone to have them. Every time somebody's shown up with another one, it's confiscated."

"He doesn't want to open the rest of the gates?"

Stipe shrugged. "Not yet, I guess. Probably wants to finish remaking the world in his image so he can show it off to the other gods."

Detwiler glanced around at the carved interior, the canted doorways, vaulted ceiling, rough and narrow steps. "Seems to be having some success with that."

"I got a place picked out we can move everything till we need it."

"Place?" Detwiler asked.

"Yeah, awhile back I found an old abandoned subway line that I don't think has been in operation since like forever. The tunnelers covered it up to bore one of Cthulhu's tunnels, but I made sure to leave one way into it. It's so close to the Temple of Yuggoth, though, that nobody else'll go near it."

"Why not?"

"You haven't been there, have you?" asked Stipe.

"How would I know?"

"'Cause if you had you'd be a gibbering mess now. The place exudes cosmic dread like a noxious gas. You hallucinate loathsome star clusters, and feel your very atoms come apart in slow motion, in agony so terrible that most people hurl themselves to their death at the very start of it."

"Yeah, I think I'd remember that."

"We only get together and chant there like once a year."

"How is it anybody's left?"

Instead of answering, Stipe went on, "I figure we can pull whatever we want out of the other temples, store it down under there. Sell it back to them if we have to, but otherwise we sit it out till we need some capital. Then we bargain."

"You're talking about the seals."

Stipe smiled broadly. "You always were a smart guy, Detwiler."

"Not smart enough."

"That's why you got me."

Detwiler closed his eyes and said nothing.

And so they'd spent days worshipping Cthulhu and his in-human underlings at various sites around New R'lyeh, and their evenings scouting each elephantine temple and slimy tunnel until they'd located the collected Seals of Kadath, a matter made harder by the repeated denials they heard, mostly from the Cthulhulians themselves, that the seals had ever existed at all.

With the stone pulled out, the two slipped into the unguarded vault beneath the Temple of Ultimate Chaos, which Detwiler observed looked like a greenish-black intestinal polyp.

They filled the duffels with the five seals, and Detwiler took time to add as many of the rough-cut diamonds as he could scoop up before Stipe nervously said, "They stopped chanting."

It had indeed grown silent overhead. But no one was making their way down the Stygian stairways to this vault either. Detwiler snatched a few more jewels.

Stipe grunted as he hauled his duffel over to the hole. It took the two of them to lift it up and over, and lower it down the outside. The weight of the bag almost pulled Stipe out the opening. They repeated the act with the other two before climbing out. Stipe was dirty and sweating. Detwiler imagined that he looked much the same. "We're gonna have to come back for the third one of these."

"Just to the end of the tunnel for now," said Detwiler.

"You're crazy."

"I must be." He lifted his duffel and started walking, bow-legged and slow. Stipe followed him. At the mouth of the tunnel, Detwiler set his bag down and went back in for the third one. He carried that with less trouble, and set it on top of Stipe's bag. They looked out into the night. This was the part of the journey that presented the most peril. The duffels had to travel to the subway entrance, a good half a mile away. But Detwiler had worked that all out. After checking to be sure no one was watching from outside the glowing tunnel, he crept off into the dark and returned a few minutes later with a dinged up wheelbarrow.

"Where'd you find that?" Stipe asked.

"I used to move with it before your twinkies caught me."

"You're a genius, John."

"Now and then." They loaded the last of the duffels and then Stipe's into the barrow. "We're still going to have to leave the third one here. Three's too heavy."

"Yeah."

"I'll stay with it," Detwiler said. "I know how you like to make off with the goods. And I can wait."

Stipe lifted the wheelbarrow onto its single wheel. "Yeah, I can handle this okay. I'll be back in under an hour."

"Be careful."

Stipe headed off, shortly disappearing over the rise and into the landscape. Amazing how dark it got without streetlights, Detwiler thought. No wonder we invented them.

He rested a bit, then set to work. First he recovered his satchel, which he'd been careful to hide near the tunnel's mouth. Now, in the dull greenish glow of the fungi at the opening, he pulled out the battered copy of Beckman's *Necronomicon*, and with a few loose bricks set it up so that he could read from it. Next he unzipped the duffel. He'd put two of the seals in the bag in order to ensure that Stipe could transport the remaining duffels by himself. Now he hauled them out one at a time, afterwards rolling each to where he could see it clearly in the pulsating glow.

A low, shambling sound caught his attention, and one of the twinkies slid sluglike into the edge of the tunnel's luminescence. Detwiler edged back to the book and flipped through the pages. "Regna'd kesin," he read. The twinkie flexed as if something invisible had poked it. "K'la ye'hah!" It turned and scuttled away. "Bug-shoggoth."

Detwiler glanced from the book to the seals. The runes on each were distinctive, and only one bore the correct symbols as illustrated in Beckman's book. When he was absolutely certain he rolled the other one across the rubble to where an old fire hydrant still stood, anchored to pavement below the debris. Certain he'd end up with a hernia, he lifted the round stone over his head and then as hard as he could dashed it on the tip of the hydrant.

The seal shattered. Somewhere, distantly in the night, something squealed like a lobster being immersed in a pot of boiling water. The sound faded. Thunder rumbled.

"Hey!" a voice called.

Detwiler turned. Stipe was approaching with the empty wheelbarrow.

Detwiler walked back over to his duffel and the remaining seal. He knelt beside the book and placed the seal face up on the ground in front of him.

Stipe set down the barrow. "What'cha doing, man?"

"Oh, this and that."

Stipe stopped. "That's the *book*, Detwiler," he said. "Beckman's book."

"Yes, it is. Makes for interesting reading. For instance, I can tell you why Cthulhu's been hoarding all these seals."

"Really?"

"Oh, yeah. But give it twenty minutes and he'll be here anyway."

Alarmed, Stipe looked around, up at the sky, at the repulsive towers. "He will?"

"Yeah, I got his attention." He gestured toward the hydrant, the broken pieces of seal standing out in greenish contrast to the gray debris.

"John, you have any idea what even one of those is worth potentially?"

"Kind of. Pretty much all of humanity."

Distantly, the air vibrated, a quiet, slow rhythm.

Detwiler gestured with his thumb at the book. "According to Beckman, this world of ours used to be Cthulhu's domain. About eight or twelve millennia ago. He's responsible for this local area, which is big, but not compared to all space and time. The realm he got booted to from here was a kind of limbo between dimensions. Thing is, honestly, he's a cousin to the Old Ones. I mean the *real* Old Ones. They're not like him."

"No?"

"Infinitely worse," said Detwiler. "They'd likely have scorched the whole solar system by now, melted the planets and reassembled them as something you and I can't even comprehend, Stipe. We don't perceive enough dimensions."

"How you know this?"

"Well, I don't, exactly. It's what the book says. I mean, Beckman could just be nuts, like we both thought."

The "whump" of huge and unseen wings grew steadily louder.

"If that's the case, though," Detwiler continued," we're in trouble here."

"What have you done?" Stipe stood as if ready to bolt.

"This—" he tapped the remaining seal "—this is the second seal. Your Old Ones think of Cthulhu as the cousin you don't invite to the wedding because he picks his nose and wipes it on the bride's gown, you know what I'm saying? They gave him our backwater swamp to manage, just to keep him off on his own. The gates are in place to keep him out as much as us in. *This* seal is Yog-Tetharoth."

The sound of wings seemed to be nearly overhead.

"You open this one"—he glanced at the book and yelled, "krel'bo'yni Kadath nar'whal Kaekeeba!" then went on as if nothing had happened— "and you'll reopen that buffer space between Cthulhu and the *rest* of the family. Suck him right back out."

Stipe's eyes were huge. "What are they like, the Old Ones?"

"All it says is, you can smell them, but you can't see them."

Something huge, writhing, with red glowing eyes emerged out of the clouds above. Detwiler drew the crowbar from his duffel.

"Of course, it requires a sacrifice. Nothing personal." He drove the sharp edge of the crowbar straight into the seam down the middle of the seal. With a flash, the greenish stone split in half.

Stipe put his hands out as if to push away from something. His mouth opened in a scream, but the more thunderous scream from the creature above him drowned him out. Cthulhu turned and vanished back into the clouds.

"That's not right," Detwiler muttered.

Stipe hadn't moved or vanished. A pure blackness arising from the broken seal spread up and out, surrounding him but leaving him untouched, save that his face contorted into a mask of revulsion, his eyes watered and he clamped both hands over his nose. The blackness rose like smoke upon a breeze and faded.

Lying flat on the ground, Detwiler glanced over at the book. He read the relevant passages again. "Krel'bo'yni Kadath nar'whal Kaekeeba—that's what it says. That's what *I* said. I don't get it." Then the stench reached him. It was like the distilled essence of sulphuric eggs run through an oil refinery and then fired out of a skunk's butt. He pressed his face into the dirt and groaned.

Stipe, on his knees, coughed and wheezed, "What did you do, John?"

"I—I was sending Cthulhu back to where he came from." He leaned up on his elbows. "You know when I said Beckman was nuts?"

"Yeah?"

"Well, his translation's screwy, too."

Overhead, clouds floated, drifted. Then, as if a titanic soap bubble had reached them, they flew apart. Moonlight spilled down, but distorted and sickly yellow as though projected through old cellophane. Detwiler could feel phantoms nearby, invisible, amorphous things that swelled against the very fabric of reality.

"You let in the Old Ones," Stipe said.

"Uh, yeah. Let's not mention that to the others, okay?" He got to his feet. He wiped at his eyes, sniffled, choked. "Listen, if we're lucky, he was wrong about them melting the planets and stuff, too."

Stipe got up, shook his head like a dog. "I can't get that stink off me."

The ruin of a nearby building suddenly flexed and distorted. As if liquid it drew together, the top of it curled like an ocean wave and then stretched into the clouds. The night filled with distant piteous cries of horror, not all of them human.

"We, ah, we might want to go back into the tunnel awhile," Detwiler suggested. He bent down to pick up Beckman's book. The stars in night sky shuddered. "Just till things settle down." He headed into the phosphorescence.

With a final glance at the world, Stipe stumbled into the mouth of the tunnel, too, but abruptly drew up. "Detwiler," he yelled, "what did you mean you needed a sacrifice?"

LOCK UP YOUR CHICKENS AND DAUGHTERS— H'ARD AND ANDY ARE COME TO TOWN!

with MICHAEL SWANWICK

I t was a hot, blue-sky August day and little dust devils were playing in the street in front of the First National Bank of Nacogdoches when H'ard and Andy pulled into town. Their flivver was coughing and almost out of fuel when one of the new "visible" gas pumps rose up out of the shimmering pavement air ahead of them, topped by a glass tank to show off the golden quality of the gasoline, a big red star, and the word TEXACO.

"Now that is a fine sight," Andy commented. "A very fine sight indeed."

H'ard was slouched back in the seat with his hat down over his eyes. With one finger he pushed up the hat just far enough for him to take a squint, then pulled it down again. "Yup."

Pulling the car over to the curb in front of a sundries store, Andy said, "I'm going to get us some gas money. You want anything?"

"Pack of smokes. Chesterfields if they got 'em."

The screen door slammed shut behind Andy, jangling a little bell. Assuming a benevolent smile, he went to the counter, manned by a clerk who looked to be half as old as Methuselah and said, "A good day to you, sir, and lordy but it is hot! I'd like to buy me some Chester—lord have mercy, are those Cravens? I ain't seen a pack of Craven 'A's since I was knee-high to a gopher, back in the Big Fog Country. You ever been out that way? Normally you don't see the sun one day out of seventeen hundred. When this drought first struck and dried up everything, the children ran and hid because they thought the sky was on fire. Folks got their first good look at how raggedy-ass their homes and farms was and it like to broke their hearts. Put some pressure on a lot of marriages, I'll tell you that. Knew a man had a vacation cottage a little west of town and when the daylight come flooding in, it just plumb wasn't there no more, nor the mountain neither. Turns out it was just a mass of cloud compacted down so dense that the county paved a road over it, sent out a surveyor, and started selling lots. I'll take that pack of Cravens, thank you, and here's a five dollar bill to pay you with."

As the clerk, a little dazed by this torrent of words, counted out four ones and six dimes, Andy went on talking: "Been traveling all my life and still got a stretch to go, all the way south to Beluthahatchie. Now there is a destination. It's a far piece, three station stops beyond Hell. The train that takes you there when you die passes on to West Hell, Ginny Gall, Beluthahatchie, and Diddy-wah-diddy. Good folks don't go to that last place, though. They's low-class people there. And West Hell's just a suburb of Hell, there ain't nothing doing there at all. Saturday night's as dead as Monday morning." He opened his wallet. "Tarnation! Look at all these ones. This thing is so fat I'm like to tilt over sideways when I sit down. Tell you what, old hoss, let me swap you ten singles for a sawbuck, if you'd be that kind."

They exchanged bills. Andy pocketed the ten and returned to his soliloquy: "Now, I'm not saying Ginny Gall is bad or nothing, but the barbeque there is second-rate and that's the plain and simple truth. All the quality folks of Hell go to Beluthahatchie for a big night out, and that includes the Head Fella his own self, so you know they don't cut no corners."

"Say," the clerk said sharply. "You're a dollar short. There's only nine ones here."

"Are there? Well, never mind, I'll give you one more and add a ten and you can just give me a twenty instead. That's right perfect, and I thank you muchly."

"Don't forget your cigarettes," the clerk said.

"**W**ell?" H'ard asked when Andy returned to the car.

"Worked me the short-change, made us ten dollars."

"So where're my Chesterfields?"

"I got you some Cravens instead. Finest Virginia tobacco and a cork tip to boot."

H'ard opened the pack, knocked out a cigarette. Then he bit off the cork tip and spat it out the window. Lighting the ragged end, he muttered, "Hell of a note when a man can't even get a pack of Chesterfields."

"It's a free pack of smokes, what did you expect? Egg in your beer? You certainly do demand a lot from the world for someone who hails from Oklahoma." Andy went outside to crank the car. Then he got back and drove up to the gas pump.

The attendant was a hatchet-faced young man with a rash of pimples across his forehead. "Two dollars and sixty cents," he said when the tank was full. He accepted a five and added, "Exactly change only."

"Well, but I don't have anything smaller. I just now traded away all my singles."

"Then you're plumb out of luck, I reckon." The young man made an insolent face and, tucking the bills in his shirt pocket, swaggered away.

"Well, don't that just take the cake?" Andy began. "Don't that just fry your shorts? Don't that—"

"Don't get mad," H'ard said. "Get even." He stared at the gas pump long and hard. Then he said, "Let's go."

The flivver pulled out of the gas station and headed down the road.

Behind them, goldfish swam happily in the glass tank of the pump.

The next town they came to was Paradise Lake. It was ten years overdue for a coat of paint, but at least Main Street was paved. There was a booth restaurant, a five-and-dime Woolworth's, a hotel that had seen better days, and a cluster of other buildings, all in an uneven line and every single one topped with a wooden façade to make them look taller and more prosperous. Those few people idly watching their passing—barefoot children, men in dungarees, women in dresses with faded splotches of color that once were flowers—could have been statues stuck in the dirt for all that most of them moved.

At the end of the row, a little separate from the rest, like the whiskey in-law at a family picnic, was an unpainted clapboard hardware store with the flaking words BAIT and CRAWLERS painted across the plate glass. There was a water pump out front with the handle chained and padlocked so nobody could use it on the sly.

"Stop here," H'ard said. "I got me a yen to go fishing."

The land beyond the shack sloped away to a dry and cracked expanse that, by testimony of a pair of tumbledown docks at its edge, had once upon a time been a lakebed. But all the open water for a hundred miles around had disappeared so long ago that there were children nowadays who'd bray like a donkey if told it used to flow out in the open with no one needing to pump it up from the aquifer. There was no telling how long ago it had dried up.

Three men lounged on a bench on the bait shop porch, and another atop a barrel, looking about as friendly as so many snapping turtles and as immovable as mules.

H'ard got out first and passed indoors without a word. Andy stayed outside. "Might I sit a spell?" he asked, and lowered himself onto the edge of the porch, his back to the men. Nobody spoke.

Five minutes later, H'ard emerged from the store, assembling the parts of a split bamboo fly rod with a cork grip. Andy recognized it for a Montague Rapidan, which was a high-end product for a cheap rod but low-end for an expensive one. Probably it was the best the place afforded. Trailing behind him were a skinny elderly gent with gray muttonchops and a bowler hat who must be the proprietor, and two indoors cronies of no distinguishing features, all talking and gesticulating at once.

"Don't see what the problem is," H'ard commented. "I said I was going to catch me a trout and that's just what I aim to do."

"Mister, there's no *water* in that lake!" the proprietor said.

"It's a poor fisherman who blames the lake," H'ard observed. "Izaak Walton said that. I'll bet you any amount of money you care to name that I pull out a two-pound trout on my first cast."

Andy stood up. "Now be reasonable, H'ard," he pleaded in the tone of a man who had seen this impractical scenario repeated many times. "There ain't no point in riling everybody up. Nobody's going to believe a word you say, anyway. It just stands to reason. These folks can't possibly believe you can pull a trout out of hard-baked mud. Why, that stuff's as hard as concrete!"

"Is your friend simple?" the barrel-sitter asked in a low voice.

"Not as such," Andy replied equally quietly. "But he caught a shell in Belleau Wood during the Great War, and it changed his outlook considerable. Ever since he survived that, he's been convinced he can do anything he puts his mind to."

The idlers exchanged looks and one of then cleared his throat. "Five dollars says you can't," he said decisively.

"You're on. Andy, hold this man's money."

"Oh, this is just ridiculous. These good people are going to line up to take your money away from you. Thank you, sir. They're going to dig out every fin and sawbuck they can find in their pockets to bet against you. You're going to end up betting every penny you have and then some. Two twenties? Well, I reckon we can cover that."

In no time, Andy was holding two fat wads of banknotes.

"I'm going to need some water, though," H'ard said.

"You intend to refill the lake?" The idlers were really hooting now, warming to the possibilities of this entertainment. Nothing this good had happened in Paradise Lake for a long while.

"A tin cup's worth will do."

The hardware store proprietor sent a crony to fetch a cup and solemnly unpadlocked the pump. Some vigorous elbow action later, H'ard strode out onto the dry lakebed, cup in hand. There, he poured the water with great care upon a shallow depression, creating a slick the size of a puddle, as reflective as a mirror and no deeper than a sheet of paper.

By now, in the mysterious manner that news got about in a small town, the number of bystanders had doubled.

H'ard stepped back a number of measured steps, his eye never leaving the slick. Then he took a fly caddy from his shirt pocket and unhooked his favorite lure which, as Andy knew from long experience, was a Basilisk Hair Caddis. With unhurried care, he tied it to the tapered line. Then, after pumping his casting arm up and down a few times to limber it up, he took the bamboo rod in hand and drew out a loop of line. In one deceptively simple gesture, he made the back cast. The line flew out behind him and to one side. When it was as far back as it was going to go, he made the front cast.

The line floated gently through the air in an arc was a pure pleasure to behold. The fly dropped down in the very center of the newly-created slick spot.

Everybody held their breaths.

A trout exploded up out of the water, hook in mouth. It leaped high in the air, its tail swinging, and landed with a wet slap upon the dry lakebed.

"Sweet merciful Jesus," someone in the crowd moaned.

H'ard trotted over to the fish, picked it up by the line, cut its throat, and carried it back to the crowd standing on the shoreline. They parted as if beholding the miracle of the loaves and fishes.

Andy had, meanwhile, walked to the flivver and returned. "I'm ready to weigh," he said. He indicated a set of spring scales as if they'd been sitting in the dirt the whole time. The cash that he had been holding had already disappeared into his pockets. H'ard hung the trout from the hook at the bottom of the scales then turned away nonchalantly to disassemble his rod.

With a *screech*, the weight indicator lurched downward, stopping at two pounds even.

"I'll be go to hell," said the proprietor.

There was a moment of stunned silence, and then Andy laughed merrily.

"Well, I reckon we've all had our spot of fun," Andy said, digging out the money from his pockets. He started handing it back to its original owners "But I cannot take your money on false pretenses. H'ard here is, as you might well guess from what you just saw, a half-breed water elemental on his mother's side. Water will simply do whatever he wants. A gift such as his comes along but once in a lifetime and even though he is a bit of a practical joker, which it goes without saying comes from his father's line, there is simply no way that we can take your money under false pretenses. Here you go, sir. Not that we could not use it—we have a big-ticket engagement in Albuquerque but that is a week away and gasoline prices are ruinous nowadays—but it would be flat-out wrong. No, sir, you only bet three dollars, I was most particular careful to take note of that."

A laugh of relief gusted through the crowd as banknotes were crinkled back into wallets and socks. H'ard, meanwhile, raised one eyebrow ever so slightly. To which Andy responded with an equally microscopic jerk of his head down the street, where a great bull of a man in a sheriff's uniform was leaning against a pole of the Woolworth's arcade, watching the scene intently.

H'ard gave the man only the slightest glance. Then he returned to seeing to his bamboo rod, the two halves of which seemed to twitch in his hand.

"You might as well have this," Andy said, unhooking the fish and handing it to the hardware store owner. "H'ard pure and simple loves to fish, but ain't neither of us can stand the taste."

All the way back to the flivver, the bamboo sticks rattled and shook in H'ard's hands.

After they had stopped by the hotel to book a room for the night, the two men went into the Hot Griddle Restaurant, which was almost without customers. On every empty table, the cups and plates were turned upside down. A less than chipper waitress, who looked like she was saving up to someday buy a decent meal for herself, took their dinner orders. Meat loaf with gravy and mashed potatoes, collards on the side, for Andy and chicken fried steak with succotash for H'ard.

"That was never a two-pound trout," Andy said when the dishes had been cleared away and they were waiting for their coffee. "That fish was a pound and a half, a pound and three-quarters tops. If we'd had to use anybody else's scales, we would have lost every dollar we had."

"Can't lose what you don't possess," H'ard replied philosophically.

At that moment, a slim girl with a tremendous mass of red hair and freckles to match slid into the booth alongside Andy, locked eyes with H'ard, and said, "I'm not wearing any underwear."

"Heaven help us," Andy said. "What kind of a way to begin a conversation is that? No how-dee-do, no 'Hi, my name is—' no big sunny smile that declares as good as words that you hope we might all of us wind up as friends. No, just a bald declarative sentence that combines a complete ignorance of the social niceties with a distasteful disregard for the importance of personal hygiene. I don't know when I've ever felt half so offended this early on in an acquaintanceship."

H'ard grunted. "Let's start over." He extended a big hand across the table. "Name's H'ard. My friend's Andy. What's your name, sweetie?"

The girl took his hand and shook. "It's Jezabel."

"Oh, it is *not*," Andy said. "Nobody's going to believe decent Baptist folk gave their daughter any such ridiculous name as that. I don't believe it, H'ard here don't believe it, and I don't believe you're fool enough to believe for an instant that we believe it neither. Your real name is probably Susan or Ellie or Mildred or something sensible like that."

The girl turned as red as her freckles. "It's Lolly. And you ain't no gentleman for forcing me to admit to it."

"Pleasure to meet you, Lolly," H'ard said. "Now why don't you tell us just what it is you're up to, talking to two strangers on no pretense at all. Not that I object. But I *am* curious."

"I intend to get the hell out of this nothing-happening town."

"Ambition is admirable in a child," Andy said. "Only, exactly how is talking with us going to accomplish that?"

"Gonna hook up with you two. I'll let you pop my cherry in return."

"What in the name of God's little green apples are you talking about, girl? Your lips are moving but listen hard as I might, I don't hear a single syllable of sense coming out from between them."

Lolly scowled. "I don't see what's so difficult to understand. Y'all got a car and I overheard my father saying that you're obviously criminals of some sort or other. We can come to terms. I've got a few heavy petting sessions under my belt and I'm ready to move on to unfettered moral depravity."

"Heaven help us," Andy moaned. "Could this situation get any worse?"

H'ard, who had been listening intensely, said, "Tell me something, little darlin'. What exactly does your daddy do for a living?"

"He's the sheriff."

"Heaven help us!"

"So I reckon you got to cut me in on whatever you got going on here, and promise to take me away with you when you go. Or else I'll tell my father you done to my fair young body what any sensible men *would* have agreed to do just now."

H'ard's eyes shifted away from her and his craggy face sprouted a ghost of a smile. "Well," he said, "no time like the present."

Lolly's head spun around so fast her hair hit Andy in the face.

By the time her father was all the way through the door, she'd ducked into the kitchen and fled out the back way.

"Evening," the lawman said. He was everybody's caricature of a big-bellied, squinty-eyed, snapper-jawed small town bully of a sheriff, but that didn't make him any the less dangerous. "Just came by to caution you boys not to leave town anytime soon."

"My apologies, sir, but who might you be?" Andy asked politely.

"Samuel Cooke. Sheriff Cooke to you boys."

Andy introduced the two of them, using last names he was almost certain had no criminal records attached to them (H'ard nodded so slightly it might be mistaken for a man catching himself from nodding off), then said, "Would it be forward of me to ask you why we're to stay in this fine metropolis of yours?"

"You boys look questionable to me. I wouldn't be surprised if that vehicle of yours is stolen. Gonna telegraph the State your particulars and license number, see if maybe you are of interest to anybody."

"Well, I don't mean to be negative, sir, but I've got to tell you: I just simply do not believe in the telegraph, and that's a fact. New-fangled nonsense device like that is prone to breaking down exactly when you need it most. Why, wires get broke and then all the electricity goes astray and flies helter-skelter all over the place, frightening horses and inconveniencing honest citizens. Fella writes down a two-dollar message and a puff of wind blows the paper right out the window. In all the confusion nobody even remembers who sent the darn thing or what it said. No, sir, put not your trust in machines. One man, one mule, and a leather sack of paper envelopes with a magenta two-cent George Washington stamp and a hand-cancelation on the front does the job best, is what I say. Takes a little longer but a dozen times more sure."

"If you want our particulars," H'ard said, "just ask."

"All right, I will." Sheriff Cooke folded his arms and waited.

"I, sir, am an adjunct professor in metaphysical studies, currently on sabbatical from Frostburg State College of Thaumaturgy, situated at the head of the beautiful Georges Creek Valley in the great state of—"

The sheriff snorted like a bull. "Stop. I never yet met a college professor that talked anything like you do. As for your friend—I know what you told those gullible souls down by the lake, and I'm going to let you boys in on a little secret: I come from a long line of witch-finders, and I got me a touch of the third eye." Addressing H'ard directly, he said, "Half-breed elemental, my maiden aunt's foot! You are nothing but a common fish wizard."

"No crime in that," H'ard said.

"Whether you doubt our credentials or not, it is a plain and simple fact, sir, that we do have business elsewhere. In Albuquerque, to be precise, where the city fathers have contracted us to meliorate a certain unfortunate natural . . ." Andy's voice trailed off, for the sheriff's ugly mug had just split in a big, mean grin.

"Now it all makes sense," Sam Cooke said. He placed his hands on the table and, leaning forward, said in a low voice, "You boys are intending to run the Dust Giant scam, aren't you?"

"What? No!" Andy cried in alarm. "I don't even know what you're talking about, officer!"

"Well, I'll tell you what. I am going to *let* you run your little grift. In fact, I'm going to help you do it. In return for which, I ask only for half the proceeds and your immediate departure afterwards."

"I see three people here," H'ard observed. "One-third would be fairer."

"Half," Sheriff Cooke said, pulling away from the table. "I'll provide you with the dynamite at no additional charge. Oh, and since we're partners now—" he picked up the check and tore it in two "—your meal's on me." Over by the cash register, the waitress looked daggers into his back, but said not a word.

On the way out, the sheriff paused and added, "By the way. If you see my daughter again, tell her she gets the strap tonight for consorting with strangers."

The next day, H'ard and Andy were the talk of the countryside. Their returning the money lost on a sucker's bet was a magnanimous gesture which particularly impressed those who privately doubted that they themselves would have done as much under similar circumstances. Furthermore, the revelation of the exceptional nature of H'ard's purported powers was bolstered by rumors which Sheriff Cooke had judiciously planted here and there about town. The upshot of which was that in no time at all, it was a known fact throughout Paradise County first, that the two strangers had the ability to break the drought. Second, that this miraculous talent they perversely intended to squander upon Albuquerque, an out-of-state city with no known positive qualities whatsoever. And third, that something should be done about this lamentable situation.

After feverish consultation, a committee of the town's civic leaders was deputed to call upon H'ard and Andy. They arrived at the Terminal Hotel (so named because it was located at the end of an interurban spur of the Atchison, Topeka and El Dorado Railway) in three separate automobiles, scattering dust devils before them, one of which paused to flip them the finger before spinning away, giggling, to join its compeers. There they found the two men, with a maximum of fuss and delay, loading luggage into their flivver.

"Sirs," said the eldest, grayest, most dignified, and by testimony of his collar, only ordained member of the three, "a word with you, if you please."

Andy straightened from the trunk, smiling. "Well, Reverend, my associate and I were just on the verge of setting out to put eighty or perhaps a hundred miles of our journey behind us before nightfall, which I know you will agree is an ambitious undertaking, requiring not only determination and grit but all the free time we can give it. However, being genial souls and courteous to a fault, I can see no reason why H'ard and I should fail to give you and your friends a fair hearing."

"Sure," Howard agreed.

At this they all ambled into the nearby hotel bar. There, the city fathers introduced themselves as the Reverend Aldis Singletary; Hiram Aloysius Bergstralh, mayor; and F. W. Showalter, undertaker. Sliding behind the bar, Reverend Singletary poured them all a schooner of beer apiece, to establish an amiable tone.

"Sirs, I will get right to the point," Mayor Bergstralh said, when all had wet their whistles. "Word is that you have the power to break the drought that has been oppressing our city, our county, and indeed our beloved state for the past six years. Is this true?"

"Only the Almighty has the power to compel nature to do His bidding, as I am certain the Reverend here will assure you is good, solid Christian doctrine. In normal times, H'ard and I could no more order the heavens to split open and bestow life-giving rain upon your dry fields and empty reservoirs than flap our arms and fly away. Howsomever, not all weather is natural. This drought, for one, surely nobody could mistake it for the work of Divine Providence. No, sirs, what you have here is the doings of a Dust Giant which has settled down into the land itself, and made this county its home. We could not help but note how the cups and glasses in your fine restaurant were inverted. You have already encountered it and have no notion when it will next decide to bury your houses, silt up your doorways, sift in through your every crack and window seam. Such creatures are inhospitable to water and so, by their very presence, they drive it away. Hence, your drought."

"Stands to reason," H'ard amplified.

"But the drought extends across seven states," Rev. Singletary objected. "How could one creature—even one exhibiting the strongest supernatural power—cause all that?"

"The drought extends across seven states *now*," Andy explained. "But if you cast back your memory, you'll find that it started in one region, and spread outward, bit by bit, county by county. Exactly as if—and it is my conviction that this is precisely how it chanced to occur—a female Dust Giant had a litter, and her cubs proceeded to spread out, each one finding a welcoming environment and settling into it as they come of age."

"Nevertheless," H'ard said.

"Nevertheless, all this is of merely theoretical interest, gentlemen, compelling to an academic such as myself, less so to others. In practical terms, using H'ard's tremendous inborn powers over water and my own deep reading into such forbidden tomes as the *Livre d'Eibon, the Mysteries of the Worm, Al Azif* (a negligible work, to be honest, its reputation notwithstanding), the *Pnakotic Manuscripts*, the *Unpronounceable Cults* of . . . well, they're unpronounceable. Not to bore you, gentlemen, but the solution to your problem proves to be laughably simple: an exorcism. Now, I am sure that you have tried that already. What sensible man would not? Even if it wasn't exactly sanctioned by his bishop, he'd . . . I see you blushing, Reverend. But the truth of it is that just as the angels in heaven are organized by rank into Seraphim, Cherubim, Thrones, Dominions, and so on down the line, so too do the chaotic powers have their own hierarchy of Fate Demons, Elementals, Gobelines, Incubi and Succubi, Drudes, Cambions et cetera. A Dust Giant, I am very sorry to have to inform you, is a full-fledged Gobeline and there are not many human beings who have the inborn fortitude to stand before one without dying instantaneously, usually through spontaneous desiccation."

"But I can," H'ard said.

"H'ard is that rare natural exception. Which, gentlemen, and I do apologize if I have gone on rather long here, is why we are urgently required in Albuquerque."

The mayor cleared his throat. "It just may be that we are interested in contracting your services."

"Sirs, I don't know if you are aware of how much money a full-scale exorcism would entail. Now, I know what you're going to say, that casting out the Dust Demon would pay for itself many times over in the first year alone. And of course you could amortize some of the cost by selling tickets to what is, admittedly, a crowd-pleaser of a spectacle. Heck, some of you might even turn a profit by providing concessions selling wiener sandwiches, ginger beer, helium balloons, and other such gimcrackery. But we cannot in all good conscience charge you less than an exorbitant fee for our services, when the fine city of Albuquerque, withering under the curse of their own demon, is waiting for us to bring them relief. Further, I am here to tell you that exorcising a Dust Giant is not like casting out a garden variety demon or nameless horror, which task could be safely left to the Reverend here, no. It takes a lot out of a man. When H'ard is done his work, I will have to immediately whisk him off to a sanitarium, where he will lie abed, weak and helpless for months, living on gruel and weak tea like a dry Methodist, and dreaming of the day when he can rear up and tear into a watercress sandwich."

"It ain't no fun, I'll tell you that," H'ard said.

"So you see, I flat-out don't think you can afford us. I say that as a friend and someone who genuinely cares for your wellbeing."

Mayor Bergstralh looked like a man who had just bit into a sausage sandwich and found a dead mouse. "Exactly how much would it cost to buy your services out from under Albuquerque?"

Andy named a figure.

"Plus expenses," H'ard added.

"Expenses?" F. A. Showalter, the undertaker, who had been silent up until now, said. "What kind of expenses?"

"Well, first of all," H'ard said, "we're going to need bleachers."

Three days later, H'ard and Andy were standing before the half-built bleachers when Lolly, sullen as usual, appeared to say, "Got another message for y'all from my sorry excuse for a father. He says to tell you the dynamite and such are in the boot of your car."

"The boot? Surely you must mean in the trunk. What in heaven's name is a well-brought-up Southern girl like yourself doing using a nonsensical Brit word like that? Next thing you know, you'll be getting knackered and gobsmacked and eating bangers and mash or toad-in-the-hole and for all I know parping on the hooter and where will civilization be then, I want to know? The question as good as answers itself."

"Where'd you pick up that word, sweetie?" Howard asked.

Looking down at the ground, Lolly mumbled, "From a book."

"That's good. Read all the books you can and someday you'll be as smart as Andy."

"I don't *want* to be smart!" Lolly said in a fury. "I want to get the hell out of town. And be deflowered. And lead a life of wealth, adventure, and debauchery." She began to sob.

Both men watched her with interest.

"Not bad," H'ard said eventually. "But it needs work."

"The lack of actual tears gives you away," Andy explained. "It's them little details you got to watch. That's why experienced ladies always dab at their eyes with a delicate lace hankie when they cry. Sometimes they might spit on it on the sly, so as to smear their mascara. Not that a young lady your age should be wearing mascara. But the day is coming."

"Lolly, darlin', have you considered that your life would be a whole lot easier if you weren't all the time fighting with your daddy?" Howard said.

"You mean being a goody-goody simpering little girlie-girl

like he wants? You try doing that yourself sometime, if you think it's such a smart idea."

The two men looked at one another. "You fill her in on the theory, p'fessor," H'ard said. "I'll get her started on the application."

Adopting his gentlest, kindliest tone, Andy said, "Listen to me, child. It is a sad but incontrovertible fact that we live in a patriarchal society. Legally, women are treated as being little better than chattel. Your gender is in fact a subject population, bullied and ruled over by outside conquerors, which class of oppressors we may call, for lack of a better term, 'men.' Now, traditionally, the powerless have had only one weapon available to them, and that is deceit. All slaves, from the time of the Old Testament through the ancient Greeks and Romans to the unfortunate years before the War Between the States, have acquired a reputation for having a slippery way with the facts, this being the only sensible response to their situation. What H'ard is telling you is to *lie* to your father. It's the simplest act in the world, it costs not a penny, and there's nothing like it for easing a man's—or woman's—woeful journey through the Valley of the Shadow of Death. I recommend it without compunction. In fact, I am ashamed of your mama for not telling you all this a long time ago."

"My mother died when I was a baby."

"Oh," Andy said. He started to say something more, but then clamped his mouth shut again.

H'ard took over the conversation. "Tell your daddy we got his message. Then tell him you want to go shopping for the kind of dresses you hate. Men have got no idea how much women's clothes cost. Easiest thing in the world to doctor the receipts and pocket a dollar or three." He glanced over to Andy. "We'd best see to the banners now. Saturday's coming down on us fast."

They left Lolly behind, her eyes wide with surmise.

By Friday night, all the dried lakefront accessible from the roadway had been fenced off, the concession stands had been built and decorated with bunting, the bleachers were ready, the tickets and souvenir programs had been printed, and an ostentatiously reluctant Sheriff Cooke had been coaxed into holding H'ard and Andy's fee ready to be paid out to them at the successful conclusion of the exorcism. People from towns around had flocked to Paradise Lake and bought up every available room and set up tents at the edge of town, in order to be early in line for the best seats. Further, a banquet was held in the Terminal Hotel ballroom in honor of the drought-breakers, it being established that immediately after tomorrow's ceremony, H'ard would have to be whisked away to a sanitarium to recover from the ordeal.

After giving and receiving many speeches—H'ard's "Much obliged and I thank you," being by far the shortest—the two men excused themselves early, pleading weariness and a hard day ahead. To resounding cheers, they retired to their room and then, after a judicious waiting period, slipped out the window and down the fire escape.

Arming themselves with a dark-lantern, a pickaxe, two shovels, and the demolition kit Sheriff Cooke had provided, they made their furtive way out onto the dry lakebed. The sky was moonless, cloudless, and thick with stars.

"Right here looks good to me. Insofar as I can see anything in this godless murk, which I purely cannot."

"Not there," H'ard said. He paced off at least a hundred steps more, leaving long behind them the spot where he'd pulled the trout. "Here."

"Why this is smack dab in the middle of the lakebed, where the mud is baked the hardest. It's going to be genuine, back-breaking field-hand labor digging here. Why on earth would you be making difficulties for us like this?"

"Dunno. Got me a feeling. Best you not describe our toil any further."

They set to work. A long, sweaty time later, the hole was done. Cautiously, they lowered the roped-together dynamite sticks and blasting cap into it, attached the detonator wire, and then covered it over again, gently patting the surface flat. Next, they reeled out the wire toward the far shore. From the bleachers, it would probably be unnoticeable. But just in case, they laid it out crooked and irregular, like one of the hundreds of cracks crisscrossing the dried mud. H'ard dribbled a little of the excess dirt from the excavation over the wire here and there, moistening it with water from a canteen he carried at his belt, for further verisimilitude. "There," he said when they reached the crumbling, dry-as-dust reeds directly opposite the bleachers. "If anybody can spot that, then good luck to 'em." He unspooled the last of the wire as he walked through the patch of reeds, disappearing from sight on the far side of them.

Out of nowhere, Lolly said, "What are you two up to?

Andy shrieked and clutched his heart. "Land's sake! Don't you never sneak up on a man like that, girl! I like to had a coronary, which I imagine would have given you a good giggle at my expense but which from my own admittedly biased perspective would not have been one bit funny at all. No, ma'am, it would not."

H'ard, who had excellent night vision, stepped out of the reeds and said, "I see you got on an unflattering dress."

"Right as rain, mister, and I like it too!"

"Just a frazz less perky and I believe you've got it."

"Well, hell," Lolly said. "There sure is a lot of nuance to being deceitful."

"Why, of course there is," Andy said. "That's why its practitioners are called confidence artists and not confidence businessmen or confidence housewives or confidence sewing machine repairmen or any such nonsense as that. You certainly don't know much about the world, girl."

"No, I don't. But I'm fixing to change that right now."

After a long, hard silence, Andy said, "That sounds ominous."

"I've been running my feet off carrying messages back and forth between y'all and my alleged father to the point where I reckon I know enough now to put the pair of you *and* him behind bars. I guess you know me well enough to know how much pleasure that would give me. But much as I'd like to stick it to that worthless, no-account sumbidge, I want to get out of this here town even more. So I'm entertaining suggestions. Boys?"

"Well, this is ingratitude put into human form and taught to sass her elders. Here you are, out past curfew, with money in your pocket and a brand-new ugly dress to boot, all thanks to us, and you're thinking of putting the squeeze on two men who were your only benefactors in your time of need. I—"

Howard held up a hand. "Andy, stop. Lolly, we give in."

"You do?"

"We do?"

"We'll cut you in on the scam. We'll take you with us when

we vamoose. You have my sworn word on that. Plus we're going to give you something any young lady your age would give her eyeteeth for."

"What's that?"

H'ard parted the reeds and turned the lantern on them. The narrow beam of light revealed a small plunger box in the shallow gully behind them. "Miss Lolly, we are going to let you blast a honking big hole in your hometown."

There was a moment of awed silence. Then the girl said, "Well, damn."

Saturday dawned hot and clear. Assorted vehicles began rolling into town by eight. People crowded into the Hot Griddle to watch H'ard and Andy eat their breakfasts as if beholding exotic zoological specimens transported from deepest, darkest Africa to be displayed in an unconvincing simulacrum of their natural habitat.

By eleven the heat was so fierce that the surface of the lakebed rippled like a mirage. The far-off reeds might have been cobras weaving in the air.

The ceremonies began at noon with a marching band and some shopworn-looking floats, resurrected from the local high school's Reunion Day parade, depicting various tableaux from the Bible or the Book of Thoth, which didn't exactly fit the day's theme, but had pretty girls waving from atop them, so everyone agreed that was all right.

Then there were speeches, of which H'ard's, "I thank you and much obliged," was easily the best received. Finally, however, the preliminaries were done. To enthusiastic cheering, Andy then drove the Model T, decked out with dyed turkey feathers and strings of faded pink paper Christmas bells, across the lakebed to the south shore. There, he and H'ard climbed out and strode purposefully back toward the lake's center.

Again, cheers rose up from the crowd, enfeebled by distance but growing as a sense took hold of the crowd that this was *really happening*, that somebody was *finally doing something* about the drought. From so far away the only person identifiable was Mayor Bergstrahl, who wore a straw boater.

Andy took his handkerchief and swiped at the back of his neck. "I declare, this must be the easiest money we have ever earned. It would be just like shooting ducks in a barrel if the afore-mentioned waterfowl had previously been duped into assembling the staves and bands of that barrel, jollified into hauling buckets of water until it was full, and then sweet-talked into diving head-long into it immediately after clipping their own flight feathers."

H'ard said nothing, just looked up at the naked sun.

The previous night Andy had explained to Lolly how the event would play out: "H'ard starts out right by the spot where we buried your daddy's whizz-bangers and then throws back his head and screams in a most astonishing fashion. After which he does his interpretation of the howling dervish dance, while fling-ing all sorts of colored powders into the air. While all this is go-ing on, I unobtrusively retreat some distance away and then wait. H'ard will be whooping and hollering and carrying on in a man-ner that will look to be random but will end up right by where I'm standing, which is well away from the explosives.

"Suddenly, H'ard goes still. Not a twitch, not the least mo-tion of any kind. This signifies that he is locked in spiritual com-bat with the Powers of Hell. I will then raise my arms to the heavens to call upon the Merciful and Almighty to deliver us from the clutches of Drought and Evil. When I do that, I want you to count to five and then push down that plunger. About half the lakebed will then fly up into the sky, looking very much like a Dust Giant being cast out of Paradise Lake. It will be a ter-rifying sight and the cause of such confusion and chaos that we will easily be able to disappear into the clouds of dust. If we're quick enough, it will look like the demon gobbled us right down and they'll even put a wreath on our marker. Ordinarily, this is when we would leave. However, we must then collect our share of the proceeds from your father, who would be alarmed to see you in our company. So you will skedaddle to the bar in the Ter-minal Hotel, where we three will rendezvous after that chore is attended to. Thereupon, we will hightail it down the state road so fast and far that by sundown this town will be a distant mem-ory and within a week you wouldn't be able to recall its name, even if you wanted to."

"Got that?" H'ard asked.

Lolly's eyes were bright. "Oh yes," she said giddily. "Yes, I will. Yes."

And that was exactly how it went, at first.

H'ard flung blue powder into the air and, shouting crazy made-up words, began to stomp and hop and dance in great looping circles. In a seeming frenzy, he spun and leaped, hair and face glittering with sweat and the blue powder that fell back upon him in the dead still air. There were several pouches at his belt. He dipped a hand into the one that contained red powder.

Abruptly, a wind out of the south, as hot as the blast from an open oven, buffeted Andy. He took his eyes off H'ard, put a hand across his brow, and squinted through the roiling heat. The distant horizon seemed to be rising slowly into the air.

A second gust of wind hit him, from the east this time. He looked back at H'ard.

H'ard had pulled off his shirt and thrown it into the air. Something gleamed in his right hand as he twirled. Horrified, Andy recognized it as his fish-gutting knife with the hooked blade. H'ard's eyes were completely white, rolled up in his head.

Andy reflexively started forward. But then H'ard swung the knife down once, twice, and an "X" of blood sluiced down his chest. Droplets rained onto the parched earth. Andy froze in his tracks. "What in heaven's name do you think you're doing, you damfool you?" he cried.

From the bleachers came a delayed collective "Oooooh!"

The wind kicked harder, shoving Andy first one way then another. A low but powerful rumble, like a highballing freight train coming down the tracks, shook the ground underfoot.

H'ard began chanting again, but the words were *words* this time. Ancient and strange though they were, they sounded familiar to Andy. He'd heard them or something very like them recited by a shaman from some Plains tribe—he could not recall which one exactly because he was distracted by H'ard's voice, grown louder and more resonant than any human's should properly be, and by the screams of the people in the bleachers as they leaped to their feet, pointed in terror at the clouds, ran off in all directions but toward the lake. A straw boater spun up erratically into the sky.

In the south the swelling horizon had become an onrushing

wall of certain doom, billowing so high that soon it must inevitably blot out the sun.

H'ard dropped to one knee, stabbed the fishing knife into the ground again and again and again, then sprang up and returned to his whirling, knife held out at arm's length. Andy shrank away just in time to avoid its blade.

Involuntarily, almost as if he were merely a puppet and had no choice but to play his part, Andy flung out his arms. "Dear Lord," he prayed to the deity he had not believed in since the seventh grade, "please spare my half-witted friend from the consequences of whatever idiot notion he has taken into what passes in him for a brain. And if—"

Which was as far as he got before the gust front of the monstrous dust storm struck, turning the whole world orange.

Which was when the center of the lakebed exploded.

Which did not play out as expected.

Having dug down into that packed earth the night before, Andy knew that what the blast should have produced was just about anything but the geyser of water that shot up into the air as if it were trying to punch a hole in the sky. Nor was it natural that the moisture that rained down upon the lakebed, the bleachers, and the fleeing citizens of Paradise County was no heavier than the spray off a waterfall. The bulk of the water hung in the air, where it flowed itself into a shape recognizable as the form of a woman a hundred feet tall.

Andy's skin ran cold. His mouth went dry. He could think of not a word to say. Not one.

H'ard, meanwhile, continued stomping about in circles and slashing and stabbing his knife as though engaged in a life-and-death struggle against the thick dust now engulfing him. Where the giantess's feet touched the ground, water boiled up around them, spreading outward fast. In a quarter of an hour at most, by Andy's reckoning, a man standing where he was now would be completely underwater. It was time to leave. Yet he could only stare in awe as the titanic woman opened her arms wide, as if welcoming the dust storm into them. The air crackled around her and lightning sizzled within the onrushing cloud.

The bleachers were lost to sight now. The town might have been a myth. Andy could see nothing but H'ard before him, and

H'ard was flagging, stumbling. He pitched forward and Andy caught him.

H'ard's head collapsed on Andy's shoulder. The knife fell to the ground.

At times of crisis, Andy found strength by talking. "H'ard," he said, "I did not at any moment imagine you would need to recuperate in a sanitarium for real, although to be fair I also did not at any moment anticipate that you would tap into the powers of the First Mother, which achievement would be of the greatest anthropological interest to me were it not for the fact that we are in danger of drowning if we don't get our butts in gear." A surge of water ran over the toes of his shoes. He stepped quickly back from it, dragging H'ard after him.

They had to get to the flivver. Assuming they could find it. Andy couldn't actually see the thing in all the dust.

H'ard coughed and drew himself upright. "First Mother?" he muttered. "Wuzzat?"

"Corn woman," said Andy, "known to some as Selu, Yellow Woman, or Iyatiku, unless of course you're a Zuni, in which case there are eight of her—"

"We catch us any trout?" H'ard asked muzzily. He was barely able to walk at all, but he let Andy tug him away from the pursuing water. Their feet splashed in it now but they seemed to be keeping pace with its growth. H'ard's head turned back toward its source, then craned upward to behold the giant woman pulling the dust storm closer to herself, concentrating its stuff into something almost solid. "Huh."

Andy could see their automobile up ahead, if dimly, its tires yet untouched by the advancing waters. He began to hope that there might yet be a happy ending to this particular story.

"Corn Woman, you say."

"I expect it's Iyatiku, as she's known in particular to come from deep underground."

"Then who's the fella?"

Still pushing against the dust and the wind toward their destination, Andy risked one quick look back. The clear water of the giant woman's naked shape contrasted with the dark dust clouds she embraced. Nevertheless, they did seem to be consolidating into a male form. It was odd that the dust and the water did not repel each other. Opposites, he supposed, attracted. These two, at any rate, certainly seemed attracted to each other. In fact, they . . .

"Lord love a duck!" Andy cried. "Whatever are they doing? And right out in the open too!"

H'ard's energy was returning to him at an astonishing rate. He took the lead now, flinging open the flivver's door and shoving Andy behind the wheel. As he turned the crank to get the motor going, the two giants crashed down to the earth, clenched together—away from H'ard and Andy, fortunately—and began to roll around in passionate abandon, with no regard for the town beneath them. Andy heard the sound of buildings collapsing, of cars tumbling down a street as they were washed toward the lake.

"I surely hope Miss Lolly's not watching this disgraceful spectacle," Andy commented as he frantically put the car in gear. "It is far too educational by half."

"Say," H'ard said. "What happened to my shirt?"

They were a good three miles down the road when H'ard said, "Uh oh."

"Uh oh? What do you mean by that? Uh oh indeed. That phrase tells me something is wrong, but I'll be dogged, flogged, and tied up like a hog if I have the faintest idea what. I swear, sometimes you are taciturn to the point of being one degree off comatose. If there is a less communicative man on face of this sweet planet, I have not had the honor—"

"Police car."

Andy looked in the mirror. Sheriff Cooke was just visible through the dust-streaked windshield of his prowler, face red and hands clenched on the wheel. He was a fair piece down the road, but gaining on them rapidly.

"I cannot say that I am favorably impressed that the sheriff would take the time to pursue a personal grudge in the middle of the supernatural destruction of a town which it is his sworn duty to protect. To say nothing of the extremely short gestation period of such primal creatures, which means that within hours he will find himself dealing with an entire litter of—"

"Think you can outrace him?" H'ard asked.

"Oh, that thing can't catch us," Andy scoffed. "Anybody can

tell just looking at it that it's a rattletrap that's fixing to fall apart
at the slightest provocation. Any minute now, the radiator is going to explode, the hood is going to go flying off, and all four
tires are going to burst at once. That thing is about to throw a rod
and go right off the road and into a field where it'll sink to the
axles so deep in the dust that they'll need a team of plow horses
and a blacksmith to pull it out. It'll be a plain and simple miracle
and one that makes men gawk in disbelief that Sheriff Cooke will
climb out unhurt."

Behind them, a gout of white steam blew the hood off the
police car while, simultaneously, all four tires disintegrated underneath it. Skewing wildly, it plowed into a cornfield, exploding
the ancient stalks into powder.

A mass of flame-red hair surrounding an ungodly lot of
freckles popped up over the back seat, causing Andy to shriek
and swerve off the pavement.

"How'd you do that? How'd you make that happen to that fat
old bastard's car?" Lolly demanded.

"What in the name of all that is righteous are you doing,
alone and unchaperoned, in our vehicle, young lady?" The flivver
bumped and jolted over fallow farmland. "I am scandalized just
being in your presence."

Lolly turned to H'ard. "*You'll* answer my question, won't
you?"

Howard nodded. "Sure." He thought for a moment. "Andy's a scoffomancer." He thought for another moment. Then he
shrugged. "That's about it."

"Lord God of Mercy," Andy said when he'd pulled the car
back onto the road. "Whatever did I do to deserve this?"

"I took your advice about lying to my patriarchal oppressors,"
Lolly said. "So instead of waiting in the bar where you solemnly
swore you'd meet me, I stowed away in the backseat."

"Right smart of you," H'ard said. "If duplicitous."

"Also," Lolly said, hauling a leather satchel up over the seat
and dropping it between the two men, "I took advantage of the
dust storm coming on to nab the money my daddy was supposed
to share with y'all out of the boot of his police car."

H'ard picked up the satchel, looked inside, held it up for Andy
to see. There was a great deal of money within.

"So the way I figure it—" Lolly began.

"Two things," H'ard said, before Lolly could say another word. "Ain't neither of us gonna touch you. Not today, not tomorrow, not ten years from now, not never. You can just put that thought right out of your head. Capisce?"

Lolly folded her arms and pouted. "Well, damnation," she said. "What's the other thing?"

"You ever heard of the badger game? 'Cause I think you'd be right good at it.'"

"Heaven help us all," moaned Andy.

STORY NOTES

THE DINGUS

"The Dingus" was the lead-off story in *Supernatural Noir*, edited by Ellen Datlow. As the title of the anthology suggests, this is a collection of stories that incorporate the darkness of *noir* film and literature with some element of the fantastic. Ellen's invitation to participate immediately made me want to write a story about a monster we'd never seen before. No werewolves or vampires. I'd had an idea for a while about a box in an attic that contained something that, if let out, gathered everything within range to create a kind of makeshift golem. I hadn't written that story, but it gave me the perfect monster for this one. The rest was pretty much a matter of researching boxing in Philadelphia in the mid-1950s. And the cherry on top was the title, borrowed from Sam Spade. I didn't think he would mind.

SO COLDLY SWEET, SO DEADLY FAIR

Once upon a time there was a truly awful film called *Van Helsing*, and a call went out to horror and fantasy writers to whip up stories for an anthology that was to be released at the same time, a companion volume if you will. At the time I had spent about eighteen months being unable to write anything at all. My father had died. My mother had died many years earlier and had not affected me the same way. With his, it was as if what I thought of as the "swamp" in my brain where stories thrive and interbreed had suddenly been drained dry. I could *feel* the vacuum where stories normally lived. I asked other writers, and almost everyone who had lost both parents seemed to have gone through something similar. For some it lasted a few months, for others much longer. The late Carol Emshwiller assured me this was all normal. She said that when her husband, Ed, died, she hadn't been able to write for two years, and that when she came back to it, what she wrote was unlike anything she'd written before his death. Anyway, the call went out for Van Helsing stories, and I thought about it. I had recently re-read *Dracula*, and recalled a passage in a coach where Van Helsing mentions that his wife is institutionalized and that, had his son lived, he would be about the age of Jonathan Harker. Two little clues hinting at a grim and tragic backstory. And suddenly, there was a story in my head. A story where Van Helsing encounters his first vampires, and is so focused on them that he doesn't see what's close to him—that his wife is spiraling into a kind of madness regarding their son, who is discovering his own sexuality. "So Coldly Sweet, So Deadly Fair" is the story that resulted, the first thing I wrote in the aftermath of my father's death. It wasn't until it was finished (too long for the anthology it had been written for, it went to *Weird Tales* instead) that I realized I had written a cathartic story about fathers and sons.

THE PROWL

"The Prowl" was written for Nalo Hopkinson for her *Mojo: Conjure Stories* anthology. I recall mostly digging deep into the research for the story. I knew a little about slave trafficking and slave ships, but nowhere near as much as I do now. The reality of such voyages outmatches any fantasy horror element I could have invented, but then that wasn't the point of "The Prowl" anyway. Mostly I did my best to hear the voice of Morgan Freeman as narrator. And as with most stories, I expect I'm the only one who does hear him.

THE FINAL ACT

"The Final Act" is another story written for Ellen Datlow, in this instance for her *Poe* anthology. Each story was to spin from something of Poe's, with all of us vying I suppose for choices. I picked Poe's story "The Imp of the Perverse," which reads like an essay penned by someone who commits a murder and then cannot keep the impulse to divulge this tamped down. It's like watching a car wreck that's just about to happen, where all you *can* do is watch.

NO OTHERS ARE GENUINE

And then there are the stories that just come out of nowhere. "No Others are Genuine" is one of those. There's a character in the story named for a writing student of mine. When I was a boy, my grandparents owned a 1919 model Victor Victrola, with a crank motor and needles that seemed as big as ballpoint pen tips. I started with that memory, but the story quickly took me backwards in time to the period of Edison wax cylinders. Why Chicago? I've no idea. The Chicago World's Columbian Exposition didn't even show up in the initial draft of the story. I took that draft to the Sycamore Hill Writing Workshop. I believe Christopher Rowe gave the story its title. Sometimes stories are an accretion of happenstance, impossible to untangle and explain. No straight lines between any two points in the process exist. In this case, the story ended up a finalist on the Bram Stoker Award ballot.

RUBBISH

"Rubbish" is a story set in an apartment complex where I lived for a time in Raleigh, NC. The setting is more or less the same townhouse unit I lived in. I'd gone through junior high and high school wanting to be an illustrator (or so I thought). By the time I wrote this, I'd met any number of real cover artists and illustrators, but none of them is my main character. The only thing that's real here is how spooky it was to carry the trash down to the dumpster at night in that complex.

THAT BLISSFUL HEIGHT

In writing classes I always tell students to keep some means of taking notes on them—voice memo app on your phone, or a pocket notebook—because you never know when or where you'll run into a story you want to write. "That Blissful Height" is a perfect example. I was touring the Second Bank of Philadelphia, nowadays a portrait gallery brimming with famous Philadelphians from the Revolutionary War period and later. One portrait in particular stopped me in my tracks. It was of Robert Hare, who, in the 19th century was considered one of the greatest inventors and scientists in the United States. The accompanying plaque explained that he was chair of chemistry at the University of Pennsylvania for three decades, and creator of "the oxy-hyrdrogen blowpipe," an amazing heat source for the time. Then, almost as an afterthought, the plaque noted that he was also the inventor of the spiritoscope. *The what?* I took out my notebook and wrote down "spiritoscope." As it happened, I was working as a program administrator at U of Penn at the time, which gave me access to the library's more esoteric collections, including its extensive collection on spiritualism—which includes the book Hare wrote about his experiences of spiritualism. I could blather on and on about what I uncovered, but then, that's what this story is about. I will say only that about 90% of what's depicted here is exactly what transpired when Robert Hare decided to investigate communication with the dead. I hardly had to warp reality at all. If this were a film, there would be that little disclaimer that while the events depicted herein are true, a few characters have been fictionalized or combined for the purposes of telling the story.

ILL-MET IN ILIUM

Editor and author Darrell Schweitzer has invited me to submit fiction numerous times throughout my career. Darrell has co-edited *Asimov's Science Fiction* and *Weird Tales* magazines, and edited numerous anthologies. One of the latter is *The Secret History of Vampires*. The premise is simple: Take any real historical event and inject it with vampires without altering the outcome very much. Well, if that's your premise, you aren't going to write a story that goes "Surprise! They're vampires!" It becomes more an exercise in having fun with the notion. In this instance, I had just finished reading Robert Fagles' translation of *The Odyssey*, and in a demented fit of hubris, I decided to try my hand at mimicking the epic verse of *The Iliad* to tell the story of what *really* happened in the siege of Troy. Note: Hiding inside a giant wooden horse with the intention of sneaking out at night to slay the Trojans is not such a hot idea when said Trojans are night creatures themselves.

THE BANK JOB

Another Darrell Schweitzer co-edited anthology, *Full Moon City*, is an anthology of werewolf tales. I happened to have a werewolf lying around from a novel that had never panned out, and he'd been looking for something to do for some years. This was also my first drift into the world of the late Donald E. Westlake, whose work I have admired for decades. More on that later.

TRAVELING ON

"Traveling On" is a story I wrote to take to a Sycamore Hill writing workshop. It's an attempt to write a narrator who is not particularly likeable or self-aware, but it all came from a single sentence written in another notebook: "Three days after the Rapture the kitchen faucet starts dripping again." I've no idea where the sentence came from, but I kept going back to it, staring at it, for a couple of years. Sheila Williams at *Asimov's* bought it, though in retrospect I think the story and magazine weren't a particularly good fit.

ELLENDE

"Ellende," written for Jonathan Maberry at *Weird Tales,* takes elements of my childhood—my grandparents, the ones who owned that crank Victrola mentioned above, had two cabins in northern Minnesota where my family summered many times as I grew up. So once again, here I am stripping some of my own reality for parts. The names of the two characters—Floyd and Jessie—were the names of those grandparents. They were right for the time period, and just felt right attached to the two characters. Jonathan had asked for something Lovecraftian, so I sort of walked off with Innsmouth and dropped it in Minnesota.

SWIFT DECLINE

"Swift Decline" is another Cthulhu-influenced tale. It evolved from an article I had read about real late-20th century private eyes and how they really operated as opposed to your TV-generated Magnum P.I.s.

THE SEALS OF NEW R'LYEH

"The Seals of New R'lyeh" is the third story here written for a Darrell Schweitzer anthology, and the most Westlake-influenced piece I've penned. As I said above, I'm a huge fan of Donald E. Westlake and in particular of his "Dortmunder" novels, starring the hapless criminal John Dortmunder, who is a brilliant strategist but whose schemes somehow always go awry. Though there are three Lovecraft-themed stories herein, I'm not particularly interested in Lovecraft, or maybe I should say, I don't take him too seriously. In this case, given the Cthulhu theme of the anthol-

ogy, I asked myself what would happen if my version of Westlake's Dortmunder were to accidentally screw up and let the Old
Ones in, thereby devastating the world. This then, like "Ill Met
in Ilium," became an overt exercise in voice. One of my friends
here in Philadelphia for many years was the terrific science fiction
author Tom Purdom. Tom was himself a huge fan of Westlake's
Dortmunder tales. So this is a rare instance where I wrote a story
with one very specific reader in mind. If Tom approved of it, then
I had succeeded. When I read the story for a local reading series
and Tom was in the audience—and he was laughing—I knew I'd
hit the mark. Needless to say, the world is a less entertaining place
without Tom in it.

LOCK UP YOUR CHICKENS AND DAUGHTERS,
H'ARD AND ANDY ARE COME TO TOWN

And so, speaking of entertaining . . . the last story in the collection is a collaboration I wrote with Michael Swanwick. To be
more accurate, "Lock Up Your Chickens and Daughters, H'ard
and Andy Are Come to Town" is a premise conjured by Michael
and discussed over a lunch. He and I have been friends a long
long time and have talked about other collaborations over the
years. This is the first time the pieces fell into place. There are
many different approaches to collaborations: Here, Michael wrote
an opening scene and handed it off to me. I tweaked that and
pushed on through a second scene, then handed it back. This immediately became an exercise in one-upmanship: Who could get
the weirdest. Trust me, it is very very difficult to out-weird Michael Swanwick. At this point, I can't even tell who wrote what in
this story. But then, that's not what matters. *Asimov's* magazine
took it, and it won their readers' poll, proving, I think, that weird
is good.

ABOUT THE AUTHOR

Gregory Frost is the author of highly-regarded novels that include *Rhymer*, *Shadowbridge* (*Shadowbridge and Lord Tophet* from Del Rey), *Fitcher's Brides* (Tor), the "PK Dickian" sf novel, *The Pure Cold Light*, and others. His short fiction has appeared in many anthologies and magazines, including *Asimov's Science Fiction*. Follow him on Facebook (gregory.frost1), Bluesky (@GregFrost.bsky. social), or Mastodon (@gregoryfrost@wandering.shop)

PUBLICATION HISTORY

"The Dingus" first appeared in *Supernatural Noir*, June 2011 | "So Coldly Sweet, So Deadly Fair" first appeared in *Weird Tales*, April 2006 | "The Prowl" first appeared in *Mojo: Conjure Stories*, April, 2003 | "The Chimera Transit" first appeared in *Asimov's Science Fiction*, February 2007 | "The Final Act" first appeared in *Poe: Nineteen New Tales of Mystery and Suspense*, January, 2009 | "No Others are Genuine" first appeared in *Asimov's Science Fiction*, October/November 2004 | "Bean There" first appeared in *Asimov's Science Fiction*, Oct/Nov 2013 | "Rubbish" first appeared in *The Magazine of Fantasy & Science Fiction*, February 1984 | "That Blissful Height" first appeared in *Intersections*, January 1996 | "Ill-met in Illium" first appeared in *The Secret History of Vampires*, April 2007 | "The Bank Job" first appeared in *Full Moon City*, October March 2010 | "Traveling On" first appeared in *Asimov's Science Fiction*, Sept/Oct 2020 | "Ellende" first appeared in *Weird Tales #364*, 2021 | "Swift Decline" first appeared in *The Stories in Between*, October 2009 | "The Seals of New R'yeh" first appeared in *Cthulhu's Reign*, April 2010 | "Lock Up Your Chickens and Daughters, H'ard and Andy Are Come to Town" first appeared in *Asimov's Science Fiction,* April/May 2015

OTHER TITLES FROM FAIRWOOD PRESS

Liberty's Daughter
by Naomi Kritzer
trade paper $18.99
ISBN: 978-1-958880-16-6

The American Writer
by Jack Cady
trade paper $19.99
ISBN: 978-1-958880-17-3

The History of the World Begins in Ice
by Kate Elliott
trade paper $20.95
ISBN: 978-1-958880-19-7

Two Hour Transport 2
ed. by NIB, Ramona Ridgewell
& Keyan Bowes
trade paper $18.99
ISBN: 978-1-958880-20-3

Egyptian Motherlode
by David Sandner & Jacob Weisman
paperback $18.99
ISBN: 978-1-958880-21-1

Storm Waters
by Kat Richardson
trade paper $18.99
ISBN: 978-1-958880-22-7

Alibi
Sharon Shinn
paperback $18.99
ISBN: 978-1-958880-25-8

Substrate Phantoms
by Jessica Reisman
trade paper $18.99
ISBN: 978-1-958880-23-4

Find us at:
www.fairwoodpress.com
Bonney Lake, Washington